"You are an infinitely kissable woman, Kat McBride, even dressed up like a frumpy old woman."

Jake caught her hand and brought it to his mouth. He stared into her eyes and sucked her fingers, one by one.

For the first time in memory, Kate thought she might swoon. The man had stumped her—nothing was going as planned. He was supposed to be with Emma at the fishpond, not here, kissing her, sucking her fingers, sending her senses into a tailspin. She should slap his face. She should kick him in the shins.

Although, if he'd kissed her for merely snooping, no telling what he might do if she attacked him....

GERALYN DAWSON

HER SCOUNDREL

HQN™

ISBN 0-373-77072-3

HER SCOUNDREL

Also by Geralyn Dawson

Her Bodyguard
My Long Tall Texas Heartthrob
My Big Old Texas Heartache
The Pink Magnolia Club
The Bad Luck Wedding Night
Sizzle All Day
Simmer All Night
The Kissing Stars
The Bad Luck Wedding Cake
The Bad Luck Wedding Dress
The Wedding Ransom
The Wedding Raffle
Tempting Morality
Capture the Night
The Texan's Bride

This one's for the next generation:
Mary Ann, Catherine, Holly, Christina,
Molly, Caitlin and Sarah.
Reach for your dreams, ladies.

HER
SCOUNDREL

PROLOGUE

The Himalayas, 1880

THE COLD CAME out of nowhere. Fierce, bitter wind whipped down from the snowcap and blasted through the mountain passes, a brutal blow of nature that attacked the small caravan winding its way along a rocky, ill-defined trail. Jake Kimball gasped a breath against the cold. The air was painful, a jagged shard of glass slicing his throat and lungs. Within minutes he was chilled to the bone.

Jake thought they should find cover. Of course, he also thought they should have turned back toward civilization weeks ago. They'd spent almost three months on the trail, on a trip the guides had claimed would take one, and now the first weather front of the season had swept down upon them like a witch's cold heart. Jake didn't trust their guides, three Kashmiri men who communicated with silent looks and surreptitious hand gestures that caused his hackles to rise.

Two weeks ago, with winter on the horizon, the rest of their party had given up and turned back. Jake had talked himself hoarse trying to convince his older

brother, Daniel, the expedition leader, to call off this
year's search for Shambhala. Daniel wouldn't listen to
him, however, arguing that Jake was only sixteen, that
this was his first expedition. He didn't have the experience to form an opinion about native guides or trip de-
lays or mountain passes heavy with an aura of
foreboding.

Right.

Now the howling wind bombarded him and a spitting of moisture stung his cheek. Ice. Sleet.

The lead horseman kept plodding ahead.

To hell with this. Jake pulled his horse out of line,
gave him a kick, and moved forward to speak with Daniel, who rode right behind the lead guide. The mountain trail had narrowed, forcing Jake to guide his mount
with care. It'd be just his bad luck to take a tumble off
the side of a mountain during a sleet storm in the middle of nowhere.

"Dan!" he called through the howling wind.
Hunched down in the saddle, his brother didn't respond.
Jake reached out and grabbed his shoulder, giving it a
shake. "Daniel!"

Daniel Kimball looked up, his eyes glassy and feverish. "We're almost there, Jake. I can sense it. Shambhala.
Magic fountains. Flying horses. Trees covered in dia-
monds and rubies and garlands of jade. It's waiting for us."

Oh, hell. Fear rippled through Jake. Daniel was sick,
and it was more than the sickness of obsession that had
ruled the man's actions for years now. Daniel was feverish, swaying in the saddle. They needed to find
cover now.

"I can smell it, Jake. Can you? Perfume. The perfume of life."

Jake couldn't smell anything because his nose was frozen. "Hold on, brother. Just hold on. I'll take care of you."

He nudged his horse forward, calling toward the lead guide. "Hey! My brother is sick. Find us shelter now!"

The Kashmiri gazed at him through icy blue eyes, then he lifted a long, bony finger and pointed up the trail. Peering through the swirl of sleet and snow, Jake spied a dark indentation in the rock up ahead. A cave. Thank God.

It took ten long, laborious minutes to reach the cave, the opening of which proved large enough to admit the men and their horses. Jake welcomed shelter from the howling wind with a sigh of relief, then quickly slid from his horse and turned his attention to his brother.

Daniel's knees buckled when he dismounted, and he'd have fallen had Jake not been there to catch him. One of the guides spread a blanket against the cave's wall, and Jake guided his brother to it. "Shambhala," Daniel murmured. "After all these years."

Daniel burned with fever. Jake grabbed his canteen off his saddle and put it to his brother's lips. "Drink," he demanded. "You need the water."

His body trembling, Daniel spilled as much as he swallowed. "I heard the sacred call, Jake. *Kalagiya!* Now I know the way is open to me." Then he lapsed into a language Jake couldn't identify, and his worry escalated.

Hell. Jake didn't know what to do for his brother, how to care for him other than to keep him hydrated, warm and dry. He wished they were home where he could send for a physician. He wished he'd listened to their sister, Penny, who'd wanted Jake to learn medicine rather than follow in Daniel's footsteps obtaining items for their father's various collections.

Most of all, Jake wished his brother had never heard of Shambhala.

Fourteen years older than Jake, Daniel Kimball was seldom around when Jake was growing up. Yet, the times his brother did spend with Jake had had a huge impact on his life. Once he'd actually saved Jake's life, rescuing him from drowning in a rain-swollen creek. Daniel had acted part father, part brother and part hero to the impressionable boy. He'd encouraged the dreams and desires and goals that had forged Jake's life path and brought him here, now, to this cold and lonely mountain.

Six years ago their father had announced his acquisition of a new prize, a chunk of meteorite he called the Kalikhari Stone. Bernard J. Kimball had then told them the legend of Shambhala. Captivated by the tale, Daniel threw himself into the study of ancient texts, languages and the science of the occult. He studied Sanskrit and Hebrew and Arabic, and amassed a great library of books, both modern and ancient. He devoted his life to finding the hidden paradise and center of wisdom in the highlands of Central Asia. Jake now feared that his brother's obsession might cost them both dearly.

Suddenly Daniel whipped out his arm and grabbed Jake's forearm, his fingers gripping like a vise. "The stone. The Kalikhari Stone. It belongs here. In the King's Tower. Get it from my saddlebags. Bring it to me."

"You took Father's hunk of meteorite? Jesus, Daniel. He'll kill you."

Daniel believed that the Kalikhari Stone was part of a larger, magical meteorite that had originated in a solar system in the Orion constellation and possessed occult properties. According to Daniel's research, the Kalikhari Stone was capable of bestowing extraordinary psychic talents upon its possessor.

So far, Jake hadn't noticed any sign of psychic abilities in his father, though he had made yet another fortune in railroad stocks of late. Jake considered the legend a crock of nonsense, but he knew his father and Daniel both put faith in it. He also knew their father would split a gut upon learning that Daniel had stolen his magical stone.

Lying on his blanket, Daniel started shuddering. Jake glanced toward his brother's saddlebags. It wouldn't hurt to do as he asked. Hell, if it could turn a man into a mind reader, maybe it could heal him, too.

It was only when Jake stood and crossed to his brother's horse that he noticed the quiet inside the cave. Except for the supply horses, he and Daniel were alone. The guides had disappeared. "What the hell?"

Jake rushed to the front of the cave, stepped out into what was now swirling snow. He looked up the trail. Down.

Nothing.

Dread snaked down his spine. "Don't panic," he

murmured to himself. "It's all right. Maybe they've gone for help."

Yeah, right. Maybe he was back at school in New York, too, passed out and dreaming after a night of drinking single-malt whisky. Maybe this was all just a bad dream. A really bad, really cold dream.

But in case it wasn't, he'd better see about survival.

Jake ducked back into the cave, found his brother sleeping, then spent a few moments seeing to the horses. Once that was done, he built a fire with hands that shook as much from fear as from cold.

"Jake?" Awake again, his brother watched him with glassy, feverish eyes. "Bring it to me."

"The guides are gone, Daniel," Jake said, hearing the desperation in his own tone. If only he were older, wiser, more experienced! "What do I do? We have a medicine kit somewhere, don't we? Tell me what I should give you."

"The stone."

Hell, why not? They could use a bit of magic right about now.

Jake grabbed Daniel's saddlebags and began rifling through them. He pulled out a spyglass, a small book of poetry and...a rock. *The* rock. It was the size of his fist and as black as a tomb. The last time Jake had seen it, the stone was safely beneath display glass in his father's study.

"Here you go, Daniel." He placed the stone in his brother's hand and wrapped his fingers around it. His brother's skin radiated heat. *Oh, God.* Jake's stomach churned. His heart raced. "What else do I do, Dan? Tell me. Should I leave and look for help? Where should I go?"

His brother smiled wearily. "Rest, Jake."

"But—"

"Rest. Sleep. Everything will be just fine."

Jake didn't believe that for a minute. He added wood to the fire, then walked to the front of the cave. Outside, the world was white. He spent a good five minutes arguing with himself about whether to leave Daniel in search of help or whether to stay. In the end, he listened to his instincts and decided he'd be foolish to leave the shelter. Where would he go in an ice storm?

Where would he go when the ice storm ceased?

Jake raked nervous fingers through his hair. Retracing their steps wasn't an answer—if it were even possible. It'd been weeks since they'd seen another human being. He hadn't a clue of what lay ahead. Better to stay here and nurse Daniel through this illness as best he could.

Decision made, Jake sifted through the supplies, searching for the medicine box and taking stock. They had food for a week, if they were careful. The medicine box held bandages and sewing supplies, headache powders and laudanum. Jake glanced over his shoulder toward his brother. Daniel cradled the rock against his chest, his eyes closed. When he awoke the next time, Jake would give him the headache powder.

He grabbed a blanket and took a seat between the fire and his brother. In all his sixteen years, Jake had never recalled feeling so helpless, so alone.

What did it mean that the guides had left all the supplies behind? Maybe they *were* coming back. Maybe they'd gone for help. It was a comforting thought.

The fire crackled. Outside the cave, the snow fell. Jake pulled the blanket tighter around himself and wondered how he'd ended up in a cave on the far side of the world when he'd wanted to spend the summer playing baseball.

Eventually he slept.

Then Jake Kimball dreamed.

The sun shines and warms the earth. Birdsong fills the air and a rainbow of flowers dots the landscape. Peace envelops him like a warm breeze.

A woman appears beside him. She's tall and slender and beautiful, with long, thick, honey-blond hair and eyes the rich green of springtime. Her cheekbones are high and defined, her nose thin and straight. She wears a flowing gown of emerald silk and a long gold chain around her neck from which dangles a clear crystal the size of a robin's egg. Her expression is kind.

Jake sees Daniel walking away. "Dan?"

His brother doesn't respond, doesn't even look back.

"You must leave here, Jake Kimball," *says the woman.*

"Where is here? Who are you? What is going on?"

"I am one of many names, in many times, many places. Simply know that I am enlightened. It is time for you to return to your place, Jake Kimball."

"Yes. Great. There's nothing I'd like better. Let me get my brother and we'll—"

"Daniel Kimball shall stay."

Dissonance tugs at Jake's sense of peace. "But Dan…"

"Daniel Kimball returned the Kalikhari Stone to its rightful home. From this time evermore he is blessed and guarded by Rigden Jye-po, King of Shambhala."

"That's nice, but it doesn't mean he has to stay here." Jake tries to move forward, to follow his brother, but an invisible force, a wall of energy, blocks his way.

"Peace be to you, young Jake. Be joyous for your brother's good fortune. Know that he will enjoy perfect happiness, that he will never know suffering or want or old age. In Shambhala love and wisdom reign."

Anxious now, the peace within him dispersed, Jake struggles against the invisible shield, calling his brother's name. Finally he rounds on the woman. *"Let me talk to him. I want to talk to him."*

"Go home, young Kimball. Know that your brother is safe and happy. Go home." She steps past Jake, through the shield that remains impenetrable to Jake. The vision begins to fade.

"I won't leave him!" Panic surges through him. *"I can't. He's my brother. He's my family. Let him go. Or let me stay. I'll stay. Daniel, make them let me stay!"*

In the blink of an eye, Daniel stands beside the woman, his warm, western clothing replaced by a robe similar to what she wears. The vision wavers, as if Jake is watching through water. He opens his mouth, attempts to speak directly to Daniel, but no sound emerges.

"He is not pure of heart," says the woman.

Daniel Kimball laughs. *"No. My brother has a bit of the devil in him, but that is how it should be. His place is in the other world. However, family is important to my brother. He will not understand. We must give him his family."*

Solemnly, for a long moment, the woman studies

Jake, drawing Jake's gaze to her. Holding him captive. Finally she nods. "He has fought hard for the love of family. Very well. Hold out your hand, Jake Kimball."

With a will of its own, Jake's arm lifts, his hand extended. A jeweled necklace appears in his palm.

The chain is long and gold, the pendant rectangular, a large, glowing emerald surrounded by gold filigree. The warm piece seems to vibrate in his hand. It is beautiful, but Jake hasn't a clue what a necklace has to do with anything.

"Find the necklace, Jake. Find your family."

The vision dissolves right before his eyes, and a bone deep chill chases away the warmth.

Jake's eyes flew open to a hazy half light. He lay flat on his back, his heart pounding, his pulse racing. Where the hell was he?

The cave. He must have fallen asleep. He'd dreamed. A vivid, colorful dream.

A frightening dream.

Jake sat up, rubbed the back of his neck and attempted to get his bearings. How long had he been asleep? It felt like forever. Last he remembered was Daniel…Daniel. Oh, hell.

He twisted his head toward the blanket where his brother had lain, saying, "How you feeling, Dan? Dan!"

The blanket lay wadded in a ball against the wall. Daniel was nowhere to be seen. Jake rolled to his feet and hurried to the front of the cave. Outside, the sky had cleared and the wind had warmed. Snow and ice were melting.

The Kashmiri guides had returned.

Jake breathed a sigh of relief. "You're back. Good. Where's my brother? He must be feeling better, right?" He'd probably gone looking for a bush to take care of personal business.

One of the guides gestured toward Jake's horse, surprisingly saddled and waiting in line, a line pointed down the mountain, back in the direction from which they had come. "We leave now."

"Good. It's about damned time." Jake strode over to his horse, took the reins and put one foot in the stirrup. He gazed up and down the trail, searching for sight of his brother. "Hurry up, Daniel," he called. "Time is awastin'."

The lead guide moved out. Jake put his foot back on the ground. "Hold on. Wait a minute. Daniel's not back yet."

The man on the horse in front of him twisted around in his saddle. "Daniel Kimball will not return. Daniel Kimball will remain in Shambhala."

Everything inside Jake went cold. "What did you say?"

"You must leave here, Jake Kimball," the guide responded, echoing the words Jake had heard in his dream.

His dream. No. That's all it was. It was just a dream. Jake drew a long, deep breath, then shouted, "Daniel!"

All Jake heard was the echo of his own voice.

Then above him, high on the current of air, soared a golden bird. It swooped down toward him, circling once, twice. It let out a haunting cry and the guides dropped to their knees, bowed their heads and cried, "Great One. Oh Great One of Altai."

The bird dipped, flying so low that Jake could see its eyes. Deep green. Emerald green. The color of a woman's eyes. The color of the necklace in his dream.

The bird cawed once, twice, then a third time. Then it rose on the wind, soaring high, the graceful beat of its wings carrying it rapidly away until it became but a spot in the sky. Until it vanished.

That's when Jake knew. It hadn't been a dream. The verdant oasis. The earthly paradise where only the pure of heart could reside. His brother, his hero, had found his Shambhala.

And he'd left Jake out in the cold.

CHAPTER ONE

Galveston Island, Texas, 1891

HE STOOD WAIST DEEP in water, shirtless, broad of shoulder and corded with muscle, his deeply tanned skin glistening beneath the winter sunshine. His dark hair was sun bleached and shaggy, and hung over his face as he gazed down at the object he carefully washed in sea water.

"Is that him?" Kat McBride asked her brother-in-law, Luke Garrett. "Is that Jake Kimball?"

"I think so. Most of our dealings were with his father. I only met him in person once, and at the time he was knee-deep in women and drowning in alcohol." Scowling, Luke added, "He looked different then. He had clothes on."

Seated beside Luke in the carriage, Kat's flamboyant grandmother, renowned sculptress Monique Day, glanced over her shoulder and winked at Kat and her sister, Mari. "Aren't we the lucky ones?"

Kat didn't care if the man was naked or clothed or wearing a dress, she intended to have a chat with Mr. Jake Kimball. The newspaper might call him an adventurer, a treasure hunter or an explorer, but she knew better. Jake Kimball was a scalawag and a thief.

But he was also the man who would make things right for the fatherless child Kat carried in her womb.

Kat wrapped her woolen shawl securely around her shoulders, climbed down from the carriage, and stepped to the edge of the grass-covered dune. "Mr. Kimball?" she called. "Mr. Jake Kimball?"

The man looked up, and Kat caught her breath. Kimball's scruffy beard didn't hide the rugged, masculine beauty of his sharp jaw, thin straight nose and eyes as blue and hard as the sapphire necklace hanging around Mari's neck. Something stirred inside of Kat when his gaze met hers, and she felt a flutter of awareness unlike any she'd known before. Different, even, from anything she'd felt with Rory when he'd drawn her under his spell. She clutched her shawl closer.

"Well, now." Monique clucked her tongue as she linked her arm with Luke's. "Isn't he a fine specimen? Reminds me of the model I used for the bronze Apollo Mrs. Astor bought for her Manhattan home."

Kat thought he looked more like a pirate than a Greek god, especially with the gold hoop earring dangling from one ear and a jeweled knife in his hand.

"Yeah?" His mouth lifted in a slow smile as he studied her face. "I'm Kimball."

Then his gaze slipped lower, locked on Kat's belly. He frowned, and a hint of alarm entered his eyes. His gaze flew back to her face, and he examined her features again. The alarm faded.

No, I am not a ruined lover come to seek the father of my babe. From his reaction, Kat suspected he'd experienced such a scene in the past. No wonder he did business with Rory. The two men were just alike.

"What can I do for you?" he asked as Luke stepped up beside her.

You could put a shirt on. Kat was annoyed that she found the man appealing. He was a means to an end for her, that's all. She'd had her fill of scoundrels.

She placed a protective hand upon her swollen stomach as Luke shot her a quick, curious glance, then took the lead. "I'm Luke Garrett, Kimball. My stepfather, Brian Callahan, worked for your father. You and I met once at his home in New York. May my family and I have a few moments of your time?"

"Yes, I remember you. I'll be right out."

Kimball sloshed toward them, and despite her best intentions, Kat couldn't drag her gaze away from the slow revelation of tanned, toned skin rising from the water. The man obviously spent a good deal of time outdoors without his shirt. The wet, dark hair on his chest lay flat against his skin and arrowed down his flat stomach to his navel and—

Kat gave herself a mental shake. Her mother had warned her that a pregnant woman's emotions ran the gamut, but Kat *never* expected to find herself staring at a man's washboard stomach and wondering how it might feel beneath her fingertips. *This isn't good.*

Luke stepped in front of Kat, blocking her view. "Perhaps you could join us at our buggy once you're, uh, decent?"

"He looks rather decent to me," Monique observed, she and Mari having joined Luke and Kat on the dune.

Luke muttered beneath his breath as he herded the women back to the carriage. Kat picked up words like "scoundrel" and "thieving bounder" and "home knitting booties." At the last, Mari glanced at Kat and rolled her eyes. Baby booties recently had become a rallying cry for the men in her family. Three days ago, after reading an article in the Fort Worth *Daily Democrat* about Jake Kimball and his discovery of a cache of treasures attributed to the pirate Jean Laffite, Kat proposed this trip to Galveston. Her father, Trace McBride, suggested she stay home and knit baby booties instead. Then he compounded the mistake by suggesting the rest of the females in the family join her.

Needless to say, the suggestion didn't go over well with the McBride women. Though the females in the family understood that Trace equated knitting with safety, Kat, her sisters, her mother and grandmother dealt with the issue by rolling their eyes, wrinkling their noses and going about their business.

In Kat's case, her business was planning the trip to Galveston to confront Jake Kimball. Her father argued against her going, but she presented her point just as strongly. Then, because Trace McBride had been unable to refuse her much of anything since she'd returned to a family who for months had mistakenly believed her dead, he'd given in. Mari volunteered to accompany Kat, naming her husband's history with Kimball and the opportunity to visit his sister who lived in Galveston as justification to make the trip. Monique tagged along because she claimed to be suffering a case of ennui and yearned for the scent of salt air.

"So here we are," Kat said softly as the babe in her womb gave her a kick. Kat didn't care that the newspapers called Jake Kimball a courageous explorer, a brave adventurer. To her he was nothing more than a criminal.

A criminal who even now climbed the sand dune while buttoning a blue cotton shirt. Kat's eyes widened at the sight of his dripping denim pants cut off above the knees. He was barefoot.

"Luke Garrett." Kimball's mouth quirked in a crooked smile. "I wondered if I might run across you or your brothers during my time here in Texas. How are Rory and Finn?"

"Dead."

Kat didn't believe Kimball's expression of surprise, and she stepped into the fray by announcing, "I married Rory Callahan, Mr. Kimball." It was true enough, in spirit if not in fact.

The pirate arched a brow.

"You've made quite a discovery here on Galveston Island, sir, and I believe it's fair to say that wouldn't have happened if not for Rory."

Kimball's gaze swept her from head to toe, pausing again briefly upon the bulge of her seven-month-gone belly. Sympathy colored his tone as he said, "I employ many individuals in the course of my pursuits, Mrs. Callahan. I pay them well for their assistance, extremely well, whether their help results in a find or not. I do not offer shares in the discovery, ma'am, so if that is what you seek, I am afraid—"

"I want the altar cross."

His gaze shifted from her to Luke, then back to her. The slight narrowing of his eyes told her he knew very well what she meant. "The altar cross?"

Kat lifted her chin. "The Sacred Heart Cross that was lost almost a hundred years ago when pirates attacked the Spanish ship bringing it to America. It is solid gold and encrusted with jewels, including a heart-shaped ruby at its center. You stole it from Rory Callahan. I want it back."

He studied her, taking her measure. His gaze once again slid to her swollen womb, and pity softened his eyes. "I'm sorry, ma'am, but I did not steal the cross from your husband. Rory sold the piece to me for a substantial amount of money."

Eyeing the sincerity in Jake Kimball's expression, Kat's stomach did a slow somersault. Had Rory lied about that, too? Lied as he lay dying? As Mari reached over and took her hand, Kat went hard and brittle inside. Had Rory Callahan been totally without redemption?

No. No. No. He'd saved Mari, hadn't he? In the end he'd done what was right. In the end he'd tried to provide for Kat and their child.

"I don't believe you." When the pirate simply shrugged, Kat continued, "He told my sister that the altar cross was our child's inheritance. He said it as he was dying. Not even Rory would lie at a time like that."

"Maybe he referred to the money I paid him," Kimball suggested. "The account is in a New York bank. As his widow, you must have records of it. Perhaps the money is still there."

"I'm not," she said softly. "His widow, that is. It turned out our marriage wasn't legal."

"Oh." He glanced at a scowling Luke. "I see."

Kat closed her eyes against the pity in Jake Kimball's gaze. She'd seen too much of that from her family in the months since returning to Fort Worth. It made her feel like a fool.

Of course, that's exactly what she was. She'd married the King of Liars, hadn't she? A man already married, already a father. If he'd lied about that, why wouldn't he lie about the cross?

Luke placed his hand on her shoulder. "If the money is there, Katrina, we'll get it for you. Rory would want your child to have it."

"Perhaps I can help with that," Kimball said. "Let me write to—"

"No." Kat shook her head. "No, I don't want money."

She wanted the cross. She had to have the cross. It was the answer. It was the key to everything! It would fix the trouble she'd caused, help wipe away the shame.

Kat straightened, her chin came up. "Very well, sir. I will buy it back from you. I trust we can reach a fair price. I won't begrudge you a profit over what you paid Rory."

"I'm sorry, but the cross is not for sale."

Frustration rolled through her like a storm. "Everything is for sale, Mr. Kimball."

"Not the Sacred Heart Cross."

Beneath her skirt, Kat's toes took to tapping. "Mr. Kimball, I come from a family of business people so I appreciate the fine art of negotiation. However, at this particular moment I have neither the time nor the inclination to dicker. Please, sir, name your price."

He folded his arms and shook his head. "Listen to me, lady. The cross is not for sale, not under any circumstances, for any price."

"Why not?"

Kimball looked toward Luke. "Your father worked for mine for many years. Surely you recall my father's passion for his quests?"

"Brian was my stepfather," Luke was quick to correct.

Even in her agitation, Kat noted how he always made the distinction that her family hardly ever made with Jenny. It illustrated one of her great worries for her child. Her baby should have a stepfather who was simply a papa, just like Jenny was a mama to the McBride girls.

That's one reason why it was so important for Kat to succeed in securing the Sacred Heart Cross. She needed it for her child, for the hope its restoration to its rightful place could bring.

Kimball continued, "My father collected art, coins, toys and even butterflies, but his special interest was artifacts related to Texas. With your family's help, he amassed quite a collection of Texana before he died. While he continually added and deleted items from his other collections, he never surrendered a single piece of Texana. That is the way of collectors."

Impatient, Kat interrupted. "What does your father's Texana collection have to do with my cross?"

Jake's expression hardened. "First off, Mrs. Callahan, the cross isn't yours. Second, the Sacred Heart

Cross was the last gift I gave my father before he died. It was the crowning piece to his Texana collection. That collection is his legacy, and I'll not break it up."

He sounded frustratingly sincere, and Kat sensed she'd need to use her strongest arguments to sway him. "How did your father die, Mr. Kimball?"

Curiosity at her question registered in his eyes. "He was playing golf and a thunderstorm blew in. My father was struck by lightning."

Kat nodded, totally unsurprised. "It's bad luck. I knew it. Rory died because of it. That altar cross has brought bad luck to everyone who's come in contact with it."

Kat's grandmother leaned toward Mari and murmured, "The Bad Luck Altar Cross? I'll go along with Bad Luck Dresses and Bad Luck Cakes, and even Bad Luck Brides. But religious artifacts? That's taking this family trend a bit overboard, wouldn't you say?"

"Kat," Mari added in a chiding tone.

Kat turned toward her sister. "It's true, Mari. I know it. The cross is cursed and it's all part of the Curse of Clan McBride, don't you see?"

"Oh, honey." Mari glanced toward the men. "Excuse us a moment, please?"

She led Kat away from the buggy, then lowered her voice and said, "Kat, what's going on here? I thought you wanted the cross because Rory left it to you and the baby. I thought you wanted the money it would bring so you wouldn't be dependent on Papa. You never said anything about the curse. Please, tell me you don't truly believe that the cross is bad luck."

Fury surged like fire through Kat's veins. "Stop it! How can you do this? How can you revert to your old, skeptical self? You believe in the McBride bad luck and in the curse and the cure, Maribeth. Don't try to tell me you don't."

"I believe," Mari snapped back. "But, Kat, this makes no sense. Why would you think that Rory's lost cross has anything to do with breaking the curse? It hasn't a fig to do with anyone named McBride!"

"But it does. This is *my* task, Mari. It's been revealed to me, just like Roslin of Strathardle said would happen!"

Two years ago, prior to their elder sister, Emma's, wedding, the three sisters had visited a gypsy fortune-teller in Fort Worth's Hell's Half Acre. Instead of Madam Valentina, they'd encountered an ethereal Scotswoman who gave them each a beautiful necklace and told them a fantastical story about a family curse— the Curse of Clan McBride. She imparted the news that if the three McBride sisters each completed a mysterious task, and in doing so found a love that was powerful, vigilant and true, they could end the curse for all time. McBrides could once again be lucky in love, without going through significant trials such as those suffered by their father and Uncle Tye.

Mari had believed the woman to be a charlatan, and she'd dismissed Roslin's claims until last year when she found her true love, Luke Garrett.

Now Kat believed her turn had come. Reaching beneath her shawl, her left hand grasped the emerald necklace hanging around her neck while her right rested over the child in her womb. "You figured out your task, and now I've figured out mine. I must deliver the Sacred Heart Cross to its rightful place. That's my task, Mari. Once I do that, then *I'll* find a love that is powerful, vigilant and true. I'll find a father—not a stepfather—for my baby so she can grow up safe and happy and secure!"

"Oh, Kat." Mari hugged her sister, then took a step back. Her blue eyes gleamed with sympathy. "I understand now. I do. You've had us all fooled, you know. The family thought you were taking this pregnancy so well, that you felt positive about the future. You must be so frightened."

Tears stung Kat's eyes, but she batted them back furiously. "I'm not frightened," she declared, trying to convince herself. "I'll be fine and my baby will be fine. I won't need to worry about being a scandal or having to live off Mama and Papa the rest of my life. I know that we'll be all right, that we'll have a man in our lives to support us and comfort us and love us. There is a great love waiting for me out there somewhere, a man who will love my baby as his own. The first step in finding that love is to get that cross from Jake Kimball and put it where it belongs!"

"All right," Mari soothed. "Settle down, now. Don't get yourself all worked up. It can't be good for the baby."

Kat glanced over at the buggy where Monique sat regaling the men with one of her never-ending stories, attempting, Kat realized, to distract them from the scene the sisters were making.

"What do I do, Mari? He doesn't seem to want to cooperate."

"No, he doesn't, does he?" Mari glanced at Jake Kimball, then clucked her tongue. "Monique was right—he is a fine specimen of manhood."

"Mari Garrett... What a thing for a newlywed to say."

"I'm married but I'm not blind, Kat." She let out a sigh. "Well, if you're certain this is your task, then I'll do everything I can to help you." She paused a moment, then asked, "Do you really think the cross is bad luck?"

"Taking its history just from the time of its discovery..." She ticked off on her fingers. "The poor man who dug it up was almost killed, the men who took it from him are in jail, Rory took it from them and he's dead. Kimball's father was struck by lightning, for pity's sake. Jake Kimball, here, is an accident waiting to occur."

"I believe in the Curse of Clan McBride, but it still goes against my nature to accept that an altar cross, of all things, is bad luck. However, since you're sure, then we need to come up with a plan for you to get it."

Kat grinned. "I love it when you sound like your old Menace self."

Mari shrugged. "It's who I am. I've accepted it. In fact, since we're talking about the curse and the cure, you should know that I've come to believe that the task I needed to complete to fulfill my part of breaking the curse was not to find you and bring you home but to find myself."

Kat wrinkled her nose. "So finding me was just what? An afterthought?"

"Finding you was the best day of my life."

"Even counting your wedding day?"

A man's voice answered, "Even that." Luke stepped up beside them and said, "We love you, Kat. We want you safe and happy. The sun's going down now, and the air is beginning to cool. Why don't we go back to my sister's house and have a cup of tea?"

Kat glanced back toward Kimball, who was chuckling at something Monique had said. "But what about him?"

"I think we should take our time with Mr. Jake Kimball. He's obviously no pushover. We need to get Emma in on this, too, and develop a plan fit for a McBride Menace."

A smile played on Kat's lips. "He won't stand a chance."

"No, he won't."

Amusement glinted in Luke's gaze as he looked from one woman to the other. "I pity the man. I probably ought to warn him about tangling with the likes of the Menaces, but I think I'll stay on the sidelines this time out."

"Good decision, dear." Mari patted his arm.

"Are you ready to leave, then, Kat?" Luke asked.

"I am. Let me have a minute to visit alone with Mr. Kimball. I want to try one more time. It's only right that he be warned that he's risking a run of bad luck by keeping the Sacred Heart Cross. I won't have his death on my conscience."

Kimball continued to laugh with the girls' grand-mother as Luke escorted Kat and Mari back to the buggy. Kat imagined that Monique had relayed one of her more colorful tales, because the man now had a wicked glint in his eyes and a mischievous slant to his smile.

Mari leaned toward Kat and whispered, "Now that's one pirate most damsels wouldn't mind boarding their boats."

Kat elbowed her sister in the side. "Hush. You're terrible. It's obvious you've been spending far too much time with our grandmother."

"Girls!" that same grandmother said as they approached. "Guess what? Jake and I have mutual friends in London. Isn't it a small world?"

"It's not the world that's small, Monique," Kat said, her smile indulgent, "but your circle of friends that's so large. The only reason you don't have friends on the moon is that you haven't found a way to visit the place."

"Give me time, Katrina. Give me time."

It was as good a segue as Kat could hope for.

"Time does change things." She met Jake Kimball's gaze. "Sir, may I speak with you alone for a moment?"

Kimball glanced at Luke, who shrugged. Kat tamped down her annoyance at the implied seeking of permission from her brother-in-law, and walked far enough away not to be heard by inquisitive relatives. Kimball fell in beside her, and though she didn't look, she felt the weight of his gaze upon her.

Out of the blue, he stated, "You have beautiful hair. The color reminds me of—" he reached into his pocket, pulled out a coin, a Spanish doubloon and handed it to her "—old gold that's been rescued from the sea."

The coin was fascinating, Kimball's comparison to her hair disconcerting. Kat tried to hand the coin back to him, but he wouldn't take it. "For the child."

Her child. Yes. Kat could not, would not, forget about her child. "Have you had enough time to reconsider? Will you sell me the cross?"

"Sorry, but no."

Kat lifted her shoulders in a casual shrug that belied the intensity of the emotions churning within her. Her action caused her shawl to slip. "You're making a mistake. Just remember, Mr. Kimball, when bad luck begins to haunt your door, I know a way to turn the tide. I'll stay in touch, Mr. Kimball. Believe me, there will come a time when you'll be only too happy to be rid of the Sacred Heart Altar Cross."

"That sounds like a threat. You know—" the scoundrel winked at her "—if you weren't so gorgeous, with all this talk about bad luck and curses, I'd worry I'd stumbled across a witch."

Cocky pirate, Kat thought as she readjusted her shawl by taking it all the way off, then resettled it around her shoulders. "I'm no witch, Kimball. But you should still beware. I'm a McBride Menace."

Jake Kimball appeared thunderstruck, and it took Kat aback. Had the McBride sisters' reputation traveled farther than she'd thought?

A calculating look flashed through Kimball's eyes and caused Kat a shiver of unease. "A menace, hmm?" he murmured, reaching out and touching her hair. "What is that, some sort of witch? Have you cast a spell on me? Will you turn me into a toad? Somehow I can't see a woman like you chanting incantations over a pot."

The man was flirting with her! What sort of scoundrel would flirt with a woman seven months gone with another man's child while her family stood within shouting distance? He must have ulterior motives. Yet, her feminine side couldn't help but respond to the attentions of this alluring man. She leaned forward slightly. "You'd be surprised at what a woman like me might do."

His grin flashed wicked. He touched her hair again, gently tugged a strand from her braid and let it slide across the skin of his fingers. "Oh, yeah?"

"McBride Menaces don't rely on spells to get what we want, Mr. Kimball. Our methods are far more creative."

"Is that a fact?" His gaze focused on her mouth.

"Oh, no." Kat licked her lips, swayed toward him. His eyes narrowed, blazed heat, and power washed through Kat like an ocean wave. *Typical man. Typical scoundrel.*

"No, Mr. Kimball," she repeated, stepping away and grinning. "It's a promise."

She all but strutted back toward the carriage. Halfway there, his voice stopped her in her tracks. "Do you want the Sacred Heart Cross, Katrina McBride?"

Kat turned around. "I do."

"Then I propose a trade. I'll give you my cross for that pretty necklace you're wearing."

Kat clutched her emerald pendant. "My necklace? You want my necklace?"

The pirate shrugged as he walked toward her. "I like baubles. It will be a bad trade on my part, I know. One jewel compared with dozens on the cross. However, you, too, are a jewel, my dear. You make a beautiful picture, standing here beside the sea, ripe and luscious and glowing. The necklace will remind me of you."

What a load of nonsense. "It's the bad luck, isn't it? I convinced you. You know you need to get rid of the cross and, pirate that you are, you recognize the value of my necklace and you're trying to make the best deal you can."

"I can show you appraisal papers for the cross. It's worth nine times the amount I paid Rory for it."

Kat's eyes widened. "I can't pay that much."

"It's not for sale. It's only up for trade. I want the necklace, Kat McBride."

"Why?"

"I told you why."

She shook her head. "You spun a nonsensical story."

"You are a beautiful woman."

Kat realized just how dangerous a man he was when the utter conviction in his voice almost convinced her he meant it. "I cannot give you my necklace. It's a family heirloom."

"Family?" His eyes lit. "Tell me everything you know about the necklace."

She wasn't about to stand here and explain about Roslin of Strathardle. "It's one of three that came to me and my sisters from our Scots ancestors. I cannot split the set, not even for the cross. My sisters would kill me."

He opened his mouth as if to protest, then apparently

reconsidered. "If you change your mind, I expect to remain here in Galveston for another month. After that, letters can reach me through Kimball Incorporated offices in New York."

A cool breeze swept in off the water, and Kat gathered her shawl around her shoulders once again. "I can be reached in Fort Worth through my sister's candy shop, Indulgences. Feel free to contact me when you're ready to change your luck."

Kat felt his gaze upon her as she made her way to the waiting carriage. As Luke helped her up into her seat, the breeze picked up, and Kat lost her slight grip upon her shawl. It swirled into the air, fluttering toward the water's edge, until a tanned hand reached up and grabbed it.

"Y'all have a nice trip back into town," Kimball said as he handed Kat her shawl. When their fingers touched, a shiver of foreboding swept over her. The calculating look in his eyes made her uneasy. What was he thinking? What was he planning?

Jake tipped an imaginary hat and winked. "Guess I'd best get back to digging. All of a sudden I'm feeling lucky."

Now, why in the world did that sound like a threat?

CHAPTER TWO

JAKE KIMBALL WAS a pragmatic man.

He didn't believe in luck, good or bad. He didn't believe in fate or fancy or fantasy, not since his journey a decade earlier on the far side of the world. Doing so might take him into that obsessive world that ultimately had destroyed his brother. Be damned if he'd travel down that particular path.

No, Jake believed in research. Extensive, comprehensive, relentless research. He believed in the tangible. He believed in what could be proven.

So why, then, was he sneaking through the window of a private residence in Fort Worth, Texas, searching for a piece of jewelry because it resembled something he'd once seen in a dream?

He wondered if he hadn't lost his mind.

With the McBride family congregating at Tye McBride's home for a birthday celebration, Jake decided to take advantage of the opportunity to search Willow Hill for the necklace he'd seen twice in his life—once in a dream, then again around Kat McBride's neck.

He'd spent much of the last month in Fort Worth

learning everything he could about the trio of necklaces worn by Kat and her sisters. Hanging around a rel-
atively small town for weeks while asking questions
about one of its most prominent families without drawing their notice had taken both skill and cunning. Yet
what he'd learned had intrigued him.

The McBride sisters began wearing the necklaces
two years ago. Publicly they told the story Kat had
given him on the beach in Galveston, that the necklaces
were old family heirlooms. Privately they told a ridiculous story about a magical Scotswoman and prophecy
foretold. Jake considered it all a bunch of hoohaw and
had twice left town, determined to put the matter behind
him. Nevertheless, old dreams about Daniel haunted
him, and new possibilities plagued him, which was why
he now found himself tiptoeing through Willow Hill's
kitchen salivating over the lingering aroma of freshly
baked ginger cookies.

Upstairs, thankful the family had left a hall light
burning, Jake checked two bedrooms before finding
one with clothing suited to an expectant mother hanging in the wardrobe. He didn't truly expect to find the
necklace—apparently she seldom appeared in public
without it. What he hoped to identify were likely places
she'd store it while at home. That way he'd shorten his
time inside her bedroom when she occupied it.

He'd decided to steal the damned thing and be done
with the speculation once and for all.

More than ten years after the fact, with his father
gone and no longer able to rake Jake over the coals for
having come home from Tibet alone, Jake had almost

let go of the guilt and made peace with his brother's disappearance. He believed his brother died on that mountain, either in the cave or by wandering into the cold in fevered confusion, though he never found a body. He'd searched hard for a full week, until the guides conveyed the message that they were leaving, no matter what. He'd searched again on two subsequent expeditions his father organized and funded. He'd given his best effort to finding his brother. He could feel good about that.

Yet, ever since Kat McBride paid him that visit on the Galveston beach, Daniel's ghost had haunted him.

Jake was a pragmatic, down-to-earth fellow. He believed man made his own luck and was the master of his own destiny. He didn't believe in witches or ghosts or mythical, magical cities hidden within a ring of snowcapped mountains.

Still, if the slightest chance existed that he was wrong, that there was something to this otherworldly folderol, well, he couldn't ignore it. He didn't *like* stealing a treasured piece of jewelry from a young woman who'd already suffered her fair share of hard licks, but he didn't see a way around it. He'd tried to trade for it, to no avail. He'd tried to buy it through intermediaries, but that didn't work, either. But because the necklace was a perfect replica of the one in his dream, because it involved his *brother,* his hero, his greatest failure, Jake couldn't afford to be nice.

He searched her dressing table, opened drawers, sifted through keepsakes in a cigar box, and then, because he was, after all, a man, he took a moment to sniff the scents in the perfume bottles. With the alluring, spicy scent of bergamot lingering in the air, he turned his attention to a chest of drawers. A wooden box with carved-ivory inlay sat atop it. Jake flipped open the lid and murmured, "Yes."

Kat McBride's jewelry box held a modest cache of baubles. A locket, pearl earrings. More earrings. A pair of gold bracelets. Not a single ring. Guess she didn't keep her faithless "husband's"—or Rory Callahan never gave her one.

The bastard. It was too bad a nice young woman like Kat McBride had gotten tangled up with the likes of Callahan. She didn't deserve it.

It's too damned bad she got tangled up with the likes of me, too.

Jake shut the jewelry box, then continued his survey of her bedroom and tried to ignore his conscience. The table beside her bed offered a likely spot if she removed the necklace last thing at night, then donned it again immediately upon rising in the morning. Jake subtly shifted the lamp and short stack of books beside her bed, leaving room for the necklace to allow for a clean pickup, if need be.

That ought to do it. He'd watched the house for the previous two nights. Half past three in the morning looked to be a good time to burgle Willow Hill. His intention was to slip back outside, settle down in his observation spot, then keep watch as the McBrides returned home and went to sleep. Then, if all went as planned, he'd slip inside the way he'd come in tonight, head straight for Kat's room, grab the necklace and go. He'd head back to Galveston first thing tomorrow morning.

He was halfway to the bedroom door when he heard the sound of footsteps pounding up the stairs along with a man's panicked voice. Jake froze, listened intently, then quickly dove for the only hiding place in sight. He crawled under her bed just as her door burst open. Jake spied a man's pair of shoes and his trousers from mid-calf down heading toward the bed.

"Jenny!" Trace McBride called. "Hurry. Pull down her sheets so we can get her to bed."

"Papa," Kat McBride said in a long-suffering tone. "I don't need to go to bed. I don't need to be carried."

"You don't know what you need. You've never had a baby before. I've had six!"

A woman's slippers and skirts shuffled into view. "Put her down, Trace. You'll hurt your back."

"Jenny! She's having a baby!"

"Yes, but not this second, Trace."

Kat added, "That's right, Papa. I haven't had a single pain."

"But…but…but…your, um… You're all…um…"

Jenny McBride clucked her tongue. "Put her down, darling, and let me help her change. Remember when I had Tommy? My pains didn't start until six hours after my water broke. This is a first baby. We'll have plenty of time."

"The bed—"

"Let her change first."

Trace set his daughter down, mumbled something about hardheaded women, then exited the room. Jake heard the door shut.

"Thank goodness," Jenny McBride muttered. "I'm

afraid that man will drive us both crazy before this is done."

"He's nervous, isn't he?"

"Terrified. You're his little girl."

Jake heard the rustle of clothing, then petticoats dropped. The women discussed feminine birthing details he'd never considered and would just as soon not know. Vaginal tearing? Afterbirth? When the bed above him dipped and Kat McBride wiggled her bare feet, Jake broke out in a sweat and wished he was anywhere but here.

Then he heard the soft clink of chain against wood. She'd set the necklace on her bedside table, right in the spot he'd cleared for it, he'd bet.

Damn. His fingers itched to reach up and grab it, but prudence won out.

Above him, Kat and her mother spoke briefly about the birthday party they'd been forced to leave early before talk returned to the subject of labor and delivery. Listening, Jake wished there was something to the whole witchy business. He'd give just about anything if a sorcerer could whisk him out of here.

What a humiliating position he found himself in, hiding beneath a woman's bed. He'd hidden from a husband in a wardrobe once or twice before, but never beneath the bed. If his friend Dair MacRae could see him now, he'd bust a gut laughing.

When the women's discussion turned to the possibility of breast engorgement, Jake considered giving himself up. If he didn't think it likely that doing so would put the necklace out of his reach for good, he'd roll out from beneath the bed this second.

How long did having babies take? An hour? Two? He had no experience whatsoever in that respect.

"I don't want to stay in bed, Mama. I'll go crazy sitting around waiting for this to happen."

"What do you want to do?"

"I'd like to take a walk."

Yes! Jake held his breath and waited anxiously for Jenny McBride's response.

"I think that's a good idea," Jenny McBride responded, stating the best bit of news Jake had heard all night. "Let's get your coat and shoes on, then we'll go deal with your father."

"Can't I just sneak out?"

"Kat," Jenny chastised.

"Oh, all right."

Moments later the door closed behind the women. Jake waited half a minute before crawling from beneath the bed. A quick glance toward her night table had his lips stretching in a grin. The large emerald pendant surrounded by gold filigree, ancient and Gaelic in appearance and suspended from a heavy gold chain, lay just where he wanted it.

Jake slipped Kat McBride's necklace into his pocket, then sneaked out of Willow Hill.

THE BRUTAL WAVES of pain washed over Kat McBride, one on top of the other, allowing little time to rest in between.

"That's it, darling," her mother, Jenny, said. "You're doing fine. You're doing great. It won't be long now."

"Hurts," Kat gasped out as the agony eased.

"I know, baby." Jenny wiped her daughter's brow with a damp cloth.

"I can't do it, Mama. I can't. Make it stop. Make it go…oh…" The pain bore down once again, vicious and intense. Heat flashed through her body, and Kat thought she might vomit. Her huge belly was as hard as granite.

"Maybe I could rub her stomach," her sister Emma suggested. "Would that help?"

Unable to verbally respond, Kat snapped at her sister's fingers.

"I think that means no," Jenny observed.

Mari nervously patted her younger sister's hand. "Try to think of something other than the pain, Kat. Think of a peaceful, gold and scarlet sunset. Or of a paper boat floating on the Trinity River. Or maybe, if peaceful doesn't work, think of something that will capture your attention. I know. Think about Jake Kimball and his latest reply to your letters. That'll certainly make you stew. That'll take your mind off the pa—"

As the contraction peaked, Kat let out a loud, agonized scream.

"—in. Or maybe not," Mari concluded as a loud crash sounded outside Kat's bedroom door.

"What in the world?" Emma said.

"That's just your father," Jenny reassured them. "Don't worry about him. He always throws things at this stage of the proceedings."

Panting for breath in the fleeting seconds of ease, Kat envied her papa. She'd like to throw things, too. Instead, she reached for the necklace she'd left lying beside the bed. The necklace had become her talisman in recent months, a symbol of hope and promise. A symbol of love.

Her fingers felt around the night table as her womb began to tighten once again. It tightened…tightened…she forgot all about the necklace. *Oh, let it stop.*

This frightened her. She had no control over her body. Over her life. "Oh," she groaned as the pain intensified. "Stop…make it stop…damn you, Rory Callahan!"

As she screamed the name, Kat felt a sense of pressure like she'd never known before. Instinctively, she rose onto her elbows and began to push.

"Thatta girl," said the midwife. "You listen to your body. Jenny, you might want to send the other girls away now."

Kat couldn't talk with her teeth clenched so hard, but she gave her head a definite, negative shake. She needed her sisters.

Time passed, Kat didn't know how much as she remained only vaguely aware of the world around her. Her focus remained on the work of giving birth. And it *was* work. Hard, physical, sweaty work, and Kat truly didn't think she could make it without her family's help. Her mother held her hand, never once letting go, not even when Kat squeezed hard enough to bruise. Her sisters took her back, holding and supporting her as she pushed with the pains. They cajoled her when she whined and encouraged her when she lost heart. Then, when the miracle occurred and the wrinkled, wriggling infant slid from her body, the McBride women cried together—all five of them.

"A girl!" Mari exclaimed in delight, wiping tears from her cheek with the back of her hand as the midwife placed the squalling infant in Kat's arms.

Love, warm and sweet and enormous, flowed from Kat's heart as she gazed down at her newborn daughter.

"She's beautiful, Kat," Emma said, sniffing daintily. She reached out and touched the infant's tiny hand. "Just beautiful. Look at all that hair. And it's blond as her mama's!"

Jenny let her tears flow freely. "My first granddaughter. Another little girl for Trace to spoil."

"Another McBride Menace," Mari offered with a grin.

Jenny laughed, then smiled warmly at Kat. "Shall we get you and our little love presentable so that you can introduce her to your father? You know he's downstairs chomping at the bit. Or would you rather sleep a little first?"

Though Kat could feel exhaustion tugging at her limbs, a strange sense of energy continued to course through her body. She knew she couldn't sleep. "I want Papa."

Twenty minutes later, Jenny McBride opened the bedroom door and called, "Trace?"

Kat heard her father's footsteps pound upstairs. He burst into the bedroom, his eyes wide and bright with panic, his hair mussed. His shirt had a whisky stain on the front. Probably his reaction to one of her screams, Kat thought.

"Katie-cat?" he asked, stepping toward the bed, his

stare sweeping his youngest daughter up, then down. "You all right, baby?"

"I'm fine," Kat replied past the lump of emotion clogging her throat. She shifted the receiving blanket and added, "Papa, I'd like you to meet your granddaughter, Suzanne Elizabeth."

Kat saw her sisters exchange a look of surprised delight as a smile as big as Texas split their father's face. "After your sisters," he said. "You used their middle names! Ah, look at her."

Trace rubbed the infant's tiny hand, then murmured with delight as she curled her fist around his finger. "She's gorgeous, honey. Pretty as you were."

"I thought I'd call her Susie."

Trace nodded. "Susie Beth. I like it. Rolls right off the tongue."

Kat, her sisters and their mother shared an indulgent smile. They all knew that no matter a child's given name, Trace McBride would invariably convert it to one of his own.

Kat gazed down at the infant sleeping in her arms, then up at her sisters and mother. "Would y'all mind if I spoke with Papa alone for a few minutes?"

Jenny kissed Kat's cheek, then asked, "How about I take Susie and introduce her to her uncles? I'll bring her right back. I know your arms will feel empty without her."

At Kat's nod, Jenny lifted the baby and cuddled her close. As Mari and Emma followed their mother, Mari said, "Don't let the boys hold her, Mama. They seem to have been awfully clumsy of late, and I don't trust them. In fact, I'm not even sure Luke should hold her."

"Luke needs to hold Susie," Kat called out. "He needs the practice."

Mari grinned and gave her still-flat stomach a maternal pat as she trailed Emma from the room. When the door shut behind the women, Trace moved the desk chair beside Kat's bed, straddled it and sighed. "I'm glad this is over. Having a baby is just about the hardest thing I do. It was a trial with your mother, but now with you and before long, Mari...I don't know if I'll live through it. You did a fine job, though. She's a peach. I think...wait a minute."

He reached out and used the pad of his thumb to brush away the tear that had escaped her eyes to trickle down her cheek. "What's this?"

"Nothing."

He studied her, frowned. "That's not a happy tear. What's wrong, baby? Talk to me."

Concern softened her father's blue eyes and brought tears to Kat's. "I'm frightened, Papa."

"What about, Katie-cat?"

"What if I prove to be a bad mother?"

Trace shook his head. "Now, don't be silly."

"I'm not being silly."

"Sure you are," he replied in a placating tone as he tucked in the bed sheet, then fluffed her pillow. "It's to be expected, though. I've had plenty of experience with this. Trust me. Giving birth to your child is one of the most emotional events in life, and it'll take you a few days to find your feet. But you'll be fine. You'll be a fine mother."

Emotion rolled through Kat and tears swelled, then

spilled. "I can't be sure. What if I'm like my mother, my blood mother? She was a terrible mother and I have her blood. What if it's cursed?"

Trace set his teeth. "Katie, Katie, Katie. You need to let this curse business go. That's all a bunch of nonsense."

"I've seen my mother's portrait. I look like her." Kat pulled at a loose thread on her blanket. "I've been wicked like her."

"Dammit, Katrina!"

It was a sign of the extent of her father's distress that he used salty language in front of Kat, but she refused to let it deter her. This was important to her. Something she'd pondered for weeks. "It's the truth, Papa. History is repeating itself. I had relations with a man out of wedlock. A con man! A criminal. That's who fathered my child. How can you even stand the sight of me? I must remind you of—"

"Stop that!" Trace shoved to his feet and began to pace the room. "Today should be the happiest day of your life and I'll not have you waste a minute of thought about that sorry sonofabitch two-timing liar Rory Callahan."

"But he's my baby's father."

"He donated the seed. That doesn't make a father. Believe me, I know. Even when I thought you weren't my daughter by blood, I always knew I was your father. And as for your mother…"

He sighed heavily, then sat back down. His brow wrinkled in thought for a long moment, before he said, "That was a long time ago and entirely different. Constance chose to betray her wedding vows. She chose to betray me and her children. You would never do that, Katrina. Never! You're going to be such a good mother."

"How can you be so certain, Papa?"

"There's not a single doubt in my mind about that." Watching her, his smile turned bittersweet. In a wistful voice he said, "Let me tell you something else about your mother. Yes, you remind me of her, Katrina. You're beautiful, full of life and have a laugh that touches my soul. Today I can look back and remember only that Constance gave me my three beautiful girls. She gave me you, Katie-cat. I'll always be grateful for that."

Kat closed her eyes. Time and Jenny and his children's love had healed her papa. Maybe there was a chance that she could heal, too. She wanted to believe that, more than anything else.

"I'm trying," she said softly. "If only I can convince Jake Kimball to…"

"No," Trace interrupted. "Kat, I've heard enough about this supposed Curse of Clan McBride. I know you girls are convinced there's something to it, and I'll admit that those necklaces of yours seem to have a special…well…something, but this fixation you have on pirate treasure has got to stop. You've barraged the poor man with letters the last month, and it's just a waste of postage."

"But, Papa, if I can fulfill the destiny of the cross, then Susie has the chance to have a good life, a wonderful life. Papa, I want her to have a father like you! What if I never meet anyone that wants us?"

"Oh, baby. You break my heart. You truly do." Trace again took his seat beside the bed and clasped Kat's hand in both of his. "One of the things I've always loved about you is the way you take on the world with such drama and flair. Such enthusiasm. What I haven't liked is your stubbornness. I want you to put that aside for a moment and open your mind and listen to your old papa. Can you do that?"

Emotion clogged Kat's throat, so she simply nodded.

"I know you've done a lot of growing up in the past year, but you're still only nineteen years old. You haven't lived long enough, haven't lived hard enough, to see that there's light beyond the dark days."

"I think I'm living pretty hard, Papa. I just gave birth to an illegitimate child whose father died as a result of breaking out of jail the man who swore to kill my sister."

Trace's jaw hardened and cold, icy anger frosted his eyes. "If Callahan wasn't already dead, I swear I'd kill him."

"Papa," Kat chastised.

"You're right. I'm sorry. I got off track. This isn't about him, it's about you." Trace reached out and tucked a stray strand of hair back behind Kat's ear. "The point I'm trying to make, Katie-cat, is that I think it's time you sat back and let life happen for a time instead of always trying to take it by the horns. This whole bad luck business, the stuff about the curse—if there's anything to it, then I suspect it'll work itself out in time for you, just like it did for Mari. You'll meet someone. Someone who will be damn lucky to have you.

"What you need to do now is to concentrate on loving little Susie Beth. That's what'll make you a good mother, Katrina. You love her and let her know she's loved and you'll do just fine at motherhood. And let me tell you one more thing. You need to treasure these days with Suzanne Elizabeth. Little ones grow up awfully fast. You don't want to look up one day and realize you've missed the best parts because you were too busy running to the post office to mail letters."

Kat took her father's words to heart. He was right. But then, he was always right when it came to the important things. And yet, a tiny flicker of fear still existed within her. Part of her wanted to crawl into his lap and tell him to make it all go away.

Still another tear slipped from her eyes to slide slowly down her cheek. "I'm afraid I'll mess motherhood up, too, Papa. Just like I've messed up everything else."

"Hmm? And that little angel downstairs? Is she lumped in with all your mistakes?"

"No! Of course not!"

"See there?" Trace wiped the wetness away with the pad of his thumb. "Susie born less than an hour ago and already you're a mama bear. You see what I mean, baby? You'll do fine. Beyond that, any questions you have about motherhood, any doubts you have, you look toward Jenny. There's no woman in the world who is a better mother than my Treasure. You agree?"

"I do."

"Good." He leaned over and kissed her brow. "Now, I'm gonna go see what's keeping your mama and Miss Susie Beth. I hardly got a chance to count the little one's toes. She did have ten of them, I trust?"

"Yes," Kat replied. She waited until he'd taken three steps toward the door, then added, "Ten perfect toes and eleven perfect fingers."

Trace whipped his head around, his eyes wide. Kat laughed. "I'm kidding, Papa. Now, why don't you go get her and bring her to me, and let's count them together, shall we?"

"Such a Menace," Trace muttered as he proceeded to the doorway. There he paused and added, "Katrina? I meant every word I said. I think you're gonna be a terrific mother."

In the days and months that followed, Trace's words proved prophetic. Kat had her daughter christened Suzanne Elizabeth McBride when the baby was ten days old, and the only cloud in her personal sky was the fact that her necklace had gone missing in the hours following Susie's birth.

Though Kat and her family had searched high and low for the necklace, they'd concluded it must have fallen to the floor and been accidentally discarded with gift wrappings or other trash. Kat still felt awful about the loss, though Mari still believed it would turn up. Mari believed in the magic. Kat didn't have time to worry about it.

Being a mother took all her energy. She faced the town gossips with her shoulders squared and her head held high, and, challenged by her grace and honesty and her family's united front, the scandalmongers eventually lost interest in throwing around the "bastard" label. Life settled back to normal, as normal as the McBrides ever managed, anyway. Trace and Jenny stayed busy trying to keep their three young sons out of trouble. Emma's budding romance with the widowed father of two of her students ended for reasons she wouldn't share with her sisters. She took a new job as a teacher at a private girls' school in Dallas, living there during the week but spending her weekends at Willow Hill. Mari and Luke welcomed their firstborn into the world, a little boy they named Drew, after Andrew Kent, hero of the Alamo. The Garretts remained blissfully happy, Luke enjoying his job with the sheriff's office and Mari splitting her time between child rearing and managing her chocolate shop, Indulgences.

Kat's life settled into a rhythm. Immersed in motherhood, she quit writing to Jake Kimball and put all thought of retrieving the Sacred Heart Cross out of her mind. Shortly before Susie's first birthday, Kat ignored her father's protests and moved into the McBride family apartment above her aunt Claire's bakery. Once a day, one of Luke's deputies, Marcus Wagoner, knocked on her door when he dropped by the bakery, ostensibly to indulge his sweet tooth. Nobody liked cookies that much, and Kat knew someone in her family sent him to check on her. She liked Marcus—he always had a compliment for Susie—so she didn't protest the supervision. She helped Mari run Indulgences and used her spare time to supplement her income by writing articles for the Fort Worth newspaper, thus providing an outlet for the creative energies that continued to hum inside her. Mostly, though, she devoted herself to her daughter.

Kat took to motherhood like a cowboy to campfire coffee. She loved everything about it. She loved making a home for Susie, teaching her, playing with her, helping her grow into a happy, well-behaved, well-adjusted young child despite the fact that Susie's family didn't include a father. Kat had family and friends who stepped into that role, Luke and Marcus primarily. Marcus was obviously head over heels for Susie, and Emma claimed he was sweet on Kat. Kat didn't want to explore that possibility. After Rory's betrayal, she wasn't ready yet. Besides, she didn't much miss male companionship. Susie filled up her life.

That made the events of a beautiful spring afternoon when Susie was four years old all the more tragic.

It happened so fast. One minute Susie walked beside Kat on the downtown sidewalk, happily munching on an apple and chatting about a friend's new doll. The next she'd dropped her fruit and dashed after a puppy that had streaked from an alley into the street.

Kat grabbed for her daughter's skirt, her fingers brushing fabric, but failing to find a grip. The wagon driver didn't have time to swerve.

Susie McBride was buried in Pioneer's Rest Cemetery next to her father's grave.

Kat McBride's shattered heart mourned.

CHAPTER THREE

Two years later, London

OVER THE COURSE of the past two decades, Jake Kimball had swum underground rivers in the Yucatan, scaled snow-covered mountains in the Himalayas and descended ancient trails into subterranean caverns in the wilds of the American West. He'd battled wolves in Canada and a tiger in India, and he'd stared into the soulless eye of an anaconda in Brazil. Yet for all of his adventures, all of his dangerous scrapes, he'd never known sheer terror such as he felt here, now, in the well-appointed drawing room of a London town house.

Sitting on a sofa sipping tea from a delicate china cup, the woman who'd always owned his heart, the one woman who knew him better than he knew himself, and the one woman who could change the course of his future, waited patiently for Jake to summon up the nerve to address the matter at hand.

"Darling," she said, her voice knowing. "Quit resisting. You have no choice but to make the commitment."

Commitment. The word made his stomach take a long, slow roll.

A little voice interrupted, "Uncle Jake?"

Seizing gratefully upon the delay, Jake turned toward the sound. A mop of yellow curls topped a round face with rosy cheeks, a button nose and a bow-shaped mouth. Big blue eyes framed by impossibly long lashes solemnly held his stare. His niece wore pink and white ruffles and a smear of strawberry jam. She reminded him so much of his sister that his heart gave a violent twist.

His voice gruff, he asked, "Which one are you?"

"I'm Belle, Uncle Jake."

Isabelle. The eight-year-old. *How the hell am I going to keep them all straight?* He looked for something unique about the girl to help him put face with name. Maybe that dusting of freckles across her nose? "Do your sisters have freckles?"

She nodded. "It's a family curse."

Defeated, he sighed. "Is there something you needed, Belle?"

"Yes, sir, Uncle Jake. It's Miranda. She's stuck in the chimney."

"Again?"

"Yes, sir."

Luke glanced down at his navy jacket, pristine white shirt and buff-colored trousers. He sighed once again, more heavily this time. "How long has she been down there?"

"A while. We didn't want to bother you, since we know you have an important meeting, so we tried to get her out ourselves, but we didn't have one bit of luck."

Jake closed his eyes. "How many of you are on the roof?"

"Theresa stayed on the ground with the baby."

Thank God for small favors. Amusement gleamed in his guest's eyes as Jake made his excuses, then took his leave of the drawing room. In the hallway, he shrugged out of his jacket and tossed it on a chair as he headed for the servants' stairs. He'd learned the shortcut to the roof his second day in London, and after one full week in residence and at least a half-dozen trips up the stairs, he could no doubt make the climb blindfolded.

Better not say that in front of the little hoodlums. They'll put me to the test.

Moments later in the attic, Jake yanked off his necktie before stepping out onto the slate roof. There the morning sun beamed down upon him as he paused to remove his boots and socks. Bare feet gave the best purchase on the slippery surface, he'd learned. He padded across the roof to the chimney where another blond girl waited expectantly. She smiled, but didn't speak.

He frowned down at her. This was the one out of the group that he recognized. "You're Caroline."

She nodded, but still didn't speak. The only other person in the carriage with her parents that fateful day, six-year-old Caroline hadn't uttered a word since the accident.

"I understand your sister's been playing chimney sweep again."

The girl nodded, then pointed at the chimney.

Jake winked at her, then called out, "Miranda? Are you all right? You're not hurt or anything?"

"I'm fine, Uncle Jake."

Miranda was the tall one, Jake recalled. The eleven-year-old. The oldest of his sister's children. Of his sister's *five* children. Four girls and a baby boy. Four orphaned nieces and a toddling nephew—a toddling marquis, rather. With only Jake and a bitter, aging, spinster aunt on their late father's side to look out for them.

God help them all.

Recently well-practiced at extracting children from chimneys, Jake accomplished the task in quick order. When they had all made it safely off the roof and into the attic, Jake leveled his most ferocious glare upon them. Three little round, cherubic faces smiled innocently back. *Angelic little devils.*

Jake cleared his throat. "Please correct me if I'm wrong, but did I not specifically forbid any more gadding about the rooftops? Did I not promise severe punishment should you indulge in such foolishness again?"

"We're sorry, Uncle Jake," the tall, sooty, guilty one— Miranda—said.

"That's what you always say." Jake donned his boots, then brushed at the soot now soiling his shirt and trousers.

From behind him at the top of the attic stairs another young female voice said, "Uncle Jake? Your friend is here. That Mr. MacRae. He's in the drawing room, too. I gave him some of the biscuits we made yesterday, and I said you'd be down right after you got out of the chimney."

"Thank you, um..." Jake's gaze darted from the blond, blue-eyed, pink-and-white-ruffle-gowned girl at the top of the stairs to the other blond, blue-eyed, pink-and-white-ruffle-gowned girls in front of him. Ah, no smear of strawberry jam—not Belle. No soot—not Miranda. Baby dribble on her collar. The nine-year-old. "Thank you, Theresa."

The four girls beamed at him for having gotten the name right for a change. Sweet, silent Caroline twirled a curl around her finger.

Jake shook his head in frustrated wonder. Their father had been a carrot top, their mother, olive-skinned and dark-haired. How in the world had that couple produced four—count them, *four*—blond-haired, blue-eyed girls who look so much alike that Jake, who had a good eye for detail, couldn't keep them straight? "We need to adopt a color system. One color per girl."

"You're silly, Uncle Jake," Belle said. Or was she Theresa?

"No, I'm desperate. I'll get a seamstress on it right away. Now, where's the baby?"

"He's in his crib in the nursery. He fell asleep."

Hallelujah. It was the best news Jake had had all morning. The little terror was a climber, and when it came to getting into trouble, he made his sisters look like pikers. "All right. Here's what we're going to do next. I want all of you to go to the nursery and stay there until I call for you. You can draw straws over which one gets to wear pink."

"But, Uncle Jake!" voices said in unison.

"If you behave," he continued, holding up his hand palm out, "we'll make that trip to the zoo I promised this afternoon." The girls started clapping and hopping and cheering, and he raised his voice to be heard over the squeals. "However, if I see so much as a ruffle or a hair ribbon downstairs, we'll forget about the zoo, and you'll all be sent to bed with only bread and water for supper. Now git."

The girls snickered with laughter as they made their way downstairs, recognizing his threat as nothing more than hot air. Jake knew he failed dismally at discipline, but he was new at it. Up until now, his role in these children's lives had been limited to gift giving and a visit every year or two. A man couldn't just switch from indulgent uncle to father with the snap of a finger.

Or the roll of a carriage.

Damn. Jake closed his eyes and absorbed the wave of grief before continuing downstairs. Daniel. His parents. Now Penny. Never would he have guessed that he'd be the last one alive. He was the one who'd been living his life on the edge, the one thriving on physical risk and dangerous circumstance. By all that was right, he shouldn't be the one remaining.

Find the necklace. Find your family.

What a crock that had been. He'd found the necklace and waited for his family to turn up. Waited for years. And what happens instead? He loses his family. Loses his sister. Just goes to show, that dream had been nothing more than a nightmare after all.

A crash from the general direction of the schoolroom jerked him back to the present. He needed to get downstairs. He wanted to hurry and get this over with before the little hoodlums escaped the nursery once again. Judging from past experience, he figured they'd listen to him for at most ten minutes.

His mind on his troubles, he neglected to pick up his

jacket from the chair as he passed it, and entered the drawing room wearing shirtsleeves and a scowl. He dropped all pretense at civility and sprawled in the chair opposite the sofa where Alasdair MacRae had taken a seat next to Jake's female guest.

"Hello, Dair. Glad to see you back so quickly."

Dair MacRae shrugged. "The business didn't take long."

Jake could tell from his face that the news his friend brought wasn't good. Suppressing a sigh, he turned to his other guest.

Marigold Pippin was the one woman, other than his sister, whom Jake had ever loved. She was the one woman on earth he trusted. She was the woman who'd changed his diapers as a babe, kissed his hurts when he bled and swatted his behind when he'd deserved it. She'd never once let him down. "All right, Nanny Pip. I'm ready. Tell me you have a solution for me. Their stunts grow bolder by the day."

"As do their cookies," observed Dair, staring oddly at the cookie in his hand. "Tastes like they added cayenne pepper to the recipe."

Jake winced, then sent a pleading gaze toward the woman who'd taught him his ABCs. "Well?"

Marigold Pippin gazed over the top of her wire-rimmed glasses and frowned in disapproval. "Look at you. You've soot all over your clothing, and you've absolutely ruined that chair. You could have taken five minutes to change clothes."

"In five minutes, they'll be listening at the keyholes. Please, Nanny Pip. What am I supposed to do?"

"You always were impatient." Marigold Pippin set down her teacup and saucer, then said, "I enjoyed spending yesterday with the children. They've grown so much. Miranda and Theresa were little more than babies when I retired. And little Belle, she reminds me so much of your sister at that age. Such a long time ago." Smiling sadly, she lost herself in memories for a moment. Then, in a matter-of-fact tone, she added, "They're sweet as spun sugar, for a fact."

Sweet? Jake and Dair shared an incredulous glance.

"I didn't need an entire day to determine the cause of their...shall we call it high spirits? It's as I suspected—the little dears are frightened down to their bones."

"Frightened? Frightened of what?" Jake sat up straight. "I haven't touched a one of them, Nanny Pip. I may threaten, but I never follow through. It was the boiling-in-oil comment, wasn't it? I knew I went too far, but they'd scared me to death sneaking out of the house at night like they did. I don't care that the park across the street is private and fenced. They had no business going there alone. When I think about who or what could have been hiding in the bushes..." He shuddered.

"They are testing you, Jake. They need to know if you're going to stay."

"Stay?" Jake could all but hear the hammer fall against the first nail in his coffin.

Commitment.

Marigold Pippin folded her hands across her prodigious bosom. "Has anyone told you what it was like for those poor little dears after our dear Penny and her husband were taken from them? And now you plan to leave. What do you expect?"

Jake propped his elbows on his knees and rubbed the back of his neck. Guilt sat in his stomach like a stone. "No one had to tell me it was awful. They went from beloved children to orphans in the blink of an eye. The physician I hired to examine Caroline said he could find no physical reason why she doesn't talk. He diagnosed mental trauma as a result of the accident."

Mrs. Pippin clucked her tongue. "Of course she's been traumatized! They've all been traumatized. And not only from the loss of their parents. Jacob, I know you were in the African jungle and that delayed your receiving the message about Penny. I know you came for the children at once upon learning the news. Nevertheless, they spent months with that awful Clarinda Barrett. Miranda told me all about it. Why, it's hard to imagine that she and Harrington were brother and sister. Harrington was so loving with his children. Clarinda all but abused them."

"Abused!" Jake exclaimed.

"She neglected the children, Jacob. She's a cold, bitter, old maid of a woman who offered the children not a bit of attention or sympathy or support in their time of great need. Clarinda Barrett swept down upon their home like a vulture, dismissed almost all of the servants, sold anything she deemed to be of monetary worth and went to Bath in search of a husband. A dowry is all that woman wanted. At her age! She left the little ones to fend for themselves almost entirely. For months!"

The stone in Jake's gut grew another five pounds of weight. He'd come as soon as he knew about the accident.

But he'd never intended to stay.

He glanced down, halfway expecting to see iron shackles clamped around his ankles. He glanced around the room, but saw nothing familiar. He'd grown up in New York, in America. Not bloody England. He didn't want to stay here. To live here. This was his father's house, one of dozens he owned across the world. It wasn't Jake's home.

Jake didn't have a home. He didn't want one. Ever since that ill-fated trip to Tibet, staying in the same place for more than a month or two made him antsy. His home was the road, an unexplored trail through a forest, an uncharted course upon the sea. That's what he wanted. It was who he was—a wanderer.

Wanderers had no business dragging children along with them.

Jake's jaw hardened. "Nanny Pip, I don't know what to do. I can't be a parent. Already, in the space of a single week, three governesses have quit on me. One girl didn't even last half a day!"

"Half a day?" Dair interjected. "Was she the one they tied up and pretended to burn at the stake simply because her name was Joan?"

"No." Jake sighed. "That was the one from Chesterfield. This one said something about toads in her wardrobe."

Nanny Pip smiled. "I know from Penny's letters that they've always been of the mischievous sort, but now they're using their pranks to test the limits of your love. They want to know if it's safe to love you."

"Safe?" He pushed to his feet and began to pace the room. Safe to love him? What kind of talk was that?

"What do they think I'm going to do? Feed them poisoned mushrooms?"

"They're afraid you're going to abandon them. That's why they're testing you, Jake. They're afraid you'll leave."

"Of course I'll leave! I'm leaving in six weeks, in fact. I wrote you about this. I'm going back to Tibet." He shoved his hand into his pocket and fingered the gold chain he carried with him always. "The trip has been in the planning for years, and I have to go."

The expression in Nanny Pip's eyes softened. "Darling, you know I love you, and I have your best interests at heart. It's time you let Daniel's ghost go. These children are the ones who need you now."

Jake's hand found the pendant. His thumb stroked the emerald. "I'm not going in search of Daniel's ghost or his mythical city. I don't believe in such nonsense. I'm going because I'm being paid a very nice commission by a prominent European museum to acquire certain items from the Panchen Lama's monastery."

Nanny Pip's expression said she didn't believe him one bit.

She knew him well.

"Those children need you," she said quietly.

Jake closed his eyes as everything inside him rebelled against the statement. "I wouldn't make a good parent. I'm not what those children need." He opened his eyes and stared straight at his former nanny. "They need you, Nanny Pip. They'd be so much better off with you. They already love you. They'd be happy."

Marigold Pippin said nothing in response, but simply sipped her tea. Jake heard the echo of yet another nail in his coffin. "Please?"

"Jake," Dair said with a sigh. "You know better. Nanny Pip has earned her retirement. In fact, I don't doubt she earned two retirements taking care of you."

"But—"

"Nanny Pip isn't the answer to your problem. She might be able to handle the children, but she'd be powerless against Clarinda Barrett."

Jake fired a look toward Dair MacRae. "Why would Nanny Pip need to worry about the aunt? What did you learn about her?"

"Enough to suspect she might go after the children legally if you're not around to stop it. The woman is still in Bath. She hasn't found a husband."

Jake's spirits sank with the news. "When I came back and assumed guardianship of the children…"

"You cut off her gravy train," Dair confirmed. "I doubt she'd attempt to take you on, but if you're out of the country and the children are left in the hands of paid caretakers—"

"Nanny Pip is family!"

"Not in the eyes of the law. Clarinda Barrett is a blood relation. This is England. It's all about blood. And the Barrett blood is bluer than most. No court would deny Clarinda's claim if you weren't around to stop her."

The final nail in his coffin was set. Yet it wasn't in Jake's nature to give in without a fight. "I could make prior arrangements with the lawyers to fight her, couldn't I?"

"You could." Dair stretched out his legs and crossed

them at the ankles. "If you're willing to trust the children's lives to lawyers."

Jake snarled at his friend, then raked his fingers through his hair. His sister had left him her babies. Her *five* babies. What was she thinking? He had no more business being a daddy than the man in the moon. "I can't believe Penny would do this to me!"

Nanny Pip sniffed. "Penelope protected her children. Remember what it was like when you were young, Jacob. Your parents left you and your sister and brother alone so very often."

"We weren't alone. We had you. Even before our mother died, you were always more a mother to us than she was."

"A sad statement, that. It's a situation I'm certain Penelope didn't want repeated with her little ones. Family is important to children, and you and your siblings suffered for the lack of one."

"We had family. We had each other, and after Mother died, Father didn't travel all that often." Jake recalled sitting in the study of the house on Park Avenue, poring over old maps with his father and brother.

"Your father may have been there in body, but not in spirit. Not for you and your sister, anyway. It was better for Daniel because he found a way to connect with the man by traipsing around the world bringing home dustables for him to fawn over. You were like a puppy trailing after him all the time."

"Dustables," Jake muttered with disgust, glancing at Dair. "Daniel brought home priceless treasures, and she calls them dustables."

Dair linked his fingers behind his head and shrugged. Nanny Pip smiled, then sobered. "Your sister loved her children, Jake, and she trusted in you to love them, too. You cannot abandon them to Clarinda Barrett."

The stone in his gut grew to boulder size. He couldn't abandon those little ones to their awful aunt. He wouldn't do that. But there had to be a way out of leg shackles in London.

Jake shut his eyes, hung his head and sighed.

Dair leaned forward, rested his elbows on his knees. "I have people working for me in that part of the world who could oversee the trip for you."

Jake grimaced but gave it serious thought for a moment before shaking his head. "Thanks, MacRae, but I won't give up my work. I love it. I love the travel, the adventure. The excitement of a new find. I'm going to Tibet."

With the necklace.

"Tell me you're not planning on taking those children with you, Jacob," declared Nanny Pip.

"No." Jake reached for a cookie as he slumped back down into his chair. He took a bite, chewed, studied the cookie much like Dair had done, then popped the whole thing into his mouth. Spicy sweet. Not bad, actually. Kind of like the way he liked his women.

Marigold Pippin shook her head in disapproval, whether at the size of his bite or from reading his mind—she was his former nanny, after all—Jake couldn't say.

Dair eyed his friend curiously. "If you're not turning the children over to Auntie Awful, and you don't intend to take them to Tibet, then just what do you have in mind?"

Jake dusted his hands. "I know my sister. She knew me. There's an out for me in this guardianship, or I can't find north by looking at a starry sky."

Actually, he'd already figured out his "out." He'd just hoped to find a less drastic solution. However, since none had occurred and time was ticking away, it looked as if he had no choice but to make the leap.

Jake reached for another cookie, took a nibble, then said, "Spicy sweet. I need to remember I like that as I go about the hunt."

"The hunt?" Dair's brows arched. "What hunt?"

"The hunt for a woman. A wife. A mother for my sister's children." Jake grimaced a little as he said it. A wife. First he's a father, now a husband?

"A wife," Dair repeated.

"Yeah." Jake's stomach took a nauseated roll. What the hell was in those cookies, anyway?

"Jacob," Nanny Pip said in a chastising tone.

Determinedly quashing his doubts, Jake plunged ahead. "If either of you can think of something else, please, let me hear it. Otherwise, I think that under the circumstances, if I want my freedom, then I'm going to have to get married."

Dair's mouth lifted in one of his rare smiles. "Your plan is to marry some woman, dump five kids on her, then sail off to Tibet for a two-year expedition? You'll accomplish this feat in six weeks?"

"Hmm…" Jake murmured. "You have a point. I probably can't get the job done in six weeks." He rose and crossed the room to the rosewood lady's writing desk in front of the window. From the center drawer, he removed a small calendar book and flipped through the pages. "Better make it eight. After all, I'll want a honeymoon."

Marigold Pippin slumped back against the sofa cushion and closed her eyes. "He always was a dreamer."

KAT MCBRIDE HATED zoological parks. She hated the smell and the small, dismal cages. She hated the sad-eyed stare of the animals trapped in a life, an existence, they must despise. Gazing at a tiger sprawled in the far corner of his cage, she wondered if he wished he were dead.

Sometimes when she looked in the mirror she imagined a set of bars in front of her own face.

"Kat, darling," called her grandmother. "There you are. Emma and I have been wondering just where you'd run off to. The reception is winding down."

Kat fought to summon up a smile, then turned around. Almost despite herself, she laughed. Her bold grandmother wore a paper mask with an elephant's trunk for a nose. "Where did you get that, Monique?"

"It's wonderful, isn't it? A precious little girl gave it to me. A little blond angel." Pausing just a moment, she pinned Kat with a shrewd gaze and added, "She reminded me of Susie."

Kat flinched. She couldn't help it. Even after two years, the sound of her daughter's name sent a spear of painful longing through her heart. Monique was the only family member who dared mention Susie's name aloud. The others walked so carefully around Kat, as if she were a fragile piece of glass that would shatter on the breath of a word she couldn't bear to hear. Monique said hogwash to that.

Six weeks ago, three hours after Mari hesitantly announced to the family at supper that her doctor believed she was carrying twins, Monique had knocked once on Kat's bedroom door at Willow Hill and barged right in. Finding the shades pulled, the room dark and her granddaughter lying listlessly on her bed, Monique had slapped Kat's hind quarters and ordered her to pack. She'd decided that Kat would accompany her on her upcoming trip to Europe for the dedication of the statue she'd completed for the entrance to the London Zoological Park. Kat's objections fell on deaf ears, and within a week she found herself in Galveston boarding a ship with Monique and Kat's sister Emma, who, surprisingly, had decided to tag along.

"Do you remember that time your father took Susie to P. T. Barnum's circus, and she roared back at the lion?" Monique asked.

"I do," said Emma as she slipped her arm through Kat's. "Her chubby little cheeks got so red, she roared so hard."

Kat smiled at the memory, and kept smiling even as they moved on to the next exhibit. It was getting easier to smile, she decided. Lately, she'd smile at least once a day. That was a great improvement over going weeks without one.

Maybe Monique was right. Maybe it was a good thing to think about her baby, to talk about her baby. Maybe it was a healing thing.

Kat was desperate to heal, for herself and for her family. She knew it hurt Mari that she couldn't be around Mari's little Drew or his sister Madeline.

Couldn't hold them, couldn't ruffle their hair. Couldn't kiss *their* chubby little cheeks.

Yes, Kat was desperate to heal. But no matter what her head said, no matter that common sense and every person in her life had declared her blameless in regard to the accident, her heart didn't believe it. Her heart couldn't fight free of the dark, heavy sadness that surrounded it.

Yet. Kat sucked in a deep breath, recognizing the tiny kernel of hope sprouting to life inside her.

At that moment a quartet of little girls came skipping toward them. Blond-haired, blue-eyed girls. One of them paused, looking at Emma, and her eyes went round. She elbowed another of the girls, then pointed. The second girl gave Emma a brief glance and nodded. "You're right. It's just like Uncle Jake's necklace, only his is green." Then, the girl pointed toward the giraffe house. "Look! You can see its nose peeking out the top."

The girls lost all interest in Emma at that. Kat watched them, her heart twisting. Lucky little girls. Susie never got to see a giraffe. Kat turned away. Tears swam in her eyes.

Emma's encouraging smile dimmed. "Oh, Kat."

"I'm sorry. Never mind me. Y'all had best be getting back to the reception, hadn't you? You're the star of the hour, Monique. People will be looking for you."

"I'm not the star." Monique smoothed her gray hair below the brim of her hat and batted her eyes as if she were fifty years younger. The woman never seemed to age, Kat thought. Monique lifted her dainty nose into the air. "My work is the star. Tell me, girls, have you ever seen such a delectable merman in your life? It's just a shame they wanted me to cover up his private parts with the scales of his tail. I do such a fine penis, if I must say so myself."

Emma and Kat looked at each other and burst out laughing. Monique winked and added, "It must be all the studying I've done, don't you think?"

"You are so wicked, Monique," Emma said.

"Thank you, dear. It's a matter of pride with me, you realize. I believe in being free and tossing caution to the wind. I believe in living life for the joy of it. Personally, I think the two of you would be happier if you'd take after me just a little bit more."

Emma leaned over and kissed her grandmother's cheeks. "When I grow up, I want to be just like you."

The sentiment caught both Kat and Monique by surprise, and they shared a curious look. Kat couldn't recall any recent time when her eldest sister expressed a desire to be wicked. Since being widowed, Emma remained cautious in her personal life. Except for a minor bit of talk when she'd ended her halfhearted romance with the widower, she never caused a stir or created even a hint of scandal. Emma was the good sister. So good, in fact, that she'd become downright boring. She did nothing to rock the boat.

Kat usually considered that a good thing since Kat's own boat invariably teetered at the point of capsizing.

She opened her mouth to comment, then changed her mind when Monique expressed interest in returning to the reception. Kat eyed the wrought-iron bench across from the tiger's cage.

"Why don't you go on? I'll catch up with you in a few minutes. I'd like to sit and enjoy the sunshine for a bit."

Kat sat by herself for a time, her eyes closed, her face lifted toward the sun as she tried to soak warmth into the chill in her soul. Then, suddenly, a squeal of frustration caught her attention. Kat turned toward the sound and gasped. One of the giggling girls who had scampered by earlier now stood at the corner of the tiger's cage. An elephant mask similar to the one Monique had been wearing lay inside the cage.

The skinny little girl was trying to squeeze between the bars.

Kat's heart all but stopped.

In her mind's eye, she saw a little dog dart out into the street. She heard the sound of wagon wheels clattering on the street. The soft cotton of a pinafore brushed her cold fingers.

In front of her, she watched the big cat's eyes light up with interest and his tail sweep slowly across the cage floor. The girl inched into the cage. *Susie McBride darted after the dog.* Kat dashed forward, running on winged feet. Her hand reaching. *Brushing Susie's dress.*

She heard a man cry out. Saw the animal rise to his feet. "Susie, no!" she cried as the girl stood with one arm and leg inside the tiger's cage, reaching…reaching…toward the mask.

The tiger growled, then crouched, ready to spring. *"Mama!"* the child in Kat's memory screamed. The child before her froze. The animal leapt.

"Susie!" Kat grabbed for the girl, gripped her arm and skirt and yanked her from the cage just before the tiger slammed against the bars.

Her heart pounding, her mouth dry as dust, Kat wrapped the sobbing girl in her arms and sank to her knees, cradling the child to her bosom. "Suzanne Elizabeth McBride. What were you thinking! That animal could have killed—"

She choked off the words as reality sank in. *This isn't Susie.*

Kat drew back from the child and looked at her. Really looked at her. This warm, wiggling little girl wasn't Susie. Wasn't her little girl. Her baby was dead. Lying cold and still in a dark grave beneath the winter snow at home.

Kat hadn't had another chance to save her daughter, after all.

Then, someone was tugging on the little girl. A man trying to pry the child from her arms. "Belle! Oh, Jesus. Thank God. Dammit, Belle!"

The man's voice shook. Color had bleached from his skin. His hands trembled and fear swam in his eyes. "Oh, Jesus. Lady, thank you. Thank you."

"Help me!" the little girl, little Belle, cried out. She wrenched herself from Kat's arms, leaving them empty. Empty.

Kat's arms flopped to her side. Tired. She was so, so tired.

The girl threw herself into the man's embrace. "That kitty almost eated me!"

In a flash, fury scorched through Kat's blood like steam, flowing into her fingertips, her toes, the tips of her ears, filling places within her dead to emotion for oh, so long. She stood and rounded on the stranger. "How dare you! How dare you neglect this precious child, this gift from God! How dare you pay her such little attention while out amongst the dangers of the world! Why, you should be arrested. You should be charged with child endangerment. You, sir, should be thrown into that tiger cage yourself so that—"

The girl hiccuped, and Kat noted her wide eyes, her trembling bottom lip. Kat realized that she'd been screaming at the man while he held his child. A frightened child. *Oh, Kat. Why didn't you think?* She reached up and wiped her brow.

The man's eyes widened. "Wait a minute," he said. "I know you. We've met before. Who… Oh, now I remember. You're Kat McBride."

Kat finally saw past the red of her own temper and the colorless wash of the man's complexion to the brilliant blue of his eyes. Jake Kimball.

He slowly straightened, hefting the crying child into his arms, absently patting her back in comfort.

"You." Kat gave her head a shake. "I can't believe it's you…."

"Small world, isn't it?"

Jake Kimball. If before Kat had steam in her blood, now it burned liquid fire. "You! You horrible, neglectful man. Do you know what almost happened here?"

"Yeah," he breathed. "Whoa, that was awful. I thought my heart would stop." He raked a hand through his hair—still long and fallen loose from its leather tie at the back of his neck. "Thank you, honey. Thank you so much. You saved my Belle. I don't think I could have made it in time. They caught me by surprise, sneaking off the way they did. Then for Belle to end up at the tiger's cage." He paused, shuddered. "They may look like angels, but believe me, they're demons in ruffled skirts."

He crooked his head toward the right and Kat saw three more blue-eyed blondes lined up watching the scene by the tiger's cage, their beautiful, rosy-cheeked faces filled with a combination of worry and trepidation.

"They're yours?" Kat asked.

Kimball glanced at them, hesitated, then said, "Yes. They're mine."

The girl in his arms lifted her face from where it was buried against his shoulder, smiled tremulously at Kimball, then popped her thumb into her mouth. She wriggled and he set her down. She scampered off to stand with her sisters.

It wasn't fair, Kat wanted to scream. A scoundrel, a thief and God-only-knew-what-else had four beautiful little girls warm and laughing and alive. Perfect. Life simply wasn't fair.

Kimball shoved his hands in his pockets and rocked back on his heels, his own gaze on the girls. He didn't see her distress. Her fisted hands. Her trembling.

"I guess I shouldn't have tried to bring them to the zoo by myself," he mused, "but I'd promised. When a friend offered to watch the baby at home, I decided to risk it."

A baby. Something inside of Kat twisted. What had

she done to deserve this? She wanted to climb into the tiger cage herself. "There's a baby, too?"

A glint of pride entered his eyes. "Yeah, a little boy. I'm hoping that as time goes on I'll be able to relate to him better than I do these girls. I don't understand them at all. I thought girls were supposed to have imaginary tea parties for their dolls. Not this group of girls. See the tall one over there? She got stuck in the chimney this morning. I had to go up onto the roof and pull her out. I think that's the third time, maybe even the fourth, that I've had to chase a child off the rooftop since we've been in London. It's only been a week."

Rooftops? He allows them to climb on London rooftops?

"Anyway—" he grinned at her, a carefree, devil-may-care grin that reminded her of Rory at his most charming "—I thank you for your help. You truly saved the day."

Kat was finding it difficult to breathe. She doubted she could force a word past the constriction in her throat. She didn't recall that he'd been married, but it must be so. And here he'd flirted so shamelessly with her that warm winter day in Galveston! The bounder!

The girls might well be feminine versions of their father—those blue eyes were unmistakable—but she'd bet they had the same mother, too. They looked too alike to be the products of different parents. Kat recalled what she'd learned of his travels during the time before Susie had been born when she'd pursued the Sacred Heart Cross. He'd been off on some expedition of a sort all the time. Judging by the ages of his children, he must have dragged his wife with him everywhere. Had they produced a child, dumped it with a caretaker, then gone off on their treasure hunts only to do it all over again? Or worse, maybe they took their children with them! Exposed them to fevers in South America. Cannibals in the South Pacific.

Tigers in the wilds of Africa.

Coaches in Fort Worth.

And he has five healthy children. Children he boldly claims not to understand or be able to control.

"So, are you here on holiday with your family?" Kimball asked, glancing around, awkwardly trying to make conversation. He had no clue that he skated on thin ice with his question. "I seem to recall that you were in a family way when you sought me out on Galveston Island. Was it a boy or a girl? Is the little one enjoying the zoo?"

Emotion churned inside of Kat, so much emotion she thought her head just might explode. Jake Kimball watched her curiously, waiting for her to respond. All Kat could manage was to give her head a quick, negative shake and whisper, "A girl."

His smile was perplexed, the light in his eyes wary. "Well, then. I'm sure you know all about little girls and their ways. I guess I'd best get back to my own little curtain climbers. Again, my thanks to you, Miss McBride. It's our good luck that you happened to notice what Belle was about."

"Good luck?" Kat repeated softly, unbelievably. It was the final straw. He had kept the cross. *He* was supposed to have the bad luck. Instead here he was catting about the London Zoo with his four healthy daughters? It wasn't fair! Good luck, he claimed? "I'll show you good luck."

With that, Kat shocked Jake Kimball's girls, other zoological park patrons who happened to be passing by and more importantly, Jake Kimball himself when she made a fist, drew back her arm, then let loose with a roundhouse punch to the jaw.

The unexpected blow caught him off balance and knocked him flat on his behind. Kat dusted her hands and smiled.

For the first time in forever, the smile went all the way to her eyes.

LATER THAT NIGHT as Kat lay in bed aching for Susie, wishing as she did at least once every day that she could have that one horrible moment in time back to live differently, her thoughts drifted back over the events of the day. She smiled into the darkness as she recalled the picture her grandmother made wearing that silly mask. She flexed her fingers as she replayed the moment she knocked Jake Kimball flat on his derriere, and the sense of power the moment gave her flowed through her once again.

Feeling stronger, she thought of his girls as they'd appeared before the tiger incident. Giggling, all pretty and pink, their blond curls bouncing as they skipped toward her along the path. A picture of joy. Brimming with laughter, with life. Jake Kimball was so darn lucky and he—

Kat sat straight up in bed. Her heart began to pound.

They'd slowed down, looked at Emma. What was it those girls had said? Just like Uncle Jake's except his was green? His what? Kat pictured her sister as she'd been at the zoo. His dress? His parasol? His purse?

His necklace.

"Oh, my God."

The clues fell into place. She *hadn't* lost her necklace. It *hadn't* dropped to the floor to be accidentally discarded with gift-wrapping paper.

Jake Kimball—scoundrel, treasure hunter and thief— had stolen it.

CHAPTER FOUR

"ARE YOU ABSOLUTELY CERTAIN you want to do this?" Dair MacRae asked, his tone resonant with doubt as he eyed the messenger waiting impatiently in the entry hall of Jake's town house.

"I'm certain." Jake passed over an envelope, tipped the messenger, then closed the front door behind him. "Everything's ready. Nanny Pip has promised to stay until we remove to the country, and by then I hope to have a full staff of appropriate servants hired. She's still well connected in the service industry. She believes she can find help with the right temperament to last in this household, from a governess all the way down to a scullery maid."

"I'm not concerned about the servants. It's the women that worry me."

"When have you ever let a woman worry you?" Jake asked with a snort. Almost subconsciously he rubbed his still-sore jaw.

A shadow passed briefly over Dair's expression, momentarily distracting Jake from his own troubles. There was a story there, Jake thought, but even after a decade of friendship, he didn't know the details. Women flocked to Dair, attracted by his dark and brooding air. He enjoyed their attentions when it suited him, then dismissed them with nary a second thought. Jake had never known a woman to get beneath his friend's skin.

"I'm not the one considering marriage," Dair replied. "If you go through with this scheme of yours, you'll be bound for life. A marriage of convenience is still a marriage. This is insane, Kimball, even for you."

Because Jake did value his friend's judgment, he considered Dair's words. *Was* he doing the right thing? *Would* Penny have approved of his plan? *Will* the girls be happy with a new "mother" in their lives?

Yes, to all of it. "True, it is a marriage of convenience. And since it's convenient for me, I don't see a drawback. As long as I choose the right woman, then matters should work out well for everyone—me, the children, the woman. Hell, even the servants."

"Therein lies the rub," Dair said gloomily. "Choosing the right woman. What a gamble that will be. Woman are like ready-made shoes, my friend. If you choose the wrong pair, they'll make you long for barefoot weather."

"Oh, quit being pessimistic." Jake slapped his friend on the back. "I am an excellent judge of character, and besides, I'll have the benefit of Nanny Pip's assistance. The woman was a nanny to dozens of children during a career that spanned over forty years. She helped me define the character traits I should look for in a potential wife and mother to Penny's children. She wrote many of the questions, and she's agreed to sit in on the interviews themselves."

"Why is it I see a runaway train heading right for us?" Dair mused.

Jake laughed. "It'll be all right, my friend. You'll see. I'll find myself a wife, settle her and the children at Chatham Park, and make it back to London in plenty of time to sail with the expedition."

"I do hope you're right."

It was indicative of Dair's distraction that he lifted a finger to massage his temple in front of Jake. Ordinarily, Dair went to great lengths to hide any sign of weakness.

It'd been that way as long as Jake had known him. They'd met over a decade ago during a robbery attempt of the Kimball collection. Late one night, Jake had sauntered into his father's study and caught Dair on the way out the window with a particularly nice Mayan fertility totem in his hand. Curious as to the thief's choice—he'd passed up precious gems and paintings by Renaissance masters—Jake had invited his uninvited guest to take a seat and discuss the burglary.

Encouraged by the gun in Jake's hand, Dair had accepted the invitation, then shared brandy and information. Four hours later, the two men had forged both a friendship and a working relationship. Over the years Jake had seen his friend wrestle against nature, battle wild animals and even wilder women. He'd never seen him hesitate, never seen him stumble, until about a year ago when the headaches began to plague him.

"They're getting worse, aren't they? Your headaches?"

MacRae slowly lowered his hand and scowled. "If they are, it's because thinking about this plan of yours would give anyone a headache."

Knowing he'd get no more from the man, Jake allowed the change in subject. "If it bothers you so badly, you don't have to stay and watch."

"I wouldn't miss this for all the whiskey in Scotland," Dair replied with a smirk. "It's bound to be a real zoo."

Later, when the women began arriving, Jake recalled his friend's words. He peeked out the window and spied the line forming outside the iron gate. He had a vision of little Belle reaching between the iron bars, and one of the women growing fangs and snapping at the girl. Then he thought of himself in the cage, trapped, with the women penned in with him.

Maybe this wasn't such a good idea after all.

Finally he thought of Kat McBride. He remembered the quickness of her movements at the tiger cage, the fierceness of her defense. A tigress herself where children were concerned. She was right to give him the sharp side of her tongue.

That boulder of guilt returned to his gut as her words replayed in his mind. Belle could have died. Died a horrible death, right in front of her sisters, and it would have been his fault.

Hell, he wasn't cut out to be a father. The incident at the zoo proved it. He was doing the right thing, finding them a new mother. A new guardian. A new protector.

He should look for someone like Kat McBride.

Jake mulled the idea over. A strong woman. Fiercely protective. A supportive family to turn to for help.

Yes. That's what he *would* do. He'd find a tigress. Someone equipped to take care of children.

If his sister were gazing down from heaven while that

scene at the zoo had been taking place, she'd be the first to agree. Finding someone like Kat McBride to mother these children was the best idea he'd had in years.

"IT'S A GREAT IDEA!" Kat exclaimed, waving the newspaper in her sister's face. "It's the perfect plan. In fact, I think it's worthy of the title of a true McBride-Menace escapade. If only Mari were here to take part in the fun."

In their suite at the Savoy Hotel, Emma lifted her nose from a bouquet of roses sent to her grandmother by one of her numerous admirers, then turned toward Monique. "I think she's lost her mind."

Monique met Emma's worried look in the reflection of the dressing table mirror. "Maybe she's found it, dear. I have not seen such life in her eyes or purpose in her manner since the accident. It's good to see her enthused about something again."

"Thank you, Monique." Kat smiled smugly.

Emma rolled her eyes. "You're happy to see her enthused about this, Grandmother? Have you paid the slightest attention to the words Kat's been rambling? The plan she's proposing? She wants to auction me off!"

"Careful, Emmaline," Monique warned. "I may be inching upward in years, but I am neither deaf nor senile. I happen to agree with your sister's plan. I think it's just the sort of escapade you girls need. I don't see why you're set against it, Emma. If I recall, you wished to join me on this trip because you felt the need for adventure in your life."

Emma snatched the folded newspaper from Kat's hand. "This isn't adventure. It's insanity!" She scanned the paper, found the advertisement and began to quote.

"Eligible bachelor seeking wife. Must be of good character with unsullied reputation. Must love children and country living. Independent personality a plus. Interested parties may apply for the position of Mrs. Jake Kimball at Bankston House in St. James Square.

"You know, I've heard of mail-order brides, but this is ridiculous. The London Season is about to begin. If he wants a society wife, why doesn't he simply go to the parties and balls like other men looking for a mate?"

"Because, Emma," Kat drawled, sounding closer in age to four than twenty-four. "He's not looking for a mate. He's looking for a mother. Monique and I heard all the ugly details while at the dressmaker today. He's richer than Midas himself, and he wants to find a woman who will care for his sister's children while he runs off to Timbuktu to add to his coffers. And you know how these vipers are here in London. They'll line up like hogs at a trough."

"I believe Mr. Kimball is headed for Tibet," Monique observed. "That's what I heard at the milliner's. He's scheduled to leave in a few weeks, and he's expected to be gone for up to two years."

"Two years? Two years!" Kat cried. "But he's responsible for those…never mind. Whatever. It doesn't matter." Jake Kimball could be departing on an expedition to Mars for all that she cared. "It doesn't matter at all. What matters is that you fit his stated desires perfectly. Your reputation is above reproach. You love children. You're very independent. You're perfect!"

"I'm not interested!"

Monique twisted around in her chair and eyed her eldest granddaughter speculatively. "I don't doubt that she'll satisfy the other requirements he failed to mention in his advertisement, too."

"What requirements?" Kat pursed her lips. She hadn't considered other requirements.

"He's a man, isn't he? The advertisement didn't mention a marriage of convenience or a platonic relationship. But I heard that much at the hat shop. He'll want a beauty to take to his bed. A girl with some spirit to her, I suspect. Emma's perfect."

A vision of Jake Kimball flashed in Kat's mind. He sat naked in bed, the white sheet draped casually across his groin a vivid contrast to his deeply tanned skin. He smiled his pirate's smile. His eyes gleamed with desire as he watched the woman approach. He watched *Emma* approach.

Kat shoved that thought right out of her mind.

"Emma's perfect, you say?" her sister repeated. "Emma thinks you've both lost your wits!"

Taking her grandmother's observation to heart, Kat eyed her sister in a new light and tried not to think about how the idea made her feel. "Of course he'll want to bed his bride. You're right, Monique. I should have thought of that. Emma, you should wear your yellow silk to the interview. For a totally proper day dress, it's very seductive."

"Aargh!" Emma threw up her arms, letting the newspaper go sailing. The door slammed behind her.

"She'll do it," Kat said, her arms folded, her toe tapping as she mentally reviewed the requirements for putting her plan into action.

"Yes, she'll do it," Monique agreed. "Although you'll need to work on her a little more."

The door burst open again and Emma, who didn't ordinarily flounce, flounced back inside. "If this is so important to you, Kat, why don't you marry the man? I don't see why *I* have to be the person to do it."

"Oh, Emma. Quit being so dramatic. It's out of character for you, and you don't quite pull it off."

Emma stopped abruptly, her lips thinned. "Out of character? And just what do you think my character is, Katrina?"

"Perfect is the word that comes to my mind."

"That's not very nice," Emma huffed. "I'm not perfect. I'm not perfect at all."

"But you're good and kind and considerate. That's a given, Emma."

"A given." Emma scowled. "So, you're saying I'm predictable?"

"Usually, yes. Although you have been acting a bit, well, more flexible on this trip. I like that. I think it's good for you, and in light of that fact, I'll apologize for my comment about you being perfect."

Emma's chin came up. "As right you should."

Monique dusted her cheekbones with rouge, then idly added, "You know, Emma, dear, she's not asking you to actually marry the man."

"That's right," Kat said, nodding. "I simply want you to interview for the job and impress him well enough to be invited to his country home for the house party, so I can tag along as your lady's maid and search the place for my necklace and the Sacred Heart Cross."

Emma dropped onto the settee. "How do you know they're there?"

Encouraged, Kat sat beside her. "I don't. But they could be. They say that Jake Kimball's father kept collections at all of his houses."

"Fine." Folding her arms, Emma added, "You want to search, then *you* be the bride on the auction block."

Kat shook her head. "I can't. He knows me. He knows how badly I wanted the cross five years ago. He might guess I'd be looking for my necklace, too. Besides, I'm not a woman of unsullied reputation."

Emma massaged the bridge of her nose. "Say I do this. Say I get invited to the country. How will you…?"

"I'll go in disguise. If Rory Callahan taught me anything, it was how to disguise myself."

Monique spoke up. "You know, darlings, it occurs to me that I won't be able to participate in this mission. Kimball knows me, too, from that lovely day in Galveston when he was sans a shirt. If he sees me with Emma, he'll glean the connection between the two of you and the jig will be up. I'll stay here in London and gad about, enjoying the Season."

"Well, that's it," Emma declared, seizing on the excuse. "If Monique can't go, than neither can we. We can't leave her in London alone. It isn't safe."

"Oh, for heaven's sake," Monique said. "That may

well be one of the dumbest things to come out of your mouth in years."

Emma had the grace to look sheepish. After all, Monique Day could well be the most independent woman ever born. She'd traveled the world by herself and been perfectly at ease while doing so. Age might have slowed her physically, true, but her character and sense of self were just as strong now as they had ever been.

"Come on, Emma," Kat urged. "Please? For me?"

"But what if…say you're right, Kat. Say he did steal your necklace. He would have had to break in to Willow Hill to do it. He might have seen me. He might recognize me, too."

"I've considered that, but I think the risk is minimal. Besides, what's the worst thing that can happen? He won't invite you to his party. Of course, in that case, I'll just get to work on finding another way to locate my necklace."

"That's a good idea," Emma said. "Why don't you wait until he leaves for Tibet and you can—"

"I can't wait," Kat said. "What if he takes it with him?"

"Why would he do that?"

"I don't know. I don't know why he stole it in the first place, but he did. I'm sure of it. If you'd been there that day on the beach, seen the avarice in his eyes, you'd know it, too, Emma. I can't risk that he'll take it with him when he goes to Taiwan."

"Tibet," Emma corrected glumly.

Monique rose from her chair, crossed the room and took Emma's hand. "Darling, you know I don't like to interfere…"

The sisters shared an eye-rolling glance.

"...but I want you to look at your sister. When was the last time you saw Kat shine this way?"

"Why?" Emma asked. "Why is this so important to you, Kat? I thought you'd stopped believing in the power of the necklaces. That's what you said after yours disappeared. And the cross—that doesn't belong to you. Stealing it from Jake Kimball would make you no better than he is."

"True, but I don't care." She cleared her throat and tried to make sense of the nonsensical. "I want my necklace back because the necklaces are something special the three of us share. As far as the Sacred Heart Cross goes, I think it belongs in the San Antonio church where it was intended to reside. I think if I helped it reach its intended destination, I might...well...look, I sinned by running off with Rory. I sinned against our family, against God. Maybe Susie..."

"No, Katrina," Monique snapped. "Don't you dare think that Susie's accident was some sort of Old Testament punishment. That's nonsense. Pure hogwash."

A lump of emotion hung in Kat's throat. "Nevertheless, I need to make amends. I need to pay penance."

Emma's sad eyes chided her sister. "Oh, Kat, that's not true."

"You're not even Catholic," Monique added.

Kat met first her grandmother's gaze and then her sister's. Flatly she said, "I allowed my child to die."

"Stop it," Monique demanded. The green silk of her dressing gown stirred as she rose regally from her chair and marched toward Kat. She took her granddaughter's chin in her hand and stared deep into her eyes. "It was an accident. A simple, tragic accident. You've punished yourself long enough, Katrina. Mourn your daughter as long as you need to. Miss her each and every day. But stop punishing yourself." Now she brought her other hand up, cradled Kat's face between her hands, leaned down and kissed her granddaughter's forehead. "Listen to me, child. It wasn't your fault."

"I know." But, she didn't *know.* Kat closed her eyes and stepped away. Turned away. Fought back tears. What *was* this scheme of hers all about? Why did it matter so much that she find her necklace, find the cross?

It didn't matter why it mattered. It didn't have to make sense. If she wanted to be irrational, she could be irrational. It was her legacy. The right of a McBride Menace. The right of a mother who'd lost the better part of her soul.

Finally in control of herself, Kat faced her sister and fought hard to summon up a real smile. "All right, then. Leaving my daughter out of it, you ask why this mission, why besting Jake Kimball, is so important to me? Here's why. I don't have a good reason. I just want to do it."

Emma met Kat's stare for a long moment, then said, "Now, *that* makes sense." With a sigh, she capitulated. "All right, I'll do it. When does this farce begin?"

Excitement chased away Kat's melancholy. "He's conducting interviews today and tomorrow. I think we're better off waiting until almost the end of the process. By that point, he'll recognize that you outshine most everyone under consideration."

"If you think that's best, Kat. This is your show."

"That it is. Let's plan for the curtain to rise about three tomorrow afternoon, shall we?" Anticipation stirred her soul. "This afternoon we'll need to pay a call on a costume shop. What type of a maid do you want, Emmie? Fat? Thin? Older with wrinkles? Younger with spots on her face?"

"No spots." Emma wrinkled her nose. "That's a touchy subject with me. I still get one or two upon occasion. Look." She pointed to the very corner of her left eye. "See that? It's the beginning of a wrinkle. I'm going to have spots and wrinkles at the same time. Now where's the fairness in that?"

Monique bubbled with laughter. "My goodness, Emma. You sounded just like Kat right then. The Kat of old."

Kat made a show of huffing and they all laughed, then Monique suggested, "Regarding your disguise, why don't you pattern your disguise after someone from home? Kat, you're a born actor, and you'll have no trouble staying in character. Emma, however, might benefit from having a slice of the familiar in the game. Lying doesn't come as naturally to her as it does to you, Kat."

"Thank you, Grandmother," Kat replied dryly.

"That's a good idea. Hmm…" Emma tapped a finger against her lips. "Who should you be? I think not a maid, but my companion. It will give you more access to events. You can't be Aunt Claire or Mama, of course."

"No one in the family," Kat agreed.

"I was thinking of Wilhemina Peters," Monique said, studying her nails.

Emma's gaze met Kat's, and they both burst out laughing. "I don't know," Emma said, eyeing her sister's bodice. "The Menaces have all been blessed with a substantial bosom, but to mimic Wilhemina... well...Kat, do you think you could navigate with that much extra cleavage?"

Kat glanced down at her breasts and mentally added a dozen inches. "I think I'll do all right—as long as I stay away from table lamps."

"WOULD YOU LIKE some peanuts?" Dair offered Marigold Pippin a sample from his bag when the parlor door closed behind bridal prospect number—Dair checked his notes—ninety-two. After sitting through yesterday's sessions, he'd come prepared for the circus today. "Or perhaps some popcorn?"

"I'm fine, thank you," Marigold said with a heavy sigh. Glancing toward Jake, she confirmed what everyone in the room already knew. "Another no?"

Two heads covered in blond curls simultaneously peeked out from behind the window draperies. "Definitely a no!"

Jake merely shook his head while continuing to make notes on the papers in front of him on the desk. Nanny Pip scolded the girls, "I thought you two promised to keep your comments to yourself if we allowed you to stay."

"They've been giving hand signals to Jake for an hour," Dair said.

"Girls." Nanny Pip clucked her tongue, then caught Jake's gaze. "You're as much a problem as they are in

regards to discipline. If you don't enforce your demands, they'll never mind you."

Jake thought a moment. "You're right. Let me make
a note before the next prospect." He searched for the
proper sheet, then wrote: #22. Discipline enforcer. "All
right, then. How many do we have left?"

The answer came from behind the drapery. "I see
three outside and two inside. I think two of the five are
companions for the ladies, though."

"Hmm...only three left." Jake glanced at Dair.
"We've only said yes to four. I'd thought to have more
to choose from. I didn't realize finding a bride would
prove so difficult."

"You're a picky man, Jacob Kimball," Nanny Pip declared.

"Well, it's a picky job. Penny would expect no less
of me."

"I doubt she'd have expected this," Dair said as he
popped a peanut into his mouth. "Shall I send in the next
dancing bear?"

"Yes. I'm ready to get this nonsense over. But give
me one of those peanuts first, would you?"

Jake's brows lifted fractionally as the next hopeful
bride-to-be walked gracefully into his study. She was
accompanied by a gray-haired, big-bosomed woman
wearing wire-rimmed glasses and an air of disdain.

The girl was beautiful, older than many of the matrimonial prospects who'd answered his advertisement;
with strawberry-blond hair and a delectable figure. She
had a look of strength about her that Jake found appealing. "Good afternoon, Miss...?"

"Mrs.," she corrected. "Mrs. Tate. I've been widowed for some time. This is my companion, Mrs. Wilhemina Peters."

Ah, Mrs. Tate was an American. Being half-American himself, Jake counted that as a plus. He nodded toward Mrs. Peters, then addressed the widow. "My condolences on your loss. I am Jake Kimball. This is Mrs. Pippin—" he gestured in her direction "—and Mr. MacRae."

Dair nodded, his gaze never leaving Emma.

Everyone said a cordial hello. Jake shuffled through his papers for the one containing questions he'd developed specifically for widows. Then, he began. "So, Mrs. Tate. Judging by your delightful accent, I gather you're from America?"

"Yes."

"Where in America?"

She glanced at her companion. "Dallas. Dallas, Texas."

The companion beamed a pleased smile. Curious, Jake thought. His gaze narrowed on the older woman. Something was off. Something…oh, a wig. She wore a wig.

Satisfied, he returned his attention to the younger woman and smiled. "I've spent some time in Texas. Summers there can be brutally hot."

"Yes, sir." She smiled, appeared to relax somewhat. "Winters in Fort Worth are pleasant enough."

The companion piped up in a nasal, annoying tone. "Fort Worth, Dallas, Weatherford, Grapevine. They're all towns close together. Weather is the same all those places."

Mrs. Tate briefly closed her eyes. Her cheeks flushed.

Hmm. Jake referred to his questionnaire. "Tell me a little bit about yourself. Age, occupation, hobbies…"

"You want to know her age?" the companion asked, slapping a hand to that prodigious bosom. "A man shouldn't ask a woman her age. It's downright offensive!"

Mrs. Tate rolled her eyes. "I don't mind sharing my age, Mr. Kimball. I'm twenty-nine. I'm a schoolteacher, and I have tutored privately, also. My hobbies are reading, needlepoint and fishing."

"Fishing?"

"I find it relaxing."

Jake waited a moment for her to expound on her reply. He'd found during his interviews that most women loved to talk about themselves. Apparently, Mrs. Tate was different.

From the corner of his eye, Jake caught the flash of frustration flaring in the companion's eyes before she abruptly leapt into the conversation. "Mrs. Tate is an excellent teacher. She has an honest love for knowledge that she passes along to her students. She has a way of making the boring topics palatable and her students adore her. Not that she allows them to run roughshod over her. Quite the contrary. She's a firm but fair disciplinarian, and she has earned the respect of her students, their parents and everyone in town. Parents compete to have their children placed in Mrs. Tate's class. Once, a local merchant offered her a hundred dollars if she'd make room for his son in her class."

"Did she take the bribe?"

"She certainly did. Not only did the money buy an extra desk for the merchant's son, it also bought school-books for the entire class, slates and chalk and a globe and new shoes for a few of the students who couldn't afford them and…and…" She glanced at the widow. "That bead thing. For arithmetic. Emma, what is it called?"

"An abacus." Emma's smile was tight.

"An abacus. That's right. So you see, Mr. Kimball, it would have been foolish of her not to accept the bribe. Everyone benefitted, even that mean little Henry Wilkins who thought he was better than everyone else in the class because his father had money." She folded her arms across that wide bosom and huffed.

Jake tapped his pencil on the desk. He'd learned more from that outburst than she might have known. The widow's name was Emma, she inspired loyalty in her friends, and the companion wore a disguise.

The question begged why. Anyone was allowed to attend this interview. No need for disguise…unless he knew the woman.

Jake took a closer look. He wanted to know more. Addressing Mrs. Peters, he said, "And her hobbies, what does she like to read?"

"History books. She's interested in foreign lands. She has a particular interest in Scotland as her family originated in that country, and she fell in love with the Highlands during one of our visits there."

"An intelligent beauty," Dair commented from the sidelines, winking at the Widow Tate, who blushed. "Scotland is one of the finest places on earth."

Emma Tate smiled shyly. "You're a Scot, Mr. Mac-Rae?"

"By blood, if not by birth. Actually, I was born in Texas. I'm a wanderer by nature."

"Oh?" Emma leaned forward. "What's your favorite place to visit?"

"The islands of Hawaii are particularly appealing."

"The Hawaiian Islands?" Interest lit Emma Tate's lovely blue eyes. "I've always been fascinated by that part of the world."

While the widow and his best friend beamed at each other, Jake addressed Mrs. Peters. "What about novels? Is she one who believes reading should always be educational, or does she support reading just for fun?"

"Emma reads adventure novels, sir. She loves a good story."

Hmm. Jake knew he was hearing one of those now. Who was this woman in disguise? She was younger than the character she portrayed, that was obvious once he started looking. What could her goal be? Was she a thief casing his home with intentions of committing robbery? Or were her motives more personal in nature?

Jake intended to find out. Referring to his notes, he chose a question at random. "Mrs. Tate, can you sew?"

Emma dragged her attention away from Dair and glanced at her companion. Both women winced. "My mother is a talented seamstress, sir," Emma said. "She's a magician with a needle and thread. That's a fact. From the time I was a little girl, she tried to teach my sisters and me her skills. Finally, after years of trying, she threw up her hands in defeat. We're hopeless, Mr. Kimball. If you want your wife to teach your nieces embroidery, I'm afraid you need look elsewhere."

Once again, the companion threw in her opinion. "Embroidery is a useless skill in this modern day and age, anyway, Mr. Kimball. Machines are taking over all aspects of the garment trade. The quality of ready-mades is rising, and I predict that in another ten years, custom dressmaking will be the exception rather than the rule."

"You consider yourself a modern woman, Mrs. Peters?"

"I do."

"I suppose you support female suffrage?"

"I do."

"You don't consider bicycling a vulgar pastime for a woman?"

"Absolutely not!"

It was the flash of fire in emerald eyes that did it. He reached up and gently prodded the fading bruise on his jaw. A grin tugged at his lips.

Well, well, well. Kat McBride. Of all the women he'd considered might show up for this event, she wasn't one of them. But why the disguise?

The cross, of course. She thinks to get her long, slender fingers on the Sacred Heart Cross. But does she intend to steal it?

Yes, he thought she probably intended just that. Intrigued, he settled back into his chair to enjoy the moment, and for the next ten minutes, Jake and "Mrs. Peters" debated equal rights for women, the concept of freedom of the press and the propriety of female presence in the workplace. When Jake suggested that women shouldn't engage in work outside the home, he thought she might take yet another swing at him. It was the most enjoyable conversation he'd had with a woman in years.

Finally, Dair interrupted. "Excuse me, Jake, but perhaps I should mention that you've run over time with Mrs. Tate, and you have asked hardly any questions on the list."

"Oh, yes. You're right. I apologize." Jake jerked his attention away from Emma Tate's most fascinating companion and scanned the list for a question that truly intrigued him. Seconds later, he looked at Emma and gently said, "You said you've been widowed for a while. Why have you not yet remarried?"

"I loved my husband deeply," Emma said, honesty ringing in her tone. "I've yet to find another man who will share with me a love that is strong, vigilant and true."

Jake bit back a grin when "Mrs. Peters's" eyes rolled and she let out a soft, but audible groan. But he was curious, so he asked, "Will you not settle for less, Emma Tate?"

"No, I will not."

Jake sat back in his chair. He liked Emma Tate. He liked her honesty and her sincerity and her gentle smile. But it didn't intrigue him like Kat McBride's fire.

Her companion reached across the distance and gave the widow's arm a quick, but apparently hard, pinch. "Sorry, there was a fly on your arm. Just shooing it away."

"I see," Jake said. And that he did. Quite clearly. Nanny Pip and Dair MacRae remained in the dark, however, so they were obviously surprised when he reached into his desk drawer and removed an engraved invitation. Standing, he handed it to Emma Tate. "It's been a true pleasure to meet you, my dear. I hope you'll be able to join us at Chatham Park next weekend for a small soirée I'm hosting?"

Shock registered on the faces of every person in the room. Every person but the ones behind the draperies, that is. They peeked out, grinned, and signaled Jake a thumbs-up. Jake thought they were Belle and Theresa. However, one of them might have been Miranda.

Emma rose from her seat and accepted the invitation, a look of puzzlement on her face. "Why, yes. Thank you. We'll be pleased to attend, although, I must say I'm surprised. I didn't think—"

"We didn't think you'd be so perceptive, sir," the companion interrupted, bounding to her feet. She elbowed Emma in the side. "Some men don't recognize treasure when it's right in front of their face."

"Oh, I recognize treasure. You can count on that." He stared deeply into her eyes. "I am a treasure hunter, after all. And just so you know, once I find a treasure, I don't give it up."

"Hmm," Kat McBride murmured, a secretive, satisfied smile on her face.

It was all Jake could do not to kiss that smile right off her lips. Instead, he escorted the women to the door, then bowed over their hands, one at a time. "Until the weekend."

"The weekend," Emma's companion replied.

Jake returned to his desk with a spring to his step. "Well, now," mused Marigold Pippin. "That was interesting."

"*Interesting* isn't the word I'd choose," Dair said. "Does somebody want to tell me just what's going on here?"

Jake took his seat, leaned back in his chair, threaded his hands behind his head, his elbows wide, and grinned. "Girls? I'm done here this afternoon. Why don't you go find your sisters, and see if your brother is up from his nap? I have a mind to take us for ice cream."

"Ice cream!" Draperies flapped in the whirlwind created by a pair of departing children.

"If you've completed your interviews for the day, then I think I'll toddle along after Belle and Miranda," said Nanny Pip. "I want to check on the new nursemaid, make sure she's all right with the little master."

When the study door shut behind Mrs. Pippin and the girls, Dair hooked his thumb over his shoulder and asked, "What about the women still outside?"

"Belle and Miranda," Jake mused. How could she tell? How can anyone tell?

"Jake? The women outside?"

"Oh, I'll send them away, tell them I've...no, wait. They have waited quite some time." Jake reached into his drawer once again and brought out two more invitations. "I'll give them these, then send them on their way."

"You're inviting two more women to Chatham Park? Sight unseen? Not interviewed? That makes how many? Seven? Are you a madman?"

Jake strode toward the window, looked outside. "Well dressed, decent appearance. They'll do. The more, the merrier, I always say. Now that the situation has changed, though, I guess I should invite a few men along to take up the slack. Don't want to leave the ladies completely disappointed."

Dair reached for his peanuts. "And here I thought the circus was almost over. What's going on, Jake?"

"A change of plan. I don't need the weekend to test the women to see who best meets my qualifications for a bride because I've already found her."

"Yes, that much I figured out. You've settled on Mrs. Tate. But I'm curious as to why. Sure, she's beautiful. Intriguing. Intelligent. But you've turned away a number of beautiful, intriguing, intelligent women these past two days. I imagine you like that she's an American, but I distinctly remember three other attractive Americans in the line whom you didn't invite to your country house. What's so special about Emma Tate?"

"What's special about Emma? Quite a few things, I would imagine. She seems like a lovely young woman. However, she's not the woman I intend to make my wife."

"She's not?"

Was that relief in Dair MacRae's eyes? Interesting. "No, I have no intentions toward Emma."

"Then you have me totally confused. Who the hell is the woman you intend to marry?"

"The companion."

"What companion?"

"Mrs. Tate's companion."

Dair froze, blinked twice. "The old battle-ax? Her bosom nearly took out the Grecian urn when she walked in."

"Padded today, I am certain." Jake chuckled softly.

"Well." Dair folded his arms. "Obviously I wasn't paying attention."

"It's not like you. But then, I don't think you ever took your eyes off Mrs. Tate."

"So what did I miss?"

Again, Jake probed the sore spot on his chin. Then, grinning wickedly, he said, "It all has to do with cookies, you see. Spicy sweet."

"Having children has driven you insane."

"That is a possibility I will not argue with. However, my sanity or lack thereof is not an issue in this instance. 'Mrs. Peters' is the perfect choice."

"Why?" Dair shuddered. "She may have been interesting for you to talk to, I'll allow, but Jake, she's rather...well...old. And she's...she's...spread out. I thought you intended to share a bed with your bride."

"Oh, I do. I certainly do." Now, he laughed out loud. "She's actually a good bit younger than me, and she's not fat at all. In fact, her figure is quite lovely, as is her face without the stage paint."

"Stage paint?"

"Subtle and well done, but those wrinkles were painted on. Her hair isn't gray, but quite the same shade as her sister's."

"Her sister! So you *do* know the woman."

"Oh, yes. I've met her on two previous occasions and

they've both proved memorable. Dair, I need you to put your investigative talents to use for me again, if you will. I want to know everything you can find out about Kat McBride of Fort Worth, Texas."

CHAPTER FIVE

KAT FELT ALMOST GIDDY as the carriage turned on the drive that led up to Chatham Park ten days later. "Oh, my. Look at that, Emma. It's a palace."

"Owned by an American upstart," Emma added. "That's what those women were saying at the theater last night. As if they were better than Jake Kimball's father because he worked for his money rather than inheriting it. Personally, I think a man who makes something of himself, by himself, has much more to preen about than a man who is wealthy just because somebody else died."

"That's very American of you, Em."

"Well, I am an American and I'm proud of it! I tell you what, Kat, if these snotty English primroses start giving me grief because I'm from Texas, well, they just might get their clocks cleaned." Emma folded her arms and sat back against the seat in a huff.

Kat smiled at her sister's vehemence. It was nice to see Emma loosening up. She suspected this bit of Menace-like behavior would be good for her in that respect. Her sister had become almost stodgy in recent years.

Kat turned her nose back toward the carriage window. Her pulse pounded with anticipation. She told herself it was due to the hunt. Certainly the prospect of seeing Jake Kimball again, tangling with Jake Kimball again, had nothing to do with it.

The man was a scoundrel. According to Monique, who made a point of becoming privy to the *on dits,* society was aghast at Kimball's plot to advertise for a bride, then pit the finalists against one other in a contest disguised as a country house soirée. Draconian, they accused. Gauche, they declared. Positively reprehensible—even for a Yank. Yet, for all the whispers, the muttering, the yammering about scandal, an invitation to Chatham Park this weekend had been the hottest ticket in town.

And somehow, despite Emma's unfortunate tendency to tell the truth and Kat's own tendency to let her mouth run away from her, the McBride Menaces had scored the invitation of the year. Maybe even the decade.

"Monique said she subtly asked around about Jake Kimball. Nobody mentioned his having a necklace that looks like yours, but she did learn that Jake Kimball's father kept collections at Chatham Park," Emma said.

"Which collections?"

"That, she couldn't find out. Someone said something about butterflies, and someone else talked about fossils."

"No Texana?"

"She heard nothing about Texana, but that doesn't mean it's not here, Kat. Look at it. Chatham Park is huge. We'll be lucky to find the water closet."

Kat let out a long sigh. "Emma, don't you dare say anything that will get us sent away before I've searched the house."

"Excuse me? I'm not the one who let her mouth overrun her brain during the interview. I couldn't believe you talked about women's suffrage! I thought you'd ruined our chances for sure."

Kat agreed. She still couldn't believe they'd actually won an invitation. After their return to the hotel with the prize in hand, Monique had gone on the prowl for gossip. She'd returned with the news that he'd interviewed almost a hundred girls. One hundred! Really, did women here have no pride? Out of all those interviewed, only seven had received invitations to the weekend's festivities. Two were shop girls, one a baron's daughter, and the rest an impoverished knight's widow, a sea captain's daughter and the bastard niece of the Duke of Worrell. And, Mrs. Casey Tate. Betting books at the gentleman's clubs had the baron's daughter as the odds-on favorite. Most considered Emma a long shot.

Kat had been insulted on her sister's behalf, which was totally foolish of her since the entire exercise was a farce.

"Look at the lake, Kat. See the swans?" Excitement gleamed in Emma's eyes, and she flashed Kat a Menace grin. "Papa would kill us for pulling a stunt like this."

Peeking through the avenue of tulip trees lining the winding road she spied swans and fountains and flowers galore. The estate was a delight for the eye. She glimpsed a folly and a hidden flower garden, statues and fountains and what appeared to be a maze. When their carriage rounded a curve and the house came into view, both sisters caught their breath. "It's huge," Emma mused.

The massive mansion rose in front of them like a general on a battlefield, commanding all within sight. The building was a collection of styles—a baroque front, Greek Revival portico, and a high tower, or belvedere, that added a suggestion of the medieval to the place. Kat counted at least four three-storied wings off the main building.

Then, as the coach pulled into the circular drive, standing on a third-floor balcony, she saw him. Jake Kimball, thief, scoundrel and one audacious American.

Kat shook her head. "Look at him. It's as if he's a prince awaiting the arrival of his princess. Only, it's a princess contest, isn't it? What do you think he has planned for this weekend? Competitions? The woman who can darn socks the fastest earns five points, woman with the most points at the end of the weekend wins?"

"My," Emma said, gazing up toward the balcony. "There is something appealing about a man surveying his kingdom. Jake Kimball certainly is handsome."

"You should see him without his clothes," Kat said absently.

"Mari did tell me he made one fine-looking pirate. I was disappointed he didn't wear an earring at the interview. Mari said it added a dashing touch."

Dashing didn't begin to describe the man. *Handsome* was an understatement. "As if he needs more *handsome* and *dashing*," Kat grumbled. "Any other man would have been laughed out of the country for wearing an earring and publishing that advertisement. He gets a hundred women lined up to compete to be his bride. A woman he can wed, bed and kiss goodbye with nary a second glance when he runs off to Tokyo."

"Tibet," Emma corrected.

"It's appalling that women would put up with such nonsense."

"Hmm," Emma murmured. "I wonder if he plans to hold a kissing contest?"

"Emma!"

Kat's sister laughed as the carriage rolled to a stop, and moments later they climbed a broad flight of stone steps and entered Chatham Park. The great hall took Kat's breath away. A painted ceiling, paintings on the wall, marble sculptures and rich Persian carpets on the floor—and a host who fitted his surroundings perfectly. Monique would be the first to say the man was a work of art.

Halfway down the staircase, Kimball said, "Ladies, welcome. I'm delighted you could join us. Alasdair MacRae, you remember Mrs. Tate and Mrs. Peters."

Her attention fixed totally on Jake Kimball, Kat hadn't noticed the man who'd come to stand in a doorway that opened into what appeared to be a library. Mr. MacRae's shoulders all but spanned the doorway. He wore his clothes casually, his chocolate-colored jacket the same color as his hair. His knee-high boots were scuffed and worn and comfortable appearing. Not the typical English country gentleman. Of course, he wasn't English, he was Scots-American, and they were a different breed, anyway.

"I certainly do. Ladies, it's a pleasure to see you again."

Emma smiled shyly at him and a touch of color stained her cheeks. Kat's eyebrows winged up. Was her sister attracted to MacRae? Oh, lovely.

Kimball continued, "We will show you to your room so you can freshen up. Three carriages arrived no more than ten minutes ago, so I'm afraid I'm a bit short-handed of servants at the moment. You won't mind Mr. MacRae and me showing you the way, I trust?"

Emma darted another look toward MacRae. "That's fine."

Kat wasn't so certain.

Kimball gave them a brief history of the house as they climbed the stairs. The estate had been a minor holding of Sir John Cowper, who sold the property to Kimball's father years ago. "My father expanded the house substantially. He wanted beautiful spaces to display his treasures."

"Oh?" Kat responded with what she hoped came across as casual interest. "What treasures?"

"His collections." He smiled, his eyes gleamed, but he didn't elaborate.

Kat felt almost as if she'd been challenged. She persisted. "What sort of collections?"

He waved a hand. "Oh, this and that. Ah, here we are." They'd arrived at the third-floor landing. "Dair, if you'd show Mrs. Tate to her room? It's the snow globe room. I trust you'll find it satisfactory. I'll have your bags sent up as soon as possible. Mrs. Peters, if you'll come with me?"

"Wait!" Kat exclaimed. "Mrs. Tate and I are not together?"

"Heavens no. I've chosen rooms with each guest in mind. After our discussion the other day, I am quite certain you'll find it to your liking."

As Kat followed Kimball down a long hallway, she decided she had a bad feeling about this. Had Kimball separated all his brides from their chaperones? Had Emma been on to something? Did he intend a kissing contest, or worse, a bedding comparison?

She wouldn't put it past the scalawag. Heavens, some of the women probably wouldn't complain. Some of the women probably fantasized about a man like Jake Kimball taking them to his bed.

Kat focused on the man in front of her. Foolish women, they'd like to tug that leather tie from the back of his neck and run their fingers through his thick, unfashionably long hair. They'd look at his broad shoulders and want to smooth their hands over his muscles. They might even want to run their tongue down the curve of his spine.

Kat's gaze followed the path of her thoughts. They'd certainly want to cup their hands around the hard, naked plain of his buttocks and—

"Here we are."

Kat jerked her stare up and willed away a blush as Kimball glanced over his shoulder and smiled. "It's the equal-rights-for-women suite."

That announcement effectively distracted her. "What?"

"Come inside and see." He grinned his pirate's grin,

and were it not for her disguise, she might have mentally added, *Said the spider to the fly.*

However, protected by the battle-ax persona she'd adopted, Kat brushed past Jake Kimball into her room. *Did he just sniff at me as I went by?*

Then, Kat forgot about her host as she realized what awaited her inside the bedroom. Framed newspaper articles decorated the walls: the *Daily Telegraph,* the *Times,* the *Eclectic Review,* the *Guardian.* Forgetting herself and her disguise, Kat laughed. "It's wonderful."

"It's subversive. Look at what some of these women proposed—divorce, equal pay, admittance to Gentleman's clubs. Can you believe that? Such nonsense would set back men's and women's relations for a hundred years."

Kat walked toward an article hung prominently on the north wall. A Victim of Bigamy Demands Justice for Her Children, read the headline. Kat swallowed a lump in her throat. Bigamy. Good heavens. "Where did this come from?"

"The *California Spirit of the Times.* I understand bigamy was quite a problem in California during the gold rush days."

California wasn't the only state with bigamists, Kat thought, a wave of sadness washing over her. "Not this article. All the articles."

"I told you my father was a collector."

"He must have been an interesting man."

Kimball was staring at her peculiarly, as if he could sense her melancholy. Kat frowned. Perhaps her acting abilities weren't quite up to snuff.

"My father was...driven," he finally said. "It brought him great success, great wealth. I cannot say it brought him much happiness. As much as he wanted to possess things, he didn't care much about human contact. His family paid the price."

"You?"

His mouth quirked in a crooked grin. "Not until now," he said, his tone wry. "I'm thinking of my sister. She wanted things from my father that he wasn't able to give her."

For the first time, Kat caught a glimpse of the man beyond the treasure hunter, beyond the scoundrel. Then Jake Kimball gave himself a shake and the maudlin tone of the moment disappeared. "My apologies. I did not intend to go off on such a tangent. Please make yourself at home, Mrs. Peters. The bedroom is through that door." He motioned toward the wall to her left. "You'll find a private water closet off the bedroom."

A private water closet? If she, the mere companion, had one, then Emma's room must be as well-appointed. The McBride Menaces certainly had landed in the lap of luxury this time. It's too bad their grandmother couldn't see them now—Monique would be so proud.

"And this door?" Kat asked, as much to fill the void in conversation as out of curiosity.

"It leads to another suite."

"Another companion's?" It would help Kat to know what other rooms around hers were occupied.

"Actually, Mrs...." he drew the word out "...Peters. Those rooms are mine."

"Yours?" she squeaked.

"Mine." His blue eyes stared into hers with a mesmerizing intensity. His voice dropped as he added, "If you should require anything during your stay, do not hesitate to knock. It's my personal mission to make your stay here at Chatham Park a memorable one."

With that, he lifted her hand to his lips for a gallant kiss. Kat didn't move until the door shut behind him, and then, she only swallowed hard and stared at the back of her hand. Surely she'd imagined the quick stroke of his tongue against her knuckle. Hadn't she?

JAKE'S FOUR NIECES lined up before him like little soldiers. Dressed neatly in white pinafores trimmed in blue, green, yellow, and pink respectively, blue eyes shining with excitement, they listened intently to their instructions. Feeling rather like a field commander, Jake marched back and forth in front of them, his hands clasped behind his back, his tone serious as he repeated their instructions one last time.

Then, movement out on the lawn caught his attention. Three of his invited bridal hopefuls now congregated on the lawn like geese. "All right, girls. The battle is about to begin. Are you ready?"

They nodded.

"Very well, troops. Go and be yourselves."

As the children scampered away, Dair commented, "You are a diabolical man, my friend. I salute you."

Jake slipped his hand into his pocket and fingered Kat McBride's necklace while he watched the McBride sisters join the ladies congregating on the lawn. "I have to say, I'm enjoying the game. I feel as if I'm on the trail of a particularly enticing treasure."

"Refresh my memory. When was the last time you didn't find the prize you searched for?"

Daniel. Jake's heart took a little hitch, then he shoved that sorrow aside. "Quite some time. Remember the Rasmussen diamond?"

Dair nodded. "That proves my point. If that's the last time you came up empty, it supports the idea that you're ordinarily quite careful about the prizes you choose to pursue." Jake shrugged and Dair continued. "I suspect this one might give you a run for your money."

As the children swooped down upon the bride contestants, Jake grinned. "I'm counting on it."

The purpose of the inaugural event of the weekend was to introduce the girls to the "brides" and vice versa. Jake understood he needed to give the appearance of going through with his original plan. He needed the women to stay through the weekend to give him time to work things through with Kat McBride. Besides, he did entertain a tiny seed of worry that the lady could surprise him. Might refuse him.

Not if you do this right, he told himself.

Walking out onto the lawn, he prepared himself to do just that. "Good afternoon, ladies. I hope you've all rested from your journey."

The competition began with a bevy of smiles from the beauties who subtly jockeyed for position in the front of the field. Emma Tate didn't dance around to catch his notice, Jake observed. She was too busy surreptitiously watching Dair. Who, Jake was surprised to see, cast his own intense glances back.

When Belle made a hurry-up motion with her hands, Jake winked at her and continued. "I imagine you're all curious about the itinerary you've been provided. I admit they are not all usual activities for a house party. However, this is not an ordinary house party."

"That's an understatement," Mrs. Peters, aka Kat McBride, drawled.

Jake smothered his grin. Damn, but he'd made a fine choice.

"First, allow me to introduce you to my beloved nieces, Miranda, Theresa, Belle and Caroline Barrett. Their young brother, the Marquess of Harrington, is in the nursery asleep."

"Aren't you darling little angels," one of the brides—the knight's widow—said.

The girls beamed. Jake resisted correcting the young woman and continued. "As you undoubtedly are aware, I intend to provide my nieces and nephew a home from now on, and my wife will be intimately involved in their upbringing. Consequently, it's important for the girls to get to know you, thus they'll be spending time with each of you alone. I trust you'll give them the attention they require during these entertainments?"

The women all murmured their agreement.

Jake removed a folded slip of paper from his jacket pocket and addressed the baron's daughter, a shop girl and the ducal niece. "Miss Walker, Miss Yancy and Miss Wainwright, Miranda requests that you accompany her on a walk to the folly. Is that agreeable with you?"

The three women smiled and nodded.

Jake winked at Miranda, who skipped over to her assignments and said, "This way, please."

Theresa, the sea captain's daughter and the other shop girl prepared to take a pony cart ride around the lake. Belle challenged the knight's widow to a game of checkers. All departed, leaving the McBride sisters with Caroline and Jake. Jake gave his niece's hand a squeeze. "Mrs. Tate, Caroline would like to spend time with you this afternoon. Would you care to join her at the fish pond?"

"That sounds delightful," Emma replied. She offered Caroline a winning smile and added, "I've been a fisherwoman since I was your age. I've spent many a pleasant summer afternoon beside the Trinity River fishing for catfish."

Caroline's eyes went round and she shot her uncle a questioning look.

"Catfish are one of the ugliest fish you could ever see, sunshine," Jake explained. "Picture a big fish with whiskers."

To Emma he said, "Caroline doesn't speak, but if you pay attention, her eyes tell it all."

Then he addressed Kat McBride. "Shall we tag along behind them, Mrs. Peters?"

Kat pursed her lips as if pondering his question for a moment, then she briskly shook her head. "Thank you, but I think I'll just spend the time resting in my room."

I'll bet. "But you're her chaperone. Shouldn't you stay with her?"

"Heavens, no. She's not a young ingenue. She's a widow. Not a young widow, either."

"Well, thank you," Emma interjected, a bite to her tone.

"I'm not really her chaperone," Kat continued. "I'm simply Mrs. Tate's traveling companion, her friend. You go along with them, Mr. Kimball. You can help take the fish they catch off the hooks. Emma loves catching, but she hates unhooking."

Emma's smile was sheepish. "She's right. I can do it if I must, but I prefer pawning that task off on someone else."

"No worry, there." Jake playfully tapped his niece on the nose. "Caroline is a champion fish-taker-offer. Right, sunshine?"

The girl's eyes glittered with laughter and she nodded.

Dair spoke up. "I'd be happy to accompany you ladies and assist if needed." He winked at Caroline and added, "I wouldn't mind having help removing fish from my line, myself. Squirmy, slimy things scare me."

Caroline rolled her eyes at that bit of nonsense.

"There you go." Jake stuck his hands in his pockets, then said, "All right, Mrs. Peters. We'll leave you to your rest."

She backed away from them, waving her fingers and smiling. "Good luck, Caroline. Here's wishing you a record catch."

Kat turned and walked sedately toward the house. Jake would bet his favorite fertility totem that she dearly wanted to run. He'd allow her twenty minutes, he decided. That would give her plenty of time to get into trouble. In the meantime, he'd walk along with Caroline and Emma Tate. Who knows what interesting tidbit he might learn from his sister-in-law-to-be?

"All right, ladies. Let's proceed to the fish pond and dig some worms for your hooks, shall we?"

Then I'll meander back to the house and see if the little minnow has taken my bait.

KAT REALIZED SHE NEEDED an organized approach to her search, so she chose to work from the top down, right to left. That meant she'd begin in Chatham Park's north wing. Just to be thorough, she made a quick sweep of the servants' quarters, then she descended a floor to the guest bedrooms where she tried the handles on every door.

Most wouldn't open, and rather than waste time trying to pick the locks—a skill she'd learned while on the road with Rory—she made a mental note of the rooms requiring a return visit. The rooms she was able to enter proved to be unoccupied bedrooms and, like her own, were decorated in themes. She discovered a room of dolls, one of wooden train models, one of seashells. She didn't find anything the least bit Texan or religious oriented, but she wasn't worried. Jake Kimball's father had been passionate about his Texana collection. She expected him to have it housed in a more prominent location within the huge house—if it were even in Chatham Park.

Her necklace posed a different problem. If Kimball owned a collection of jewels, she doubted she'd find them lying around waiting to be stolen. What she hoped to find was a room with signs of having more substantial security than she noticed elsewhere in the house.

"Maybe I should have started at the bottom and worked my way up," she muttered. Knowing the other guests were either out of the house or in the saloon taking tea made snooping easier. Nevertheless, it wasn't until she descended to the common rooms on the next floor that her pulse sped up and the speed of her search slowed down. In these rooms, themes were not so readily transparent.

Kat shut the door of the ante-library behind her. The scent of leather and tobacco permeated the air, and a section of bookshelf immediately caught her notice. "*A History of Texas,*" she read aloud. "*Flora and Fauna in the American Southwest.*"

Did this room hold all or part of Jake Kimball's father's collection of Texana? Could it be this easy?

She made a quick visual search of the room, but saw no sign of an altar cross. No, it wouldn't be this easy.

The room was filled with treasures, however, and she tried to figure out what theme tied them all together. From the mythological scene of the painted ceiling, her gaze trailed down the walls, across bookshelves interspersed with a painting of a gentleman with a tricorn hat, another of coaches on a dusty mountain road and a third of cattle and deer in a park. Furniture consisted of gilt wood armchairs and sofa in a neoclassical design, and two easy chairs upholstered in contemporary needlework. She spied a large collection of oriental blue-and-white porcelain, a group of Minton figures and a jeweled ormolu-and-white-marble mantel clock beneath a glass dome.

"What pulls it together?" she murmured, picking up a Copeland figure of a girl feeding birds.

A voice behind her rumbled, "Blue. The color blue. Chatham Park boasts a room dedicated to each of the primary colors. Why are you in my blue room, Mrs. Peters?"

Kat whirled around. Jake Kimball hadn't made a sound as he'd entered the room. *Darn.* She ordinarily had better hearing while acting improperly.

One dark eyebrow arched. "Stealing the porcelain, perhaps?"

Kat asked herself what Wilhemina Peters would do in a situation like this, then she descended into character by going on the offensive. "This house is ostentatiously large, Mr. Kimball. If you are going to invite guests here, you should have manners enough to provide them with a map. I've been lost for hours, and I am quite devastated by the event. It's downright rude to leave guests in such turmoil, sir, and it doesn't reflect well upon your hospitality."

Kat finished the harangue with her best imitation of Wilhemina Peters's full-bosomed *harrumph* and attempted to brush past him and out of the room.

He stopped her by gripping her arm just above the elbow. Then he reached behind him with his free hand and swung the door shut. "Not so fast, my dear," he said, his voice a low and somewhat threatening purr. "You'll pardon the forwardness of my upcoming action, but we've been beset by theft here at Chatham Park. It is my duty to protect the premises."

He stood so close, Kat could feel his body heat and his masculine scent, a combination of sandalwood and leather. Wary, she narrowed her eyes. "What do you mean, 'protect the premises'?"

His grip on her arm firmed, and his free hand slid slowly down her side. Kat didn't have to fake her gasp at the boldness of his touch, and when his hand slipped into her dress pocket, she protested, "Sir!"

"What is this?" He removed a small figure of a trapper.

"How did that get there?" Kat asked in honest confusion.

"It's impolite to steal from one's host, madam." He set the figurine on a table. "What else do you have hidden away?"

"Nothing. I didn't take that. I don't know how—" She broke off abruptly as his hand smoothed upward from her hip and along her waist. She attempted to wrench away from him to no avail, before his hand swept across her bodice.

"Well. What have we here?" he asked, his fingers prodding the stuffing in her corset. "Your flesh feels rather feathery."

"Get your hands off me," Kat snapped, trying yet again to pull away. This time he allowed her to go. But when she attempted to sweep past him, out of the room, he stepped in front of her, blocking her way.

"You're not at all what you seem, now are you? This discovery begs the question Why the disguise? What are you concealing? What do you fear my finding out? Your identity? Your purpose for sneaking around my ante-library? Could it be you are looking to steal something more valuable than a figurine from me?" She struggled as he removed her eyeglasses, then tugged off her wig. His blue eyes gleamed with satisfaction. "A jeweled cross, perhaps, Miss McBride?"

Kat put both hands against his hard chest and shoved. This time he let her go.

"How did you know?" she asked, her voice trembling. Whether from anger or reaction to his nearness, she wasn't sure.

His lips stretched in a slow smile. "You're an unforgettable woman, my dear. I don't believe I've ever known a woman with eyes as green as yours. What color would you say they were?" He moved toward her. "Celadon? Malachite? Serpentine?"

Kat backed away. "Green. They're just green."

"No." He kept advancing.

Kat felt the wall of bookshelves against her back. She thought she should probably make a dash for the door, but she couldn't seem to make herself look away from him. His stare was intense. Mesmerizing. She had a quick mental vision of how he'd looked the first time she'd seen him. Naked and wet and gleaming beneath the warm Texas sun.

Her mouth went dry.

"Your eyes are more than just green," he insisted. "They're like cat's eyes. Kat's eyes. I'm curious to learn if they glow in the dark."

Holy Hannah. Now she was flat against the bookshelf, his hands against the wall on either side of her. Trapping her. Her fingers searched book spines, gripped a thick volume, a weapon should she need it.

His gaze dropped to her lips. "What are you doing here, Katrina?"

Getting into trouble, I'm afraid.

Again.

"I'd thought you'd given up on your quest for the Sacred Heart Cross. Your letters quit following me around the world."

No mention of the necklace. He obviously wasn't aware that his niece had spilled the beans, so to speak. Kat cleared her throat. "I lost interest in you."

"I'm crushed." He moved closer and his body heat toasted her skin. "I quite enjoyed your entreaties. They showed such imagination. I admire a woman with imagination. Perhaps I can…entice your interest once again?"

Oh, my. Oh-my-oh-my-oh-my.

He leaned forward, inhaled her scent. "Mmm. Spicy. Perfect."

Perfect?

"You still want the cross, don't you?"

Her heart fluttered like a hummingbird's wings. She licked her dry lips and his eyes narrowed. "I do."

"I'm glad." His head dipped toward her. He nuzzled her hair.

Her blood hummed and her eyes drifted shut. "You're glad?"

"I'm…excited."

So was she. Heaven help her, she was excited and needy and achy for the first time in years. For the first time since Rory. Rory. Another scoundrel. What was wrong with her? Why was she attracted to the wrong kind of men?

His lips brushed the sensitive skin just behind her ear,

and Kat shivered. She tilted her head, allowing him better access to her neck. He immediately accepted the unspoken invitation, and his teeth gently scraped her skin. Kat caught her breath. She wanted to sink against him, to press against his hard, hot body. She wanted to trail her fingers across his naked skin. She wanted...she *wanted*.

"Kiss me." Deep and persuasive, his voice caused her nipples to tighten beneath the mounds of padding.

"No," she breathed, her tremulous voice just above a whisper. She couldn't believe her body was reacting this way to this man. It frightened her.

He drew back. Stared deeply into her eyes. He didn't speak, but Kat heard him nonetheless. *Yes. Oh, yes, Katrina. Say yes.*

"No," she said, with a little more force.

He stroked his finger across her bottom lip. "Is that intended for me or for yourself? Do you truly want me to walk away, sweeting?"

She felt herself drowning, and instinct took control. She lifted her chin, offered her mouth, yearning for that sweet, savory taste of life she'd gone without for so long. "No," she whispered. "Don't go."

Lightly Jake Kimball's mouth touched hers, his lips moving with tantalizing expertise across her tender skin. The taste of him, brandy and passion, filled her senses, and Kat's lashes fluttered, then drifted shut. Sighing, she swayed into his arms. Jake murmured a sound of victory.

Locking his arms around her, he drew her against his chest. The heat of him burned through the layers of their clothing and seeped inside her, warming her. Making her hot. Hotter than she'd ever been in her life.

Her pulse pounded and arousal rippled through her, coaxing her, stimulating her.

Affecting her.

He said her name once, softly, then deepened the kiss. His tongue thrust into her mouth, hungry and demanding. Kat wound her arms around his neck and accepted the intimacy of his tongue with an eagerness that surprised them both.

Yearning, naked and hot, built within her. Passion. It was passion, and it exploded out of Kat like Fourth of July fireworks. It had been so long since she'd known a man's touch. So long since she'd felt alive.

So long since anyone had held her.

It felt good. So good.

She almost wept.

His hands moved restlessly over her back, stroking up and down. Her fingers delved into his thick hair, then drifted to his shoulders, clutching the layers of muscle that stretched across his broad frame. She clung to him, her senses reeling, giving as good as she got. Their mouths mated, their tongues battled, their breath mingled. The kiss went on and on and on.

Part of Kat knew she should be shocked by Jake's bold behavior, or at the very least offended. A part of her was screaming for her to resist him. To resist her own weakness.

But the biggest part of her wanted it never to end.

Lost in his kiss, Kat forgot her worries, her troubles and strife. Her blood rushed warm through her veins.

Her nerves sizzled with pleasure. Sensations dormant for years flowered into full bloom. Lost in his kiss, Kat came to life again.

Had he lowered her to the floor right then, she'd have murmured not a sound of protest.

Instead, he pulled away, and the cold sense of loss seeped back into Kat's bones.

He stared at her, his blue eyes darkened with passion like a stormy sea. Satisfaction gleamed in his expression. Slowly he reached out and traced her lower lip with the pad of his thumb. "Spicy sweet. Just as I suspected."

Kat shivered at his touch and tried to calm her pounding heart. "Mr. Kimball, I—"

He moved his index finger to her lip. "Call me Jake. I think we've moved that far, don't you, Katrina?"

She didn't know what to say. She didn't know what to think or feel or do. She was caught inside a whirlwind of emotion that left her battered and baffled. "How did this happen?"

"It's rather simple." Amusement lightened his eyes. "You were snooping, I caught you, and I kissed you."

That was more than just a kiss. He'd stripped away first her disguise and then her defenses. "Why?"

Now he chuckled. "Because I wanted to, sweeting. And I always get what I want."

He winked devilishly, and Kat's guard went up. She might be attracted to him, but she wasn't stupid. Looking at Jake Kimball now was like seeing Rory all grown-up and dangerous.

How frightening was that? This was no youthful,

playful rogue like her late not-quite husband. This was a mature, sexy, wealthy, successful, seductive, infuriating scoundrel.

Katrina Julianne McBride, get your bustle back to London as fast as the carriage will carry you.

Jake caught her hand and brought it to his mouth. "You are an infinitely kissable woman, Kat McBride, even dressed up like a frumpy old woman."

He stared into her eyes and sucked her fingers, one by one.

For the first time in memory, Kat thought she might swoon. The man had stumped her. Nothing was going as planned. He was supposed to be with Emma at the fish pond, not here, kissing her, sucking her fingers, sending her senses into a tailspin. She didn't begin to know how to respond to that. She should slap his face. She should kick him in the shins.

Although, if he'd kissed her for merely snooping, no telling what he might do if she attacked him.

A delicious shiver went down her spine.

Kat closed her eyes. What was wrong with her? Had she lost every last shred of self-respect?

Jake Kimball didn't seem to care about self-respect. And it was patently obvious he didn't care about propriety. Nor did he even notice Kat's distress.

He took her hands in his and his gaze swept her from head to toe. His lips twitched with a rueful smile. "When upon the rare—very rare—occasions in the past I have considered doing what I am about to do, I never pictured it like this. Nevertheless, especially after that kiss, I am confident of the question."

Foreboding rippled through her like a dark tide. "What question?"

"*The* question. The question of the weekend. The prize sought by dozens, if I'm forced to immodesty."

Kat's eyes widened and her stomach dropped to her knees. Surely he didn't...he couldn't. He wouldn't!

"So, Katrina McBride. Will you marry me?"

Oh, my God. He did.

CHAPTER SIX

JAKE COULDN'T RECALL having this much fun since the time he rode the waterfall in Tahiti. He'd shocked her speechless, and he suspected that was difficult to accomplish with the likes of Miss Kat McBride. This wasn't the way he'd planned to go about gaining her cooperation, but that reckless streak inside of him had taken control, and he honestly couldn't regret it.

Her mouth worked, but no sound emerged. Tempted to dive in for another kiss, Jake's instinct held him back. He stepped away from her, propped a hip upon the Chippendale desk, folded his arms and waited.

It took some time, but she finally managed to squeak. "What did you say?"

"Hard of hearing, cookie? I asked you to marry me."

She gave her head a shake. "Cookie? Did you just call me 'cookie'?"

"Spicy sweet. It's a taste that grows upon a man." He offered her his best wicked grin.

"You're crazy." Mumbling, she brushed past him, headed for the door. "First advertising for a wife. Now proposing to a woman who is trying to steal from you.

It's ludicrous. Insane. Were you always this way, or did you catch some sort of malady during your travels?"

Damn, she was going to be a pleasure. "Don't go, Kat. Please."

It was the *please* that slowed her retreat, of course. That one little word coming from the mouth of a man who knew how and when to use it could sure pack a punch.

"What do you want from me?" she asked.

"I told you. I want you to be my wife."

"Why? Why me? I wasn't one of those women who stood in line for hours for the dubious honor of applying for the job."

Her eyes glittered, color painted her cheeks. Her lips still glistened from his kiss. She was beautiful, sparkling with life and brimming with energy. Jake drank in the sight of her and replied, "You're the one I want."

The certainty of it rolled through him like a shot of good whiskey, and the strength of his reaction left him a bit unsettled. She was a means to an end. A pleasant diversion. Why did the need to win her, to claim her for his own, hammer at him so?

It must have been the kiss. Those lips of hers truly packed a wallop.

"That's it?" she asked, temper flashing in those emerald eyes. "I'm the one you want so you think you can have me?"

Yeah, he did. He thought he could have had her on the ante-library floor if he'd put a bit more effort into it. Not that it would have been an effort. Taking that kiss to an ultimate end would have been the easiest thing in the world to do. "It's not a one-sided proposition, Kat. I have quite a lot to offer."

"Oh, really," she drawled, sarcasm dripping from her words.

Jake wanted to nip the curl in her bottom lip. "That's right. My wife will be mistress of Chatham Park and five other substantial estates in Great Britain and America, along with a few lesser properties scattered about the world."

"How lovely. A mistress without a mister. You are off to Tasmania soon, I believe."

"Tibet."

"Yes, well, wherever."

Snippy bit of baggage. "My wife will have wealth to indulge any whim."

"Moneygrubbing females take note."

Jake's lips twisted with a smile. "My wife will have social standing on both sides of the Atlantic, and the doors open to her will include palaces and statehouses. Even the White House, I daresay."

"Church doors, however, would be a different matter altogether. The devil's bride is seldom welcome in a house of God."

"Kat," he chastised. "I'm crushed. Why would you think so poorly of me?"

With dramatic flair, she clapped a hand against her chest. "Could it be the fact that you're a thief?"

He dismissed her comment with a wave of his hand. "In my younger days, perhaps. I acted under the influence of a scurrilous group of scalawags, men like Luke Garrett."

She narrowed her eyes and glared at him at the mention of her brother-in-law's name. Jake bit back a grin and continued, "I am a *reformed* thief."

She gave an unladylike snort.

"I go to great lengths to ensure that the treasures I hunt today can be legally obtained. In this instance, I'll use a marriage license."

"Now you're equating the bride-by-advertisement with a treasure? Please."

"You would be a prize. Of that I have no doubt." Jake risked taking a step toward her. "Marry me, Kat McBride. I'll give you homes, I'll give you wealth…I'll give you independence."

That, he saw, scored a point.

Momentarily.

Kat drew herself up, lifted her chin. She was, Jake thought, magnificent. "You'd give me grief, is what you'd give me. No, thank you, Mr. Kimball. I must decline your proposal. I have experience with a man like you, sir. You're no different from Rory Callahan, and I'll not tangle with a blackguard again. Thank you for your hospitality, but I'll be leaving Chatham Park. Immediately."

Jake waited until she'd reached out to open the door before saying, "Would you like to see the cross before you go?"

Her hand on the doorknob, she froze.

"The majority of the Texana collection isn't housed here. My father built a special display for it at his castle in Scotland. When I realized you'd be visiting Chatham Park, I sent for it. It's upstairs."

Kat's arm dropped to her side. "What sort of game are you playing?"

"No game. This is very much real life. So, can I tempt you with my treasure, darling?" Taking her hand before she could nod or demur, he led her into the corridor.

Jake moved quickly, anticipating she might plant her feet and protest at any moment. He'd hate to have to pick her up and carry her the rest of the way, but that's what he'd do if need be. Although on second thought, having her in his arms again didn't sound like a bad idea at all.

"This is the wing where my bedroom is, isn't it?" she murmured. Now the feet dug into the Persian carpet. "Don't tell me the cross is in my room."

"It's not." He gave her a tug, and all but flung her into the master suite. "It's in mine."

Jake shut the door behind them and smiled at her. Kat shut her eyes and shook her head. "From the frying pan into the fire, Mr. Kimball?"

"Call me Jake, darling. Don't be suspicious. The cross is in here." He led her from the sitting room into his bedroom.

"Your bedroom," she muttered, putting her back to the bed. "Of course. My mother warned me about scoundrels like you."

"You don't listen to your mother much, hmm?" Jake walked across the room to the fireplace and the locked wooden box sitting on the mantel. "My father commissioned this case for the cross the day before he died. The ivory inlay is spectacular. It's quite a treasure."

He set the box on the table before the fireplace and took a seat on the small couch, then gestured for Kat to sit beside him. He removed a key from his vest pocket, then opened the box.

The Sacred Heart Cross nestled against rich red velvet, its old gold and precious jewels gleaming in the room's natural light. Seeing it, Kat McBride's eyes went wide.

"It's beautiful," she said. "It's a work of art. I didn't expect…my heavens, look at the size of that ruby. It's bigger than Emma's pendant."

Or yours, Jake thought. "I researched the cross extensively after it came into my possession."

"You mean, after you stole it from Rory."

Jake sighed. "Must we beat that dead horse again, my dear? I paid the man for it. I understand you accessed the funds once I informed you of the account's existence."

"My father insisted." Kat wrinkled her nose. "What did you learn about the cross?"

"The ruby is Burmese, of course," Jake replied, indulging her. "Rumor has it that it was taken from a sultan's palace during the Crusades. It, along with the emeralds and sapphires, somehow found their way to the church during the Inquisition. Cardinal Franco of Spain commissioned the Sacred Heart Cross early in this century and sailed on the *Copernicum* to the New World. As we know, the *Copernicum* fell victim to pirates in the Caribbean, and the cross was deemed lost— until your Rory brought its existence to light."

"He wasn't my Rory," Kat snapped.

Jake stifled a smile. "Someday I want to hear how a woman like you ended up with a man like him. I've wondered about that ever since we met on that beach in Galveston. Whenever I looked at the cross, I thought of you. You were so beautiful that day."

"I was seven months pregnant!"

"You were ripe and luscious. A fertility statue come to life. Your hair glistened in the sunlight, old gold in color, just like the altar cross. I look at the ne—" catching himself, Jake corrected "—at the cross, and I see the emeralds and I think of your eyes."

"You're not back to that again."

"Your lips are more enticing than the ruby."

"Are you part Irish, Mr. Kimball? You are so full of blarney. Besides, I'm pretty sure it's sacrilegious to look at a cross and think about…that."

"Sex, you mean?" She blushed an attractive pink. Jake reached into the box and set it on the table. Then he took her hand in his. "I'll ask again. Marry me, Kat. Marry me and I'll give you the altar cross as a wedding gift."

Her eyes went wide, and for a moment he thought he'd won. Then abruptly she wrenched her hand from his and stood. "I'm no whore, Mr. Kimball."

For a long moment, the ugly word hung in the air like an offensive smell.

Then, Jake shoved to his feet. "Wait a minute. Wait just one minute." He braced his hands on his hips and glared at her. "I never said that. I didn't think of it that way."

"Oh, really?" she drawled, her tone dry as West

Texas in July. "So, if I were to take you up on your…gracious invitation, you would not expect to share my bed?"

A hot wave of desire shot through Jake at the thought. He pictured sweeping her from her feet and carrying her to the next room, to his bed. "Actually, I'd want you to share mine. It's huge. Shall I show you?"

"No. I have no interest in your bed, Kimball, and I find I've lost interest in your cross, too."

He folded his arms. "Stubborn, aren't you? I guess that goes along with being spicy. Kat, think about this. My gifting you with the cross is no different from a marriage settlement, and that's been the tradition here in England for ages."

"I'm an American."

"And brides don't have dowries in America? Grooms don't bring assets to a marriage? Accepting a gift from her husband doesn't make a whore of a woman."

"Maybe not, but this entire scheme of yours is distasteful, and I want no part of it."

"The ninety-odd other women who answered my advertisement wouldn't agree with you."

"The emphasis being on *odd*," she said with a disdainful sniff.

Jake couldn't help but grin at that. "Maybe my advertisement did lean toward artless, but at least it was honest, which is more than anyone could claim about the marriage mart that is the London Season. My offer is as good as many a gentleman who dances his way into an engagement."

"At least you're not pretending love."

"No, I am not." Love wasn't something he was looking for. Ever. Or not, at least, until the desire for adventure had burned from his bones—and he didn't see that happening any time soon. Too many times in the course of his career he'd watched love fasten shackles around a wandering man's feet. Explorers like him had no business playing with that sort of fire. To do so risked the loss of what mattered most—the trip beyond the horizon.

"At risk of appearing unsympathetic, Katrina, I believe you married for love once before, and that didn't turn out quite the way you'd hoped, did it?"

She sucked in a breath. "You make Rory look like a saint."

"It's a good deal, Kat. Think about it. I can offer you travel, adventure. You seem to me to be an adventurous woman."

"At one time, the idea of adventure made me salivate. I dreamed of traveling to places like those you visit. The Orient, the South Seas. The Arabian desert. Then I had a taste of adventure, and I learned it has a sour flavor."

"Callahan again?" Having that one thrown in his face could grow old. When she responded with only a shrug, Jake frowned. "You shouldn't base a lifetime on one experience."

In a quiet, but not quite convincing, tone, she said, "I'm happy with a nice, quiet life in Fort Worth. Besides, I don't need a husband to travel. I'm here in England, am I not?"

Jake nodded, acknowledging her point. He tried another tact. "As my wife, you'd be self-supporting, no longer dependent upon your father."

She flinched slightly, proving he'd hit a nerve.

"I'm not dependent on my father," she clarified, a protest in her voice. "I work. Of late, I spend more time in my sister's chocolate shop than she does because she's too busy having babies. I earn a living wage, I'll have you know."

"So is working in a chocolate shop your dream? Is that what you wish to do the rest of your life?"

Her lack of response was as good as a no so he continued, "Is there someone else? Another man to whom you've given your heart?"

"I will *never* give my heart to another man."

Jake's eyes widened. She'd said it with such vehemence that he made special note of the sentiment. In his viewpoint, that made his choice of her as his bride all the more appealing—no attachments. "Then tell me your objections, Kat, and give me a chance to overcome them. I will make every effort to do so. You're the perfect bride for me."

"In heaven's name, why?" she asked, her frustration evident. "You don't even know me."

Jake sensed she was wavering, sensed she was close to agreeing. He took a step toward her and spoke with total sincerity. "I know what's important. I know that you're smart and spirited, Kat McBride. I know that you are of independent character. I know that I want you in my bed. And, most important, I know you'll be a good mother for the children."

"The children. I almost forgot." She closed her eyes for a moment, then looked at him and laughed. It was the saddest laugh Jake had ever heard. "Someone else once told me I'd be a good mother. That someone else was wrong. Very wrong. Look to your other guests for a bride, Mr. Kimball. I am not interested in the position."

She left him then, without a backward glance, and Jake realized he'd been mistaken. She'd shown no hesitation whatsoever in her refusal. Displayed not one bit of doubt. "Well, hell."

He'd meant what he'd said when he told her she was perfect. He needed her. He had to have her! So, what should he do? Try a different approach? Should he appeal to her sister? Turn the girls loose on her? Seduce her?

Seduce her. That particular solution had an undeniable appeal.

But what if she meant what she said? He'd already pegged her as stubborn. What if he couldn't change her mind? What if he'd do no more than waste his time by taking another run at her? What if she turned him down no matter what he did?

If she turned him down after he seduced her, his ego might never recover.

Maybe he should take a closer look at the other bridal prospects here at Chatham Park.

Jake pondered the notion for less than half a minute. No. He didn't want any of the other prospective brides. He wanted Kat. One way or another, he'd have Kat McBride.

Jake Kimball, treasure hunter, always got his prize.

KAT PICKED UP HER SKIRTS and dashed down the corridor, running away from herself as much as from him.

She was shaken, confused. Frightened, almost. What had just happened? What had she almost done?

Jake Kimball was pure temptation.

Kat didn't understand the feelings swirling inside her. She'd thought she'd put men and their temptations and their troublemaking behind her. She'd held no man, kissed no man, since Rory. And she hadn't missed it. Not at all.

Then Jake Kimball swept her into his arms, and what was dark and dead inside her burst into light and life.

Kat picked up her pace. She didn't want this. She didn't want to feel again, to need again. She certainly didn't want to love again.

A little laugh escaped her as she descended the staircase. But he wasn't offering love, was he?

In that respect he was right. It was a good deal. The woman Jake Kimball married could enjoy the lifestyle, the independence, he promised without giving her heart. How perfect was that?

All the woman needed to do was act as mother to five orphaned children.

Kat slammed the door on that thought and hurried out of the house, headed in the direction of the fishing pond and her sister. Halfway there, she spied one of the potential brides rushing up the path that led to the folly, and surprise stopped her cold.

Mud smeared the young woman from head to toe. The pins were missing from her hair, and wet, soggy strands of it hung splattered against her filthy face. She marched toward the house with murder in her eyes and a sharp, squealing screech emitting from her mouth at irregular intervals. At her side skipped one of Jake Kimball's nieces, the apologies on her lips at odds with the light of mischief in her eyes.

Kat knew that look. She'd seen it in her sisters' eyes and in her own reflection enough times throughout the years to recognize it in a flash.

Obviously, the girls weren't the little angels that Jake would have liked the bridal prospects to believe.

"I'm so very sorry, Miss Walker," Miranda said. "I forgot all about that old mud hole."

"You are a wicked, evil girl." The bride swept past Kat without deigning to speak, her nose lifted high into the air. The girl, pretty and pristine in a pinafore trimmed in yellow, skipped along right behind the furious baron's daughter and flashed Kat a brilliant smile as she went by.

"Scamp," Kat murmured.

Not half a minute had passed before she spied yet another angry bride. The shop girl, Miss George, bustled toward Kat, her stylish gown soaked and dripping. "Hoodlums!" she exclaimed as she approached Kat, her skirt hiked almost to her knees. "I don't care how much money the man has, it's not enough to put up with the likes of those little troublemakers."

"What happened?"

"What happened? I'll tell you what happened. She pushed me! She'll say it was an accident, but I know she pushed me."

Kat bit back a smile. Under other circumstances, she thought she could take a real liking to the Barrett sisters. Jake Kimball deserved a set of Menaces of his own.

But these weren't other circumstances. These were *these* circumstances. And *these* circumstances required that Kat gather up her sister and skedaddle, the sooner the better. She didn't know for certain that he had her necklace—despite his slip of the tongue moments before. She could have misheard the girls at the zoo. She'd been a fool to involve herself with that altar cross again. She'd been right about it years ago—that cross *was* bad luck!

Kat continued along the path toward the fish pond, grateful she'd studied the layout of the park from her bedroom window. She crossed a charming arched bridge, then made her way past an Ionic temple built alongside the bubbling stream. The path took a turn to the left, and Kat spied the earthen dam covered in a blue and pink swath of bluebells and rhododendrons just ahead.

Beyond the dam, the water spread out in a placid pool. Kat's gaze searched the shoreline for her sister. She spied a rowboat tied to a short wooden pier that stretched out into the water. She saw a pair of fishing poles leaning against a small stone supply building. Then her stare snagged on two pairs of shoes—Emma's pink slippers and a sturdy pair of man's boots.

A plop in the water grabbed her attention. She found the expanding circle of ripples and followed the fishing line to its source. There, half hidden by a tree, she saw young Caroline.

The girl stood at the bank of the pond, fishing pole in hand. Alone.

Kat moved toward her, watching with trepidation as Caroline reeled in her line, then set her pole on the ground. She scooped up a handful of rocks, then scampered toward the short pier. Alone. Walked out on it. Alone. Dropped a rock into the water, then leaned over to watch it.

Alone.

Heart pounding, Kat picked up her skirts and dashed toward the little girl. Where was Emma! Where was Mr. MacRae? *Please, God. Don't let me be too late.*

Her gaze focused on Caroline, Kat finally noticed Emma in the periphery of her vision. Her sister was sitting on a quilt with that Scotsman, smiling up at him. Not paying one bit of attention to the child. "Emma, how could you!"

Caroline straightened, gripped another rock, and reared back to throw. Kat's heart lodged in her throat as she darted onto the pier. The rock went flying; the little girl teetered.

Kat grabbed the girl around the waist and steadied her. Steadied her own heart. Caroline looked up at her with alarm in her eyes.

Kat released a long breath. "You scared me, honey. I thought you were going to fall in."

"Kat, what in the world are you doing?" asked Emma, stepping onto the pier.

Twisting her head, Kat shot her sister a furious look. "What am *I* doing? I think the question is what were *you* doing? How could you ignore her, Em? She almost fell in! She almost drowned!"

"There's only eighteen inches of water beneath that pier. Even if she'd fallen in, she wouldn't have drowned. And I *wasn't* ignoring her."

Kat snorted. "So you have eyes in the back of your head now? You certainly weren't looking her direction while making cow eyes at that…that—" she cast a glance toward the bank where MacRae waited steps away from the pier "—that bounder. You have to watch children closely, Emma. You know that. Trouble can happen in an instant."

Kat felt a tug on her skirt and glanced down. Caroline smiled, then pointed to herself. Next, she pantomimed swimming strokes with her arms. "You can swim?"

The child nodded, then puckered her mouth into fish lips.

"You can swim like a fish," Kat interpreted.

"I confirmed that fact before we ever reached the water, Katrina," Emma said, her voice sharp. "I understand your caution, but you should give me some credit. I've never neglected a child in my care."

"Unlike me," Kat said softly.

Emma winced. "That's not what I meant, and you know it."

Kat closed her eyes and rubbed her temples. "I know. I'm sorry. I guess I overreacted. Again."

She did that a lot. It was part of the reason she had such trouble being around her own niece and nephew. It wasn't just that she couldn't bear to be around them; she couldn't bear to be around them without hovering, without smothering them with attention. It drove Mari and her little ones crazy.

"All the more reason for me to get out of here as quickly as possible," she murmured beneath her breath.

In a normal tone, she said, "Emma, I need to talk to you. Privately."

MacRae proved himself useful at something other than flirting when he spoke up. "Hey, Caro? I think I see a rabbit peeking out from the flower patch. Want to walk with me and see?"

The girl nodded, then darted off. The McBride sisters watched them for a moment, then Emma folded her arms and said, "What's wrong, Kat?"

"He knows," she responded flatly. Then, agitated once again, she stepped off the pier onto the ground, motioned her sister to join her, and walked off in the opposite direction from MacRae. "That wretched pirate saw through my disguise. He knew who I was all along."

"Oh." Emma sighed, then looked over at MacRae. Her teeth tugged at her bottom lip. "So Dair must know, too? Hmm…that explains a couple of things he's said to me. Oh, well. You knew it was a long shot, Kat, and I can't say I'm sorry that I won't have to play the blushing prospective bride."

"Afraid it would conflict with your flirtation with MacRae?" Kat responded with a bite in her tone.

"Why shouldn't I enjoy an innocent flirtation?"

Kat shrugged. "Never mind. You're right. I'm sorry. I guess I'm not accustomed to you acting like…"

"Like what?" Emma bristled. "Like you?"

Kat's chin came up. "I don't flirt. Not anymore, anyway. But forget about that. We'll find someone else for you to bat your lashes at, but for now, we need to leave. As quickly as possible."

"Did Kimball throw us out?"

"No. It's…well…it's complicated. We can find an inn at the nearest village and stay the night. I want to leave right away."

Emma frowned and stuck her hands in the pockets of her dress. Her bare foot kicked at a stone lying just off the path. "I don't."

Kat blinked. "What?"

"I don't want to leave."

"But, Emma, he knows!"

"Then we won't have to pretend. We can simply enjoy ourselves."

Kat gaped at her sister. This wasn't like Emma. Not at all. "What's gotten into you?"

Emma's gaze trailed back along the bank to where MacRae stood skipping stones with Caroline. With both his pant legs and his shirtsleeves rolled up, he waded ankle deep into the water to retrieve the perfect flat stones to throw. Noting the interest in her sister's eyes, Kat bit back a groan. "It's him, isn't it? It's more than a simple flirtation. That man has turned your head!"

Emma's lips lifted in a smug smile. "I don't know what it is, Kat. He's…fun. I'm having fun. It's been a long time since I've had any fun. I think I need it."

Fun? She wants to have fun? Now? Kat smoothed her hair back away from her brow. "I won't argue that you could use a little amusement in your life, Emma, but it can't be here and now. I have to get away from Jake Kimball."

"Why?"

Frustration blew through Kat like a springtime thunderstorm. "Because I just do. I don't want to go into details."

"I need details."

Kat blew out a heavy sigh. How could she explain to her sister what she didn't understand herself? "He's just…I don't know…he's giving me trouble. I can't be around him."

"Trouble? What sort of trouble?"

Aargh! "Emma, you are like a dog with a bone. Why the interrogation?"

"Why *not* the interrogation? I'm supposed to drop what I'm doing and leave just because you say let's go? Who made you queen, deciding everything we do, Kat? Hmm? Why is everything always about you?"

Kat folded her arms. "Please, Emma. We're not children anymore. Don't you think you're too old to be talking that way?"

"Too old? Too old!" Emma braced her hands on her hips. Her eyes shot fire. "Maybe I *am* too old. Maybe I'm just old and tired. Tired of always being Emma the poor widow, Emma the dutiful daughter, Emma the supportive sister. Maybe I just want to be a flesh-and-blood woman. Maybe I just want to be *Emma!*"

Taking a step back, Kat gawked at her sister. She was shocked. She'd had no idea that Emma had these feelings churning inside her. She wanted to be a good sister and explore her sister's feelings but not right now. Right now she was in the middle of her own crisis! "He kissed me, Emma."

"He kissed you?" Annoyance flashed in Emma's eyes. "See? That proves my point. I'm the one who comes here pretending to want to marry our host, and you're the one who gets the kiss."

"I didn't want him to kiss me!"

"Why not? I'll bet it was good. He has that look about him."

"Emma!"

Her sister shrugged. "If you want to interrupt my weekend—a weekend you dragged me into, I might add—just because a handsome man stole a simple kiss, then I'm not going to have it."

Kat set her teeth. Simple kiss? Not hardly. "It's more than the kiss," she said softly, calmly.

"Then tell me."

Kat resumed walking, picking up her pace. Emma let out a frustrated sigh, then followed along. "Slow down, Kat. I'm barefoot."

"I noticed," Kat grumbled. Then, in the way of sisters, she added, "You have a lot of nerve, Emmaline, having fun while I'm in the middle of a crisis."

"I know," Emma replied, flashing a quick, wicked grin. "Now, what's the crisis? Spit it out. What is it you're trying so hard not to tell me?"

"He picked me!"

"Picked you for what?"

"As the winner. The winner of his stupid contest."

"The bride contest?"

"Yes!"

Emma's brows winged up. "But it's barely started. And you're Mrs. Peters, for goodness' sake. I don't mean to be insulting, honey, but you're not at your best in that outfit."

"Apparently, that doesn't matter to Jake Kimball."

"Hmm…" Emma resumed walking, her brow knitted in thought. "Of course, he *has* met you previously. You must have made quite an impression on him, Kat. Still, I'm surprised he's calling a halt to the game this soon. Personally, I had my money on that Miss Starnes. Why would he pick…? Oh. The children. You saved his niece from the tiger that day at the zoo. He thinks you'll take good care of the children when he's gone."

"Exactly." Kat glanced around on the ground until she spied another small rock, then she gave it a hard, satisfying kick. "Even if I were silly enough to consider his audacious proposal, I couldn't do it. You understand that, Emma. Right?"

"Well…"

"Look how I overreacted a few minutes ago. You know I couldn't bear to be responsible for those children."

Emma reached out and brushed a dragonfly off her sister's shoulder. Gently, she said, "*Do* I know that? Do *you* know that?"

Eyeing her sister warily, Kat asked, "What do you mean?"

"Maybe that's exactly the challenge you need."

"Children?" she squeaked.

"Yes, children."

"Don't be ridiculous." Kat shut her eyes against the frightening mental vision of herself, standing at a London intersection waiting to cross the street, attempting to hold the hands of four little girls while carrying a baby. "Look, I'm sorry to interrupt your fun, Emma, but

I simply cannot stay here. Let's go pack our bags. We can be out of here within the hour."

Emma stooped and tugged a daisy from the dirt. She plucked the white petals from the flower one by one. Finally the green stem plucked barren, she tossed it to the ground, dusted her hands and said, "I don't think so."

"Em?"

She shook her head. "I've already told you I'm not leaving just yet. This is a huge estate. If you want to dodge Jake Kimball, you can find plenty of places to hide."

Kat couldn't believe her sister was being so stubborn. It wasn't like her. Why, this was the first time she could remember Emma refusing any request of hers since...well...since Susie died.

While Kat mulled over that bit of insight, Emma turned back toward MacRae and the girl. "I want this weekend, Kat. If you absolutely must leave, then leave without me."

"You're being as hardheaded as—"

"You?" Emma replied with a mischievous grin.

Kat sighed. "If I hide in my room, will you promise to bring me food?"

"Double desserts, even."

"All right, then. I'll hold you to the double desserts. And I want...oh, my. Look at that." Kat pointed toward the manor house where Mrs. Hartman, the woman who'd retired to the music room to play a game of checkers with Belle, rushed down the west wing steps and headed straight toward the fountain. "Surely she's not going to—"

Mrs. Hartman jumped into the fountain with a splash.

"She did," Emma observed. "I wonder why?"

"I can hazard a guess, and I'm impressed. If you're bound and determined to stay here, I suggest you beware. I'm beginning to suspect that those girls could out-Menace the Menaces."

CHAPTER SEVEN

FROM THE THIRD-FLOOR WINDOW of a storage room filled with medieval armor, Kat looked down upon the lawn where Jake Kimball, his sister's children, their new nanny, Miss Parker, and his guests played an unusual variation of croquet. Oh, they used balls and mallets and wickets, but their rule book must have come handwritten from tablets in the schoolroom. Watching Miranda pick up an opponent's ball, then whack it with her mallet like a baseball against a bat and send it flying into a marble fountain, Kat couldn't help but grin with nostalgia. She'd once done the exact same thing while playing croquet with her cousins, only she'd batted the ball into the Trinity River.

It was the second day of their three-day visit, and Kat was beginning to relax. The room she'd chosen as her daytime hideout had proven safe enough so far. Jake Kimball hadn't found her. In fact, from what she could tell, he hadn't put himself out to look for her. So much for thinking he might be plagued by memories of her kiss.

Kat insisted that wasn't why she was feeling rather peevish. She hadn't slept well last night. Instead of sleeping on a hard wooden pew in the chapel, she should have risked a bed in one of the unused guest rooms. But she'd been afraid Jake would find her and weave his sensual spell around her before she was entirely awake. Uncertain how she'd react in such a circumstance, she hadn't wanted to risk it. She hadn't thought he'd look for her in church.

Apparently, judging from comments he'd made to Emma over breakfast, he hadn't looked for her anywhere. She sniffed, then muttered, "The rat."

It didn't help her mood that she'd failed in her attempts to pick the lock to his room—a lock not even utilized the day before. She knew the cross was in there. She'd bet her necklace was, too. Being so close and yet so far fired her temper.

Maybe she should have told him she knew he had it and demanded its return. That's what she wanted to do, but she didn't trust the man to do the right thing and hand it over. If she let on that she knew he had it, he'd surely hide it somewhere she'd never find it.

She feared he'd already done just that. He'd known her identity from the beginning. He wouldn't leave the necklace lying around for her to find. Not after he'd gone to the trouble to steal it.

That's something else she wanted to know. *Why* had he taken it? The man had baubles galore, many much bigger and more valuable than hers. What had made Jake Kimball sneak into Willow Hill and rob her?

"I could ask him," she murmured. Maybe she should just do it. Get everything out in the open. What's the worst that could happen? She'd leave Chatham Park without her necklace. Kat was beginning to fear that might prove to be the case, anyway.

Or maybe Emma could enlist the aid of Dair Mac-Rae. The way the rogue looked at her sister, he might be willing to steal the Crown Jewels if she batted her eyes and asked sweetly.

Outside on the lawn, Jake and his remaining guests appeared to be enjoying themselves. Yesterday's pranks had thinned the ranks a bit. In the wake of their "accidents," the Misses Walker and George had surrendered the field and departed Chatham Park.

"They're the smart ones," Kat muttered, her breath fogging the window as she leaned closer to get a better look at Jake, who stood just at the edge of her vision. He threw back his head and laughed at something that Miss Yancy said. Kat couldn't help but notice how broad and strong his shoulders looked or the way his trousers hugged his tight, firm buttocks as he put his back to the house. But when he moved to stand behind the shop girl, then reached around her and gripped her croquet mallet as though teaching her how to stroke the ball, Kat's stomach took a funny dip.

She turned away from the window, took a seat in a carved mahogany-and-leather, throne-type chair and tried to turn her attention back to the novel she'd pilfered from the library.

Five minutes later she was back at the window.

Out on the lawn, her sister was playfully struggling over a croquet mallet with MacRae. Jake had abandoned Miss Yancy and was now repeating his croquet lesson with the duke's niece, Miss Wainwright. The four girls frolicked in the middle of the field. Mrs. Hartman sat on an iron bench beneath a shade tree with the toddling marquess in her lap.

Kat startled when a knock sounded on the door behind her. "Miss McBride?" called the butler. "A message has arrived from London addressed to Mrs. Tate and Mrs. Peters. Mr. Kimball instructed me to bring it to you."

Kat let out a growling noise, then marched to the door and yanked it open. Chatham Park's butler stood in the hallway holding a silver tray upon which lay a vellum envelope. "How did you know I was here?" Kat asked, reaching for the note.

"Mr. Kimball told me."

Kat narrowed her eyes and frowned. How did he know? No one followed her up here. She'd made sure. Not even Emma knew which room she'd chosen to conceal herself in today. *He must have someone spying on me.*

Probably one of the girls, she decided. This house no doubt had hidden passages like her parents' home. Heaven knows, Kat and her sisters had spent their fair share of time spying on visitors come to call at Willow Hill.

Kat took the envelope from the tray, then closed the door. "Monique," she murmured aloud, recognizing the handwriting on the envelope. She opened the letter and read. "Oh, great. Just great."

Her grandmother had run off and gotten "married." Again. What was it? The fifth time? Tenth? Kat couldn't keep it straight.

Monique had lost her husband, Jenny's father, to

pneumonia when Kat and her sisters were still girls. She'd grieved hard for a year, then proceeded to form a series of romantic liaisons with gentlemen all over the globe. Monique saw that the couple always had a wedding ceremony of a sort, but never one that was legal, thus leaving her free to marry again at will.

Now, apparently, according to her letter, she had picked her new partner and departed England on an extended honeymoon to Greece. She wrote that the girls should continue on their travels without her. They could expect Monique to return to Texas next winter. She'd signed the missive "Monique, Countess of Wharton."

"An earl, for Pete's sake." Kat chuckled softly. Some things never change.

Well, she guessed she'd better track down her sister and give her the news. Emma would want to know this information as soon as possible.

Kat stepped out into the corridor, then paused in front of a hall mirror where she checked her hair, pinched her cheeks, then bit at her lips. Satisfied with her reflection, she hurried downstairs.

If the thought occurred that she was happy to have an excuse to join the others wearing one of Emma's dresses instead of her disguise, she didn't acknowledge it. She was too busy planning how to worm her way into the croquet game.

She couldn't wait to take a croquet mallet to Jake Kimball's ball.

MOIST BLACK SOIL clung to the white wire wicket when Jake tugged it from the ground at his nieces' request.

Bored with the relative calm of a game of croquet, the girls had requested they begin a new game, baseball.

The question had sent a wave of nostalgia running through Jake. One of his earliest memories was of his father jumping to his feet and roaring with delight as the Knickerbockers' first baseman whacked a home run in a game against the Gothams at Elysian Fields in New Jersey. Jake's 1869 Brooklyn Athletics card formed the basis of his most prized personal collection, his baseball cards. Jake recalled many a summer afternoon when he and his sister joined neighborhood children in a game. It's no wonder she'd taught her daughters to enjoy the sport.

"Uncle Jake?" Miranda ran toward him, one of four sand-filled bases clutched to her chest. "Here comes Miss McBride."

Delight ribboned through him as he turned and looked toward the house to see Kat striding toward them. She looked stunning, her eyes aglow, color in her cheeks. She wore the yellow silk dress her sister had worn to his interview. Jake smiled with masculine appreciation at seeing her true figure revealed, and around him the remaining potential brides stirred.

"Who's she?" he heard Mrs. Hartman ask.

"She looks like that woman from Texas," Miss Yancy declared.

"Hmm," murmured the brides simultaneously, as if they'd realized that the odds of winning the contest had grown longer.

Jake wondered if any of them would recognize the transformation of "Mrs. Peters."

When he'd spied Kat standing in the window of the armor room earlier, he'd been moved to flirt conspicuously with the women. He'd hoped such behavior on the heels of his marriage proposal might annoy Kat enough to draw her outside.

"Do you think she'll play baseball with us, Uncle Jake?" Miranda asked.

"I'll bet we can convince her."

"Good. The more players we have, the more fun the game is."

Jake glanced around at the remaining women. "Yes, Miranda. I do believe you are right."

Miss Yancy stepped closer to Jake and flashed him a winsome smile. "I hope you'll choose me to be on your team, Mr. Kimball."

He gave her hand a gallant kiss. "I'd be honored to have you on my team, my dear. However, Miranda and Theresa have captain's honors. Right, girls?"

"That's right," Theresa piped up. "My team is the Green Caterpillars and Miranda is calling hers the Yellow Jackets."

"We're going to sting you," Miranda added. She reached out and pinched Miss Yancy, saying, "Buzz."

"Ow." Miss Yancy's smile had some teeth in it as she slapped playfully at the girl.

Returning his attention to Kat who had now drawn within earshot, Jake decided that introductions were in order. "Ladies, allow me to introduce Miss McBride of Fort Worth, Texas. Miss McBride, these ladies are—"

"We met yesterday," Kat said, cutting him off. "I'm Mrs. Tate's sister. I came to Chatham Park in disguise."

Following a pregnant pause, Mrs. Hartman asked, "Why?"

Kat shrugged. "I'd hoped to steal something from Mr. Kimball, but he found me out." While the women gaped and gawked, Kat turned to Jake and asked, "Where is Emma?"

Jake glanced around. Both Emma and Dair had gone missing. Imagine that. "I'm afraid I didn't see her leave."

"She and Mr. Dair have taken Robbie inside to change his nappy," the new nanny explained. "I offered to take him, but Mrs. Tate insisted."

Belle skipped up to join the group. "They're coming right back. They said to go ahead and pick teams. You'll play, too, won't you, Miss McBride?"

"Please?" Theresa wound her green hair ribbon around her finger.

Miranda smiled hopefully. "Miss Emma told me you can swing a bat real good."

Kat's gaze flickered from one girl to another. Jake read the refusal in her eyes, but as she opened her mouth to respond, Miss Starnes batted her lashes toward Jake and said, "I am quite an…athletic…woman. I'd love to…play. I just need a bit of instruction. Mr. Kimball, I'd like to place myself in your expert hands." Her voice dipped into a purr as she added, "I promise you won't be disappointed."

Kat snorted.

Not to be outdone, Miss Wainwright stepped forward. "I'd like some instruction from you, too, Mr. Kimball."

Kat rolled her eyes.

After that, Mrs. Hartman and Miss Yancy chimed in, presenting their athletic qualifications and personal desires with tittering giggles and come-hither looks. Soon Jake found himself instructing the bride prospects in batting stance and swing. Of course, doing so meant he had to stand behind them, place his hands atop theirs on the bat and demonstrate the motion of the swing. Each of them used the occasion to brush and rub against him like cats looking for a good stroking.

"Oh, for goodness' sake," Kat muttered, scowling with disgust. "Have you people no pride at all?"

Jake had to stifle a laugh when Miranda met Kat's gaze and said, "They're all cooey and cuddly because they want to marry him. It makes me want to throw up."

Kat rested her hand on the girl's shoulder. "Turns my stomach, too."

At that, Jake couldn't help but sputter. He disguised his laughter by turning it into a cough and stepped away from the bride in his arms. "Miss McBride? Shall I instruct you in the fine art of how to hit a baseball, too?"

Kat paused, looked up into the sky. "I shouldn't," she said softly. "I know I shouldn't, but the temptation is so great."

"I'm a firm believer in indulging in temptation, Miss McBride," Jake said, showing a devilish grin. He held his arms out wide. "Step into my office, my dear."

As the brides muttered, Kat said, "You know, Mr. Kimball, I learn best by visual instruction. Why don't I pitch the ball to you, and you can show me how it's done?"

It was a direct challenge, a trap. *So you think you're a pitcher, do you?* "Now, why do I suspect you have ulterior motives with this suggestion?"

Her smile bordering on sly, Kat wiggled her fingers toward Theresa. The girl gave the woman the baseball. Gesturing toward the field, Kat asked, "Shall we?"

Miranda placed the bases, then Jake stepped toward home plate, the prospect of competition putting a spring in his step and a gleam in his eyes. He tested the weight of the bat and took a few practice swings as he waited for Kat to take the pitcher's mound. "One of you girls want to be catcher?" he asked his nieces.

Theresa waved her arm, then wrestled a mitt away from Belle and dashed toward home plate.

Kat whistled a jaunty tune as she sashayed her way out to the pitcher's mound. "Would you mind too much if I toss a couple of practice balls before I throw at you, Mr. Kimball?"

At me? Suspicious of her innocent air, Jake narrowed his eyes. "Be my guest."

"Give me a target, Theresa," Kat said.

The girl held the baseball mitt in front of her chest. Just the way her mother taught her, Jake thought, glowing with a sense of pride. Kat tossed the ball into the air then caught it. Once. Twice. Three times. "Ready, Theresa?"

When Jake's niece nodded, Kat made a gentle, underhanded throw that crossed the plate at a snail's pace and landed softly in Theresa's glove. Theresa tossed the ball back to Kat who made a second gentle throw. Jake wondered if he'd read the woman wrong. Maybe she did want batting tips, after all.

"All right," Kat called. "I'm ready."

Jake stepped up to the plate. "Do you want to me talk you through a swing or do you want to ask me questions?"

Kat finger-waved to her obviously shocked sister who'd returned from the house with a freshened toddler in her arms, then smiled at Jake. "How about I make a couple of throws and then we'll decide how best to proceed?"

As was his habit, Jake tapped his bat twice on the ground, then brought it back over his shoulder. Wanting to set a good example, he paid attention to his form. Bat up and back, he wiggled his wrists, waggled his butt and kept his eye on the ball.

Until Kat McBride did a bit of waggling of her own. Concealing the ball behind her back, she leaned toward the plate. Jake's eyes about popped out of his head. Her top few buttons had come undone, and he could see skin and the shadow between her breasts. Plump mounds swelled toward him. Jake's mouth went dry.

Kat moved with the fluid grace of a ballet dancer, and the ball sailed past.

Theresa jerked up a thumb. "Strike."

"Wait a minute." Jake glared down at his niece, then back toward the pitcher's mound. "I wasn't ready."

"Oh, I'm sorry." Kat sucked on her bottom lip. Her plump, rosy bottom lip. "You were standing over the plate with your bat at the ready, so I just assumed…"

Jake stepped away from the plate. *Just assumed, my ass.* She'd done that on purpose.

Theresa tossed the ball back to Kat McBride who caught it with practiced ease. The woman was a ball player. A ball player and a sneak. Bet she had unfastened those buttons herself. She should be ashamed, flashing her bounty in order to distract him.

Wonder if she'd hike up her skirts when she ran the bases?

"Is there a problem?" Kat asked, the innocence in her tone at odds with the glee in her gaze.

Little witch. Two can play at this game, by God. "No problem. No problem at all." Jake slipped his bat between his legs and held it with his thighs while he rolled up his shirtsleeves above his elbows, his gaze fixed upon her mouth. Then he stepped up to the plate.

He rolled his shoulders. Flexed every muscle he could flex. He waggled the bat. Waggled his butt. Winked at her and said, "All right, little cat. Show me what you have."

After nervously drawing the back of her hand across her brow, Kat repeated her wind-up. *Eye on the ball,* Jake told himself. *Don't notice her cleavage. The ball. The ball.*

The ball came at him hard and inside. Jake swung around just as it dropped. His swing swished smoothly through the air.

Theresa did the thumb thing again. "Strike two, Uncle Jake," Belle called helpfully from the sidelines.

Her expression perplexed, Kat tapped her lips with an index finger for a moment before she stopped, smiled and snapped her fingers. "I get it. You're teaching what *not* to do!"

Jake scowled, snarled, then said, "Enough is enough."

From behind him to the right, he heard Dair

MacRae say, "What do you want to bet that he hits this into the pond?"

Emma Tate responded. "She'll strike him out swinging. Kat has a better fast ball than the starting pitcher for the Fort Worth Panthers."

Now Jake's pride was on the line. He choked up on the bat. Focused on the ball. All business. No nonsense. He'd hit it to the far side of the damned pond, by God.

Kat wiped her hand on her dress. Right along the curve of her hip. She wiggled that hip, right to left, then right again.

Watch the ball. The ball. The ball.

She began her windup. Jake drew back the bat. He wouldn't look at the way her tongue slicked across her mouth or the creamy vee of skin dipping into her bodice. The ball. The ball.

She drew her right arm back. Her left arm got tangled in her skirt. As her arm came forward, her skirt hiked up.

He saw lace. Lots of lace. A flash of skin.

The baseball streaked toward him. Sonofabitch.

He managed, just barely and by the grace of God, to get some wood on it. Not much wood. Just enough to send it flying foul. Right at Dair.

The ball hit Jake's friend right in the nose. Dair let out a yelp.

"Oh, hell," Jake muttered as he saw blood spurt.

"For goodness' sake, Kat," Emma snapped, tossing a glare toward her sister as they all converged on Dair. "You should warn people before you pull that stunt."

Then she shoved the baby into her sister's arms and

turned her attention toward Dair, clucking her tongue and cooing in sympathy. The girls oohed and ahhed and made exclamations of disgust and interest about the blood. The brides tittered and winced. Jake glanced at Kat and halted midstep.

Kat held the baby at arm's length, her eyes round and glassy, her complexion bleached white. Her chest rose and fell in short, shallow breaths. Jake feared she might faint dead away.

"Kat?" he asked. "Are you all right? Are you hurt?"

"I'm the one bleeding here," MacRae grumbled.

"I...I..." She closed her eyes and hugged Robbie close. Tears rolled silently down her cheeks.

"I'm all right, Emma," Dair said. "Bloodied, but not broken. This isn't the first time Jake Kimball gave me a bloody nose and it probably won't be the last."

Emma clucked some more. "Let's get you up to the house and we'll put ice on it."

"But your sister..."

Emma glanced at Kat, and a myriad of emotions chased across her face. "She'll be fine. If she'll give herself half a chance, she'll be fine." Then, slipping her arm around Dair's waist, Emma Tate propelled him toward the house.

Kat stood frozen in place. Robbie's right fist beat playfully at her cheek as he gooed and giggled. His left hand tangled in her hair. Jake wasn't certain whether the little mewling sounds came from her throat or the baby's. The girls looked at one another, shrugged, then shot questioning looks toward Jake. He shrugged right back at them. He didn't know what to do.

"Is the game over?" one of the brides asked.

Without taking his gaze off Kat, Jake nodded. "Why don't you ladies go back to your rooms and rest for a while? We'll pick up with the scheduled itinerary after lunch."

Miss Wainwright sniffed. "I wanted a turn. My moves are as good as Miss McBride's."

"Goodbye, ladies." Jake then cocked his head toward his nieces, motioning them to move along, too. Miss Parker held out her hands to take the baby.

Wordlessly Kat handed Robbie to his nanny, then turned to leave. Jake fell into step beside her, keeping pace as she walked blindly away from the house, not speaking, an island unto herself. Jake shoved his hands into his pants pockets and entertained second thoughts about his proposal.

A man didn't need to be a mind reader to realize Miss Katrina McBride had an emotional hitch where the children were concerned. She was protective of them, but not comfortable with them. Being around the children made her stiff and brittle, and her smiles never reached her eyes. Oh, she was kind to them. Gentle. Considerate. But she never relaxed while in the company of his nieces and nephew. Was her reaction a result of having lost a child?

Maybe so. Jake shot her a sidelong glance. If that were the case, maybe Kat McBride wasn't the best choice for a bride after all. Maybe she wouldn't be good for the children. Or the children good for her.

It was a sobering realization, one that Jake needed to seriously consider.

Dammit, though, he wanted her. She'd be good for him. He liked her spark, her sass. God knows, he liked her body.

But he needed to put the children first. He owed it to them. He owed it to his sister.

He drew back his foot and gave a dandelion a swift kick. Yet he owed something to himself, too, didn't he? If he had to get married, it should be to a woman who appealed to him.

He needed to understand why Kat McBride acted the way she did. Maybe this problem with children was something he could fix. That would be good for everyone, wouldn't it? Maybe he wouldn't have to give up on the idea of taking her to wife.

Kat interrupted his reverie by snapping her fingers. "Shoot. I got distracted, and I didn't speak with Emma about our grandmother. I have news she needs to hear."

"Not troubling news, I hope."

"Not to me. Emma won't like it. She doesn't approve of our grandmother's thirst for adventure or her attitude toward love and marriage."

Now that was an intriguing thought. From what Jake knew of Monique Day, her attitudes leaned toward the liberal. Did Kat's comment mean she shared her grandmother's viewpoints? Maybe. She'd tangled with ol' Rory Callahan, hadn't she?

Hmm…maybe he could have his cake and eat it, too, as the saying went. He could marry a woman for the children, but take Kat McBride along for himself. A woman had accompanied him on an expedition once before, and he'd thoroughly enjoyed the experience. Of

course, that particular expedition had been to an exca-
vation in Greece where they'd slept in a hotel every
night. Not quite what they'd find in Tibet. Still… "Do
you like mountains?"

"Mountains?"

"Real ones. Not the little hills they have in West
Texas."

"Like the Rockies?"

His mouth quirked. "Exactly."

She wrinkled her nose. "I don't care for heights."

Damn. She sounded certain. Looked like dessert
wasn't on the menu. And yet, Jake tried. "Come now,
Kat. You don't ever feel the itch to climb to the top of
the world?"

"I itch to be home. It was a mistake to come on this
trip."

"Now, why do you say that? I'm trying to be such a
good host. Didn't I let you throw a couple of balls by
me?"

"Oh, please. You were a bloodied nose away from
striking out swinging."

They argued the point a few more minutes until
movement at the top of the steps of the west wing caught
their attention. MacRae held Emma's arm as they descended the stone steps, then disappeared behind a
hedge.

"That's a maze, isn't it?" Kat asked.

"Yes."

"It's private?"

"Very much so."

"Great. Wonderful. My sister saunters into an English hedge maze on the arm of a handsome stranger. Maybe I was wrong, and she will approve of Monique's news. Emma's changed."

"Sometimes change can be good," Jake observed.

Kat responded with a disdainful "Hmm."

Always a man to seize an opportunity, Jake nodded toward the maze. "Now you've made me curious. Let's go ask her, shall we?"

Kat hesitated. "I'll find my sister on my own."

Jake arched a brow. "Do you have a good sense of direction? The maze covers almost two acres. Visitors have been known to get lost inside for hours."

"That's not true," Kat scoffed.

No, it wasn't, but sometimes the truth was overrated. "I know the maze and Dair MacRae. I know where to find Emma."

Sighing heavily, she said, "Lead the way, Magellan."

Jake took her arm, leaned toward her to catch a whiff of her spicy scent, then escorted her toward the maze.

Surrounded by roses and honeysuckle and rectangular in shape, the Chatham Park maze had been fashioned from boxwood and yew. Inside, a visitor could find statuary and fountains, iron benches and clay pots overflowing with flowers and ferns. At the center of the northern section of the maze stood a miniature Greek temple. The southern section center boasted an elegant structure of eight connected marble arches called The Exedra, a place for quiet contemplation. At the heart of the whole maze stood a simple wooden gazebo furnished with cushioned benches, lounge chairs and shelves filled with novels, biographies and poetry. Jake considered it one of the prime locations for seduction on the estate.

Kat grumbled but went along with him. They were halfway to the maze when a flash of pink darted in front of them. Caroline planted herself in Kat's path, smiled big, then lifted her arms for a hug. Kat shot Jake a half-wild glance, then bent down and gave the girl an awkward hug. Caroline kissed Kat's cheek, then wiggled away, dashing back toward the croquet field.

"What was that for?" Kat asked.

"I don't know. Just because, I guess. Caroline has taken quite a shine to you. It's nice to see. A relief. You're the first woman she's taken to since the accident."

"Why me?" Kat asked, her lips dipping at the corners.

Jake shrugged. "Maybe she senses a kindred spirit. Whatever the reason, it reassures me to see her reaching out toward a female. She needs a mother figure in her life."

"Not me. Absolutely not me."

"They all need a mother figure."

"Not me," Kat repeated. "They may need someone, but that someone's not me."

"Tell me why, Katrina." Jake led her into the maze, turning left, to the south, since he knew Dair liked the maze's temple in the northern section. When Kat didn't respond to his request, he pressed, "Tell me about your daughter."

She jerked away from him and wrapped her arms around herself. "How do you know...?"

"I wouldn't ask someone to be my wife without learning something about them."

"You spied on me?"

"I don't think spying is the right word. That's what the girls do when they skitter around the hidden passages at Chatham Park, then report to me that you were in the chapel or the armor room or the like."

"Hidden passages," she murmured. "I knew it."

"What I did is more of an investigation."

"That's offensive, Mr. Kimball."

"Say 'that's offensive, Jake.' Use my name. I think we've progressed that far, don't you? Now, I'd like to know you better, to understand why you're not comfortable around the children. I suspect it has something to do with your daughter. Share her with me, Kat. She was Rory Callahan's child?"

"Suzanne Elizabeth." Kat's voice cracked. "Susie."

"Tell me about Susie."

Kat increased her pace, walking blindly. Jake let her go. They reached a dead end, and when she turned, Jake noticed sunlight glinting off the tears in her eyes. "Was she blond like you?"

Kat nodded. "I don't talk about her. None of us do. At first, I didn't want to. I couldn't. The pain…" She put one hand over her heart, her fist clenched, as her voice trailed off. Jake linked her free hand with his. "My family was careful of my feelings, and that's what we grew accustomed to. Only Monique ever mentions her."

Jake took her hand and led her back along the proper path heading toward the privacy of the gazebo at the center of the maze. Thinking of his relationship with his father after his brother's disappearance, he observed, "It's difficult to know how to respond to a family member's grief."

"I know. I'm not complaining. My family was a godsend. Without them, I don't know that I would have survived."

Silently Jake pointed out a pair of bushy-tailed rabbits feeding on the grass in front of them. Kat sighed, then said, "Susie wanted a pet bunny. Of course, she wanted a pet dog, cat, fish, snake, lizard, buffalo and frog, too. She loved animals."

A snake? A buffalo? "Apparently all kinds."

Kat McBride's smile was a gift. "She'd spend hours chasing horned toads in my father's backyard. Every so often, she'd catch one, and then her shrill little squeals would bring everyone in the house running. She never knew whether to be excited or scared."

"I'd vote for scared. Horned toads are wicked-looking animals." When that elicited a little chuckle, encouraged, Jake pressed on. "I'll bet she was a smart little girl."

"Oh, she was." Kat's voice grew animated, and light sparked in her eyes. "She learned her ABCs almost as soon as she learned to talk, and she'd even begun to read. Emma is a teacher, you know, and she said Susie was one of the brightest children she'd ever seen."

It was like lancing an infected wound. Kat started talking about her daughter, and she didn't stop. Jake encouraged her with questions as he guided her toward the gazebo. He sincerely liked listening to her tales. Once, during a story about the baby's birth, he'd come close to commenting about the moment from his perspective, and he'd literally bitten his tongue to keep from giving himself away. She was a fountain, flowing and frothing and bubbling with delight. At times almost frenetic.

Then, abruptly, she went silent and still. Her complexion grew waxen. She swayed and Jake anticipated the buckling of her knees. He caught her before she dropped to the ground.

The tears came on like a flood, hard and fast and ferocious. She wept from her heart, from her soul, her grief controlling her, consuming her. It was a force unlike any Jake had ever seen. He felt helpless, awkward and unsure as he carried her into the gazebo and laid her gently on a chaise. She rolled onto her side away from him, her sobbing unabated. Jake reached out and patted her shoulder.

Ordinarily he was good with women. He was a champion charmer, a superior seducer. He instinctively knew what to say and do in order to achieve his goals where the fairer sex was concerned. However, he was lousy at offering comfort. Just yesterday Theresa had fallen, skinned her knee and burst into tears. He hadn't known what to do for her, either.

"Oh," Kat moaned into the chaise's tufted pillow. Unbelievably, the intensity of her weeping increased.

My God, could a person hurt herself from crying? Tear an organ out of place or something? Jake patted her shoulder again. "Calm down, honey. Don't cry so hard. You're scaring me."

Kat continued to sob.

Jake muttered a curse, then sat beside her. He shifted her weight, lifting her into his arms and onto his lap. "It's all right, Katrina," he murmured, rocking gently back and forth. "Everything is all right. You're all right. Hush, now."

He kissed her head. "Calm down." He kissed her temple. "You've got to calm down." He kissed her cheek. "Find your peace, Katrina."

This time when he bent his mouth toward her, she turned her head, and her mouth sought his, found his.

Kat McBride kissed Jake as though her life depended on it. She wrapped her arms around his neck, pressing her body against him. She moaned against his mouth, and Jake was lost.

This he knew how to do.

"Jake?" She went still in his arms.

"Shh," he whispered against her lips. "I can help you, Katrina. Just let me." Anticipation roughened his voice, making it low. For a brief moment he feared she'd bolt. Nibbling at the corner of her mouth, he waited, his heartbeat drumming a beat within his chest.

Her eyes met his. In the gazebo's shadowed light, the deep emeralds shone nearly black. Such sad eyes, he thought. Beautiful, yet so heartbreakingly sad. He longed to see them alight with pleasure. With emotion. With desire.

Using great care, Jake ran the tip of his tongue along her bottom lip. He meant to go slow, truly he did. But the sound she made, the sweet sigh of surrender created a temptation too great to deny.

Reaching up, he gently speared his fingers through

her hair and pulled her head back, opening her mouth so that he could take it again. His tongue slid into her mouth deeply, repeatedly. With whispered words of encouragement, he coaxed her, gentled her to his touch. Jake wanted to dull her pain, if only for a brief moment in time.

He stroked her hair, her cheek, reveling in the way she responded, the way she made him feel. The depth of his own desire surprised Jake. An inexplicable allure to have her, possessed his every sense, every emotion. Kat McBride called to him like an ancient siren, and he was powerless to resist.

Yet the siren's song lamented the loss—a loss like no other, and one a man couldn't begin to understand. This mother's arms held only memories, and he could not, would not, take advantage of Kat's weak moment for his own need.

Well, maybe just a little.

Sliding a hand to her bodice, Jake deftly undid her buttons until his fingertips found warm skin. With an impatience he could barely rein in, he pulled and tugged until she was bare before him. Glorious, he thought, as he traced the swell of one breast, careful to resist the crowning bud at the tip. She should be painted naked on a canvas, wrapped in scarves and roses.

But for my eyes alone.

Swallowing the surprisingly selfish idea, he drank in her body's perfection. Flawlessly shaped. Soft and round with dark pink nipples begging for his attention.

When Kat murmured and sighed with pleasure, Jake smiled against her lips and teased the other breast in the same sensuous manner until she kissed him with a fervor that tempted him to abandon the idea of gallantry. His whole body tightened as he lowered his head for a taste.

Immediately her back arched. A deep, primal moan escaped her lips as her fingers squeezed his shoulders.

Pleased, his tongue captured the peak of her breast and laved it until she cried out. Then he switched to worship the other, basking in her mindless cries.

The sounds stirred Jake's blood to a boil. His whole body tightened as he drew her more heavily into his mouth. The caress changed from gentle, sweet contact to an intense, demanding passion that Jake longed to explore like no other territory.

His hand found her hip, easing her skirts up. He wanted to learn her secrets, needed to know her in the most intimate way. This was dangerous, Jake knew. Probably even stupid. But when his fingers discovered her downy cleft wet, warm and waiting...

His own growl blended with hers, and prudence flew away on the cool afternoon breeze.

While he continued to suckle her, Jake's fingers parted the lush petals and stroked the hidden bud with a slow rhythm that sang through his veins. The taste and scent and feel of her sank into him like unrelenting talons. His own breath came hard, as though he were running close to the edge of reason.

Probing insistently, he felt her body giving way, yielding to his magic. Following her signals, he slipped one finger inside her, then raised his head to meet her stare.

Kat's hot emerald gaze consumed him. Her eyes were fevered, burning. Glistening with something he couldn't deny. Something he put there.

A wave of satisfaction nearly drowned Jake. He'd done it. He'd made her burn. And like a moth to that elusive flame, he hungered to lose himself in her luster.

Falling into her gaze, Jake tenderly caressed her softness again and watched the passionate emotions play across her face. One word, one simple word passed her swollen lips.

"Please." Her eyes closed, her head titled back.

It was all the encouragement he needed. Pleasure swept through him, hard and determined. He increased the pressure of his hand, sliding yet another finger into her. He stroked, pressed, circled and tugged until she writhed upon his lap.

"Say my name, Kat."

She twisted desperately, moaning in an incoherent chant.

"My name," he repeated, this time a demand.

"Jake. Oh, Jake."

Using the pad of his thumb, he quickly brought her to the crest and watched her tumble over.

Her breath broke on a cry of completion as she convulsed, spilling warmth from her body into his hand. Her scent swirled around him like a warm, earthy caress.

He watched her enjoy the swells her body rode until the storm within her subsided. He delighted in such natural abandon. He longed to make it happen again.

Then he saw the fresh tears.

"Kat?"

Slowly she smiled.

For a moment he went completely still. Then he bent and kissed her eyelids tenderly, stealing her tears with the tip of his tongue. "Don't cry anymore, sweetheart."

For the first time in Jake's life, he found himself more concerned with a woman's pleasure than his own. He found himself wanting to hold her, protect her, to banish her sorrow.

With an unknown strength, he removed his hand from her inviting heat and simply held her in his arms. When she sighed with contentment, pressed a sleepy kiss to his throat and curled herself into his embrace, Jake's own lips lifted in a wry grin. When she woke, he predicted there'd be hell to pay. Rubbing his chin against her silky hair, he kissed her temple and leaned back into the cushions. Until then, he'd simply enjoy having her in his arms.

It was a memory he'd savor.

KAT DRIFTED AWAKE SLOWLY, warm and comfortable and relaxed. The masculine scent of sandalwood lingered from her dreams, and she smiled, luxuriating in the pleasure of one of her favorite scents. Then, abruptly, memory returned. Her eyes flew. *Oh, no. What have I done?*

She lay sprawled in Jake Kimball's arms, her skirt hiked above her knees, her bodice loose and gaping, her breasts exposed. Humiliation and embarrassment washed over her as she clutched her dress to her chest and scrambled off the lounge chair. She felt the warmth of a blush stain her cheeks. "Oh, dear. I…um…oh."

She couldn't look at him. She didn't dare. She kept her back to him as she struggled to right her clothing.

She could hear the chuckle in his voice as he asked, "Have a nice nap?"

"Oh, Mr. Kimball. I can't believe…I didn't mean… oh, I'm so embarrassed."

"Hey, now, no sense being embarrassed. You obviously needed a good cry. And again I think we are far beyond the 'Mr. Kimball' stage, don't you?"

"I'm not embarrassed about crying!" she exclaimed, darting a look over her shoulder. He sprawled on the chaise, one arm slung across its back, his shirt unbuttoned to the navel. His hair was mussed, the light in his eyes devilish and knowing. He sat with his legs spread, the bulge between them prominent and bold.

And big.

She swallowed. Temptation in all its glory.

Kat quickly jerked her stare forward as she struggled to fix her buttons. She didn't hear him rise, so the first brush of his fingers against her skin caused her to startle.

The touch of his lips to the nape of her neck made her squeak. "Surely you're not embarrassed because we played a little?"

Played a little? Playing is what they did with the baseball and the bat, not with his fingers and her…oh, no. Fresh warmth coursed through her. If that was just playing…what did he consider serious business?

Her mouth went dry with anticipation.

This was awful.

But he is so good.

Shame melted through her from head to toe.

Jake turned her in his arms. "Don't be embarrassed, Kat. Look, I caught you in a moment of weakness. I took advantage of you."

"More like I took advantage of you," she muttered, looking anywhere but at him.

He placed a finger beneath her chin and tilted her face up, forcing her to meet his gaze. Laughter gleamed in his eyes. "If that's the case, feel free to repeat the insult at will."

She sighed and closed her eyes. "Sometimes I wonder if I'll ever outgrow the Menace in me."

He waited a beat before saying, "Marry me, Kat. We could be good together."

Her eyes flew open. She stepped away from him, out of his arms. "We've already had this argument, sir. Nothing has changed. If anything, you should have a clearer understanding of why it's totally out of the question."

"What I understand is that you came alive in my arms. Doesn't that mean anything?"

"It means I have a proven weakness for men like you. Now I need to find my sister and tell her the news about Monique. Will you please show me the way out of here?"

For a long moment he gave her a considering stare. "I need a wife, Kat McBride. You're the best choice for all of us. You're the one I want."

"We don't always get what we want, do we? Choose one of the others, Jake. I'm not strong enough to act like a mother to those children."

"Oh, you're strong. Maybe one of the strongest women I know." He folded his arms and his gaze swept her from head to toe. "Any chance you'd want to make a trip to Tibet?"

"As what? A pack horse?"

"I'm thinking my personal assistant."

Her eyes widened, then she sputtered a laugh. "You don't give up, do you?"

"Not often."

She shook her head. "This time you must. Lead the way to my sister, Mr. Kimball."

He sighed, clearly unhappy with her refusal, but took her arm and escorted her through the maze. As they approached the temple, Jake paused and called, "Dair? Miss McBride has come looking for her sister."

Following a long pause, Dair MacRae called, "I owe you one for this, Kimball."

The couple emerged from the temple a long few minutes later. Emma's mussed hair and rosy complexion offered proof as to how the pair had passed their time—not that Kat had entertained any doubts about it. What did surprise Kat was Emma's apparent lack of embarrassment and the scowl her sister sent her way.

The sooner we leave here, the better, Kat decided. Or both of them might get burned. "Emma, I need to speak with you."

"It couldn't wait?" her sister snapped.

"It appears to me I waited too long as it is," Kat fired back. "We've had a message from Monique. I'll give you one guess as to what she's done now."

Emma waited a beat, then said, "She's remarried? Again?"

"And off on her honeymoon trip. Will you come upstairs with me, Emma? Please? We have some decisions to make."

CHAPTER EIGHT

LATE IN THE AFTERNOON, gunmetal gray clouds rolled in and an unseasonably cool wind began to blow, effectively putting a halt to outdoor activities at Chatham Park. As raindrops began pattering against the rooftop, Jake poured himself a glass of whiskey and stood at the window, staring outside, sipping his drink and brooding.

He tried to tell himself he was glad for the change in weather. He needed to talk to the girls, and he'd have an easier time locating them knowing they were somewhere inside the house.

Miss Parker did her best to keep the children corralled and Jake was eternally grateful for her help. However, once she turned the girls loose outside, they tended to leave her in the dust. To complicate matters, the young nanny was plagued by a lingering head cold. When Jake had returned to the house after leading Kat and her sister from the maze, he'd been met by the butler who'd informed him that the new nanny had confessed to the upstairs maid that she felt absolutely awful, that she'd had difficulty sleeping of late and missed her mattress at home.

Jake had ordered Nanny Parker to bed, then retired

to his study where he poured himself a drink and faced the inevitable.

He'd run out of time. He had to solve this marriage problem now.

He had to give up on Kat McBride.

He drained his glass, then sighed. This truly went against his instincts. He wasn't a quitter. To Jake, the word "no" meant only that he needed to try a different tact, take a different path. Ordinarily, he'd view Kat McBride's "no" as a challenge to be overcome. Today, he'd accept it. Period.

If his decision had anything to do with her heart-wrenching tears, well, he wasn't about to admit it. He refused to recall that each tear she shed had sliced him like a knife.

Jake set down his glass, then left the room. Keeping a sharp eye out for wandering brides—he'd have enough of their company later that night during the ball—he headed up the nearest flight of stairs in search of the children. The baby, he quickly discovered, was in the nursery napping. The girls took a little longer to locate, and when he did—even when he saw the proof with his own two eyes—he had trouble believing the scene before him.

Miranda, Belle, Theresa and Caroline each sat primly in a chair at a small, square table in the third floor, east wing playroom. Each girl wore a lady's hat and gloves. Each girl held a doll in her lap. Each girl pantomimed sipping tea from the miniature china tea set.

A tea party? The wild, raging hooligans-in-petticoats were having a quiet tea party with their dolls? A shiver of worry crawled up Jake's spine. They must have done something really awful to be behaving so good.

He cleared his throat. "Hey, ladies. What are you doing?"

"We're having a party, Uncle Jake," Theresa said, twirling her green hair ribbon around her finger.

"Nanny Parker is sick." Miranda dabbed her doll's mouth with a yellow napkin.

Caroline pooched out her lip and nodded sadly.

"We're trying to be good for her," Belle said as she fussed with her doll's blue hair ribbon.

Jake was momentarily distracted when he realized his nieces had taken his color-coding idea and made it their own. He felt a surprising sense of pride at his own influence. "That's nice."

"Miss Kat told us that if we behaved real good for just a few days, Nanny Parker wouldn't worry so much, and she'd get well faster. We like Nanny Parker, Uncle Jake. Nanny Pip picked just the right person."

Jake stepped farther into the nursery. "You've been talking to Miss McBride?" When the girls nodded, he grabbed a child-sized chair and straddled it. "Tell me about it."

Caroline grinned and covered her mouth with her hand. Belle giggled and said, "You look funny, Uncle Jake. Your knees come up all the way to your chin."

"Always glad to be a source of amusement. Now tell me about Miss Kat."

Theresa said, "She came looking for us to show us her sister's necklace and ask about yours."

Jake went still. "My necklace?"

"The one you keep in your pocket, Uncle Jake," Belle said with a smile.

Hell. "Miss Kat knows about that?" When the girls nodded, he added, "How?"

"We told her."

"How do you know about it?"

"We snooped, of course. We needed to know about you."

"I see." Jake rubbed the back of his neck, his mind racing as he attempted to assimilate the possible consequences of this revelation. He had to expect that Kat would come to him and demand to see his necklace. He didn't have a similar one on hand to substitute, so that pretty much limited his option to lying. Lying, or returning her necklace.

Jake drummed his fingers on the chair back. Hmm…return the necklace. Should he do it? Probably. Would he do it?

No.

Jake might well be a practical, pragmatic man, but even after all these years, the dream he had in that Himalayan cave wouldn't turn him loose. *Find the necklace. Find your family.*

It was nonsense. Penny was dead, wasn't she?

Yet, in a couple of months, he'd return to Tibet on an expedition he'd planned for years. His first trip to that part of the world since stealing Kat's necklace from Willow Hill. A good man, a righteous man, would return the woman's treasure.

Jake would carry the necklace with him to the Himalayas.

"Look, girls. We'll talk about this snooping business another time. Right now we need to talk about the brides."

His nieces visibly tensed. Miranda asked, "What's wrong?"

"I need to know who you like best among the contestants who are still here." Four pairs of eyes went round with worry. Caroline reached out and grasped Belle's hand. Jake sighed, then laid out the truth. "I know we all wanted Miss Kat to marry me, but I'm afraid she's refused my offer."

The girls exchanged a look. "Make her change her mind!"

"I tried. Believe me, I tried."

"We don't want any of the others, Uncle Jake," Theresa explained. "We only want Miss Kat."

"I know. I feel the same way. However, this time, we're not going to get who we want."

They argued with him until he was ready to bang his fist onto the table in frustration. He talked to them about Kat's Susie, tried to make them understand how deeply the loss of a child had wounded the mother, but they didn't want to listen. They wanted Kat McBride.

Until Caroline managed the impossible without saying a word. She shut her sisters up by the simple act of standing.

Jake watched in amazement as Belle, Miranda and Theresa stilled, waiting for their youngest sister to "speak."

Caroline simply shook her head. The other three girls frowned. "Why not?" Miranda asked.

Caroline closed her eyes, placed her hand on her heart, and dropped her chin to her chest. There was a long moment of silence, then Caroline took her seat. The quiet continued for another long beat, then Miranda sighed and said, "All right."

She looked up at Jake. "Would you please go somewhere else, Uncle Jake? My sisters and I need privacy to figure out which of the brides we want."

Unease crawled up Jake's spine. "I think maybe it's better we work together on this."

All four girls shook their heads. Damn. "Girls…"

"No, Uncle Jake," Theresa said. "This is our business."

"But—"

Miranda folded her arms. "We need to pick a *mother.* That's much more important than a wife."

He could see their point. Still…

"You're planning to leave us. We need someone who loves us and who won't go away."

Jake winced as the arrow struck home. "I…uh…I love you, girls. And I'll always be your uncle."

Theresa frowned. "Uncles aren't worth much if they're a billion miles away."

"We'll vote for who we want, Uncle Jake," Miranda said. "Then we'll come tell you. Since you're leaving, you don't get a vote. Now, if you'll excuse us, please?"

Jake slowly unfolded himself from his chair, then returned the chair to its spot against the wall. He stuck his hands into his pants pockets, then rolled back and forth on his feet. "Uh…you know, girls, uh…your mother understood what my life is all about. I hope you'll try to understand, too. Your mom…by making me your guardian…well, she knew I couldn't be around all the time. She knew I'm not cut out for family life. She knew I could never be a real father to you, but she trusted me to do what's best for you and your brother. That's what I'm trying to do here."

"It's all right, Uncle Jake," Theresa said. "We always knew you wouldn't stay."

Belle nodded in agreement. "That's why we won't love you with all our hearts, only little pieces of them."

With that, catching his breath against the pang in his chest, Jake walked away.

KAT MISSED TEXAS. She missed the prairies and the huge blue sky. She missed the scent of the honeysuckle outside her bedroom window and the sound of her mother's laughter when her father chased his wife around the kitchen table. She missed Mari and her brothers. She was ready to go home.

The trip had helped her, she thought as she stepped beneath the stone arch leading into the rose garden. It'd been good to get away from Fort Worth for a while, to step outside the routine. Now she felt stronger, more in control. She thought she'd taken a big step forward.

"With maybe a few steps back," she said on a sigh as she watched Jake Kimball stroll along the garden path with Miss Starnes on his arm. A flame of jealousy sparked. Blasted man. How dare he make her feel…

Defeated. Kat sighed. He'd also made her feel alive for the first time in ages. However, the interlude in the gazebo was merely that. An interlude. A moment of pure fantasy.

A serious lapse in judgment.

"Miss Starnes is welcome to you," Kat told his retreating back.

Liar.

Ignoring the taunting voice inside her head, Kat gripped the archway's mossy wall for support and frowned. She suspected that the sea captain's daughter would get the matrimonial nod from Jake. He'd been particularly attentive to her during last night's ball, and now again this morning.

Kat turned away from the garden and wandered back into the house, deciding to spend some time with the Texana collection. Maybe it would soothe this malaise she chalked up to homesickness, but suspected was something more.

Kat made her way to the west wing second floor parlor currently utilized as a Texana print room. There, she gravitated toward the caricatures hanging on the wall. Sam Houston at San Jacinto. A longhorn getting his first look at barbed wire. Outlaws on the run from a Texas Ranger carrying a very large gun. She wondered if Emma had seen these yet. She'd enjoy the drawing of the ranger. Kat and Emma liked to tease Mari about the size of her former-Texas-Ranger-husband's "gun." If Emma hadn't explored this particular room yet, maybe the two of them could pay a quick visit here before their departure tomorrow morning.

Kat had wanted to leave Chatham Park today, but Emma had pleaded for one more day with Dair MacRae. Now Kat worried tomorrow might be too late.

Emma was obviously infatuated with MacRae, and Kat worried about her. She'd suffered some rough times, romantically speaking, in the past and didn't need another broken heart.

Kat remained in the parlor for over an hour, and she honestly enjoyed herself. The pieces of Texana were fascinating, and it did provide Kat with a little taste of home. As a result, both her heart and her step was lighter when she left the room. She was even able to laugh when Jake's nieces skipped past her squealing at the antics of an irritated goose they, for some reason, had on a leash. Inside the house.

They reminded her of her old Menace days.

Kat wasn't prepared for the youngest one—sweet, silent Caroline—to turn around and run back to Kat. She lifted her arms to Kat, an unspoken request to be picked up.

Think of it as a test, Kat told herself. *If I can do this, surely I'll be better with Mari's little ones.*

Caroline put her little hand over Kat's heart. Her big blue eyes filled up with tears. Kat felt herself tremble, and she moved to set the girl back on the ground. But just as she shifted her weight, Caroline removed her hand, replacing it with a gentle kiss. Then she wiggled, signaling she wanted down.

Kat placed a hand over the little girl's kiss, cradling its healing warmth against her broken heart. What a sweet, sensitive child.

Once Caroline disappeared down the hallway, Kat went looking for her sister. She wanted to show Emma the caricatures. Not finding her in the house, she tried the stables and arrived moments after Jake had just departed on a horseback ride.

Watching her host gallop across the wide expanse of park, Kat sighed. She'd have loved to have gone for a gallop herself. A good hard ride was just the exercise she needed.

The thought gave rise to a mental vision of another sort of ride, and she groaned in self-disgust. He was a thief, a liar, a scoundrel. He'd stolen her most prized possession, for goodness' sake! Why did he intrigue her so?

"What's wrong with me?" she asked herself as she made her way back to the house. Why was she attracted to dangerous men?

She couldn't leave Chatham Park soon enough. In fact, she'd leave right now if it were possible. She'd forget about the last ditch effort she had planned for retrieving her necklace. She'd leave the altar cross in its box. She'd flee the magnetism of the man who'd tempted her in ways she'd never before imagined.

The rattle of wheels against cobblestones caught her attention, and she looked around to see a well-appointed carriage departing Chatham Park. "Missed my chance again," she murmured, idly wondering who occupied the coach. One of the brides, most likely. Someone who'd also seen the writing on the wall regarding Miss Starnes.

Though she had no concrete reason for it, Kat didn't care for the sea captain's daughter. She wondered why, out of the remaining women, Jake appeared to have chosen her. She was beautiful, true. Witty. Intelligent. Nice to the girls. Protective of the baby.

Kat couldn't stand her.

Such were the thoughts on her mind when she passed the doorway into the music room and saw the remaining brides sharing tea and conversation. When she heard Jake's name, Kat couldn't help but stop and eavesdrop.

"…ride alone in order to make his decision."

"He'll announce it at the luncheon, I'm told."

Kat moved to where she could see into the room. Talk moved on to Jake's nieces.

"It's interesting that while we all recognize what a problem those girls are, Jake doesn't agree. Any time I've raised the subject, he puts a stop to it immediately."

"It'll just have to wait until he's left the country," said Miss Starnes.

The other women shook their heads in agreement. Mrs. Hartman said, "It's not like we'd be breaking faith with him."

"That's right." Miss Starnes smiled with satisfaction. "He *is* leaving one of us in charge of their welfare. I wouldn't make any decision I didn't think was in their best interest. However, if I decide they'd be well served attending a boarding school where they'd learn manners and control, well, it will be my decision, won't it? He'll be a million miles away."

Boarding school? Kat's heart pounded. The women's voices were a buzz in her ears.

"Those girls are out of control."

"They certainly need discipline."

"The baby is sweet as can be, though. He's better apart from those girls. They're a bad influence."

"Especially the mute. She doesn't set a good example for the dear little marquis."

Miss Starnes sighed loudly. "So true. I know of a lovely sanatorium outside of Bath that would be perfect for her."

"Yes." Mrs. Hartman nodded. "I know of that place."

"It will be the best thing for her," agreed Miss Wainwright.

A sanatorium for Caroline? Kat shuddered with anger. Why, those…those…those…witches!

Intending to show them the sharp side of her tongue, she took one step forward, then stopped. Anything she had to say would fall on deaf ears. These women were vicious, moneygrubbing harpies. Why, Jake's ship wouldn't even be out of the harbor and the girls would be off to boarding school. Dear little Caroline off to an asylum.

Well, we'll just see about that.

Kat had heard all she needed to hear. Jake needed to know what these wicked women planned. He needed to hear just what kind of woman he was choosing. She backed away from the music room doorway, then whirled around, picked up her skirts, and dashed for the stairs.

She'd wait at the stables, speak to him the moment he returned. Surely he'd believe her. But, what if he didn't?

Maybe she should…no! No. No. No. Kat pushed the dangerous thoughts out of her mind. Short of kidnapping Caroline and the rest of the children, Kat had no options.

Save one.

The one that lingered, refusing to die. In the middle of the entry hall, she abruptly stopped, breathing hard. Did she dare? No, she couldn't. She wouldn't. She needed to leave this house. Immediately.

Before she did something truly stupid.

Kat turned around and headed in a different direction. Moments later, she burst into Chatham Park's kitchen. "Excuse me," she said to the startled cook, "but may I please borrow a hammer and a screwdriver?"

"Umm...?"

"Shoe repair," Kat lied. "A heel."

It was enough, apparently, to allay the woman's fears. She rummaged through a wooden box, then handed over the requested items. Kat dashed back upstairs. She had to hurry. She had to get her business done fast, get her sister, and get out of Chatham Park before Jake returned from his ride.

She hurried into her bedroom suite, slamming the door behind her, then locking it. She crossed the room toward the door that led to Jake's suite of rooms, her gaze on the hinges, her grip tightening around the hammer. Halfway across the room, in the periphery of her vision, she noticed the envelope propped against the desk. Her sister's handwriting penned "Kat" across the front.

Kat halted midstep. Her stomach sank to her knees. The tools slipped from her grip to bang against the floor. Somehow, she knew what was in that letter. She felt it in her bones. Emma's letter would change her life.

Kat's mouth was dry, her heart heavy, as she opened the envelope and removed the folded note.

Dear Kat,

I'm leaving Chatham Park today with Dair MacRae. Please tell Mama and Papa not to worry, that I'm fine and safe and happy. I hope you all will understand. I'm off on an adventure. It's my turn.

I'll write often.

Love,
Emma

Kat closed her eyes. She set her teeth. Everything inside her went hard.

No! No, no, no!

"I need you, Emma. I'm in the middle of a crisis here. How could you run off and leave me!" She sank onto the bed, breathing hard. What was she to do?

For a good five minutes she sat rocking back and forth, her mind blank. Then, breathing like she'd just run five miles, she grabbed the tools up off the floor and approached the door to Jake's suite, dragging a chair with her. She set the chair in front of the door hinges, climbed up on it, positioned her screwdriver, and began pounding the hinge pin.

She worked for five minutes, then ten, making too much noise, but not caring. She heard someone knocking at her door, calling her name. She ignored it. Finally, the pin fell free.

She went to work on the second hinge. It proved easier to manipulate and took her less than five minutes to free.

She wiped her sweaty hands on her skirt, grabbed the door and pulled with all her might. Finally, thankfully, she heard wood split as the lock gave way and she opened a large enough space to slip through.

Jake's rooms smelled of sandalwood and leather and him. Kat noted the box containing the altar cross on the fireplace mantel. Leaving it there for the time being, she moved into his bedroom and began a thorough search. First the tables, then his wardrobe and every pocket she could find.

Desperation made her movements jerky. It had to be here. She had to find her necklace. She had to leave right away, and she wanted to take it with her. Emma's run off with a man. Monique's run off with a man—again. She was all alone in a foreign country rifling through a man's bedroom. Some would claim she was the one who should be committed.

She opened the chest of drawers and rifled through his handkerchiefs and socks. Teardrops she didn't realize were falling splatted against the back of her hands. It wasn't here. She slammed the drawer shut, gazed wildly around. Where else could she look? Damn that man! Did he have it on him even now?

Running entirely on emotion now, she went to his bed and yanked back the covers. "Where?" she cried, throwing a pillow. "Where is it? I'm running out of—"

"Where is what?" his incredulous voice demanded. "What the hell is going on here, Kat?"

"—time." Kat's knees went weak and she grabbed a bedpost to keep from falling. She'd waited too late.

"Which one, Jake?"

"Which one, what? Kat, talk to me. You're as white as those bedsheets. Why are you crying?"

"Which bride did you choose?"

There was a long silence. His expression went blank. Then, in a quiet, matter-of-fact voice, he said, "Miss Starnes."

I know a lovely little sanitarium outside of Bath. Kat closed her eyes. That cold-hearted bitch.

"I want my necklace back, Jake Kimball."

Another long moment of silence passed and she expected him to deny stealing it. Instead, when the thief finally spoke, he said, "I'm sorry, no."

"Why?" she demanded.

After another pregnant pause, he said, "I think it might lead me to my brother."

His brother. Kat knew the story. He'd had a brother who'd been lost for years. But, damn the man, he had nieces who needed him now. "The children need you more."

"They'll be fine with Miss Starnes. Better off than with me. She'll make them a good mother."

Kat could tell him what she'd overheard. Even if he didn't believe her, he'd have second thoughts. He wouldn't have Miss Starnes.

But what would that really solve? He'd just find another Miss Starnes. Another woman who'd put money and power and position ahead of the needs of those poor orphaned children. Another woman who'd wait till his back was turned and send sad little Caroline to an asylum.

There was but one thing Kat could do. God, help her.

Decision made, slowly, she turned. She straightened her spine, squared her shoulders, and wiped the tears off her cheek. She looked him dead in the eyes. "I'll have the necklace as a wedding gift."

His brow knotted. "I…uh…that's a wedding tradition that's new to me—the groom giving a bridal gift to a woman other than the bride."

"I'll be the bride, but I want the necklace and the cross."

Jake's eyes widened, then narrowed. "You're saying you'll marry me?"

Now, her gaze skidded away from him. Jerkily, she nodded.

He moved toward her. "Why?"

Her mouth twisted in a bitter grin. "It's either that or the sanitarium. So…" she held up her hand, palm out. "Do we have a deal?"

His stare focused on her mouth, then dropped to her hand. "You can have the cross. However, the necklace…"

"It's non-negotiable. And it's mine."

His gaze slowly lifted, lingered on her breasts, before returning to her mouth. He took another step closer. "I guess I can work with that."

"And I want those brides out of this house by sunset."

Now he stood but an arm's length away, so close she could feel his body heat. "Consider them gone," he told her, his voice low and raspy.

The sound, the scent of him, the heat of him brought a shiver to her skin. It took conscious effort to keep from swaying toward him, and she cleared her throat. "I won't give you children, Jake Kimball. You must vow to take precautions."

He hesitated just a moment before slipping his hand into his pocket and slowly withdrew her emerald necklace. Kat's breath caught as sunlight caught the faceted jewel and it gleamed. "So we have a deal?" she asked.

He placed the chain over her head and down around her neck. When the pendant nestled against her breasts, a sense of rightness, of homecoming, of peace engulfed her. She breathed a sigh of relief.

Heat fired in his eyes, twin blue flames that burned into her. "So many times I've imagined how you'd look wearing this and nothing else. We have a deal, Katrina. Now take your clothes off, and let's seal it."

CHAPTER NINE

JAKE COULDN'T BELIEVE the turn of events. Just when he'd thought all was lost, when he'd decided for once in his life to let something—in this case, someone—he wanted go without a fight, Kat McBride turns up in his bedroom. Damned if he wasn't a lucky son of a bitch.

Reaching out, he traced the scooped neckline of her morning dress and savored the contrast between the cold, hard chain of her necklace and warm softness of her skin. He wanted his mouth there. Now.

"You're not moving fast enough, Katrina. Let me help." He searched for the buttons on her dress. When he'd worked his way down to the third, Kat came to life.

"No," she stated, pulling away from him. Her eyes looked a little wild. "By God, I'm not doing this again. You want to seal this deal, we'll do it with a handshake. No naked anything until it's legal. In fact, this time I want references. References and a sworn affidavit that no legal impediment exists to this marriage. I want vows before a minister and a judge and…and…and all the children. And all the servants."

Dammit to hell, thought Jake. Rory Callahan rears his ugly head from out of the grave again. This was getting old. "While I'm at it, shall I sign the marriage license in blood?"

"It wouldn't hurt."

Jake waited a beat before saying, "As much as it disappoints me and adds to my physical frustrations, we'll do this your way. However, just so you know, I'll abide only the two of us in our marriage bed." When she wrinkled her brow in confusion, he clarified, "Rory Callahan needs to stay dead."

Her chin came up, but she didn't respond verbally. Jake continued, "I've already arranged for a license, so we won't be delayed in making it legal. We could do it this evening, in fact. Emma and Dair can stand up with us and—"

Kat interrupted. "You don't know? They left."

"Left? What do you mean?"

She explained about the note she'd found and the carriage departure she'd witnessed. Jake wasn't too surprised that his friend had taken off with Emma Tate in tow. Dair had obligations that often changed his plans, and Emma…well…she wasn't the first woman to fall for MacRae's brooding good looks. "We have plenty of other witnesses available. Shall I arrange the matter for this evening?"

She closed her eyes, swallowed hard, then shrugged. "All right. Fine. Whatever." Following a moment's pause, she added, "Just make sure those women are gone first."

"Your wish, bride-of-mine, is my command." Then, because Jake couldn't help himself—didn't want to help himself—he sealed the deal, anyway, with a kiss.

It had him humming for hours afterward.

Memory of the kiss kept him warm during the deep freeze that settled over the dining room when he made his big announcement during lunch, then shuffled the disappointed ladies to the train station. It distracted him while writing notes to the village minister and telling the children his good news. Memory of the kiss had him slipping into fantasy, off and on, imagining the upcoming night, up until the ceremony itself.

The bride wore gray and cried her way down the aisle of the chapel at Chatham Park. Instead of a floral bouquet, she carried a cat. When she reached the altar, Jake said, "I think I can figure out the reason for the color, but the cat has me stymied."

"I eloped the first time I wed. I missed not having a McBride family wedding. This is as close as I can come today."

"All right," Jake replied, understanding only that she held on to her composure by a thread.

He glanced over his shoulder to where the children sat dressed in their finest beside Nanny Parker. The girls beamed at him, and he couldn't help but preen a bit beneath their regard. The minister began his spiel, but Kat cut him off midsentence. She spent a full five minutes quizzing the man regarding the legalities of the marriage. After that, she turned to the magistrate there at Jake's request. Once he, too, had satisfied her questions, she nodded her readiness for the ceremony to go forward. When, moments later she repeated her vows, Jake let out a relieved breath he'd been unaware of holding.

It was done. He'd married Kat McBride.

As he took her into his arms and dipped his head toward hers for a kiss, the strangest thing happened. He'd swear he heard laughter echoing through his mind.

And damned if the laugh didn't sound just like Daniel.

KAT HADN'T EXPECTED a honeymoon. As a result, when Jake led her to a carriage and explained they'd be gone a week, she was caught flatfooted and unable to protest... If she even wanted to protest. She hadn't had time to figure out how she felt. Everything about this was so different from her first wedding.

Which was probably his purpose, she decided as he assisted her up into the carriage, then took a seat opposite her. Yet, as she settled back against the plush velvet seats, she decided this time spent away from Chatham Park might be for the best. She'd have a week to adjust her thinking, a week to prepare herself for the task of taking on the care and raising of his sister's children.

A week to overcome the grief that might harm those poor orphans if Kat didn't finally learn to deal with it.

"I think you'll like the hunting lodge," Jake said as he gave a final wave to his nieces. "It will remind you of some of the cabins you can find in the Texas hill country. It's cozy and comfortable, and I've had the larder stocked. It's far enough away from Chatham Park so that the girls won't come looking for us, but if a problem arises, we can get back quickly."

He kept up a running dialogue about the area, the entertainments, the menu he'd planned for their days away. None of it was threatening or demanding. She suspected he was trying to put her at ease.

It worked. The farther they traveled from Chatham Park, the more Kat relaxed. The weight she'd carried since agreeing to this marriage seemed to roll right off her shoulders. Like most scoundrels, Jake could be a charmer when he put his mind to it. He was trying hard this afternoon.

Kat suspected her attitude had as much to do with being *away* from the children as being *with* their uncle. With no children around, she could let down her guard.

She wasn't worried about being alone with Jake. After she'd made the decision to marry him, she'd decided she might as well enjoy the physical aspects of their relationship. They were obviously well suited in that regard.

The man excited her. That gleam in his eye, the mischief in his grin. The bold stroke of his touch. Jake Kimball appealed to the shameless hussy inside of Kat, the part of her she'd thought died with Rory Callahan.

Well, the hussy in her was alive and well and looking forward to the evening. Her grandmother would be proud.

Her grandmother would tell her not to waste a minute. After all, the man planned to leave in a little less than a month.

When he paused in his recitation of the benefits of a brisk walk in the woods, Kat fired her first shot. "I suspect you and I will get along quite well together in bed."

Jake's elbow slipped off his knee.

Kat hid her smile, her spirits lifting. She'd forgotten how much fun teasing a man could be. "I enjoyed marital sport with my first husband—although I guess to be honest, you are really my first husband. Rory was my first lover. He did have a way about him. I must have been the most satisfied bride in Texas."

"Damned scoundrel," he muttered.

"It's a point in your favor, of course. You and Rory are two peas in a pod, so I suspect you'll be quite pleasing."

"Wait just one minute." He lowered his brow and glared. "Remember what I said about a crowded marriage bed?"

Kat rolled her tongue around her cheek. "Hmm. Tell me, Jake, would you consider yourself bold in such matters?"

This time his mouth gaped open, and he stared at her as if she'd grown two heads. "Bold?" he croaked.

Kat shrugged. "As opposed to athletic. I don't doubt you're athletic. It's another reason why I believe we'll suit."

Jake waited a few seconds before giving his head a little shake. "You surprise me, Mrs. Kimball."

It was the first time she'd heard her new name spoken. Kat cocked her head, considered it. Kat Kimball. A smile played across her mouth. She liked it.

She snuggled back against the coach's velvet seats and tested her wings. "I've always been a bit of a free spirit. It's a natural tendency that's been encouraged by Monique and even my mother. They're both strong women, and they nurture that strength in their loved ones. The women in my family don't follow society's rules as much as we follow our own sense of right and wrong."

"I have noticed that."

"I try to be honest and forthright in my dealings with others and with myself," she added, playing with her necklace's chain.

"This from the woman who arrived at my home dressed in disguise and under an assumed identity," Jake said dryly.

Kat acknowledged his point with a grin, then said, "When I was younger, I aspired to be an actress. I've always enjoyed the drama of a play, the freedom of fantasy. I was especially enamored of the idea of happy endings. However, life, I've learned, is very real. It's real and it's heartbreaking and it's heavy to bear. The way I see it, though this marriage is legal—I'm confident of that, by the way, and I thank you for the reassurance—this marriage of ours is more illusion than real life. We're not in love, or pretending to be in love. Ours is not even a traditional marriage of convenience. So for us to have a honeymoon, well, it's like a week-long theatrical play. It's pure fantasy. If I'm going to indulge in fantasy—" Kat shrugged "—I might as well enjoy it."

Jake remained silent for a time, his brow knitted in thought. Then he propped his boot on the opposite seat. "This is the most peculiar situation. I feel as though I should protest, but I don't quite know why. Doing so would not be in my best interest."

"It's a week," she replied with a shrug. "A guilt-free

week away from reality, away from responsibility. A week of freedom to indulge ourselves. I look forward to sharing a marriage bed with you, Jake. I find you incredibly appealing, and we do seem to have a certain…sizzle between us. I think it will be fun to see how hot we can burn."

Jake studied her for a long moment, then leaned forward and banged on the window, alerting the coachman. "How much farther?"

"Fifteen minutes or so, I'd say."

"I'll double your tip if you make it in ten." Jake settled back into his seat as the horses picked up their pace. He drummed his fingers against his knee, and his gaze never left her face. "You are a most surprising woman."

"I'll take that as a compliment."

"It is meant as one."

They didn't speak again, but the tension inside the coach grew thicker every minute. Kat's body hummed beneath her husband's smoldering regard. She stoked the fires with little, deliberate movements—the sweep of her tongue across her bottom lip, a sensuous roll of her shoulder, a sinuous stretch of her leg. His nostrils flared and the angles on his face seemed to sharpen, his body grow hard. In response, Kat felt herself soften.

The coach rolled to a stop, and Kat had her first look at the hunting lodge. Red stone walls and brown wooden shutters gave the two-story structure a solid, masculine look, but the flower boxes at the four large windows softened the facade. He'd been right about it resembling hill-country stone houses, though she'd never seen a Texas cottage this big. "It's welcoming," she said, breaking the silence between them.

"It's comfortable." Jake opened the coach door, and jumped to the ground. Reaching up to assist Kat, he fitted his hands around her waist, then lifted her down, sliding her body against his until her feet touched the ground. Rather than release her, his fingers tightened, drew her closer. "Welcome to Paradise, Mrs. Kimball."

"Paradise?" It startled a laugh from her. "You have no doubt about your talents, do you, Mr. Kimball?"

He smiled his scoundrel's grin, then cocked his head toward a sign above the door. "Paradise Lodge."

"Oh."

His hands slipped from her waist and slid slowly down across her hips until he cupped her buttocks. He gave her a quick, hard kiss, then said, "I trust it will live up to its name."

Releasing her, he stepped aside to speak to the driver before sending him on his way. He shoved his hands in his pockets and rocked back on his heels, watching the coach depart. Kat kept her gaze on him, appreciating the handsome sight he made. He'd forsaken a jacket and stood in shirtsleeves and trousers, his cuffs rolled halfway up his forearms. Sunlight glistened off his dark hair and flashed from the gold hoop earring he'd donned for their exchange of wedding vows. She was reminded of the first time she saw him, standing shirtless and wet beneath the Texas sun. A pirate.

Then he looked at her, his eyes hot with desire. A pirate ready to ravish.

Warm, honeyed lust washed through Kat.

A smile played upon his lips. "The answer to your question is yes."

"What question?"

"I like boldness in my bed."

Kat's pulse leapt as he advanced on her. She backed away. She didn't mind joining the spirit of the game, but she feared she'd given him the wrong impression. She'd heard whispers of unusual appetites involving whips and pain that left her cold. She cleared her throat. "What sort of boldness appeals?"

Jake toed off his boots, then worked the buttons of his shirt. "The grass is green and thick. The sunshine warm. We're alone. I want you here, Kat Kimball. I want you now."

"The lodge is only twenty feet away."

"Too far."

Outdoors? All right. Yes. She could do that.

"I had planned a slow seduction, but that will have to wait for another time. You've teased me long enough." He shrugged off his shirt and Kat's mouth went dry. Broad and bronzed and sculpted, he took her breath away. He took yet another step closer, and this time, Kat held her ground.

Jake's gaze burned as he reached out and pulled the pins from her hair. "So lovely," he murmured, his eyes hot and hungry. "Old gold. I never forgot that about you, Katrina. I never forgot you."

His lips took hers, raided, captured, ravished. Heat flowed from his body into hers, engulfing her like a firestorm. His hands gripped her hips and he yanked her against him.

Kat pressed right back. She wrapped her arms around his neck and moved against him, sliding and rocking and rubbing. Her blood boiled. This man. This moment in time. It felt right and wonderful, and it had been so long.

"Take me, Jake." Desperate, she arched against him, offering herself as her heart pounded and arousal thrummed in her blood. "Touch me. Take me."

"You're mine." His hands ripped at her buttons and yanked at her bodice and finally filled with her bare flesh. He fondled her breasts as his mouth slid to her throat. Kat arched her neck, giving him access. His greedy mouth nipped at her skin and she wanted to scream.

His hands were everywhere at once and his mouth chased right behind. When he took her breast into his mouth the sweet pull of suction on her nipple drew a moan from her lips. He let out a hum of satisfaction in response.

So lost was she in the sensual spell he wove that she only vaguely noticed the brush of breeze against bare skin as her skirts fell away and her underclothes disappeared. Jake Kimball was a forbidden dream suddenly within reach, and she sank into the dark, hungry fantasy.

Her fingers threaded into his hair, tugging the thick, silky strands free of the tie at the base of his neck. Her hands streaked across his shoulders and back, molding the firm cords of muscle, learning his long, lean form. He smelled of sandalwood and male and tasted of temptation and spicy hidden pleasures.

Kat wanted the rest of him, so she tugged at the waistband of his trousers. Desire nipped and gnawed and clawed through her as his hands swept down her spine, cupped her bare buttocks and lifted her against his straining erection. She whimpered as he ground himself against her.

Suddenly he returned her feet to the ground and pulled back. Stepped away. Her empty, aching arms drifted slowly to her sides. Then, she saw the hot, greedy appetite in his eyes as his gaze trailed slowly over her nakedness, and the sense of feminine power drew her up short. She'd long been self-conscious about her curves, but now, watching her husband literally tremble with need at the sight of her, she was filled with a soaring pride.

She lifted her arms to take off her necklace, but he stopped her by saying in a thick, hoarse voice, "No. Leave it. You're just as I pictured. You take my breath away, Katrina."

He stripped away his trousers, and Kat's throat went tight, her mouth dry. He was a pagan god, elemental and erotic and larger than life. He turned her knees weak.

His expression appeared chiseled in granite as he strode toward her, then swept her up into his arms. Her hands caressed his broad shoulders as he carried her around to the back of the lodge to a spot where the grass grew thick and green and sweet. He lay her down like a prize, then rose above her like the conqueror he was.

Jake lowered his head and feasted, savoring her inch by inch. His big hands explored her, his touch firm and just a little bit rough. Kat's eyes fluttered closed as she surrendered to the sensual pleasure of the moment—the whisper of the gentle breeze, the earthy fragrance of the grass, the warmth of the sunshine against her skin, and the pure delight of his intimate attentions.

He nibbled his way along her shoulders. "Your shoulders intrigue me, Katrina. They're delicate, soft and round, but they bear so much weight."

She gasped a breath as he trailed his tongue along her collarbone. "You're too beautiful for such heavy burdens. Shed your burdens and fly with me now."

She hissed out his name as his fingers found her woman's core. As the tension built, she arched her back, opened for him, breathing in throaty moans until he captured her mouth in a kiss almost savage with desire.

His heart pounded beneath her fingertips as he skillfully, ruthlessly, drove her to a peak. She cried out and her wetness poured into his hand.

Jake growled low in his throat, then rose above her, positioned himself at her entrance. "Mrs. Kimball. Mine," he murmured, then he drove himself home.

So long, Kat thought as she took him deep. And never like this. Never this full, this hot, this…complete.

She rocked against him, matching his rhythm, until the savage tension built within her once more. Her body went taut, and as the tremors began, clutching him, working him, Jake let out a shout and yanked himself from within her, spilling his seed safely on the ground.

Breathing hard, he gathered her against him, and they lay without speaking beneath the warm springtime sun. Kat's thoughts spun. Lovemaking with Jake

Kimball had been bigger, grander, more powerful, more physical than anything she'd known before.

So why did she feel so empty?

ADVENTURE.

Upstairs in the master suite, Jake's eyes flew open on the word, and he smiled with satisfaction. His body ached as if he'd galloped a horse up a rocky Himalayan mountainside, but he wasn't about to complain. Earning battle scars like these had been the best time he'd had in…well…he couldn't remember when.

He turned his head on his pillow and gazed at the woman sleeping beside him. When he'd made plans for this honeymoon, he'd expected to have to coax her into his bed. Instead, he'd had her three times before they even came close to a mattress. First outside, then on the sofa in the main room, then up against the wall on the staircase landing. She'd been a randy man's fantasy, and heaven knows, he was a randy man.

He rolled onto his side and propped up his head with his arm, then watched her. Sunlight filtering through the bedroom window bathed her creamy complexion in soft light. Sleeping beauty, he thought. He twirled a strand of her silky, spun-gold hair around his finger. Sleeping puzzle, too.

She'd been right there with him every time. In fact, she was the one who instigated the exchange on the stairs. Yet, for all her enthusiasm, for all her obvious satisfaction, each time they finished, he noted a strange light in her eyes. A light he couldn't quite place. Or maybe it was more of a dimming.

Was it the fact that he'd followed her wishes and withdrawn from her before spilling his seed? Possibly. He could understand how her feelings about conception might be conflicted. Jake suspected her reaction more likely involved that damned bounder she'd "married," but damned if he'd ask her about Rory Callahan. The son of a bitch's ghost already hovered in the air of their intimacies. Jake wanted an exorcism.

How to go about it? Leaning forward, he inhaled her scent. Sleepy, sunshine sex. Mmm. What would please the lady and rid her of her ghost? What would keep the light shining in her eyes?

He considered what he knew about Kat McBride Kimball. She was smart and courageous. Beautiful. Witty, energetic, kind.

Her lips curved and she sighed in her sleep. *Pleasant dreams, beautiful?* Dare he hope she was dreaming of him?

Hell, she might as easily be dreaming about baseball and striking him out at the plate. He shouldn't leave *competitive* out when describing his Kat. She was definitely competitive, adventurous and…

Adventurous. Hmm…

She'd told him she didn't like adventure. What exactly had she said? Something about the reality of adventure not being as exciting as the fantasy of it?

But then, she'd said something about fantasy, had she not? The freedom of fantasy. Hmm.

Fantasy. Adventure. An idea hovered just beyond his reach.

Her eyelashes fluttered, then opened. Her eyes glittered like the emerald she wore around her neck. "Good morning."

The rasp in her voice stroked him like a physical touch and he immediately went hard. "G'mornin', sunshine. So, did you have pleasant dreams? You were smiling in your sleep."

Kat chuckled softly. "Pleasant dreams? You wouldn't believe me if I told you."

"Try me."

"I dreamed about the time my sisters and I robbed a train."

Jake sat up. "You what?"

Now she giggled. "We robbed a train. It was part of our attempts to play matchmakers for our father and Jenny Fortune. We were successful, I might add."

"You were children."

"We were Menaces."

There's that word again. Jake stretched out beside her once more and trailed his finger along the supple curve of her arm. "Sounds like you were a real trial for your father."

"We were." Her smile turned rueful. "We are."

He leaned down and kissed her shoulder. "I like the sound of that. Will you be a Menace for me?"

She blinked at him. "I'm here, aren't I? Yesterday wasn't adventurous enough for you?"

Jake nudged the sheet downward, revealing her breast. "If I'd had any more adventure yesterday, you'd be burying me today. Although, let me assure you, now that I've had time to recover—" he brushed his fingers over her nipple until it hardened "—I'm hearing the call of the wild all over again."

"Grr…" Kat growled as she tugged him toward her. She nipped at Jake's shoulder, and he gave himself up to the glory of her touch, her teeth, her fingers. Later, when he heard himself howl, he was torn between laughter and lust.

When she'd left him lying vanquished on the field as she sought her bath, he knew an unusual sense of dismay as he watched her walk away. The woman was a joy, fun and exciting and, yes, adventurous. They had so little time together.

He wished she were joining him on his travels. He imagined how she'd look aboard ship, her long golden hair flowing behind her on the salty sea breeze. That fantasy led him in other directions, and he placed her in the prow of a gondola in Venice, in a pirogue on a Louisiana bayou, bedecked like a native on a South Pacific island. Her breasts bare.

Or, maybe in a sultan's tent in Arabia, wearing a silky, transparent harem costume. He could be the sultan. He'd have her dance and…hmm. Jake propped himself up on his elbow, gazing at the bathroom door. Maybe… A grin played at the edges of his lips as the idea took hold. He took a mental inventory of the contents of Chatham Park. One great thing about being the heir of a devoted collector, he had plenty of props.

Whistling now, energized, Jake rolled from the bed and padded over to the desk. He removed two pieces of paper from the drawer and began making a list on one. When he was satisfied with his plan, he took the blank page and sketched out detailed instructions. Downstairs he put his note in a basket on the front porch for a Chatham Park servant to pick up when he delivered the daily supplies.

The plan set in motion, Jake made his way back upstairs where he joined Kat in her bath. Damned if this first full day of his honeymoon wasn't off to a wonderful start.

KAT THREADED A WORM onto her hook, then tossed her line into the water, willing a fish to take her bait. She had two fish on her stringer to Jake's three, so she felt the pressure to catch up. Kat was too competitive to be happy coming in second in any contest. Yet she was too relaxed to get worked up over much of anything.

They'd passed a leisurely morning at Paradise Lodge, much of the time spent in conversation. Jake questioned her about her interests, opinions and her everyday life at home. He'd acted as if he truly wished to learn about the person he'd married.

They'd talked politics, favorite foods, tastes in music. His repertoire of bawdy-house songs was impressive, and the recipe he touted for a pecan tart had Kat itching to get to the kitchen. She found herself telling him stories about her childhood, about her father's courtship of Jenny Fortune and the McBride Menaces' contributions to the effort. He was sneaky with his questions, though, making subtle points about the value of stepmothers to children with no maternal figure in their lives.

It was when his interrogations turned toward Susie that Kat put a stop to the questioning by proposing a fishing expedition. She'd have been happy fishing off the pier that extended into the lake, but for some reason Jake wanted to take the rowboat out. He'd insisted she sit at the very front of it.

"Have you ever eaten Tagine t'Faia?" he asked out of the blue.

Kat frowned at him. "You're a very strange man."

He slashed a grin. "It's a Moroccan chicken dish. It's made with saffron and ginger. It's very good."

"I see." Feeling a tug on her line, Kat yanked her pole. Darn, something stole her worm. "So, are we having Moroccan chicken for dinner tonight?"

"Not tonight." His smile went wicked. "Tonight we're having Italian."

Suspicious now, Kat baited her hook. "What are you up to?"

"Just wanting to be sure that I satisfy your appetite." With that, he yanked another fish into the boat.

Kat wrinkled her nose at the small bass flopping in the bottom of the boat. She reacted not to the smell or to the slime, but to the fact that she truly hated to lose. Since that appeared to be the likely outcome, she fell back on a tried-and-true tactic. "You're cheating."

"Cheating? How can a person cheat at fishing?"

"I don't know, but you're doing it. This contest is over."

Jake gaped at her. "I didn't cheat. I'm using worms just like you. I can't help it if I'm a better fisherman than you."

Pulling her line from the water, she sent him a scornful look. Inside, though, she was smiling. "You cheated."

"You're being ridiculous."

She folded her arms and turned her head away, smothering the smile that threatened.

"You just don't want to admit you've lost. My sister was that way. No matter what game we played, any time she fell behind, she conjured up a reason to quit. It drove me crazy."

He continued to grumble while he added his latest catch to his stringer. Kat pretended not to listen, and in truth, her attention did drift away. She felt light out here on the boat. Light of heart. Peaceful. Almost...happy.

It was a sobering thought.

Kat couldn't remember a time she'd ever been this emotionally confused. Sitting here trading fish tales with Jake filled her heart with gladness. Being away from the children gave her a sense of relief. Losing herself in his arms left her physically satisfied but mentally discontent. Being a hussy wasn't as easy as she'd expected it to be.

She wondered how Emma was holding up under similar circumstances.

Jake dipped the oars into the water and propelled the boat toward shore. For a number of minutes, neither of them spoke, and Kat's thoughts drifted toward home. She thought of her parents and decided she was glad she'd be far away when Trace McBride learned about the most recent activities of two of his daughters. She wondered where Emma was and how Mari was doing, how her pregnancy was progressing. She'd be big and round now, the babies due soon. With her sisters on her mind, Kat's right hand drifted up to clasp the pendant on her necklace.

The weight, missing for long, felt good in her hand. Mari would be thrilled to learn the necklace was back where it belonged. Which brought up a question she'd been wanting to ask. "What does my necklace have to do with your brother?"

Jake hesitated midstroke, then resumed his rowing. "I wondered when that would come up."

"Well?"

He sighed. "You were so beautiful that day at the Galveston beach. I wanted a keepsake—"

"Oh, please. Skip the nonsense and try the truth for a change."

"I don't lie to you," he protested.

She arched a brow and waited.

"Often." He sighed heavily, pulled in the oars and propped the handles on his knees. "It's a long story."

"We're here for six more days."

Jake grimaced, rubbed the back of his neck, then said, "Six days won't be enough to make sense out of nonsense. I've been working at it for sixteen years, and I'm still lost in a fog."

Well, Kat thought, shifting on her seat in an effort to get a bit more comfortable. This was starting to look interesting.

"Daniel and my father enjoyed an especially close relationship. They were both passionate about the collections. Daniel brought Father most of his prizes." Jake rested the oars on his knees and looked out over the water. "Whenever Daniel came home from one of his trips, Father allowed me to come down from school to see him and the treasures he'd brought home. I envied

Daniel and my father their connection. I wanted to be part of it. When I was sixteen, I finally got my chance. Daniel agreed to let me tag along on a trip to the Himalayas."

For the next ten minutes or so, Jake relayed a story that kept Kat enthralled. He painted a vivid picture of a wild, wondrous land and mysterious, mystical people, and in doing so, gave her a glimpse of himself that she'd never seen before.

"Was it all a dream?" he mused. "Did I lie on the floor of that cave and hallucinate the entire thing?"

Then he turned his head and met her gaze. "I honestly don't know. What I do know is that your necklace is the exact replica of the necklace I saw in that cave. When I saw it hanging around your neck that day, I knew I had to have it. The whole thing might be fantasy, it might be a case of dehydration combined with altitude sickness added to a young man's inexperience."

"So you stole my necklace."

He heaved a sigh. "Five years ago, I still wondered if my dream hadn't been all dream, if Daniel was right and Shambhala did exist and he was living a fantastical existence in a hidden city in Tibet. I thought that if your necklace somehow had the power to reach him, then…well…I had to have it."

Yes, she could see that he would think so. If their situations were reversed, she'd likely have stolen it herself. "And the trip you've planned? You're still looking for your brother?"

"No." His gaze darted back toward her, then quickly

shifted away. "I have other reasons for going. Important reasons. I signed a contract. People are depending on me."

Uh-huh. Did he honestly believe that or was he being deliberately blind? Hiding her skepticism, Kat subtly made her point. "How long ago did your brother disappear?"

Jake thought a moment. "Going on eighteen years now."

When Kat simply looked at him, his chin came up. "I know my brother is dead. I know he's not going to show up at my door one day, that I won't stumble across him in a bazaar in Mongolia. That's all superstitious nonsense."

Kat didn't believe him for a minute. After hearing his story, she thought she was finally beginning to understand Jake Kimball. Whether he knew it or not, finding his brother motivated most of Jake's life. He might know in his head that he wouldn't stumble across his brother in a foreign bazaar, but his heart had yet to get the message.

Kat felt a sympathetic pang in the region of her own heart. He hadn't accepted his brother's death. She couldn't imagine how she'd react if one of her siblings disappeared. However, that didn't excuse Jake for planning to abandon his sister's children. The children needed him more than did his brother's ghost. Jake needed to see that.

She needed to make him see it.

Abruptly Kat sat up tall in her seat, creating a rocking motion in the rowboat. Could that be the answer? Maybe the necklace *was* working its magic, after all.

Maybe this was her task, her contribution toward ending the family curse.

Maybe in saving this family, she'd help to save her own.

"What is it?" Jake asked. "Why the strange expression?"

Kat smiled at him, the first from-the-heart, from-the-soul smile she'd ever given him. "Jake Kimball. I think I'm glad I married you."

He gave her a long stare, then blinked twice. "I think I'm glad to hear that."

She laughed, grabbed for his fishing pole, then tossed his line in the water. Almost immediately, she caught another fish. Her laughter rang out over the lake as she held up the fish with a flourish. "He's the biggest. I win."

Jake's eyes took on that heavy-lidded look she'd come to know so well. He muttered an oath as he dropped the oars into the water and began to pull. The boat glided forward.

Kat tilted her face up to the sun, closed her eyes and let the warmth sink into her bones. She stretched sensuously, inhaled a deep breath and smelled honeysuckle on the air. Eventually she wondered why the boat had yet to reach the dock, and she opened her eyes. Her brow wrinkled when she realized Jake had rowed them in circles. "Jake, is something wrong?"

"Yeah."

"What is it?"

"It's not time to return to the lodge yet."

She waited a moment for him to say something else, something that made sense. "Why not?"

"Because!" He shot her an exasperated glare. "Eating Italian takes time."

"I'm afraid you've lost me."

"I know, but I don't want to spoil…oh, to hell with it." Jake yanked the oars from the water once again, stood, rocking the boat, then shocked Kat by diving over the side.

The splash from his entry landed on the front of her dress. Kat sat frustrated and fuming, plucking the wet cloth away from her bodice, waiting for him to surface.

Jake's head broke the surface and he swam a half dozen strokes away from the boat, then a half dozen back toward it. Kat called, "Jake Kimball!"

He pulled up, treaded water and looked at her. "Yeah?"

"You splashed me!"

His gaze slid over her like melted caramel. "I can see that."

"Why in heaven's name did you jump out of the boat?"

"Actually, I dove rather than jumped, and I did it because I thought the water would be colder." His stare fastened on her bodice. "It's not nearly cold enough. Kat? Can you swim?"

"Yes. Of course. I…" Jake swam beside the rowboat. His eyes gleamed with purpose and that sexual heat she'd come to recognize so well. When he reached up for the side of the boat, she warned, "Oh, no you don't."

"Just to take the edge off, honey. C'mon." The boat tipped. Kat's balance teetered.

"Come play with me."

CHAPTER TEN

ON THE FIFTH DAY of his honeymoon, Jake Kimball whistled as he approached Paradise Lodge. Leading two horses, saddled and ready for the upcoming ride, he had a spring in his step and a song in his heart. A particularly bawdy song. Jake Kimball was a happy, satisfied man. He passed his nights feasting from a sensual banquet and spent his days in carefree harmony with his interesting, intelligent, active bride.

Kat appeared to be enjoying her honeymoon, too. Once she made it past her initial surprise during their Italian evening, she'd fallen right in with his adventures. His wife had a talent for drama, and she thoroughly enjoyed role-playing. That bit of information caused him to make small adjustments to their nighttime travelogues.

Something had changed with Kat the day of their fishing trip. Her attitude toward him had softened. Her acceptance of him had strengthened. Most important, that dull light in her eyes at the finish of their lovemaking had mostly disappeared.

Jake thought Kat was beginning to like him.

He suspected she was adjusting to the notion of having children in her life again, too. She certainly talked about his nieces and nephew often enough. Every day she brought them into the conversation, asking him questions about them, soliciting stories of his interaction with them, requesting his advice regarding potential problems she might encounter while acting as their mother. Jake took her interest as a positive sign.

He responded to her talk about Penny's babies by asking Kat about her Susie, and he'd been pleasantly surprised at the way she'd opened up about her daughter. The grief still haunted her eyes and shimmered in her voice, but she managed to laugh a time or two when talking about her child. She always looked surprised when it happened. Jake always leaned over and kissed her.

He was in the mood to have her mouth again. She'd been eating a strawberry last time he saw her. He wondered if he would taste it in her kiss. Looking up toward the open window he called, "Kat? You ready?"

Her face appeared. "Sorry, I was reading and lost track of time. Give me ten minutes?"

"Women," he grumbled up at her. She flashed him a smile, then ducked back inside. "God love 'em."

Jake hitched the horses to a nearby post, then leaned against the trunk of an oak tree and settled down to wait.

Yep, he had it good. He couldn't recall another span of time he'd enjoyed so much. Too bad their honeymoon had to end.

Two more days. Only two more nights. Damn.

On the bright side, he wouldn't leave for Tibet right

away. Just because they returned to Chatham Park didn't mean they couldn't continue their trips around the world. He had locks on the bedroom door. In fact, now that he thought about it, he had locks on most of the doors. Instead of bringing the collections to them, they could go to the collections. Hmm, maybe they'd try the jewel room. What a sight she'd be, bedecked from head to toe in emeralds and gold and nothing else.

She walked out of Paradise Lodge wearing a riding habit that had arrived with her wardrobe from London. She carried a picnic basket and looked so lovely that, were the work crew not scheduled to arrive soon, he'd have taken her then and there.

They passed an enjoyable afternoon at the ruins, and it wasn't until they'd ridden to within sight of Paradise that Kat asked about that night's menu. Since he could spy the billowing white silk of the tent beyond the lodge's rooftop, he decided to begin the play immediately. "It is not your concern, woman."

Kat reined in her horse. "Excuse me?"

"It's not a concubine's place to question her master."

"A what?" Her eyes went wide, then abruptly narrowed. "Her what!"

Jake relished the word. "Master."

Kat's eyes flashed. Her chin came out. He could see her tongue sharpening with sarcastic words. If Jake wasn't careful here, he could ruin the entire evening.

So he subtly played upon her sense of adventure. "Tonight, when the moon rises above the desert sands, and the eastern star kisses the sky, you will come to me, and I will show you the pleasures of an Arabian night."

Then, with the fluent move of a master horseman, he turned his horse around and galloped off across the fields, leaving Kat to worry and wonder.

Damn, but he enjoyed being married.

"THE MAN IS RUDE," Kat grumbled, tugging her bonnet strings as she climbed the stairs to her room. "A bounder. Master, hah! He's a barbarian. If he thinks for one minute I'm going to play slave to his sultan, well…" Whatever would make him think she'd find such demeaning nonsense intriguing? Desert sands. Arabian nights. In a tent!

Honestly.

She may have enjoyed their "trips" to Venice and Paris and Hawaii, but it was one thing to imagine oneself sipping Chianti at a trattoria along the winding canals of Venice or holding hands with a lover while walking beside the Seine. Pretending to be ravished by a desert sheik was something else entirely. Kat was not a submissive woman. McBride women didn't do submissive. She doubted she could even fake it.

She walked into the room and tossed her hat onto the bed she'd yet to use during her visit to Paradise Lodge. "Tonight might be the ni—" Colorful scraps of silk lay folded at the foot of her bed. "Oh."

Kat was too much a female not to investigate, and the first thing that caught her attention was the amazing piece of jewelry lying atop the pile of emerald silk. It was a diadem of white gold, adorned with a teardrop-shaped emerald. Had the item been from any other man, she'd have figured the jewel as paste, simply part of a costume. From Jake, the heir of the world's greatest collector, she knew the gem was real. "Typical man. Trying to buy me off with jewelry."

Almost against her will, Kat lifted the headband off the bed and carried it over to the dressing table. Well, it wouldn't hurt to try it on. She smoothed back her hair, then gazed into a mirror as she placed the diadem on her head. The emerald teardrop rested at the middle of her forehead.

A swift, strong sense of the exotic engulfed Kat. Her gaze drifted back to the bed. "Leave it alone, Kat," she told herself. "This isn't you."

Submissive, my Texas-born foot.

She could all but hear the echo of her grandmother's voice in her mind. "Don't be a stick-in-the-mud, Katrina. Be bold."

Bold. Kat's teeth nibbled at her lower lip. Cautiously, she reached out and lifted the first item from the pile. After a moment's study, she realized the linked metal chains as wide as her hand were fashioned into a belt. Dozens of filmy scarves in a rainbow of colors hung through loops at the bottom of the belt. It was a skirt, a skirt made of scarves. Free hanging scarves that would shift with every movement, revealing what lay beneath them.

"For heaven's sake." Kat blew out a tremulous breath.

The next garment on the bed was made of emerald-colored silk and trimmed in silver braid. The soft, transparent band with two thin straps was obviously meant to cover her breasts, but she doubted it contained enough fabric to do the trick.

Beneath the breast band she found a matching bolero-style jacket that would do little more than cover her shoulders. Next she found a small square veil, and below that, two pairs of bronze finger cymbals and a collection of bangle bracelets. Kat's fingers itched to try out the cymbals, but she made herself back away. She took off the diadem and dropped it beside the costume. "No. I'll not play a slave for the man. For any man. I won't do it."

Really. She wouldn't.

She moved to the sitting room adjacent to her bedroom intending to return to her book. She'd picked a delightful novel filled with mystery from Paradise Lodge's library shelves, and she was anxious to discover the perpetrator of the crime. But when she reached for the book on the table where she'd left it, she found another in its place.

"*The Arabian Nights' Entertainments?*" she read the title aloud. Frustration rushed through her. What happened to her novel? "Jake Kimball, you have the nerve of a toothache."

She glanced around the room, searching fruitlessly for her book. Sighing, she sank onto the settee and pulled off her riding boots. She stretched her legs and wiggled her toes. She drummed her fingers on her knee. What should she do next?

Her gaze returned to the book. No, she wouldn't read it. That's what he wanted. He wanted to intrigue her, to tempt her. To take her to places she'd never go on her own.

The arrogant beast.

"Well, I'll show him." She'd read, but only because that was her original plan. She wouldn't don the costume and she certainly wouldn't visit that tent. Not now. Not after dark.

She lifted the book, flipped to a random page. *"In a town in Persia, there lived a man and his wife."*

Kat quickly sank into the story and when she finished it, she began another, losing track of time. Losing herself in the mystery and allure of Shaharazad's stories.

BENEATH THE SILVERED LIGHT of a full moon, Jake waited for his bride. Honeysuckle perfumed the warm, gentle breeze that whipped ripples in the roof of the tent. An owl's mournful hoot drifted across the night.

Jake surveyed his surroundings. The tent, the pillows and the rugs had come from a friend in London whose wife had hosted an Arabian-themed ball the previous year. The mattress belonged in one of the lodge's guest rooms. The chests and their contents came from collections at Chatham Park. The *djellaba* he wore was his own, acquired during his most recent trip to El Bahar.

The silks and scents in the tent came from a trunk sent back to their father by the Kimball brothers following a visit to El Bahar on their fateful journey to Tibet. Jake recalled another night in another tent in the faraway land, sitting beside Daniel as scantily clad women danced before them. He'd been offered his choice among them for the night, and he'd spent the succeeding hours in a young man's version of heaven. He'd worn himself sore, and he'd barely managed to ride the following day. Daniel gave him grief about it until the day he…

"Hell." Jake grabbed a date from a wooden bowl, then stepped outside the tent. He wasn't going to fall into the past's trap tonight. Tonight was his. His and Kat's. He stared up toward the house, toward the bedroom window where lamplight burned. Would she come? Or would he have to go get her? Either way worked for him.

He indulged for a moment, imagining what it might be like if she didn't cooperate with his plans. He'd sweep into her room like a desert wind. She'd be sitting on the sofa, dressed uncharacteristically prim and proper. She'd have her hair bound neat and tight. She'd be sitting in a chair doing embroidery, and it'd slip from her fingers once she saw him. Alarm would spark in her eyes.

"Come," he'd say.

"No. Never."

He'd yank the corded ties from the bedroom curtains and advance on her. She'd stand abruptly, knocking over her chair. She'd gasp and put a hand against her chest and back away.

He'd bind her arms against her side by wrapping the cord around her as she struggled against him, then he'd scoop her up, toss her over his shoulder, one possessive hand cupping her buttocks, the other up under her skirt, holding her bare legs, as he headed downstairs and out of the lodge.

She'd be protesting, of course, threatening him, begging him…Jake slowed the fantasy for a moment, particularly enjoying the begging aspect...but being a manly, arrogant master, he'd turn a deaf ear to her words. He'd carry her into the tent, then toss her onto her back on the soft, luxurious mattress.

Now, she'd take a good look at him and despite herself, against her own will, her eyes would soften with arousal. Her reaction would make her angry, and she'd renew her resistance. Jake would be forced to brandish his knife.

Kat's eyes would grow round. "You wouldn't."

"Of course I would."

Taking extraordinary care not to touch her delicate skin, he'd slip the blade beneath her demure neckline and slit the material all the way to her ankles. Shocked at the boldness of his actions, she'd lie still, and he'd turn his attentions to her corset, then her underclothes, and within seconds, she'd lie naked before him like a feast. The erect, rosy nipples that tipped her full breasts would rise and fall with her rapid breaths. He wanted her. How he wanted her.

He'd throw the knife, end over end, toward the tent's centerpole, and it would wedge in the wood with a thunk. At that point, Kat's spirit would revive, and she'd scramble off the bed, slipping once or twice when her fingers and feet failed to make purchase against the satin and silk. At some point during their struggles, her hair would have fallen loose, and now it unfurled like a golden flag behind her as she fled.

He'd catch her in two strides, swooping her up into his arms, laughing. He'd dump her back on the feathered mattress. She'd bounce like an angry cat and come up spitting fire and fighting. So full of fire, his Kat. So full of life and love. She warmed a part of him he'd never before realized was cold. He'd miss her when he was gone.

It was a shocking thought that jolted him right out of his fantasy.

He didn't miss women. Ever. They came and went through his life with barely a ripple. He enjoyed them while they were there, but he seldom thought twice about them once he'd moved on.

He'd think about Kat. A lot. He'd miss her humor, her wit, her laughter. God knows he'd miss her loving.

Jake raked his fingers through his hair, then began to pace back and forth in front of the tent. This was wrong. He didn't like this. He hadn't anticipated it.

He'd let her get too close.

"Well, hell," he muttered. He'd known he might miss the children when he left, but missing Kat was something else entirely. He didn't like thinking he'd allowed her to matter. Hadn't he learned better than to care too much long ago?

Maybe this honeymoon hadn't been such a great idea, after all. He'd spent too much time with her and without any other distractions. He'd learned too much about her, about her wishes and dreams and fears and frustrations. Maybe he should take a step back, put some distance between them.

Maybe he should pack up the Tagine t'Faia and call it a night. Call it a honeymoon. He'd make up some excuse for leaving early. Hell, if she weren't enthused about the gifts he'd left lying on her bed, she might be more than happy to return to Chatham Park.

Yeah, that's what he'd do. Nodding decisively, Jake pivoted and ducked into the tent. Just for the hell of it, he gave a square pillow made of purple silk and trimmed with gold tassels a swift kick, sending it flying toward the mattress. Just as it landed, he heard a noise behind him.

Clink. Clink. Clink-clink-clink.

He turned and his heart stopped.

She stood just inside the tent, a woman right out of a man's hottest fantasy. His mouth went dry as the Sahara as his gaze trailed over her from head to toe. The diadem crowned her free-flowing hair. Around her neck, she wore her emerald pendant. The fullness of her breasts all but overflowed the top, their luscious bounty snagging his gaze for a long moment until his stare drifted lower. She held her hands in front of her bare midriff, blocking his view of her navel. He watched her fingers move as she played the *zills,* the sound of the finger cymbals vibrating to his core. He sucked in a breath as he studied the way the chain belt rested below her hips. Her swaying hips. Hips that did little figure eights and sent the scarves hanging from the belt shimmering in the lamplight, shifting with movement, allowing revealing flashes of the smooth, supple skin of her thighs.

Lord. It was a plea, a prayer. She stepped forward and he saw she wore bangles around one ankle. Her feet were bare. He wanted to suck on her toes. Her nipples. Her…

Jake swallowed hard.

Clink. Clink. Clink. The cymbals clattered. She

hummed an exotic, erotic tune, and her hips moved faster, the chains at her hips rattling. The scarves swaying.

Then she said his name, a soft, seductive, come-hither whisper of a word. The glow in her eyes teased.

He'd created a monster; that's what he'd done. Jake Kimball, the consummate seducer, man of the world, explorer extraordinaire was at risk of being soundly beaten at his own game. Damn.

Could a man die from too much of this?

Jake all but fell on his knees at her feet. All thought of leaving evaporated from his mind like a morning mist. He reached for her, but she spun away, laughing. The view from behind was almost as intriguing as that from the front.

"Kat, you are…I don't have words."

She glanced back over her shoulder, a saucy, sassy look that made him want to grind his teeth. "Quiet, slave. You've not been given permission to speak."

That stopped him. "Slave?"

"You were a gift to me from my sultan, my prize for having saved the life of his beloved son." She reached for the bowl of grapes and selected one.

Jake's eyes narrowed. "How?"

"How what?" She chewed, then licked her lips.

He swallowed. "How did you save the son's life?"

"In a drowning accident."

Jake folded his arms. "In the desert?"

Kat scowled at him. "It rained that afternoon."

"Oh."

"And you're not supposed to talk. I forbid it."

Jake sauntered over toward the baskets containing the food for their feast. He plopped down upon a plush Tabriz rug, leaned back against a pillow, grabbed a date from a bowl and popped it into his mouth.

Kat narrowed her eyes and shot him a warning stare. "You're awfully cocksure for a slave."

Nodding, Jake solemnly agreed, "Yes, I'm definitely sure of my cock."

Her lips twitched a bit at that, but she continued to play her character. "Silence, slave. I'm tempted to cut out your tongue for disobeying me, but since I have other uses for it, you're safe. For now, anyway."

"Lucky for me." Jake stretched out his leg. "So, I'm a gift, hmm? I take it you wanted a sophisticated, debonair gentleman?"

"If that were the case, I'd be out of luck," Kat replied, wrinkling her nose. "You couldn't act the gentleman if your life depended on it." Falling back into her role, she quipped, "No, I just wanted a slave tall enough to…ahem…dust my shelves."

"You're a cruel woman, mistress."

"Now, see? That's the wrong word. Pay attention, Kimball. Tonight, I intend to be the master. You wanted Arabia, after all. Now, you will submit to me in any way and in every way I choose."

"You have a vivid, if misguided, imagination, darling. I submit to no one."

She responded by arching a brow and smiling, her gorgeous green eyes lit with challenge. "Oh, my imagination is vivid. Never doubt it. It appears we shall have to work on yours."

Then, with a slow, purposeful swivel, she did that figure eight movement with her hips.

All right, perhaps her imagination wasn't as faulty as he'd thought. Jake mentally debated the exact meaning of the word *submit*.

The corner of her mouth lifted in challenge. "Do I excite you, slave?" She removed the bolero, displaying a healthy amount of supple cleavage in the candlelight.

He blinked.

"Do I?" Running a delicate finger down the length of her pendant's chain, she seemed to delight in teasing him. "How much?"

"More than you know."

"Do I tempt you?"

More than you should. "Yes."

"Very well, then." Coming behind him, she pressed one hand to his shoulder while the other picked up a dark purple grape from the bowl near his elbow. Jake's body hummed with anticipation.

Her perfume was like an elixir. All sweetness and spice blended with woman and night air. It grabbed hold of him like an exotic opiate and held him captive.

She leaned down and caressed his bare shoulders with the cold fruit. First one, then the other. Her hair a blond curtain over her shoulder, she bent and offered it to him, only to playfully snatch it back to enjoy herself. Featherlight, grape-tinged kisses teased his nape, his collarbone, his earlobe. He turned to reach for her.

She stepped back. "Dare you touch your mistress without permission?"

Did he ever. "Kat…"

"Silence!"

He blinked again. Well, hell. He'd started all this. Maybe an igloo in Alaska would have been a better choice. Eskimo women are just happy to be bedded on a pile of furs. Slaves and masters…what in God's name had he been thinking?

Idiot. She intended to make him pay.

With a click of her tongue, she shook her head. "I was afraid of this. You are far too rebellious. I shall have to resort to other methods to ensure your…cooperation."

His mouth went dry. "Methods?"

Her eyes darted around the room. Then she smiled again. A devious, seductive smile. "Ah, just the thing." Snatching up the knife from the table, she moved across the room and cut the gilded cord from the heavy velvet drapes before he could mutter a single word of protest.

Wrapping the delicate cord around her wrists, she snapped it once, then again. "Perfect. You have thought of everything, I see." She approached him like a jungle cat. Sleek, dangerous. Hungry.

He'd thought of everything. Right. Not hardly. He sure as hell hadn't banked on this. His eyes fixated on the drape cords. Surely she wasn't meaning to…? That was *his* fantasy, dammit.

"Kat," he said, then noted the gleam in her eye. "Er, mistress, master, whatever. Really, I think this has gone far en-*UMPH!*"

Flattened on his back with his wife straddled across his chest, Jake fought the urge to laugh. "What are you—*OW!* Careful, that's *not* a pillow!"

She distracted him with a kiss, and while Jake lost himself in the pleasure of her mouth, he hardly noticed the jingle of her bangle bracelets as her hands worked above him. Only when she drew back did he realize she'd twisted the cord into a knot of precarious loops and tangles. Then with a tug and a flourish, she wound the drapery tie around his wrists a last time. She'd tied him to the side handle of a chest filled with supplies. A heavy wooden chest filled with heavy supplies.

Well. This was unexpected.

As quickly as she'd landed on him, she was off. Then, to his surprise, so was his djellaba.

Naked and tied up.

Son of a bitch.

He gave his wrists a tug. Then another. The more he pulled, the tighter the cord drew. She crossed her arms. The jangle of those bracelets started to grate on his nerves. "I suggest you stop struggling, slave. The knot won't give. I know my knots."

She looked so smug, so proud of herself, that he wanted...no, he needed...his hands on her. "Untie me."

"Or what? What will you do?" she purred, walking around to view her handiwork. "Punish me?"

"I just might."

She laughed then, the sound rich and throaty. "I'll look forward to it. Until then, you are mine to...savor." Then her brows knitted. "Unless of course, you aren't interested in continuing this little...Arabian escapade?"

"I'll be happy to continue playing along. Just as soon as you untie me. I want to touch you, Katrina."

She considered that. Then shook her head, a devilish sparkle alight in her emerald eyes. "I don't think so. Not yet."

"It's a wicked thing, to tease a man so."

Tapping a finger against her chin, she looked him over, letting her eyes rest on one specific area. "It's a wicked sort of night, don't you think?"

Then she started to dance.

CHAPTER ELEVEN

KAT KNEW she'd probably never, ever, forget the look on Jake Kimball's face when she tied him to the chest and stripped off his sheik's robe. But the look on his face when she started her sultry striptease would be forever burned upon her memory. Hot, unabashed, blatant, male desire.

Her eyes swept over him. The muted light of the candles illuminated every muscle in sensual detail. Lean and rugged and hard, every sinewy inch of Jake Kimball spoke of strength, excitement and mystery.

He gazed at her, watching her sway to the silent music. His eyes were nearly black in the dim light of the tent, but glittering in the intense depths was challenge. And Kat McBride never backed down from a challenge.

From the moment she walked into the tent and found him robed and waiting, she'd decided that this would be her show. When she was finished with him, he'd be lucky to remember his own name.

Tossing him a sultry grin, she plucked at her scarves, removing them from the belted cinch one at a time, and let them flutter and fall across Jake's prone form.

Never could she have imagined such a fantasy.

Never had she undressed so slowly, so seductively.

Never had she witnessed such brazen lust burning in a man's eyes.

Jake watched her fingers as they removed each delicate scrap of silk. His throat worked, his body tense. Kat could almost hear the thud of his heartbeat as she continued her arousing performance.

When there were no scarves left, Kat unlinked her belt and let it fall to the thick carpet. Shaking her hair back beyond her shoulders, she slipped down the thin straps of the gauzy chemise. With a shimmer of emerald, she stood naked before him.

"Kat," he whispered hoarsely.

Taking pity on him, she approached slowly. Dropping to her knees beside him, she bent and touched her nose to his. "Do you want me?"

"God, yes."

She grinned. One of the scarves lay across his stomach. Picking it up, she brushed it across his face. "Perhaps my slave should be blindfolded."

He opened his mouth, yet no sound emerged. Then he shook his head in defeat. "All my fault," he whispered, more to himself, as she tied the scarf around his head. "Sultans and slaves. I'm an idiot. A fool. Igloos next time. Furs and fires and a nice big polar bear rug. No scarves. No cords. No ropes."

"Fur and fire, huh? Sounds interesting." Kat captured his lower lip between her own, effectively cutting off his tirade. "I shall hold you to it. Tonight, however, you're mine to take."

She kissed him again, catching his groan of frustration. Soon, though, his groans turned to growls, and Kat knew that even tied up and blindfolded, her husband was a man to be reckoned with. For a brief, wary moment, Kat's breath caught. Her husband. Her lover. Her man.

Hers. How wonderful that sounded. To belong. To be cherished. To be loved.

Her hands shook as they stroked his skin. She touched, teased, tantalized. Even slightly shaky, he seemed to be enjoying himself, if that shameless smile quirking his lips was any indicator. Thank heaven he was blindfolded, else he'd see the anxious look on her face.

Love wasn't part of the agreement.

The marriage, the honeymoon, it was all just a blissful wink in time. Once they left Paradise Lodge, reality would return and Kat's normal life would commence again.

Normal. Right. Married to a man who intended to leave her. Again. A man who didn't love her. Again. Only this time, she'd be left with the responsibility of five children. And she'd walked into it with her eyes wide open.

Unless, of course, she could convince him to stay.

"Kat?" His voice drew her back. "Why did you stop?"

"I didn't," she lied. Dipping the tip of her finger into his navel, she taunted, "I'm just letting you catch your breath. We've a long night ahead of us."

Tracing tiny circles on his breastbone, she kissed the skin beneath his copper-colored nipple with renewed vigor. His swift, sharp intake of breath made her smile against his skin.

He pulled hard on the cord. "Kat?"

"Not yet."

She took her time. Touching, caressing, teasing. Enjoying every sound he made, every curse, every shiver. He ordered, cajoled and demanded to be released from his bonds.

Yet she gave him no quarter.

Making a man tremble with need was the ultimate female power, and Kat reveled in her accomplishment. She wasn't about to give over her power just yet. Instead she pressed a kiss to his lower belly, and was sure he'd yank the chest right off the ground.

Oh, there was no doubt he'd make her pay for this later. There was no telling what he'd do when she finally decided to untie him. But for now the moment belonged to her.

Leaning toward him, she lifted a breast and teased the corner of his mouth with her nipple. With a determined lunge, he briefly captured the peak between his lips and smiled at Kat's surprised hiss.

"You'll pay for that," she told him.

She glanced down at his straining desire. Boldly, she ran a finger down the length, then upward. She cupped his fullness, then glided a hand up the shaft until she reached the tip.

His entire body shook. "Careful, woman."

Taking pity on him, she abandoned her sweet torture and brought her breast to his mouth once again, then moaned as his tongue circled her nipple. He licked, nibbled, even bit. She arched her body toward him, and he opened his mouth to take what she offered. He suckled her tenderly at first, then increased his ardor.

Kat stroked the back of his head with her free hand. Running her fingers along his nape, she combed the silky locks that rippled down his neck. It should be a sin for a man to have hair such as this. So soft, so silky. So…decadent.

The heat between her thighs quickened, her body eager to be joined to Jake. Slipping her leg over him, she eased herself downward, impaling herself upon him. In an instant Kat found her rhythm, rocking to and fro, enjoying the keen sensation of controlling her own desire. "Have me, slave."

The demand was easily met. Jake surged upward, moving faster within her, his hips rising in measured thrusts. Digging her fingers into the strained muscles of his shoulders, she held on for both purchase and support. The sweet feeling inside her grew hotter, tighter, piercing her womb and soul, melting her heart and bones. He'd reached the very core of her.

Liberated, Kat threw back her head and rode him.

She arched and strained and journeyed through time and space itself. Clinging to the moment, Kat drove herself further into the fantasy until reality was no more. She clung to him, feeling him drive deeper and deeper into her, carrying her higher and higher, further and further into a blur of soft sands, of night sky, of wild torment.

Crashing into the blinding light, she shattered like a million stars and answered his hoarse cry of surrender with one of her own.

SNUGGLED WARM AND RELAXED, spooned against the furnace of her husband's body, Kat awoke to the music of birdsong, and she smiled. Then memories of the previous evening came rushing back, and she flushed with an overwhelming sense of embarrassment. Had that truly been her? Had she really done those wild and wicked things last night?

She pried open her eyes and the first thing she saw was a transparent blue silk scarf dangling from the hilt of the knife buried in the center pole. The second thing she spied was Jake's hand sprawled in front of hers, his fingers stained purple from the juice of the grapes. Yes, she'd really done those wild and wicked things last night.

She wondered if Jake's skin felt sticky, too.

Oh, my. She closed her eyes in mortification. What had possessed her? Three times? Or was it four? Good heavens. Why had she lost all sense of propriety? She didn't even have the excuse that it was Jake's fault. He's not the one who used a drapery cord as a hog-tie.

Where had such thoughts come from? She'd never imagined such things before last night. But last night, she not only imagined them, she acted upon them! Kat was mortified.

Her grandmother would be proud.

Jake let out a little snore against her ear. He certainly hadn't seemed to mind that he had a wanton for a wife. Even tied up and blindfolded, he'd been smiling. In fact, last night her husband had acted as if he'd died and gone to heaven. He'd even said exactly that at one point, sometime between the grapes and the honey pot.

Oh, yes, the honey. Leave it to a man to decide his dessert needed more sweetness. Well, she'd asked for that, she supposed.

Kat felt her cheeks warm with embarrassment, and yet along with it came a sense of...well...pride. It made a woman feel good to know that she could make her man so happy. And, after all, wasn't that part of her bigger plan? To make him so happy, so content, he'd want to stay with the children? *And,* whispered a soft voice in her head, *with you.*

"Good morning," Jake's voice rumbled in her ear. Those grape-stained fingers flexed, then moved toward her, trailing a path from her shoulder to her waist. "Did you sleep well?"

"I—" Kat broke off abruptly when the sound of a man's panicked shout intruded.

"Mr. Kimball? Mr. Kimball!"

In a flash, Jake had rolled to his feet and donned that white desert robe he'd worn briefly the night before. Kat scrambled for clothes as he exited the tent. "Here!" she heard him call. "Is that you, Wilson?"

Wilson. Chatham Park's stable master. Kat's stomach sank. Something was wrong.

She pulled on the costume, such as it was, then wrapped herself in a large, fringed coverlet and dashed after Jake. She caught up with him just as the stable master began his tale.

"We've a problem, Mr. Kimball. It's bad. It's the young lordship. Apparently, he climbed out of his bed and went exploring before anyone else awoke. He was quiet, slipped right past Miss Parker. He took a bad tumble down the stairs."

Kat gasped and Jake grabbed her hand, gripping it hard.

"He's still alive, sir, but he won't wake up. We sent for the doctor right away."

"Broken bones?" Jake asked with an edge to his voice.

"Nothing's sticking out. But the little guy is so small, we can't really tell. He has a big old knot on his head. His arms and legs have twitched a bit, but he didn't let out a peep when we moved him."

Though Jake's grip on Kat's hand tightened, he showed no emotion as he instructed, "Saddle horses for Mrs. Kimball and me, please, Wilson. We'll be right down."

They hurried into the house and climbed the stairs two at a time. Jake threw off his robe the moment he entered the master suite. Reaching for trousers, he said, "Kat, I intend to ride fast. If you'd rather wait and return with Wilson, that's—"

"I'll go with you. I'll keep up, Jake."

"Good. I know this isn't the sort of thing you…" He dragged a hand down his face. "Hell, he's just a baby."

Kat didn't respond. No one knew better than she that being a baby was no protection from disaster.

They rode hard without exchanging more than a word or two. Kat spent a good portion of the ride arguing with herself, telling herself that she couldn't, wouldn't, turn the horse around and ride the other way.

Nausea rolled in her stomach. She didn't want to deal with another injured child, another—God forbid—dying child. She didn't think her heart could bear it. Again. This was why she hadn't wanted to be responsible for these or any children.

She could deal with the small things, the little accidents. Skinned knees, scrapes and scratches. She could handle illnesses, too. Head colds and stomachaches from eating too much taffy. But incidents like this left her helpless. The serious things. The heartbreaking things.

Disaster was always one step away.

She prayed they'd find the toddler awake and well when they reached Chatham Park. But if Robbie's condition failed to improve, then Jake was about to get a firsthand lesson in disaster.

The idea made Kat shudder. She recalled holding Susie's lifeless body in the middle of a dusty street.

How would he respond? Would he find it difficult to leave the children once he'd witnessed the reality of a guardian's responsibilities? Or would he find it easier to go?

Would he run as far as he could go to protect himself? After she'd climbed from her bed months after Susie's death, in essence, that's what she'd done. She'd turned away from the sight of Mari's children. She didn't hold them, didn't touch them. She'd run.

She couldn't do that this time. Whatever Jake did or however he reacted, she needed to take care of her own responses. If the worst occurred, she needed to be ready to be strong for those girls. They'd need her. They'd need her desperately, and Kat needed to be ready to help them.

Think positively, Kat, she silently chastised herself. These children have suffered enough bad luck, losing their parents the way they did. Surely they're due a break. She wanted desperately to believe that.

They rode the last hundred yards to Chatham Park at a gallop and dashed up the front steps. The sight of the four Barrett girls seated on the staircase, silent and serious and teary-eyed, stopped the adults in their tracks. Jake cleared his throat. "Girls?"

"Robbie is hurt, Uncle Jake," Theresa said.

"He climbed out of his crib and fell down the stairs," Miranda added.

"I know. Is the doctor here yet?"

Miranda nodded. "He and Nanny Parker are in the nursery."

Big fat tears welled up in Caroline's eyes, and Belle sniffled and said, "We're so scared!"

The girls all nodded.

Kat's heart melted. She glanced at Jake and said, "Go on up. I'll speak with the girls a moment first."

He nodded and started up the steps, pausing just long enough to give silent little Caroline's head a comforting pat. Kat took a seat on the staircase just below the girls. She eyed them each in turn, then said, "It's a scary thing, I know, but we must have faith. It's—"

"Our fault!" Miranda cried. "It's our fault he fell!"

Caroline reached over and clasped Miranda's hand. As the girls shared a guilty look, Kat's stomach clenched. "Why do you say that?"

Belle chewed on her fingernail. Miranda picked at a loose thread on her skirt. Theresa twirled a curl around her finger. Caroline squeezed her eyes shut. Two plump tears rolled down her face.

"Girls?"

Without looking up, Miranda said, "This morning we sneaked into the nursery. We played peekaboo with Robbie and made him all excited and giggly, and then we left. I'm sure he tried to follow us, Miss Kat. We left the door open and he tried to follow us and he fell down the stairs! He won't wake up. What if he never wakes up? It's all our fault and we'll go to hell and we'll never see Mama and Papa again in heaven!"

"Oh, girls." Kat's heart wrenched at the pain in their expressions. "Listen to me, all of you. You cannot blame yourselves for Robbie's accident. You didn't pick that baby up out of his crib and leave him teetering at the top of the staircase, did you?"

"No!" Theresa exclaimed.

"Did you have a reason to think he could get out of his crib by himself?"

"He lifted his leg a time or two, Miss Kat," Belle said, "But I thought he might be winkling 'cause that's how boy dogs winkle."

Kat's gaze trailed up the staircase as she smiled at Belle's comment. Part of her was anxious to learn what the doctor had to say. Another part of her wanted to turn around and walk right back out the front door. However, right now, these little girls needed her. "I don't think that was a good enough clue, honey," she assured Belle. "Was there anything else?"

The girls gave it a moment's thought, then shook their heads.

"Then you shouldn't feel guilty."

"But it's hard!"

"Oh, I know. I know that very well." Kat rose gracefully to her feet, then helped the girls stand, too. "Why don't the four of you go to the chapel and say some prayers for your brother?"

"That's a good idea," Theresa said.

Miranda asked, "Will you let us know as soon as he wakes up?"

"I promise."

Kat left part of her heart with the girls as she continued up the stairs. Those poor children. She knew the agonies of doubt that plagued them. She understood the guilt, the regret. She looked at them now and saw herself, her sisters, the McBride Menaces of old. She didn't look at them and see Susie.

Maybe she could do this thing after all.

Infused with a new strength and confidence, Kat made her way to the nursery. She told herself she'd be strong and ready to help if she arrived to find it time for the family to mourn. Of course, if the little one was awake and babbling, she'd join the rest of the family in celebration. If Robbie's status remained unchanged, she'd act as a calm, sturdy support for anyone who needed her. Kat approached the opened doorway prepared for whatever she'd find when she arrived.

Or so she thought.

Jake sat beside the bed, holding the baby's limp hand in his. Noting Kat's arrival, he said, "The doctor doesn't know a damned thing. He says if Robbie doesn't wake up pretty soon, he may never regain consciousness."

"Oh, Jake."

"It's his head. There's a lump the size of a hen's egg on the side. Miss Parker said he did move his arms and legs, though, so that's a positive thing." He looked at her then, anxiousness in his eyes. "Don't you think?"

"I think that's a wonderful thing." She glanced around the empty room. "Where is the doctor?"

"Bastard wants breakfast. Miss Parker took him down the back stairs. Robbie looks pale to me. Does he look pale to you, Kat?"

"A little, yes."

"I heard somewhere, I don't know where…hell, maybe I dreamed it." Jake shoved his fingers through his hair. "Anyway, I heard that having a lump is good. It's when you've bonked your head and you don't have a lump that you need to worry. Have you heard that?"

Panic lurked in his words and in his movements. Kat didn't want to tell him no. "My youngest brother fell out of a treehouse when he was just a little boy."

"He did? Was he hurt? Was he knocked unconscious?"

"Yes. My parents were frantic. He was out for almost half an hour, but when he woke up, he was his old mischievous self."

"A half an hour," Jake murmured. "It's been three times that long. Oh, God." He buried his head in his hands. "This is my fault."

Kat reached out to touch him. "Now, Jake…"

"No!" Violently he shoved to his feet and paced the floor. "See, this is why I'm not cut out to be a father. I should have been here. Instead, I'm out pretending to be the fucking Sheik of Araby while yet another family member of mine suffers a potentially fatal accident. Goddammit, what's wrong with me? Why am I such a failure when it comes to family? I let my sister down. Just like I let my brother down. Who else is going to die on my watch? See, Kat? This is why it's better for me to wander the world. When you start to grow roots, something yanks them up. Somebody dies."

"Stop it," Kat snapped. "I know you're upset, Jake, but panic and self-pity serve no purpose here. They do neither you nor Robbie any good."

"I guess you ought to know," Jake snapped, striking out in his pain. "You're the one whose self-pity makes you blanch when you have to hold a baby."

Kat sucked in a breath as the barb struck home.

But it was the agony on his face, the guilt gleaming in his eyes when he looked at the baby boy lying so still and pale against the crisp white sheets that pushed Kat to reach out to him once again.

"You're right, Jake," she said calmly, reasonably. "I do know about children and accidents. They are frightening things. Sometimes horrible things. My brother fell from the treehouse and suffered no serious consequences. My daughter darted into the street after a dog and died. Your nephew, our nephew, took a tumble down the stairs, and the outcome of that is yet to be known."

"If he dies…" Jake's voice cracked, and Kat's heart broke for him.

"If he dies, you won't be to blame. This was an accident, and accidents happen. They're part of life. As much as we want to, we can't protect children from life. They have to be free to run and grow and—" her voice faltered just a bit as she said "—play with puppies."

"Maybe. I don't know, Kat. I don't know anything about children. That's why I have no business being responsible for any."

"I understand how you're feeling, Jake. I do. You're afraid. Afraid of being a parent, afraid of getting close to these children. It's already happened, though. Can't you see it? You already love these little ones."

"As an uncle. Not a father. A father would have been here to stop Robbie from falling down the stairs."

Kat swallowed hard. "And a mother would have been there to stop her daughter from darting into a wagon's path." He flinched and she stepped to his side, touched his arm. "Don't you see? It's not that simple. Parenting is far from simple. It's complicated and messy and difficult. But it's the most rewarding, most wonderful job in the world."

"How can you say that, Katrina? Your little Susie died!"

"Yes, she did, and losing her almost destroyed me. But does that make me wish she'd never been born? Never been a part of my life? No, absolutely not. Even knowing the outcome, I'd do it all over in a heartbeat. In a sense, that's what I'm doing here with Penny's children."

Standing beside the bed now, she reached out and stroked Robbie's soft skin, his silky hair. "I didn't see it until now. I've been given the chance to be a mother all over again, and that makes me terribly lucky."

Jake shook his head. "I don't understand you."

Her smile bittersweet, Kat leaned over and pressed a kiss to the baby's forehead. "That's all right. I think I finally understand myself."

CHAPTER TWELVE

AT SEVEN MINUTES BEFORE NOON, Robbie Barrett, Marquess of Harrington, dug his elbow into Jake's chest and let out an angry cry. Joy rang through the halls of Chatham Park.

The jubilant mood continued for the next week as Jake and his bride spent their days with the children and their nights wrapped in each other's arms. They picnicked and played and laughed and frolicked. Twice Jake thought he heard Caroline let out a giggle, but he never could be certain.

In an attempt to make a fatherly difference before he left, Jake made it a goal to get the girl talking. Every day he peppered her with questions, direct and indirect, encouraging her to respond. More than anything he hoped to hear Caroline ask what's for dinner or tattle on one of her sisters or say "Good night, Uncle Jake," before he departed for Tibet.

That day was fast approaching, and never before had the prospect of an expedition left him so ambivalent. Never before had he dreaded leaving home. In fact, this was the first time in memory he felt as though he *were* leaving a home. Kat had done that. In a short span of time, she'd created a home at Chatham Park, in a place that didn't suit her at all.

Kat didn't belong in this big monstrosity of a house. She didn't belong in England. He'd watched her interact with neighbors since their marriage, with the brides before that. While she could blend in wherever she wanted—her social skills were superior—the woman was simply too American. She belonged in Texas.

She belongs with me.

The idea floated in Jake's mind like a song. Jake could live anywhere. The children could live anywhere, too, at least until they were grown. Robbie had his title, and he'd need to return to England at some point to assume those duties, but that was a long time away.

Jake eyed his wife and the children as Belle and Miranda spread a quilt upon the lawn near the orangery. Theresa carried a handful of storybooks; Caroline, the basket containing the tea cakes. Kat carried the willing-to-climb-anything marquess. They looked like a family.

Jake's gaze settled on the necklace hanging from Kat's neck. He admitted to being thick upon occasion, but it hadn't escaped his notice that the message of his Tibetan dream could have referred to the scene before him. *Find the necklace, Jake. Find your family.*

Yet, if he believed in the dream, that meant he believed in the mountain magic, which meant Daniel didn't die in that cave. After all these years—after the promise he'd made to his father that he'd never stop looking for his brother, a promise made to Bernard Kimball as the man lay dying—could Jake walk away? Could he put the past behind him and walk forward into the future?

The question plagued him while he read fairy tales to the children. It haunted him while he pretended to swipe cake off Caroline's plate and harassed him while he tickled Theresa's nose with a dandelion puff.

Perhaps because thoughts of staying and leaving weighed so heavily on his mind, Jake knew in his bones what it meant when Chatham Park's butler arrived with news that a visitor awaited Jake in his study. Jake was tempted to turn his attention back to the children and pretend he hadn't heard the butler.

"Are you expecting someone?" Kat asked.

"A business partner," he replied, shifting his focus away from her. He couldn't tell her who he suspected the person might be. He didn't want to see her reaction.

Kat never mentioned the upcoming expedition. In fact, she went out of her way to change the subject whenever he attempted to broach the topic. His departure for the Himalayas hung over his marriage like a black cloud.

Excusing himself, Jake made his way to his study where a tall, stocky man stood at the window overlooking the rose garden, sipping from a glass of whiskey. Jake's mouth twisted in a brief, humorless grin. Damned if he hadn't been right. "Captain Wallace, welcome to Chatham Park."

The captain turned toward Jake and smiled. "Thank you. It's a beautiful home. I imagine you'll find it difficult to leave."

"It's brick and mortar," Jake said, shrugging. What would be hard was leaving the people who lived there.

"I brought a message for you," Captain Wallace continued. He reached into his jacket pocket and removed an envelope. "It was a strange thing. A man claiming to have worked with you in the past called at our shipping office day before yesterday and asked that I deliver this to you personally. He was quite insistent about it."

"What's the fellow's name?" Jake asked as he crossed the room to accept the missive.

"He never said."

When Jake touched the envelope, be damned if his fingertips didn't tingle.

It bore no writing on the outside, but showed significant signs of travel—smudges, creases and bent edges. Jake frowned as he carried it over to his desk, retrieved a letter opener from the center drawer and slit the envelope.

It contained a single sheet of paper folded in half. The paper emitted a scent—bayberry, Jake believed. He flipped open the page, and the sight of the familiar handwriting punched him in the gut.

Daniel.

No, it couldn't be. Not after all these years.

Hand trembling, Jake sank into his desk chair. Shock created a roaring in his ears as he tried to focus on the words written on the page.

The sentences were brief: "Greetings, brother. I wish you fair winds and a safe journey. I look forward to seeing you soon."

Jake's heart pounded. His mouth had gone dry as the Arabian desert. Daniel was alive. His brother was alive!

Jake looked up at the captain of the *Ulysses*. "How fast can you prepare the ship?"

KAT KNEW SOMETHING was wrong the moment Jake rejoined them on the lawn. Oh, he still smiled, still teased the girls, but he had a distracted air about him. She sensed a tension in him that was new since his trip to the house. Plus he avoided meeting her gaze. Instead he kept looking to the east as if the answer to whatever troubled him could be found in that direction.

Dread clutched her stomach as a troubling thought occurred. "Is it Emma? Did you hear something about Emma?"

He gave her a blank look. "Emma?"

Her heart eased. If he'd had bad news to impart regarding her sister, he wouldn't have appeared so dense when Kat mentioned Emma's name. So what else would bother him so? She could think of one other possibility.

Jake was leaving. She'd bet her favorite hat that he'd made the decision to go. Early, at that. The visitor must have brought some news or made an argument that influenced Jake, convinced him more effectively than her efforts both in the marriage bed and out.

She caught her breath, closed her eyes. Her heart pounded.

"What's wrong, Kat? Why are you worried about your sister?"

"I'm not," she managed to get out past the lump of emotion in her throat. Anger, hurt, disappointment. Anger. "It's nothing."

Nothing but rejection. He was leaving the children. Leaving *her*. After the good times they'd shared, the joy and laughter and loving, he didn't want to stay. She couldn't hold him. She'd failed in her task.

She stewed about it for the rest of the afternoon, waiting to see what he'd say, how he'd attempt to justify his actions. Never mind that he'd been up-front with her from the first. Never mind that this had been his plan all along. Never mind that she'd agreed to it. That was before she'd changed her mind!

Jake disappeared into his study after supper and failed to appear when the time arrived to put the children to bed. Coward, she thought. As each hour passed, Kat grew more certain she'd guessed correctly. By the time she heard him coming down the hall toward the master suite, she was spoiling for a fight.

Rather than enter the suite in his usual manner through the shared sitting room, the yellow-bellied scoundrel had avoided her by using the door that led directly into the master bedroom. With that, Kat had had enough.

She marched across the sitting room and shoved open his bedroom door and let it crash against the frame. Her gaze fell upon the traveling bag lying open on his bed. It hit her like a boot to the belly.

"When do you leave?" she demanded flatly.

For a long moment, Jake went still. Then, calmly and deliberately, he added a stack of shirts to the case. "Tomorrow. Tomorrow morning. Early."

"I see."

She didn't see, of course. She didn't see at all. How could he do it? How could he walk away from this…this…this *family?* "What do you intend to tell the children?"

Standing at his wardrobe, his back to her, he froze

for a second, then yanked a pair of trousers off a hanger. "It'll be easier for them if I just go."

Easier for them, my elbow. Easier for him, he means. "And you'll be gone for how long?"

"I'm not sure."

"I thought you'd planned a two-year expedition."

His only response was a shrug.

Two years, Kat thought. He's leaving for two years, and he didn't even intend to tell the children goodbye? Kat stared at him, blinked her eyes, as icy-cold fury whipped through her. *And me, had he planned to sneak out on me, too?*

She might have made a noise because Jake glanced over at her, an implacable light in his gaze.

His look silently challenged her, and Kat took up the banner. "Well," she snapped. "You certainly had me fooled."

She detected the slightest hardening of his features, but he didn't respond, didn't defend himself. She stepped toward him, her chin up and her tone scathing. "You're good, Jake Kimball. I knew years ago that you were a thief, a liar, a dishonorable cad. Then—" she held up the pendant hanging around her neck "—I discovered proof that I was right. Indisputable proof."

She released the necklace and braced her hands on her hips. "But did that matter? Did I listen to my own instincts? My own good sense? No. Featherbrain that I am, I let a smooth-talking, slick-handed, pretty-eyed pretty boy turn my head. Again!"

He slammed his hand against the wardrobe. "Goddammit, don't compare me to Rory Callahan! Just don't. I'm sick of being compared to that bastard every time I turn around. He's dead, Katrina. Dead and gone and out of your life."

"And so are you, apparently." She sucked in a breath against the pain. "As for comparisons, I can do, say, whatever I darn well please! And do you know what? You won't be here to stop me, will you? You'll be half-way across the world."

He let out a heavy, aggravated sigh. "Kat, I have to go."

"Why? Because you might find the next Koh-i-noor diamond? Or maybe you yearn for the earthy aroma of mountain goat droppings."

"Oh, for Christ's sake."

Angry tears stung the back of her eyes. "For Miranda's sake. For Theresa's and Belle's sake. For Caroline's and Robbie's sake. What is more important than those children, Jake Kimball? What is more important than—" She bit off her sentence before she spoke the humiliating word aloud. *Me.*

A muscle worked in his jaw. "Don't do this. Please. I've been up-front with everyone about my plans. The girls have known from the first that I'd be going, and so did you."

"But that was before, damn you!"

"Before what?"

She waited, the words hovering on her tongue. Words she'd shied away from, even in her own thoughts. Did she want to lay herself bare before him this way? To sacrifice her pride, her dignity? Did she want to admit aloud something she'd never admitted to herself?

But they were words that could make a difference. Words that might make him stay.

But the risk. He might deny it, but Jake *was* like Rory. His actions today were those of a hard-hearted scoundrel. Why should she give her heart again, allow it to be trampled again, when she'd finally begun to heal? No, she couldn't trust Jake Kimball, so those words would remain unspoken.

Kat took a deep breath, then offered others that humbled, others that could hurt, but wouldn't destroy. "Before I asked you to stay."

Jake muttered a curse, dropped his chin to his chest. His arms fell to his sides.

She stepped toward him. "Stay with me, Jake. Don't go. Stay and be a father to the children, a husband to me."

"Dammit, Kat. I want…" He closed his eyes, shook his head. "I can't."

It rocked her, but didn't knock her down. "Don't ever again try to tell me that you're not like Rory Callahan."

Jake visibly gritted his teeth. He reached into his pocket, then handed her a note. "It's Daniel. I heard from my brother. He's alive, Kat. He sent this."

Scanning it quickly, she shrugged. "So, he's alive. Why didn't he come tell you that in person? Why should you drop everything, leave everyone. Why doesn't he come here?"

"Kat, I…finding him…hell…I've been searching for him half my life. Maybe I couldn't admit it, even to myself, but that goal has been the driving force behind everything I do."

And that goal was obviously more important to him than the children, than her. Kat felt a rush of relief that she'd never said those three humiliating little words. "Fine, then. Go."

A muscle worked in his jaw, and she thought he'd continue to argue or explain or attempt to justify. Instead he turned toward the door, and her heart crumpled.

Jake took a step into the hallway, then abruptly stopped. "Dammit, Kat." He whirled and returned to her, yanking her into his arms, taking her mouth in a long, deep, passionate kiss that was different than any they'd shared before. It filled her with yearning, arousal and hope.

He lifted her off the floor, carried her to his bed. With his knee he shoved the travel case off onto the floor and placed her gently upon the mattress. Jake proceeded to make love to her with intensity and devastating care. The heady, masculine scent of him filled her senses as his hands stroked her body, caressing her as if she were a precious treasure. His lips blazed a slow, sensuous trail over her face, her neck, her shoulders, before paying slow, sweet homage to her breasts. As his mouth and tongue worked their magic, the familiar heat flared within her, and Kat gave herself up to the passion of the moment. The thoughts crowding her mind gave way to feelings and a storm of sensation.

His attentions drifted lower. Her belly trembled when his tongue dipped into her navel. Her breath caught when his lips continued to descend until he gave her the most intimate kiss of all.

Through it all, he never spoke. He didn't whisper the

earthy words she'd grown accustomed to him using. He didn't tease her or murmur praise or express his own pleasure. Unlike any other encounter between them, he made exquisite love to her in almost reverent silence. So beautiful was the experience that tears spilled from her eyes even as he brought her to climax time and time again.

When at last he joined his body with hers, sliding home with an exquisitely slow, smooth stroke, he held himself still for a long moment. Their gazes met and held: his, steady and unblinking; hers, shiny with tears. As the seconds ticked by, a wrenching understanding became clear to Kat.

Jake was telling her goodbye.

She let out one little inadvertent whimper as her heart twisted, then she searched inside herself for strength. Finding it, Kat nursed it to a numbing anger.

So he's leaving. Let him go. Let him throw us away. But be hanged if I make it easy for him. Be hanged if he walks away without regret. Jake Kimball might go, but by God, he'll take memories of me with him. He won't walk away and forget me.

With that, she set about making it happen. Kat turned aggressive, rolling him over, taking control. She teased and she tormented. She used every sexual, sensual weapon in her arsenal along with her extensive knowledge of Jake's body, his penchants and preferences, to drive him wild. Time and time again she brought him to the edge, time and time again she denied him the relief of going over until finally she destroyed the tethers of his control by taking her own pleasure.

Jake let out a feral roar and flipped her onto her back. He plunged into her once, twice, then groaned out her name as he shot his seed deep within her body.

He collapsed against her, hot and heavy and gasping for breath. Kat had worn him out and wrung him dry. She knew that she'd won. Jake Kimball would have to travel farther than Tibet for longer than two years to forget her, by God.

It proved to be an empty victory.

Jake eventually found the energy to move, and he rolled off her onto his back. They lay side by side, yet miles apart. Long minutes passed while the only sound to be heard in the room was the ticking of the mantle clock.

Finally Kat could bear the silence no more. "Anyone can write a note, Jake."

His voice was a low, lonely sigh. "He wrote me letters when I was at school. I recognize his handwriting."

Hmm. Handwriting can be imitated. Could someone be playing a cruel joke? Jake was wealthy. What if someone was trying to swindle him?

Jake was a swindler himself. He should be able to tell.

"All these years and he's never once communicated with his family? How utterly horrid of him. I can't believe he'd make your family suffer like that. Your father and sister both died not knowing the truth. He should be horsewhipped."

"Kat," Jake started to say.

"You recall that for months my family believed I'd died in a fire. The moment I found out, I knew how important it was to let them learn the truth. I can't believe your brother would be so selfish as to let his family suffer for more than fifteen years."

When Jake failed to respond to that, she added, "And I can't believe you'll jump to his beck and call on the basis of a long overdue note. As if you don't have the children to think of, a life. A wife."

She felt his body tense, but again he didn't speak. He wouldn't defend himself. Wouldn't explain himself. A cauldron of emotions welled up inside her. She wanted to kick him, hit him, punch him in the gut. Make him see how stubborn and hardheaded he was being. Instead she rolled over onto her side and tried not to cry, tried to go to sleep. Eventually she drifted off.

She awoke to an empty bed. Jake had sneaked off, a thief in the night.

The sorry, no-good scoundrel had taken her necklace with him.

JAKE STOOD AT THE BOW of the ship gazing forward as the *Ulysses* sailed away from England. Two weeks into the trip, he spent all his time at the stern, looking backward. He feared he'd given up a chance at a future because of a promise he'd made in the past.

Kat's words haunted him. They rang in his ears and echoed through his mind, growing louder with every mile that stretched between them. She'd made a good argument. Daniel should have contacted the family before now. Their father had suffered over his eldest son's loss until the day he died. Jake had spent the past seventeen years being haunted by a ghost who didn't exit.

If Daniel could get a note out of his magical kingdom now, then why the hell hadn't he done it years ago?

Knowing the isolation of the region and the difficulty of travel there, Jake was willing to cut his brother a little slack timewise regarding notification. He could understand two years, three. Hell, even five.

Seventeen went beyond the pale. Seventeen was cruel.

But the Daniel Jake had known and loved was not a cruel person, so why had it taken him this long to contact the family? Why had that contact been so brief, raising more questions than it answered? Was it somehow tied to Shambhala?

Jake needed to know. He needed to know if his dream that day on the mountain had been real. He needed to know how Kat's necklace played a part in the drama. He needed to know what family he was supposed to find—his brother or the woman he'd made his wife.

The woman he loved.

It was true. Somewhere along the way, he'd fallen in love with Kat. He didn't know when it happened. Maybe that last night when she'd turned into a tigress in bed. Maybe that afternoon at the zoo when she'd jumped his butt for letting Belle get near the tiger's cage. Hell, it could have been the very first time in Galveston when he'd glanced up and seen a Madonna on the beach.

So why the hell was he only figuring it out now?

"'Cause you're dumb as a doorknob, that's why." Jake fingered the pendant in his pocket and watched the sea foam created in the ship's wake. "Stupid and confused."

What was he supposed to do? What did he *want* to do?

He wanted to verify that his brother was indeed alive and satisfy the promise he'd made his father on Bernard Kimball's deathbed. He wanted to turn this ship around and return to Chatham Park, to Kat and to the children and satisfy the yearning in his heart.

But he couldn't be in two places at once. Or could he? Who knows what magic Shambhala had to offer?

Jake had spent many years traveling the world in search of unique and wonderful things. The fantasy of Shambhala intrigued him. And yet, as England's shores grew distant, Jake realized that the reality of his wife and family intrigued him even more.

He ordered the *Ulysses* to the nearest port where transportation back to England could be found. He appointed an assistant to be expedition leader and spent the next two days writing letters to smooth his replacement's way.

He cooled his heels in Africa for days, waiting for a ship headed west to arrive. A day into that voyage, engine trouble forced another delay. The broken axle on the carriage he'd hired to take him to Chatham Park was icing on his bad-luck cake.

Or, so he thought.

Riding a horse he'd purchased from an extortionist innkeeper, he entered the wide, tree-lined avenue leading up to Chatham Park. For the first time in what felt like forever, he relaxed, and a pleasing sense of homecoming settled over him. At his first glance of the house, Jake smiled with anticipation. Finally, after weeks of trying, he'd come back to Kat.

He fantasized about how she and the children would greet him. They'd be up in the nursery playing tea party. He'd appear in the doorway; the children's faces would light up. They'd jump up and run to him, wrap their little arms around him in a hug, all talking at once as Jake's gaze would meet Kat's across the nursery, she'd smile warmly, then rise and walk toward him. Then, because she was, after all, Kat, she'd make a fist and throw a hard punch to his gut, and then when he bent over, she'd place her other hand around his neck and kiss him.

Grinning, Jake signaled his horse to run faster. The fantasy was a joy, but he was smart enough to know the reality might go a little rougher. He'd been a coward to leave without telling the children goodbye, and they might well make him grovel a bit before warming up to him. And Kat...well...she probably wasn't too happy that he stole her necklace again. He'd probably have to do some fancy talking to get back into her good graces.

He wouldn't tell her he loved her right off. He'd wait until they had some privacy for that.

Before Jake could dip into yet another fantasy, he arrived at the house. He bounded up the steps and opened the front door. Inside he looked and listened for the sight and sound of children.

He heard only silence.

Well, it was a big house, a big estate. He'd find one of the servants to tell him where to look.

Jake started toward the kitchen, but a woman's voice stopped him. "Mr. Kimball?"

Jake turned and spied a maid emerging from the library, a dust cloth in her hand, a shocked expression on her face. "Hello, Susan," he said with a grin. "Where will I find my wife?"

Her mouth worked, no words emerged. Jake felt a niggle of unease. "Susan?"

"Mrs. Kimball's not here, sir."

The niggle grew to a nudge. "The children?"

"They're with Mrs. Kimball."

"And where is Mrs. Kimball?"

Again the maid's mouth worked, and again she made no sound. Finally she sent a desperate look above him. Jake slowly looked up.

Chatham Park's butler stood at the top of the staircase, a grave expression on his face. "Carstairs!" Jake exclaimed. "Where are Mrs. Kimball and the children?"

The butler descended the stairs, straightened his lapels, then faced his employer, his shoulders squared, his hand linked behind his back. He cleared his throat. "Texas, Mr. Kimball. Your wife has taken the children to Texas."

CHAPTER THIRTEEN

Fort Worth, Texas

KAT TOOK A DEEP BREATH, shifted Robbie's weight from one arm to the other and climbed the front porch steps of Willow Hill. Home. Finally. After a long journey and a truly difficult day. Emotion clogged her throat, and she swallowed hard against it as she waited for the girls to join her. "All right, ladies. Let's have a look at you. Miranda, fix your hair bow. Belle, tie your shoe. Caroline, you've a smudge of chocolate on the side of your mouth."

"What about me, Kat?" Theresa asked.

Kat's gaze swept over the girl, noted the two splotches of cherry crème on her pinafore. Anxious for news about Mari's pregnancy and wanting to reward the girls after their sweet and sensitive behavior while Kat visited her daughter's grave, she'd stopped by Indulgences on her way home. Though Mari was home resting, Kat learned that her sister had delivered twins, a boy and a girl, early the previous week. Mother and babies were healthy and happy at home. They'd celebrated the news with a treat, and now the children were chocolate messes. Clucking her tongue, Kat said, "You're hopeless, love. My papa's going to love you."

As she reached for the doorknob, she couldn't help but remember another homecoming, the day she'd returned to Willow Hill surprising parents who'd believed her to be dead. This wasn't a surprise of quite the same magnitude, but it was close. She hadn't warned them of her marriage or of her recent return to motherhood. While Emma might have mentioned Jake in letters she wrote the family, she wouldn't have known the developments subsequent to her departure from Chatham Park. There were plenty of developments.

After returning from her honeymoon, Kat had begun a dozen letters to her parents, but she'd never found the right words to explain what she'd done. Then, when the rotten scoundrel left her and she'd decided to go home, she figured she might as well wait and explain in person. Her papa always did better learning news in person.

She opened the door, stepped inside and called, "Hello?"

Her seventeen-year-old brother, Billy, sauntered out of the kitchen eating an apple. Spying Kat, his brows winged up. Taking in the sight of the toddler in her arms and quartet of girls hanging on to her skirt, he started choking on his fruit.

Miranda dropped her hold on Kat and flew to Billy's rescue, pounding him on the back. My God, Kat thought, the boy had grown a foot in the short time she'd been gone. He must be as tall as Papa now. And he'd filled out. He looked like a man.

"You can stop," Billy said. "I'm fine. Uh, that's enough. Hey, that hurt!"

"I saved your life!" Miranda exclaimed.

Billy glared at his sister, then at the miniature mother hen. "Who is this squirt?"

"I'm not a squirt! I'm a lady."

Kat winked at Miranda, then said, "Billy, I'd like you to meet my new daughter, Miranda Barrett."

"Your what?" her brother asked.

"Your daughter?" her mother said from the kitchen doorway, her entire face alight with a brilliant smile.

"Katie-cat! You're home!" Trace McBride barreled down the hallway that led to his office. "Thank God you're home."

Kat's father swept her into his arms and held her tight, burying his face in her hair until Robbie grabbed a handful of his and yanked while he babbled, "Ya ya ya ya."

"Hello, there, bruiser," Trace said with a grin. He took a step back, his blue eyes bright with pleasure, and asked, "Did I hear right? You've given us more grandchildren?"

"Yes, Papa."

He looked closer at Kat's crew, and his eyes went wide. She could see him mentally counting. *One, two, three, four, five! Five?* "Stupendous!"

Kat's tension eased. She'd known her parents would accept the children, but it helped to have her confidence in them justified. Kat introduced each of the children, saving Caroline for last. "This little one doesn't speak, but she adores apples. Mama, do you have more apples in the kitchen?"

"I do."

Turning to her brother, Kat asked, "Billy, would you show the girls where Mama keeps the apples?"

"Sure." Then he winked at Miranda and asked, "You won't hit me anymore, will you?"

"I saved your life!"

Billy led the girls into the kitchen, where, knowing Billy, he'd find some cookies to give them along with their fruit. "Here, let me hold the little one," Jenny McBride said. When Kat handed him over, she added, "Aren't you just precious."

Robbie cooed and giggled as Jenny led Kat and Trace into the parlor. Trace took the opportunity to give Kat another long hug. "I missed you, girl. It's been a long few months without you and Emma around. And speaking of your sister, the facts in her letters are sketchy. What do you know about—"

"Trace, no," Jenny interrupted. "You'll get all worked up, and you won't get to hear about Kat and how she's managed to bring us new grandbabies." Glancing toward her daughter, she added, "Including one who doesn't speak? She's obviously not deaf. Was she injured somehow?"

"Her heart has been injured. We believe Caroline can speak, but chooses not to." Kat took a seat in her customary spot on the settee next to her mother and began her tale, sparing herself no quarter. She told her parents about the incident at the zoo and her decision to retrieve her necklace and the altar cross. She told of Jake's bride hunt and Emma's application and her own disguise.

"So that's where she met up with this MacRae fellow?" Trace asked.

Kat nodded.

His face went red as he said, "What sort of man convinces a woman to—"

"Trace," Jenny warned. Robbie snuggled his head against her shoulder and appeared to be going to sleep. "Honey, continue your story."

Now Kat was getting to the difficult part. She explained about Jake's proposition, her refusal, then what led to her changing her mind. "I couldn't abandon these children, Mama. I thought maybe I was *destined* to care for them. They needed me, but I needed them, too. And it turns out I needed them desperately. They opened my eyes about losing Susie. They helped me see beyond her loss to her life. I can remember her now with joy and laughter, not only with sorrow and heartbreak. They helped me heal, Mama, and that's enabled me to come home."

Tears welled up in Jenny's eyes. "I'm so glad, honey. So very glad."

Trace rubbed the back of his neck, then cleared his throat. "Wait a minute. Need a little clarification. You actually *married* this man?"

All right, she only thought she'd gotten to the difficult part before. "Yes, Papa. I did."

"He couldn't have named you a guardian and gone about his business?"

"We feared that might leave the matter up to challenge from another relative, an aunt who treated the children poorly during the time they spent with her prior to Jake's return to England."

"So it was like a...what...a marriage of convenience?"

Kat guessed that depended on one's definition of *convenience*. Certainly Jake, the rat scoundrel, had found it convenient. And to be honest, for a while she'd found it convenient, too.

She knew her father, however, and knew he was asking about the intimate side of marriage, never mind that it certainly wasn't any of his business. Well, those were details she intended to keep to herself.

"I'd term it more a marriage of necessity," she said, sidestepping the issue. "These children needed their uncle to marry me."

Trace narrowed his eyes and frowned. "I don't like it. It's not right that you're married to a man who's half a world away."

"Some might say that's the ideal marriage," Jenny wryly observed.

Kat chuckled softly. "I wouldn't argue the point."

Trace paced back and forth in front of the fireplace. "I think it's shameful. No matter why he married her, he married her. He had a duty to her from the moment he said 'I do.' What kind of man marries a woman intending to leave her? What kind of man abandons the care of children—*five* children—to someone who is little more than a stranger? Sure, he picked a gem in Kat, but what if she'd fooled him? What if she was a poor caretaker for those children? He can't do a damned thing about it from Timbuktu."

"Tibet," Kat corrected.

"What are your plans, honey?" Jenny asked, subtly

diverting her husband's attention as she patted the back of a sleeping Robbie.

"Money isn't an issue. I have a veritable fortune at my disposal."

"Harrumph." Trace was clearly not impressed.

"Caring for five children is a full-time job. I was able to hire help on the voyage to Galveston, but the train trip home…" She paused, shuddered at the memory. "I hope to find a nanny soon."

"You wouldn't need one if your husband was here to help," groused Trace.

Ignoring him, Kat continued. "My first order of business will be finding a house."

"You'll stay here," Trace declared.

"No, I don't think that's a good idea."

Her father frowned. "Now, Katrina."

"It's different this time, Papa. I'm able to care for the children. I want to make a home for them. Our home. All of us need that."

Storm clouds gathered in Trace McBride's eyes, but his wife stepped forward to dispel the blow. "You're in luck, Kat. I know the perfect place. It's less than two blocks away. The Braxtons decided they'd had enough of the Texas summer heat and moved back to Minnesota. That house is perfect for children. Plus it's close to us and your uncle's place, so we'll get to see lots of the little ones."

Kat pictured the sprawling home so near her parents and nodded. "Knowing you and Aunt Claire, I'll probably never see them." Then, turning to her father, she asked, "Would you see to the paperwork for me, Papa?"

Frowning, he suggested, "You're welcome to live here, you know. Your mama and I like having curtain climbers around."

"I know, Papa. Thank you." Kat rose from the sofa, crossed to her father, went up on her tiptoes and pressed a kiss against his cheek. "I think it's best I take the Braxton house, but I know I'll need your help quite a lot in the coming months. Why, I'll probably ask you to come by every day to fix something or another."

Mollified, Trace nodded. "I'll see about getting the house this afternoon. First, though…" He folded his arms and scowled. "I want you to tell me what the hell got into Emma?"

WITH THE PAPERWORK for her new home folded neatly into her purse and her children wearing clean clothes and smiles at the prospect of another delicious sweet, Kat opened the door of Indulgences and spied a new employee behind the counter. *This could be fun.*

She set her mouth in a stern frown and said, "Hello. I understand the owner of this establishment is in for an hour today?"

The young woman nodded. "Yes, ma'am."

"Would you please tell her Mrs. Kimball and her five children are here to complain about the quality of her chocolate?"

The employee's brows winged up and her chin dropped. "Uh, well, um, she's having lunch right now. With the sheriff and his deputy."

That's even better. "I don't mind interrupting her meal. Please tell her I'm here. It's Mrs. Kimball."

The woman scurried into the back room, and seconds later Kat's sister emerged with a smile on her face and insult in her eyes. Her gaze swept over the children, then landed on Kat. Shock chased the anger away. She clapped a hand against her mouth and let out a squeal. "Oh, my heavens. Kat?"

Kat heard chairs scraping in the back room and Luke Garrett and his deputy, Marcus Wagoner, rushed to the rescue as Kat smiled and said, "I hear you've added two new members to the family. I'm dying to meet them, but guess what? I've got you beat. Mari, I want you to meet my children."

Mari shook her head in confusion as she stared at the children, her gaze lingering on the toddler in Kat's arms. "Your children?"

"I've remarried, Maribeth. These are my daughters, Miranda, Theresa, Belle and Caroline Barrett. And this is my son, Robert Barrett, Marquess of Harrington."

One of the men bumped a table, and a coffee cup crashed to the floor. "It wasn't us," Belle was quick to say.

"Married?" Mari asked. "You married a marquess?"

"Actually, I married a pirate. Remember Jake Kimball?"

Her sister blinked. "The man who bought the Sacred Heart Cross from Rory?"

"That's him. He stole my necklace, too."

"Your necklace!" Maribeth grabbed the back of a chair and steadied herself. "My-oh-my-oh-my. I can't wait to hear this story. Emma didn't mention any of this in her letter."

"Can we have a piece of candy now, please?" Theresa asked, oblivious to the undercurrents in the room as her stare locked on the candy case.

Luke Garrett stepped up to Kat, bent and kissed her cheek. "Welcome home, sunshine. We've missed you."

"I've missed you, too, Luke."

"That's a handsome fellow in your arms. Of course, McBride women always pick the good-lookin' ones."

Theresa said, "Aunt Kat? That cherry crème I had earlier was the best thing I ever tasted."

Mari's curious gaze silently asked, *Aunt?*

"Jake assumed guardianship after they lost their parents," Kat explained. "Are the babies in back, Mari? I'm so anxious to see them."

Mari shook her head. "Aunt Claire and Uncle Tye commandeered them. There's a merchants' society luncheon today and they wanted to show off my boys. They should be back soon, though."

"Aunt Kat?" Theresa tugged Kat's sleeve. "The cherry crème?"

Luke took charge. "C'mere, girls. Uncle Luke will take care of you. Y'all pick whatever you want."

"You're our uncle Luke?" Miranda asked.

"That I am."

Miranda shared a delighted grin with her sisters. "After you get us our sweets, will you take us to meet our new cousins, Uncle Luke? Not the babies. They're not much fun. I mean the older ones. Aunt Kat says they're really nice and that we're going to love them and that we'll adore having cousins. We've never had cousins before."

"Well, you have cousins now, little bit." He turned

to Marcus Wagoner. "Would you mind holding the fort at the office for a while this afternoon, Marcus? Looks like I have some introductions to make."

Marcus Wagoner's smile looked a little sickly as he nodded. "Sure, boss. I, uh, I guess I'll go now."

Mari glanced at her friend. "Finish your sandwich first, Marcus."

"No, thank you. I, uh, don't have much of an appetite today." He retrieved his hat from the back room, then walked toward the front door. He nodded at Kat as he passed. "Welcome home, Kat."

"Thank you, Marcus," she replied, smiling. "It's good to be home. Very good."

"Oh, Kat." Mari blinked rapidly. "You sound like your old self!" Then she burst into tears, ran across the room and wrapped her sister in a hug. The two women bawled together like babies, and Miranda looked at Theresa and said, "Promise me we'll never act that silly."

"Never," Theresa agreed.

Once Luke left with the children in tow, headed for his own house where the Garretts' hired babysitter watched the older children a few hours each day so that Mari could keep her fingers in the chocolate, so to speak, the sisters settled down to catch up.

"It's amazing." Mari sipped from a glass of lemonade. "All these life-changing events because of an overheard remark from a child's mouth at a zoo." Sighing, she added, "I wish I'd been with you and Emma. Y'all had a good old-fashioned McBride-Menace escapade without me."

"We missed you. We could have used another pair of hands searching Chatham Park for the cross and my necklace."

Mari set her glass on the table. "So. Kimball stole the necklace from you a second time, but what about the cross?"

"It's still at Chatham Park."

"You left it behind? Why?"

Kat eyed the chocolates on a tray atop the counter and debated having one more. "I don't believe in that nonsense anymore."

"What nonsense is that?"

"The family curse. The Curse of Clan McBride."

Mari folded her arms and frowned at her sister. "Stop that. What's the matter with you, Kat? You believed in the curse and in the power of our necklaces from the first. Why are you being so cynical now?"

Kat debated how much to say. It was one thing to keep the truth about her marriage secret from her parents, but something else entirely to keep it secret from her sisters. "I've grown up, Maribeth. Finally. Look, I was little more than a girl when Roslin gave us our necklaces. I was starry-eyed and stupid and still very young when I convinced myself that Rory Callahan was my destiny. After he died, I latched on to the idea that my task was to deliver the Sacred Heart Cross to San Antonio because I was desperate for hope, needful of a dream to hold close at a time when I faced the reality of being an unwed mother. After Susie was born, I didn't have time to dream. When I lost her, I didn't have the desire."

"So why create an elaborate plan to reclaim the necklace and the cross?"

"Because I'm a slow learner," she replied with a sad laugh. "I think I'd reached the point where I was ready to step away from my grief, but I needed a catalyst to make the leap. Jake Kimball provided it. Then, when I needed an excuse to justify my actions with Jake, I latched on to the idea that caring for these children might be my task, and that Jake might be the man to offer me a love to fit the requirements."

Mari gave a vigorous nod. "Exactly."

"Exactly *wrong*. Again. I may be slow, but I do eventually learn. I don't have a task, and I don't have a love that is strong, vigilant and true. That's why I didn't bring the cross home, Mari. It's just a cross. It's not enchanted or cursed. What it is, though, is his. He bought it fair and square."

"But—"

"Jake Kimball left me, Mari. We're not headed for a happy-ever-after."

Mari twisted her mouth, sat back in her chair, and drummed her fingers on the table. After a few moments thought, she declared, "You could be wrong, Kat. The curse—"

"For heaven's sake. Haven't you heard a word I said?"

"I heard, but I disagree with your conclusions. One thing I've come to understand about the curse is that the process of breaking it is full of surprises. Although, now that I think about it, we should have seen it coming with regard to Jake Kimball. You were certainly obsessed with the man for a time. Still, I thought that when you finally got over Rory, you'd find a man here in town. Someone like Johnny Wilkinson—he's asked you out dozens of times. Or Noah Barnes. Why, I thought you might take a liking to Marcus. He's been sweet on you for years, you know."

"Marcus has been kind to me," Kat agreed. "He was such a dear when Susie was killed. Noah and Johnny are fine gentlemen, too. Maybe when word arrives that Jake Kimball slid off a mountaintop, I'll walk out with one of them."

"Katrina!"

Why not? Jake's eye was probably roaming somewhere in the world even now. "In fact, maybe I won't wait until Jake falls off a cliff."

"Would you stop it!" Mari protested. "You know, Kat, your reaction further convinces me I'm right. I hear such passion in your voice when you speak about Jake Kimball."

"A lot of good passion does me alone. The man is off climbing a mountain for at least two years. It mustn't have been all that passionate for him. Happy-ever-after, hah!"

"Roslin of Strathardle didn't promise us a time line."

Kat wrinkled her nose. "I'll tell you about a time line. The man walked out on me and those children for no good reason. Two years won't be long enough for me to forgive him. And as for stealing my necklace, twenty years won't do it. Maybe, just maybe, two hundred years would get the job done, but I don't think I'll live that long."

Mari sat back and drummed her fingers against the table. "Oh, my. You went and fell in love with him."

Kat looked away.

"You're in love with your husband!"

"No. No, I'm not. I'd be a fool to love that man, and I've sworn off foolish behavior. Jake Kimball may be charming, handsome and intelligent, but he's also a thief, a scalawag and an adventurer."

"In other words, he's just your type."

Kat bent over and banged her head against the table. "What's wrong with me, Mari? Why am I always attracted by the wrong kind of man? Why couldn't I fall for someone kind and considerate like Marcus? Why am I attracted to inappropriate men?"

"I bet it's the curse," Mari said.

"Oh, stop bringing up the curse! I swear, you must have milk fever. It's making you batty. And to think that you were the skeptic among us back when Roslin gave us our necklaces."

"Hmm…" Mari said, absently rubbing her belly. "I still think I'm right. I think the cross and your necklace brought you and your Jake together, and you simply need a little more time for the love you share to become powerful, vigilant and true."

Kat reached out, took her sister's face in her hands and stared into Mari's blue eyes. "Listen to me. There is no 'shared love.' Jake Kimball doesn't love me. I don't love him."

Mari patted her sister's cheek. "I guess time will tell, Katrina. Time will tell."

WHEN JAKE STEPPED OFF the train in Fort Worth, Texas, he halfway expected a tornado to hit or an explosion to rumble or lightning to strike from a clear, blue sky. At the very least a comet should streak down from the heavens and knock him on his ass. It had been that sort of trip.

In all his years of traveling, Jake had never had a run of bad luck like what he'd experienced since the day he'd left Kat sleeping in their marriage bed. From the trouble he'd had returning to Chatham Park, to the delay in his departure from England caused by an overzealous constable who, based on a case of mistaken identity, arrested him for being a Peeping Tom. After finally striking out for Texas, Jake encountered a washed-out bridge, another broken axle, a horse with digestive troubles, more engine problems aboard ship, a quarantine in New York harbor and three days cooling his heels in the city while taking care of Kimball Foundation concerns.

He'd almost sent her a telegram telling her he was on his way, but he'd decided that in this case forewarned might literally mean forearmed. Surprise might save them both grief in the long run.

The train trip from New York to Texas was a nightmare he'd just as soon not revisit. Suffice it to say he'd tracked the robbers down and retrieved the Sacred Heart Cross and Kat's necklace.

He glanced down at the satchel he carried in his left hand. He was beginning to think that maybe Kat had been right all along, that this religious icon was cursed with bad luck.

"All the more reason to follow through with her original plan," he murmured as he exited the train station. He wasn't an overly religious man, but he'd had quite enough of God's wrath. Hopefully, giving the cross to the Sacred Heart Mission would appease the Almighty where Jake was concerned.

When Jake had discovered she'd left the cross behind when she took the children to Texas, he'd decided to take her plan and make it his. He expected he'd need a grand gesture like giving up the Sacred Heart Cross to buy his way back into her good graces. And God's.

Jake chose to check into a hotel rather than make straight for Willow Hill and the expected confrontation with his bride. And, probably, her father. He signed an alias to the register, figuring he'd reconnoiter the area a bit before making his presence known. It wouldn't surprise him to learn that Trace McBride had put a price on the head of one Jake Kimball.

Or maybe not. Surely the children wouldn't like that. Would they? He supposed they might be pretty angry with him. Damn, but he couldn't wait to see them. He'd missed the little troublemakers something fierce. Just like he'd missed his wife.

Jake bathed away the travel dust and dressed in clean clothes before pulling on a pair of boots and heading downstairs. He figured he'd begin his search for information in the hotel bar.

With its polished oak panelling, upholstered furniture and classical art, the Cactus Bar attracted businessmen looking to unwind at the end of a workday, rather than cowboys hunting up a good time. Jake suspected a pair of sharp ears along with a well-considered question or two might pick up a bit of news about someone with the last name of McBride. Or even better, McBride-Kimball.

He ordered whiskey straight and stood at the bar, one boot propped upon the brass rail. He sipped his drink and eavesdropped on the conversations around him. He heard talk about cattle prices and oil exploration. Complaints about wives, lady friends, bosses and employees swirled in the air. Jake chuckled into his drink at a joke a preacher told about a banker. A fellow mentioned the name of Kat's sister's chocolate shop, and Jake perked up.

Then, drifting through the doorway that led from the Cactus Bar into the hotel restaurant, Jake heard a laugh. A familiar laugh. A laugh that sent a shiver of longing up and down his spine. *Kat.*

Absently he set his drink onto the bar and, drawn like a moth to a flame, moved toward the open door. His mouth went dry. His heartbeat pounded. *Damn, I've missed her.*

Stopping in the doorway, he scanned the room. There. Looking beautiful in blue, her hair a little mussed, her cheeks rosy, her smile bright and easy, Kat sat laughing with her dinner partner.

Her dinner partner was a man. A man who, judging by the gleam in his eyes, was not her brother, uncle, cousin or any other relation.

A red haze of temper descended over Jake, dulling his thought processes and allowing him to act in a manner that was…well…stupid. He marched across the restaurant to his wife's table, braced his hands on his hips and demanded, "What the hell do you think you're doing?"

Kat gazed up at him in shock, her eyes round, her mouth working. But no words emerged. Jake, on the other hand, had no trouble spouting off. Stupidly. "Allow me to remind you that you are a married woman, Mrs. Kimball."

She drew herself up. Seconds ticked by.

"With children," he added.

At that, her eyes narrowed and Kat finally found her voice. "How dare you!" she said in a scathing tone as she threw her napkin down onto the table. She shoved to her feet, her eyes flashing. "How dare you speak to me that way! Even Rory had more sense than to flap his mouth like that."

Rory Callahan? Again? Already? Jake thought his head might just explode.

"You have more nerve than a broken toe," Kat continued. "You sneak out of our home like a thief in the night—which you are, by the way—then dare say a word against me? You're lucky if I don't—"

She broke off abruptly. Her eyes blinked twice, then she looked at her dinner companion and said, "Marcus, arrest this man."

"What!" Jake exclaimed, towering over her menacingly, his gaze locked with hers.

"He's a thief. He stole a valuable necklace from me. He might even have it in his pocket right this moment. Marcus, dear, I want this man arrested!"

"Dear?" He gritted his teeth. "You call him 'dear'?"

Somewhere beneath the thrum of his fury, Jake heard the familiar click of a gun being cocked. "Back away from her, Kimball."

Jake broke eye contact with Kat long enough to snarl at ol' Marcus. "You stay the hell away from my wife." Then, turning back to Kat, he continued, "You have some explaining to do, woman. Let's go—"

A gun barrel poked his side. "Empty your pockets."

"What? I'm not going to—"

The gun barrel gouged him. "Now."

Kat folded her arms and smiled. Jake curled his lip and glared at *dear* Marcus. Then he reached into his pocket and pulled out Kat's necklace. From behind him, he heard the crowd gasp. Marcus held out his hand for the necklace, but instead, Jake slipped it over his wife's head and around her neck. The pendant snuggled between her breasts, and he sighed heavily. He'd wanted her to be naked when he did that.

Ol' Marcus cleared his throat and his eyes went hard. "You're under arrest, Kimball. Now, if you don't feel like coming along peacefully, I'll be more than happy to make Kat a widow."

Well, hell. Jake eyed the other man. He wasn't as tall as Jake, but he was sturdy. Jake would have to work to take him down. Mixed with a locked-and-loaded gun and a restaurant full of innocent bystanders, that option didn't present a good opportunity for success. Frustrated and furious with both himself and his bride, Jake raised his hands and backed away from Kat. "This is cold, Katrina."

She lifted her chin, then addressed the man with the gun. "Deputy Wagoner, if it's all right with you, I'll wait here while you lock up your prisoner. I hope you'll return when your business is done."

Then, Jake's wife, the little witch, licked her lips and added, "I've a mind to savor some dessert tonight."

CHAPTER FOURTEEN

WHEN MARCUS ESCORTED Jake out of the restaurant, Kat sank down into her seat, oblivious of the excited hum of conversation stirring around her. She trembled like a willow tree in gale. *He's here. Jake is here. Why?*

She gripped her necklace, still warm from his body heat. Oh, my. Oh-my-oh-my-oh-my. *He came after me.*

"Ma'am? Are you all right? Can I get you anything?"

Kat glanced up at a waitress. "Bourbon, please. With ice."

The liquor scorched its way down her throat and chased the numbing cold of shock from her body. Kat took a second, fortifying sip, then tried to focus. Tried to consider the ramifications of what had just happened. No matter how hard she tried, she couldn't get past one main thought.

He came after me.

She hadn't a clue how long she sat there, her mind spinning. She couldn't believe Jake was here. Here, in Fort Worth, Texas. Not in Tasmania. Here looking dapper and handsome and…jealous. He'd looked jealous.

Why had he come? For the children? Had he come to take the children away from her?

"He's not taking my children."

"Kat!" Mari said, sounding as if she'd been repeating the name for quite some time.

Kat gave her head a shake. Her sister was sitting in the seat Marcus had vacated, holding a baby outfitted head to toe in pink. Kat looked at little Jenna, and as always her heart melted. "Oh, let me hold her. Where are your other little ones? What are you doing here?"

"Drew, Maddy and Travis are at Willow Hill," Mari said, handing over the baby. "I'm here looking for you. Luke sent me a note telling me what happened."

Kat cuddled Jenna close and pressed a kiss to her petal soft skin. "He's here, Mari."

"Actually, I hear he's in jail. Your husband follows you halfway across the world and you have him arrested, Kat?"

She shrugged. "It seemed like the thing to do at the time. You should have heard him, Mari. He's the one who steals and runs, then he has the nerve to act like I was doing something wrong by having a nice, quiet dinner with Marcus."

"Why *were* you having dinner with Marcus?"

"We're Jenna's and Travis's godparents. We're planning the christening celebration."

"Oh. Over bourbon?"

"I didn't start drinking until after the men left." Kat smoothed a finger over the baby's silken blond hair. A smile tugged at her lips. "He sounded jealous, Mari."

Mari folded her arms over her full breasts and leaned

back in her chair. "I think that this is the perfect time to repeat one of my favorite sayings—I told you so."

"I don't know. I don't know why he's come or why he's not in Tasmania."

"I know why he's here." Mari snagged a roll off Kat's bread plate, tore off a piece, and ate it. "The man loves you, Kat. The power of the necklace is at work here. You wait and see, Jake Kimball has come to Texas to prove that your love is powerful, vigilant and true. I predict that soon we'll be two-thirds the way toward breaking the curse. So," she leaned forward, her eyes alight with excitement. "Shall we go bail your husband out of my husband's jail?"

Kat considered her sister's question. She recalled her shock, the fierce rush of elation when she looked up and saw his angry face glaring down at her. Then she remembered the sadness she'd felt upon awakening that spring morning to find him gone. He'd hurt her. Terribly. "No, Mari. Let's not."

Her sister blinked. "You're going to leave him in jail?"

Kat smiled down at the baby in her arms. "Yes, I think I am. You're the one who thinks he needs to prove that his love is powerful, vigilant and true. Let's see if it's powerful enough to get him out of jail—and past the McBride men."

"Oh." Mari's eyes went wide. "Papa. I hadn't thought of him."

"Papa and Uncle Tye and Luke and maybe even Billy, for that matter. He's grown up an awful lot of late."

Mari winced. "Poor Jake."

Kat bit her lip. "He'll find a blizzard on a mountain in Tibet more welcoming than the Fort Worth jail."

The sisters' gazes met and held. Together, they burst into laughter.

"I'M GONNA SHOOT HIM through his cold black heart."

Seated on a thin mattress atop a cot in a six-by-five-foot jail cell, Jake looked up into the barrel of a gun. Great. Just great. How many guns would he have to face before this godforsaken day finally came to an end?

"You can't shoot him while he's inside the jail cell, Trace," said a second man, a fellow that looked exactly like the fellow pointing the gun at Jake's head. "Luke would get into trouble for that."

Trace McBride and his twin brother, Tye. How fun was this?

"I'd just as soon you not shoot up my jail, Trace," Luke Garrett agreed. "We're still trying to get the blood-stains off the walls from last time someone got shot. Now, I could turn him loose…"

"Yeah, Luke." A young man with hair and eyes the color of Kat's fixed Jake with a belligerent glare. "That's a plan. Let him go. I want to give him a good ol' Texas welcome before you shoot him, Pa."

Must be one of Kat's brothers. The oldest one, probably. What's his name? Billy?

The four men lined up in front of his jail cell. Three of them wore a look of angry scorn and fierce determination. They were an intimidating bunch. Big and broad and mean looking. Itching for a fight. Luke Garrett simply looked amused.

Jake found that rather reassuring. For all their talk, they wouldn't actually kill him. He didn't think. Probably not, anyway.

They wouldn't think twice about hurting him, though. Jake ran his tongue across his teeth, wondering if he'd come out of this missing one or two.

What worried him more than anything was the fact that ol' Marcus, dear, seemed to have disappeared. Jake thought Kat's remark about dessert had been for his benefit—she'd wanted to piss him off—but just in case, well...*if he's sharing Kat's dessert, I'm gonna kick his ass.*

Jake needed to get out of this cell. Standing, he folded his arms, briefly met Kat's father's mean gaze, then focused on the sheriff. "What am I being charged with?"

Luke Garrett shrugged. "Doesn't really matter. You're in Texas now, boy. We do things a little different here."

"I want a lawyer."

Billy McBride snorted, then piped up. "I'll be his lawyer, Luke. Let me in the cell to confer with my client."

With that, Jake had had enough. He stepped to the cell door and wrapped his hands around the bars. Addressing Trace, he said, "This is getting us nowhere. What do you want from me?"

"Your black heart on a spit." McBride's blue eyes burned into him like a hot branding iron. "You hurt my little girl."

"I know. I'm sorry. I was wrong."

"That's all you have to say?"

"To you, yes." Be damned if he'd spill the beans to Kat's father before he had the chance to talk to her. "I have a lot I'd like to say to my wife."

Trace winced at Jake's use of the word *wife*.

"What took you so long to come after her?" Tye McBride asked, folding his arms across his broad chest.

"That's part of what I'd like to tell Kat."

"Run it by us first," Luke Garrett suggested.

Jake eyed the men, one after the other. These were Kat's relatives. People she loved. Put in their shoes, he could understand their aggression. Hell, maybe he would just tell 'em about his journey. Let 'em hear how much fun he'd had on his trip to Texas.

Jake let go of the bars and allowed his hands to drop to his sides. "I left Chatham Park bound for Tibet on a Monday."

He took them through every broken engine part, each busted axle, every washed-out bridge, broken saddle strap, illness of man, beast and barnacle on the trail. The longer his story went, the harder his audience listened. They appeared to forget their frustration and put aside their anger in the face of a trip that would have given Jason and his Argonauts a run for their money.

Jake concluded his tale with the train robbery in East Texas and his unfortunate encounter with a skunk after retrieving Kat's necklace and the altar cross from the criminals. "Then, when I finally make it to Fort Worth, I land myself in jail before I can finish my first glass of whiskey."

"Holy hell," Billy McBride breathed. "You had the worst luck of any man I ever heard!"

Tye McBride looked at the floor and rubbed the back of his neck. Luke Garrett shoved his hands in his pockets and rocked on his heels, his gaze looking everywhere but at Jake. Trace McBride reached for the back of the desk chair, then sank blindly into the seat. He closed his eyes and massaged his forehead with his thumb and fingers.

"Bad luck," he murmured. "Son of a bitch."

For a long moment, the only sound to be heard in the jailhouse was the nervous tap of Billy McBride's boots against the wood floor. Jake gazed at one man after the other. Something was up. What did they know that he didn't?

His expression troubled, Trace McBride looked to his brother. "What do I do now?"

"I think you have to stay out of it," Tye advised.

"That goes against my instincts."

"I know, brother."

Trace drummed his fingers on the desk. Jake tried to figure out just what was going on.

"You want me to let him go, Trace?" Luke Garrett asked.

Jake took a step forward at that, but his father-in-law responded, "No. She had him put here. She'll have to be the one to let him out."

"Wait a minute," Jake protested. "I want to see a lawyer."

"We'll get around to that," Luke said.

Trace McBride scratched along his jawline. "Where is that damned cross?"

"Uh, Pa?" Billy frowned. "I don't think you should mix religion and cussin'. Not when it involves the Bad Luck Cross."

Luke shrugged in agreement, then said, "Marcus has gone to get the cross from Kimball's hotel room. I thought I'd keep it here in the safe."

Jake's jaw gaped. "What? He can't do that. What about my rights?"

"You're in Texas now," Trace explained. "In my son-in-law's jail. You don't have any rights unless we want to give them to you."

"Oh, for God's sake."

Jake plopped down on his cot as Trace McBride rose to his feet. He studied Jake, scowled at the gold hoop earring Jake wore in one ear, then sighed heavily and shook his head. "It's the hardest thing in the world, being a father to girls. Those little ones of yours are precious. At least I can take some pleasure in knowing what you have ahead of you."

With that, the McBrides departed the jail. Jake gave Luke Garrett an incredulous look. "What the hell just happened?"

A wide grin wreathed his brother-in-law's face. "Can't you figure it out? Papa McBride just welcomed you to the family."

BRIGHT AND EARLY the following morning, after dropping Robbie off at Willow Hill in response to her mother's pleas to babysit, Kat accompanied the girls downtown to the jailhouse. Luke and Marcus were both on duty, and they welcomed the visitors with smiles and peppermint sticks. Kat watched the girls distract the sheriff using feminine weapons of giggles and charm. Luke never noticed when Caroline-the-criminal lifted the key ring to the cell door off the peg behind his desk and tucked it into her pocket.

Kat decided to keep the bit of thievery to herself for the moment. She remained in the outer room with Marcus when Luke took the girls back to the cell to visit their uncle Jake, although she did stand near the doorway so that she could peek down the hall and observe the conversation.

It was the best entertainment she'd had in...well... since early this morning when Mari came by to describe the scene at the jailhouse last night as shared with her by her husband. Now Kat smiled in smug satisfaction while Jake endured tears and silent recriminations, puppy dog eyes and martyred airs from his abandoned nieces. Then the girls let him have it.

They scolded him, berated him, badgered him and bullied him. Before all was said and done, he made promises to them he'd spend the next twenty years working to keep. If he meant to keep them, that is. The bounder.

Yet, for all his thieving and deceiving, she'd never known Jake Kimball to flat-out lie. He dodged the truth, avoided it, danced around it, but when he gave his word, from everything Kat had seen, it was good.

The girls asked him to promise that he'd never leave them again. Kat leaned toward the doorway, listening carefully to his reply.

"Ah, pumpkin, I can't promise that," Jake said. Kat could tell he chose his words carefully as he added, "What I can promise is never to go unless it's very important, and never to go again without telling you goodbye first. That was wrong of me, girls, and I apologize for it."

"Why did you do it, Uncle Jake?" Belle asked. "It was mean!"

"I know, sunshine. I guess I was scared."

"Scared!" said a trio of voices. "You?"

"I was scared to face y'all. I think I knew deep in my heart that I shouldn't go, but I thought I needed to."

"Because you wanted to visit your brother. Kat told us."

"Did you find him?"

"No." He paused and Kat strained forward, listening. Listening. Finally, frustrated, she peeked around the doorway. Jake was looking right toward her. Their gazes met and held. "I went a little ways, then turned around. I figured out that as bad as I wanted to find my brother, even though it was the last promise I made to my father before he died, I simply couldn't be away from my loved ones that long."

"You mean us?" Theresa asked.

"Yes, you. My family. The people I love. You, Miranda, and you, Theresa, and you, Belle, and you, Caroline. And Robbie." Then, looking his wife straight in the eyes, he added, "And you, Katrina."

Her heart stuttered. The breath whooshed from Kat's body. Her emotions whirled and swirled as if they'd been caught in the winds of a dust devil. Hope, yearning, need…and fear. Fear and distrust.

"I want to talk about why I left," he told her. "I—"

Silently she shook her head, cutting him off. She didn't want to hear his excuses. They'd just hurt her. Every time she opened her heart to a man, he hurt her. She felt bruised, beaten down.

But she wasn't defeated. Not Kat McBride. Not the new Kat McBride.

Cautious. That was a good word for how she was feeling. She'd been here before, listening to a man declare his love for her. Time and heartbreak for her and those whom she loved had proved her error in believing his words.

Still, she wanted to believe Jake. She desperately wanted to believe. But she needed to be certain. She needed to have all her doubts erased, all her fears laid to rest. She wanted to trust him. Be damned if she'd settle for less.

Kat wanted Jake's love, but only if it was powerful, vigilant and true. Then maybe she could risk loving him in return.

She drew a deep breath, then let it out slowly. *So, Jake McBride, you love me?*

His gaze burned into hers, steady and fierce.

She squared her shoulders and lifted her chin. *Prove it.*

With that, Kat exited the jail, instructing Luke to send her girls down the street to the mercantile once they'd finished their visit with their uncle.

She spent the rest of the morning glancing over her shoulder as she went about her errands, anticipating the appearance of jailbreaker Jake since she knew the girls must have slipped him the keys. The girls obviously expected their uncle's arrival, too. By midafternoon, they stood sentry on the front porch of their new house. He never showed.

By suppertime, Mari arrived to tell her why.

"Your husband is sick as a dog, Kat. Luke says he can't keep anything in his stomach. They moved him to a hotel room and—"

"A hotel room!"

Mari nodded. "Luke suggested bringing him here, but Jake was afraid of passing the illness to y'all. The doctor thinks he must have picked up a bug on his travels."

"Is he at the Pickwick?" Kat asked, frowning. "I'll go—"

Mari put out a hand to stop her. "Luke said Jake insisted you and the children stay away in case what he has is contagious. The Pickwick's manager's wife said she'd look in on him from time to time."

Kat couldn't help but worry about the man, and she checked with the hotel manager's wife periodically throughout the evening. Shortly before ten she was relieved to learn that Jake's illness had passed, and he'd ventured downstairs to the restaurant for a meal. She slept peacefully that night.

The following morning she once again waited for him to appear. By noon she'd begun to stew. Before she could work up a good anger, however, word arrived from her mother, of all people, that Jake had suffered yet more trouble.

This time the incident was more serious, her

mother's note said. A valve in Jake's hotel room had malfunctioned, and natural gas leaked into his room during the night. Luckily, another guest noticed the smell and alerted authorities who'd revived Jake. He was weak, but he would recover. He was resting at, of all places, Willow Hill.

Jenny suggested that Kat pay him a visit.

She traveled halfway there before she changed her mind, changed direction and soon knocked on her sister's back door. "I'm too worried about Jake to visit him," she told Mari.

Her sister shook her head. "That makes absolutely no sense."

"Sure it does. If I see him looking weak and vulnerable, I'll be weak and vulnerable. I won't be able to tell him no."

"Tell him no about what?"

"Whatever he asks."

Mari blinked once, then twice. "All right. You've lost me. What are you talking about, Kat?"

"I'm beginning to think you may be right, Mari."

"I'm *right?* Did you say I'm right? Hold on, let me find a pencil. I need to mark this special day on the calendar."

"Very funny."

"What am I right about?"

Kat touched the necklace that Jake had returned to her upon his arrest. "I might be making another mistake…. It's truly against my better judgment…. I honestly can't believe I'm setting myself up for disappointment again but…"

"Katrina, spit it out. What are you talking about?"

She drew a deep breath, then exhaled a heavy sigh. "Mari, I think I'm beginning to believe again. In Roslin. In the curse. I'm beginning to think it might be possible for me and Jake to fulfill the necklace's promise."

A smile burst like sunshine across Mari's face and she snapped her fingers. "I get to say it again. I told you—"

"However," Kat interrupted. "Before I commit myself, I want to be sure. I must know without a shadow of a doubt. I need proof of Jake Kimball's love."

"You need faith."

Kat shook her head. "I've had faith in the past. This time I need more, only, I don't know what 'more' is. I just have to believe that I'll recognize it once I see it."

Her sister studied her for a long moment with narrowed eyes. Then, abruptly, she snorted. "You want your love to be tested, don't you? Of all the foolish, ridiculous, short-sighted ideas. Let me tell you something about being tested, Katrina. Two words—Finn Murphy."

Finn Murphy was the villain who'd murdered Rory and almost killed Mari, who would have killed her if Luke's love hadn't driven him to continue to search for her long after most everyone else believed her dead. "Mari," Kat chastised. "I'm not looking to be kidnapped or held hostage or have my life threatened in some other way by some outlaw so that Jake can ride to my rescue. I'm not stupid. I just want…something…and I know if I don't stand my ground now, I'll never know for sure. I'll never be certain."

Mari's long, loud sigh filled the kitchen. "You always did want drama in your life."

No, Kat thought, as she made her way back home. What she'd always wanted, what she'd always dreamed of, was love.

CHAPTER FIFTEEN

A WEEK AFTER HIS ARRIVAL in Fort Worth, Jake stood outside his wife's house in the wee hours of the morning, ready to storm the fortress. Despite extensive efforts on his part to talk with her, she'd avoided him. He hadn't seen hide nor hair of her since she'd left the jail, and damned if he hadn't come close to dying three different times since then. He'd been gassed, nearly bitten by a rattler that had slithered into his boot, and yesterday, damned if a stray bullet hadn't come within inches of making the woman a widow. The coldhearted wench hadn't bothered to so much as send a note.

How the hell was he supposed to prove his love if he couldn't get within ten feet of the woman?

The time had come to settle this nonsense once and for all. Unbeknownst to Kat, Jake had made arrangements for the children with Mari and with the children themselves. Now all that remained to do was the doing.

He checked his pocket watch, then let himself into the house with the key Miranda had given him. Not five minutes later, Maribeth Garrett hurried up the walk, infants in arms. Jake opened the door, and Mari took her babies directly into the parlor, placing the sleeping children in the cradles Kat kept available for her. She switched on a light, got her first good look at Jake, and her eyes went wide. "Well, that's a strange traveling costume."

He wore knee-high boots, tight black pants, and a billowy white silk shirt. Jake winked at her and grinned, then started up the stairs. He heard Mari murmur, "My sister is so going to owe me for this."

According to the children, Kat's bedroom was on the second floor, first door to the right. Jake silently turned the knob and cracked open the door. Moonlight spilled into the room, illuminating the bed where his wife lay sleeping. Despite the need for speed, he took a moment to enjoy the picture she made. *My very own Sleeping Beauty.*

He decided to wake her with a kiss.

His lips brushed hers once, twice, then settled down to savor. She awoke, he was gratified to discover, with his name on her lips.

Then she immediately went stiff as a board. "Jake? What…how…why are you here in my bedroom!"

He gave her a slow, sensual smile. "I can't think of a better place to be."

She tried to roll off the bed, then, keeping her voice low so as not to wake the children, showed him the sharp side of her tongue. Jake subdued her struggles, though the effort got his blood humming. For the first time in forever, he had his hands where he wanted them—on her—and it felt damned good.

Until she elbowed him in the breadbox, that is.

"Hellcat," he muttered. He straddled her, holding

her captive between the strength of his thighs as he pulled his knife from the sheath inside his boot.

Kat's eyes rounded. "What are you doing?"

He sliced the cord tying back the bed curtain, then held the knife to his mouth and bit the blade as he dragged her arms above her head and bound her wrists.

"Oh!" Kat flailed about beneath him. "I know what this is. You're playing pirate. I'll tell you what, Jake Kimball. You're crazy if you think I'm going to participate in any of your honeymoon fantasies."

Once he had her arms secured, he grabbed her kicking legs and cut another cord to wrap around her ankles. Returning his knife to its sheath, he said, "This is no fantasy, love. I'm not acting a character or playing a part. This is completely real. I'm a thief, remember? Well, guess what?" He gave her another quick, hard kiss. "You're my prize."

Then, using the silk scarf he'd tugged from his pocket, he gagged her. She writhed and wiggled and squealed into the scarf. Jake scooped her up and over his shoulder, then, giving her bottom a swat, headed downstairs.

Mari waited by the front door. Kat went stiff as a fence post when she heard her sister say, "Y'all have a good time, now. Don't fret about the children. Luke and I will take good care of them. Maddy and Drew are looking forward to spending more time with their cousins."

Jake felt Kat lift her head, and he knew she must be glaring at her sister. Her body vibrated with rage. Just for the fun of it, he started to give her rear another swat, but he ended up just holding her cheek instead. Damn, but he'd missed this woman.

Outside, he laid her in the bed of a rented hay wagon and covered her with a blanket. "So far so good, sweetheart, and that's saying something for me these days. Now just relax and keep still. It's a short ride to the train station."

"Mfrwaf...mmwafhm...mfruwarh."

"Hush, now. We'll have plenty of time to talk on our way to San Antonio."

Their trip through the dark streets of Fort Worth went quickly and without incident. Jake suspected it was too soon for his luck to have turned. Nevertheless, he grew hopeful. At the train station, he pulled the wagon past the passenger platform and along the rail toward the caboose and the private car preceding it, a car he'd purchased from a railroad baron the day before yesterday. He set the brake on the wagon, then hopped to the ground. "Be right back," he told Kat.

He unlocked the railcar, stepped inside and lit the lamps. He glanced around, checking the space for potential weapons. He saw nothing he'd term as being lethal in Kat's hands. Loudness, he figured he could live with. She'd need to vent her frustration some way, and he doubted she'd be willing to do it the way he'd choose. Not at first, anyway.

In the bedroom Jake turned back the bedding and indulged himself in a quick fantasy picturing Kat against the midnight-blue sheets, her hair spread out around her like a golden waterfall. "Soon, sweetpea. Soon."

Leaving the railcar door open, Jake climbed to the

ground, took a good look around, waited for a railroad worker to disappear around the side of the station, then lifted Kat into his arms. He took only seconds to carry her inside the car.

Her eyes widened at the luxurious interior. The previous owner had outfitted the two bedrooms, bath and parlor with only the finest. Mahogany paneling, stained glass, crystal light fixtures. Kat wouldn't have cause to complain about the accommodations. This time she'd travel in style.

Jake gently placed her on the bed. Her emerald eyes shot arrows of fire. Jake idly thought that Kat Kimball, in a temper, rivaled a South Sea sunset in beauty. Stepping away from the bed, he pulled the chair away from the dressing table, set it beside the bed and straddled it.

"Mmurmphf. Frmphrumph. Mmf. Mmf!"

"Hold your horses. I'll do a little explaining to you, then I'll let you loose. Probably. If you promise to behave."

"Mmurmphf."

He interpreted that as a curse. "Shall I start with the big stuff and work my way down or begin with the details and work my way up?"

"Mfph. Mfph."

"All right, I'll begin with the little stuff. As I mentioned earlier, this train will take us to San Antonio. I've done a lot of thinking about the Sacred Heart Cross, honey, and I've decided there's something to this bad-luck business you warned me about the day we first met. It may be the last gift I gave my father, but enough is enough. I'm tired of being sick, stuck, bitten, beaten and shot at. I brought the cross with me, and you and I are going to finish that task that you've been planning for so long."

As he'd hoped, the fire in her eyes banked a bit at that. Jake continued, "I would have talked it over with you ahead of time, but we haven't exactly had an opportunity to visit since I came to town. I want to apologize for that night, by the way. I was out of line."

Now her eyes narrowed as if she doubted his sincerity. Jake didn't like her reaction, but guessed he couldn't blame her. He wasn't in the habit of apologizing.

He plowed on. "I was jealous. I didn't like seeing you having supper and laughing with another man. I didn't like the way he was looking at you. Makes me see red every time I think about it. The man is a deputy sheriff. He shouldn't be poaching on another man's woman."

"Mmrufph."

"Yes, I know. He wouldn't have had the opportunity had I been where I belonged. With you. That's something else I need to explain. I told you a little bit about Daniel, but there's more to the story. I'm hoping you'll listen and understand a little better once I'm done."

It wasn't just Daniel's story, of course. In this, as in most other aspects of Jake's early life, his father had been the driving force. Jake told her about Bernard Kimball, about always trying to please a man impossible to please. About how Daniel was the light of Bernard Kimball's world.

Jake spoke about his family for a long time, baring his heart, baring his soul. He talked so much that his mouth went dry, and he stood up to pour himself a glass of water. "Oh," he said, frowning. "You're probably thirsty, too."

Kat nodded hard.

"Hmm. There are people milling around outside now. Promise you won't scream or yell for help if I take off the gag?"

She considered it for a moment, then she nodded again.

"I'll shut you up if you try it," he warned. "I've been looking for an excuse to kiss you again."

Jake filled two glasses with water, then nimbly untied the knot and removed the gag. "I can't believe you kidnapped me and tied me up!" she said the moment she could speak.

"It was my turn." Jake helped his wife sit up, then he held the drink to her mouth. He experienced a twinge of guilt when she drained half the glass, but then he got distracted by the moisture clinging to her lips.

Jake couldn't help but kiss her then. He touched his lips to hers, a whisper of a touch, drawing the pleasure out. He'd been without this much too long. He missed her.

He sank into the kiss, tracing her soft, wet mouth with his tongue, encouraging her lips to react, to open to him. The familiarity of Kat's response both soothed him and stirred his blood. He wanted to lie beside her, to feel her full breasts pressed against him, to tangle his legs with hers. But the time wasn't right. Not yet. Jake summoned every ounce of his control and ended the kiss and stepped away.

He picked up his water glass and drained it. He considered pouring a second glass and dumping it in his lap.

Kat cleared her throat. "I didn't scream, but you kissed me, anyway."

"I was thirsty," he said, showing her his pirate's smile. "There was water on your lips."

"So you took it."

"Yeah."

"Not a 'may I' or a 'please' or a 'would you mind.'"

"I'm not a gentleman thief. Just a plain old everyday thief."

Kat wrinkled her nose. "You're a pirate. A knife in your mouth. An earring in your ear."

"Ravishment on my mind," he added, waggling his brows.

She sniffed. "You frightened me to death."

"No, I didn't. I surprised you. I intrigued you. I aroused you."

She sighed dramatically. "I'm weak."

"No," Jake fired back, all teasing gone from his demeanor. "You are one of the strongest women I've ever met, Kat Kimball. Honestly, that's one of the reasons I was brave enough to follow you to Texas."

At that, she cast him a wary glance.

"This is where we work up to the bigger stuff. I did a lot of thinking while I was adrift in my various occurrences of bad luck. I realized something important. I tried to tell you this at the jail that night, but—"

"No!" She said it violently with a furious toss of her head. "No more. Don't you dare say any more. Not this way."

Well, hell. What had he done? "Not what way?"

"Untie me, Jake."

He scratched the back of his neck. "You gonna go to San Antonio with me?"

"You really brought the cross with you from England?"

Wordlessly, Jake rose and walked to one of the railcar's built-in cabinets. He opened a drawer and removed the jewel-studded piece. Carrying it over to the bed, he asked, "Why didn't you take it when you left Chatham Park? I couldn't believe it when I saw that you'd left it behind. Especially since I absconded with your necklace."

"Again."

Jake nodded. "Again."

Her gaze locked on the treasure. "The cross is all tangled up in my mind with you. It's because of the cross that I first met you, because of the cross that you saw my necklace and decided to steal it."

"Only after you refused to sell it to me," he said.

Her lips curved and she gave a soft laugh. Hearing it encouraged Jake, and he relaxed a little.

"I thought about bringing the cross with me when I came home. I took it out of its box and stared at it for a long time the day we left Chatham Park." She paused and as the moment drew out, Jake tensed all over again. "You'd rejected me. Leaving it behind was symbolic."

"You were rejecting me." It was a knife straight to his heart.

"You and the curse and the dream," she said with a shrug. "It is a beautiful work of art, though, isn't it?"

Jake set the cross on the table. "A part of me thinks

it's damned ugly. Every time I look at it a shiver creeps up my spine and I hear your voice in my head telling me it's bad luck. Then I think of every bad thing that's happened to me and my family since I purchased that piece from Rory Callahan. Makes me wish I'd been pocket-lint poor when ol' Rory contacted me about the treasure."

Jake returned to his seat, reached out and curled a long golden lock of Kat's hair around his finger. "And yet, another part of me thinks it's the prettiest knick-knack I've ever seen. Without that altar cross, I never would have met you. What a conundrum, hmm? The bad-luck altar cross bringing me good luck. You, Katrina, are just about the luckiest thing that's ever happened to me."

"Jake, untie me. Now."

"But—"

"If you're fixing to say what I think you're fixing to say, and you do it while my hands and feet are bound, I'll never forgive you!"

Jake waited a beat before asking, "Never?"

"That's right."

"Even when we're old and gray?"

"Even then."

Yes. Those two little words allowed a great big burden to roll right off his back. She was going to forgive him. He might have to work to get there, but in the end she was bound to be his.

Actually, now that he knew he didn't have to sweat the outcome, the getting there might just be fun.

Jake rolled his tongue around his mouth and tried to

choose whether to start with her ankles or her wrists. He'd always had a fondness for shapely legs on a woman, but look at where she was holding her hands— pillowed against the soft, thin cotton of her nightgown right on top of her breasts.

He eyed the knot. He'd tied it good. The quickest way to set her free would be to use his knife, but quick didn't exactly have a lot of appeal.

He sat beside her on the narrow bed and began working the knot at her wrists, his fingers brushing her breasts both by accident and by design. "When I was trying to decide how best to approach you, I kept thinking about that first day we met on the beach in Galveston. You were so beautiful. Ripe and lush, I never forgot you."

"I felt fat and awkward and ugly. I moved with the grace of a cow." After a moment's hesitation, she added, "For a brief time that day, you made me feel feminine."

He brushed a knuckle across the peak of her breast. "I thought I made you angry."

"That, too. I couldn't believe you were so stubborn about the cross. If I'd known then that you were going to compound the insult by making off with my necklace, I think I'd have knocked you down and drowned you."

The knot loosened. Jake trailed a finger along the inside of her wrist, and Kat shuddered. "You think so, hmm?"

Jake wondered if he should confess to the circumstances of the theft of her necklace. One of these days she was bound to ask him about it. If he told her now, he'd have all his secrets out in the open. They could begin this new stage of their relationship without a single dark cloud hovering on the horizon. Wouldn't that be a good thing?

He recalled those harrowing moments beneath the bed where she lay laboring. No. No, he didn't think he'd confess. Some secrets were meant to be kept.

"I thought about you, too," Kat admitted, surprising him.

"You did?" Jake worked one end of the cord through the loop and the knot was gone. He pulled the cord free, rubbed the reddened spots on her wrists, then brought them to his mouth for a kiss. "I hurt you. I'm sorry."

"They don't hurt."

Jake continued to kiss them anyway, licking and sucking and soothing her with his tongue. "So, tell me about these thoughts of yours."

It took her a minute to gather herself enough to speak. "You intrigued me. I thought you were exciting. I've always had a weakness for intriguing, exciting scoundrels."

"I see. It's different for me, however. I've never met another woman like you in my life. Strong, I've mentioned." He turned her right hand over, kissed a knuckle. "Beautiful, too." He kissed another knuckle. "Witty." Another kiss. "Warmhearted." Kiss. "Smart. So very smart."

He set her right hand down, then turned his attentions to her left. "Generous." He kissed a knuckle. "Sensuous." Another kiss. "Adventurous." He lightly nibbled at her ring finger knuckle before kissing it. "Fun." One final kiss, then he gazed into her eyes and added, "Fascinating."

"Oh, Jake." Kat's brilliant green eyes softened and warmed. Then she smiled impishly and added, "Don't forget my feet."

He looked over his shoulder toward the end of the bed. She wiggled her bare toes at him. "Careful. I might bite 'em off." When she wiggled them again, he chuckled. "Did I mention daring?"

"I like it when you suck my toes."

With that, she defeated him. Arousal roared through him like a summer storm. Abandoning his plan to go slow, Jake slipped his knife from his boot and cut the cord. He threw the knife, sending it sailing end over end, to bury its point in the oak paneling on the opposite wall.

Kat's chest rose and fell rapidly as he knelt above her. "Do you understand now why I left you?"

Wordlessly, she nodded.

"Do you understand why I came back?"

She swallowed hard. "Tell me now."

Jake's heart pounded. His blood thrummed. He licked his suddenly dry lips and stared into her soul. "I came after you, Katrina, because I couldn't stay away. I didn't want to stay away. I came after you because I love you. I love the children. You're my family now."

Jake waited, hoping to hear similar words from his wife's lips, but the slow, sweet smile that spread across her face distracted him. She lifted her arms to him and drew him down against her, and within seconds Jake forgot everything but the woman in his arms.

GERALYN DAWSON   333

Their lovemaking was tender and gentle and reverent. So sweet it made his heart weep. At the same time, it was fierce and physical and as demanding as any encounter he'd ever experienced. Most remarkable of all, it was new. Unique. Making love to a woman he loved added an entirely new dimension to the event, and it left Jake satisfied in a way he'd never been before.

Almost. Never once during those long, pleasure-filled hours on the ride to San Antonio did she return his declaration of love. Not in the throes of ecstasy. Not in the quiet aftermath. She laughed with him, shared stories about the girls, tales about her family. Twice she wept softly at the beauty of their desire. Never once did she tell Jake she loved him.

For the first time, Jake understood how much he'd hurt her by leaving, and doubt crept into his heart. Was the damage he'd done her irreparable?

Alighting in San Antonio, he escorted his wife from their private railcar carrying an invaluable piece of pirate's treasure and a heavy heart. As they walked beside the peaceful waters of the San Antonio River, and his gaze first landed on the bell tower of the Sacred Heart Mission rising into the blue sky before them, Jake stopped short.

Wait just a minute. Since when had he become a quitter? He'd stolen her necklace twice. What made him think he couldn't steal her heart all over again?

Besides, something more than his own abilities was at work here. He gazed at the mission and considered all the events that had brought him here today. Eighty-odd years ago the pirate Jean Lafitte buried the cross in the sands of Galveston Island. Seventeen years back Jake experienced a weird, otherworldly vision in a Himalayan cave. Eight years ago a phantasmal Scotswoman gives a young Kat McBride a one-of-a-kind necklace. Two years later, the cross ends up in the hands of a man with ties not only to Jake's own father, but to Kat. Then he and Kat happen to cross paths at the London Zoo. Could all this be coincidence?

Not hardly.

Some force was at work. Jake didn't know if it was God or ancient magical beings or curses or simple fate or not-so-simple Shambhala. Whatever the cause, whatever the reason, Jake and Kat were meant to be together. She was meant to be his Bad Luck Bride.

Jake took his wife's hand and they walked up the weathered stone steps to the main entrance of the mission church. Baroque carvings framed thick wooden doors that needed some muscle to move. Stepping inside was like walking back in time.

The chapel was cool and quiet. Votive candles flickered red and blue. Frescos decorated the walls. At the center of an ornate marble altar stood a simple wooden cross.

"It's a beautiful church," Kat said in a low, reverent tone.

"Your cross suits the altar."

A sound to the right of the altar drew Jake's gaze, and he spied a round little man dressed in a friar's robe enter the building carrying a stack of hymnals. "Excuse me," Jake called out. "You're one of the priests here, I take it?"

"I'm Brother Paul. May I help you?"

"We brought…wait." He handed the box to Kat. "You do the honors, Kat. That's the way it should be."

She smiled at him warmly, then turned to the padre. "My husband and I are delivering a long-overdue gift for the church. It's taken a circuitous route to get here, but I guess it's better late than never."

Kat opened the box. The brother took one look, slapped a hand against his chest, and cried, "Praise God! It's the Sacred Heart Cross."

As Brother Paul reached into the box to lift the cross from its velvet nest, Jake placed a cautionary hand on Paul's arm. "A bit of warning to you, there, Padre. It's my opinion that this piece is in dire need of a good blessing. Give it the works—holy water, incense, whatever you have. This cross has an aura of bad luck about it, and I'd hate to pick up a newspaper in a week or two and read that the Sacred Heart Mission had burned to the ground."

So delighted was he by the unforeseen windfall that Brother Paul not only blessed the cross, but he expanded the blessing to include Kat and Jake and, to Jake's delight, their marriage.

After that he made a little ceremony of installing the cross in its place, then broke out a bottle of rum and offered a long line of toasts. As a result of the blessings and the spirits and the laughter on Kat's lips, Jake left the church with a spring in his step and a confidence in his heart.

Jake knew damn well that his luck was about to change.

CHAPTER SIXTEEN

"EXCEPT FOR BEING MARRIED to our Katrina, Jake Kimball doesn't have an ounce of good luck," Trace McBride observed, strolling into his kitchen where his wife, sister-in-law and two of his daughters sat discussing their children.

"What's happened now?" Kat asked.

Trace removed two bottles of beer and two bottles of Dr. Pepper soda pop from the ice box. "The man drew a straight flush. Bet damn near all his chips on the hand—just like any decent poker player would do. Damned if Billy doesn't lay down a royal flush. Now, what are the odds of that? Have to be about five million to one. This after winning the cake walk at the church social this afternoon only to find out he won a cake baked by Wilma Hutchins."

"Oh, dear." Claire McBride grimaced. Everyone knew Wilma Hutchins made the kind of cake one used as a doorstop.

Trace continued, "And that was on the heels of his correctly guessing the number of marbles in the pickle jar at Martin's General Store to win this month's prize. Know what prize he won? Not a good pair of work gloves like last month or a new hammer like the month before that. Seems like George Martin was getting complaints about the prizes from the ladies, so he was making it up to them. Jake Kimball won a Kabo hipless corset from the Sears, Roebuck and Company catalogue! I'm truly starting to feel some sympathy for the man." He pinned Kat with a sharp look and added, "When are you going to get some?"

"Now, Trace," Jenny said. "That is Kat and Jake's business, not ours."

Kat's father scowled. "It's my business when I have to watch the moony looks she gives him when he's not looking and listen to his lovelorn sighs when he's playing cards. Kat, I'll be the first to agree that the son of a bitch did you wrong, and I don't have a problem with you making him pay for it. Up to a point. I didn't raise you to be hardhearted, girl. Don't drag this out forever. It's cruel." With that he returned to his poker game leaving an awkward silence in the kitchen in his wake.

Five days had passed since Kat and Jake returned from San Antonio. To his unwelcome surprise, despite the closeness they'd shared on their private railcar journey, she'd refused him permission to move into her house. He'd all but chewed his tongue in two, but he'd agreed.

Then the blasted man convinced the Harrelson family next door to rent him a room. He was always underfoot, always pitching in to help with the children. Always trying to convince Kat that she could trust him with her heart.

Now, glancing around her mama's kitchen table and

seeing the curious light in the eyes of women she loved, Kat felt the need to explain to them what was in her heart. If only she knew what that was.

She'd made little progress in that respect in recent weeks. For the life of her, she didn't know what she was waiting for, except, she was definitely waiting for *something*.

"She doesn't believe his love is strong, vigilant and true," Mari told her mother and aunt, a faint note of disgust in her tone. "She wants it to be tested."

"Now, Mari," Kat started to protest.

"It's true and you know it." Mari met her mother's gaze. "It's that love for drama running through her that she wants to satisfy. Just because Luke proved the strength of our love by saving my life doesn't mean Jake has to do the same thing."

"Now, Mari," Aunt Claire chastised. "I'm sure your sister's emotions are more complicated than that."

"That's right," Jenny agreed. She leveled a stern look upon her youngest daughter and added, "It'd be downright stupid for Kat to hope some madman shows up to kidnap her and leave her in a hole in the ground to die."

"That's not what I want." Kat scowled at her sister. "I don't know what I want. That's the problem. But until I do know, Jake Kimball can just hold his horses." She folded her arms and sat back in her chair with a huff.

Mari wrinkled her nose, then sipped her iced tea. "I agree with Papa. This is dragging on way too long."

"Stop it! Just stop it." Kat shoved back her chair and

pushed to her feet. "You have no right to sit in judgment of me, Maribeth Garrett. My situation with Jake isn't a thing like yours was with Luke."

Mari scowled up at her sister. "Jake is a good man, Kat, and you're not being fair to him. He loves you and you're using that love as a weapon against him."

"No, I'm not!"

"Girls…" Jenny warned.

"Mama, she won't forgive him for leaving her even though he came to his senses and realized his mistake. That's no way to begin a marriage. Men are always making stupid mistakes, and women have to forgive them. That's just the way marriage is. You know that. You do it with Papa all the time."

"I forgive Jake for leaving," Kat declared. "I understand why he did it. I'm not so sure that I wouldn't do the same thing if, God forbid, Emma disappeared. You, on the other hand…"

"Why don't you find Papa's razor and sharpen your tongue some more, sister, dear?"

"Girls!" Jenny snapped. "Enough."

Jenny's rebuke was unnecessary, however, because Mari experienced an epiphany that drained her of anger. "You forgive him for leaving, but you don't trust him not to do it again. That's it, isn't it?"

Kat found herself fighting back sudden tears as she sank back into her chair. "I can't get past that. Since he returned, I've tried to put it behind me, tried to believe his assurances. I can't love a man I can't trust."

Aunt Claire reached over and patted her arm. "Of course you can't, darling."

"Not after what you went through with Rory," Jenny agreed, nodding.

"So what do I do?" Kat asked. "How do I convince myself that Jake can be trusted not to break my heart?"

Jenny patted her hand. "I don't know, darling. I guess you'll just have to give it time."

"Which brings us right back to the beginning," Mari said with a sigh. "I suggest you do some hard thinking about this situation, Kat. I have a niggling feeling that y'all can't go on the way you're going too much longer."

"A niggling feeling?" Kat repeated, alarm washing through her. Mari's intuition was even stronger than their father's, and when she got a niggling feeling that trouble lay ahead, a person could bet the farm that trouble was coming. Kat glanced at her mother. "What about Papa? Has he mentioned anything about a niggling feeling?"

Jenny's teeth tugged at her bottom lip. "He's troubled about Jake's run of bad luck. Your father worries it will seep onto you."

"Or the children," Kat murmured.

She lay awake in her lonely bed most of that night.

THE FOLLOWING DAY while Jake was on his way into a downtown store to buy jigsaw puzzles for the children, he heard a crashing sound above him. He looked up just in time to see scaffolding raining down upon him.

He woke up in the doctor's office half an hour later.

"He'll be all right, though?" he heard his wife's anxious voice ask.

Yeah, now she cares. Maybe if I get hurt badly enough, she'll let me into her house. That's it. He'd die, and she'd have him cremated and put his ashes in an urn on the parlor fireplace mantel.

Bruised and beaten, cut and abraded, Jake was feeling a bit sorry for himself at the moment.

He felt somewhat better an hour later after she'd tucked him into a guest bed at her house, fed him a bowl of chicken soup and kissed him on the forehead before telling him to sleep and leaving the room. He'd have preferred she kiss his mouth, but he wasn't about to complain. Besides, he couldn't do his best work with a split lip.

He took her advice and slept for a while. When he awoke, sore and aching with a headache from hell, he thought he must still be asleep and having a nightmare. Trace McBride was sitting beside his bed.

"Look, boy. We've got to talk."

Jake looked up at the ceiling. "Just shoot me and put us both out of our misery, why don't you?"

"Shut up and listen. I'm worried about my little girl."

What, did she break a fingernail? "Look, McBride, I don't want Kat getting hurt any more than you do, but—"

"She needs to fall in love with you."

Jake wondered if the scaffolding accident had done something to his hearing. "Excuse me?"

"Believe me, it makes my tongue curl to say it, but I'm a desperate man. If we don't do something, this bad luck is gonna kill somebody, and my fear is that it might be somebody other than you."

"I'm sorry. Since I suffered a head injury earlier today, you're going to have to spell this out for me."

"Very well," Trace grumbled. "Look, here's the deal. I've battled this bad-luck business off and on for all my adult life. First it was me and Jenny, then Tye and Claire. Even had some British cousins get in on the act. So a while back when the girls came home with those necklaces, yammering on about a family fortune-teller, I listened. I believe in the Curse of Clan McBride, and I think it's got hold of you."

Jake grimaced. "I don't—"

"Yeah, well, I didn't either, at first. But open your eyes, boy. What the hell are you waiting for, the earth to crack open and swallow you? You can't go on like this, and I'm not going to stand around and watch it. Katrina can't bury another husband."

As much as he'd like to argue the point, Jake felt too poorly to do so. Besides, to be honest, the man's opinion coincided with his own.

"Though it pains me to say, I suspect you're meant for my Katie-cat, Kimball. Now, your bad luck started when you left her, right?"

Jake made the mistake of nodding. The pounding in his head had him freezing fast. "Yes," he croaked.

"Getting rid of the Sacred Heart Cross was a good idea, but it obviously wasn't the answer. I've pondered this matter at length, and I think what's throwing everything all out of kilter is the fact that the two of you are married but not committed to each other."

"I'm committed to Kat!" Jake protested, snapping to a seated position despite the pain of moving. "Dammit, I'm not going to sit here and defend myself to you, McBride. If staying in Fort Worth after seventeen scrapes with death isn't 'committed,' what the hell is?"

"Well, she's not committed to you, and who can blame her? I've gotten the whole story from my wife who got it from Mari who got it from Katrina's own mouth. Your wife doesn't trust you, Kimball."

All right, that hurt. Especially coming from Trace McBride. Jake let his aching head loll back on the pillow. "I know that. So if that's the basis for your visit, gloat, then get the hell out."

"Gloat? You think I'm liking this? I gloated when Luke threw your sorry ass in jail. I laughed when that flock of geese flew over and dropped a load right on top of you in the middle of Main Street. Then things got ugly. And dangerous. I'm not gloating anymore. Do you see me smiling?"

Jake cracked open one eye. The man looked mad. He always looked mad. "So what do I do? You're the expert on this bad-luck insanity. What am I supposed to do to put an end to it?"

"You've got to fix it. The girl wants to love you, that's obvious. Disturbing, but plain as the nose on my face. What you have to do is convince her that doing so wouldn't be a mistake. She has some experience with mistakes, does my Kat. She doesn't want to make any more."

None of this was truly news to Jake. He simply didn't know what to do about it. "I've tried, McBride. I've told her that I'm in for the long haul, that I won't ever leave her again. I bought land here, for God's sake. I want to build our home."

"Land? That I don't know about. It's close to Willow Hill, isn't it?"

Jake ignored that question. "I don't know what else to do other than let time prove my sincerity."

"That's just it. We don't have time. You were lucky today for an unlucky son of a bitch. I'm not going to wait around and have my daughter or one of my new grandbabies be walking beside you when a church tower falls on top of you. Instead, we're going to do whatever it takes to wipe the doubts from Kat's mind and clear the way for her to let herself fall completely in love and do away with the damned bad luck."

"I suppose you have an idea regarding the 'whatever it takes' part?"

"As a matter of fact, I do." Trace sat back in his chair, stretched out his legs and pulled out a cigar. Lighting it, he said, "We're going to give you a test."

A test? "Like what? Mathematics? Latin?"

"Geography." Trace blew a puff of ratafia-scented smoke. "As in how you don't give a damn about it anymore."

"You've lost me."

"Katrina's the one who lost. She lost two people she loved dearly, that bastard Rory Callahan who didn't deserve her love but had it nonetheless, and our sweet little Susie Beth. When they died, a part of Katrina died with them. Then you come along, another bastard—with a ready-made family—and you give her back her dream. So, what do you do then? You leave her. After she went and fell in love with you."

Jake pondered that statement for a moment. He

didn't know how he felt about having her daddy say Kat loved him before Kat got around to saying it herself. Jake knew Kat loved him, she was just being hardheaded about saying it. Guess it wasn't so bad to hear it from her father. "She won't say it. Won't admit to it."

"Of course she won't. She's a smart girl. She's done a lot of growing up since she ran off with Callahan. I couldn't be more proud of her. Look at what she's done lately. Instead of feeling sorry for herself when you leave her in the lurch, she feels sorry for those children. She wants to do right by them, give them the very best, so of course she brings them home to me and her mama."

"I was wrong to go, all right? I know that, dammit. That's why I'm here and not out looking for my brother!"

"Exactly." Trace pointed his cigar at Jake. "But you've got to prove it to her. Convince her and the children, too, for that matter, that their hearts are safe in your keeping."

"Which brings us back to the original question. How the hell do I do that?"

"You pass a test."

"What test!"

"Luke found Mari buried in a cave, and that pretty much proved his love."

"What, are you crazy? You want to bury Kat in a cave?"

"No, stupid. That wouldn't do any good. According to her mama and her sister, who know her better than anyone, you and me included, Kat is afraid you'll get a wild hair again to go after your brother. So here's what's going to happen. Your brother is going to show up and tell you that you need to leave with him, go on an adventure. Maybe he's found the lost city of Atlantis and he needs your help to strip it of its treasures. Doesn't matter. Those are the kinds of details we can work out later.

"The bottom line is your brother will ask you to go and you'll tell him 'hell no.' You'll pass the test. Kat will feel safe, and then the damned bad luck can find another body to haunt." He paused, rubbed the back of his neck and muttered, "Worries me it'll be after Emma next, but first things first."

"It's an inventive idea, McBride, but there's just one little problem. I haven't seen my brother in seventeen years. I seriously doubt he'll show up for supper sometime in the next few days."

Trace put out his cigar. "Sure he will. I already have it worked out."

"What?" Jake's eyebrows winged up.

"He waits bar at my old place, the End of the Line Saloon down in the Acre. Looks enough like you to give me nightmares. As soon as you're back on your feet, you need to drop by and pay him fifty dollars. That's what he's charging to pretend to be your relation. Personally, I wouldn't do the job for less than seventy-five."

"Hold on just one minute," Jake said. "You—Kat's father—are telling me to lie to her? Is this some kind of trap you're setting? 'Oh, look, Katrina, the bounder lied to you again. Let me shoot him this time.'"

Trace rolled to his feet. "You put your mind to getting well, now, boy. There's no time to waste. I figure the babies' christening next Saturday would be a good time to do this. You'll have a big audience. That ought to help. Gives you a whole week to get over your aches and pains."

Jake didn't think a whole year would be enough time to prepare him to participate in this idiotic idea of his father-in-law's. But Trace had made some valid points, Jake realized. He bought into the bad-luck theory, and he agreed with McBride's assessment of Kat's position. It crushed him, knowing how destructive his actions had been, but he couldn't argue that his wife's father had it right.

Up to a point.

"It'll never work, McBride. It's a *lie.* I've done a lot of lousy things to my wife, but I don't lie to her. I won't. It's wrong. It's not a way to begin a marriage, and it's certainly not a way to establish trust in a relationship, and *that's* the bottom line."

"You have a better idea, Kimball? One that's gonna solve the problem within a week? Give it much longer, and I'll be buying a casket for somebody. My neck niggle is telling me so, and believe you me, you don't want to ignore my neck."

So I put mine in a noose instead? Son of a bitch.

But, what if he was right? What if next time the bad luck struck, the children or Kat were with him? In a war—and this by God *was* a war—wasn't a life worth a lie?

Kat would understand that. Wouldn't she?

WEDNESDAY AFTERNOON while Robbie napped upstairs in his crib and the three younger girls played dolls in the attic playroom, Kat stood in her kitchen glaring at half a dozen pie plates. She couldn't understand what she'd done wrong with her crusts. They were heavy as bricks. "I can't take these to the christening. What did I do wrong? I make good piecrusts. Light, flaky, melt-in-your-mouth piecrusts. Magical piecrusts, learned at the side of a master in Aunt Claire."

"Take 'em anyway." Jake looked up from his seat at the kitchen table where he sat helping Miranda with her homework. Not that Miranda needed his help. The girl was smart as a whip and knew her multiplication tables backward and forward, but she liked having her uncle's attention. "You can call them the Bad Luck Piecrusts. Sell 'em for doorstops."

Out of the blue, Kat burst into tears. Jake and Miranda shared a look of alarm. "Honey, I'm sorry. It was a joke. I was teasing. I didn't mean to upset you. Look, it'll be all right. You can make new piecrusts. I'll help you."

She threw out her hands. "Isn't that just what I need? A pirate in the kitchen. It's not the pies, Jake Kimball. It's you. Your being here and my being here and us being so far apart. I should have sent you back next door when you felt well enough to climb out of bed. This isn't working, Jake. I just can't do this anymore!"

She rushed from the kitchen, running blindly outdoors into the backyard. Moments later the screen door banged a second time as Jake followed. Kat marched like a soldier away from the house and ended up at the sandbox Jake had built for the baby. She stepped over the gray railroad tie forming the border and gave the sand a swift, hard kick.

Jake waited until the grains had settled back to the ground before asking, "Can't do what, darling?"

She whirled on him, her arms fisted at her side. "I'm so *angry* at you."

"Finally," he muttered. "All right, Katrina. Tell me. I've been waiting for this, and it by God needs to happen. Tell me why you're angry at me."

"You left those children. Left them! Like they were puppies to be shuffled from one family to another."

He set his jaw. "What's bringing this up now? Did something happen? Did you hear about your father's lunatic idea?"

"This has nothing to do with my father. It has to do with you. Yes, something happened. You had a responsibility to those children, Jake Kimball. Parenthood is not something you pass off to an assistant. Your sister left them to you. Not me. I can't believe you abandoned them that way."

"All right. Yes. Well, I figured we'd get around to this conversation sometime. But before you take a piece of my hide with that tongue of yours, tell me this. I've been here for weeks. Why are you just now getting around to telling me I'm scum?"

"You're not scum. You're a scoundrel who only thinks about treasure and fantasy lands and fantasy sex. When are you going to grow up, Jake Kimball? You have five children to care for. Five children who depend on you."

"They depend on you, Katrina. I knew you'd take care

of them. I knew you loved them." He shoved his hands in his pockets. "I thought you'd be better for them than I would, and you are. Look at you. You've made a home for them. You've given them a mother again."

Kat wrapped her arms around herself as she stared up at the house. Her voice calmer, cooler, she said, "I know what it's like to have a stepmother, and that's basically what I am to these children. I know how insecure a stepchild feels, how difficult it is for them to feel loved and wanted and protected, even if their stepmother is as wonderful as Jenny was to me. I know how much the older ones miss their mother and father. And what about poor Caroline? She watched her parents die and she hasn't spoken since. Did you ever once stop and consider what your leaving might do to her?"

"I didn't think it would matter," he said with a guilty grimace. He sighed and raked his fingers through his hair. "Look, Kat, did you ever think that maybe I'm feeling some of the same things you feel? Look, I loved Daniel and he disappeared. I loved my parents—they died. I loved Penny. She's gone, too. Maybe I was a little afraid to set down roots for fear they'd be cut. You've got to understand that, Kat. I know you felt that way, too."

She considered it a moment, then shook her head. "It isn't about us anymore. It's about the children."

"I didn't know—"

"Do you think anyone knows? You think I knew anything about taking care of children when Susie was born? I didn't. I knew nothing, but I did my best. I take comfort in that now. I did my best.

"Nobody knows what to do or how to act, Jake. Parenthood is a learning process and you stumble through it, doing your best. Making mistakes and making up for those mistakes. But what you don't do is pick up and leave!"

Now he yanked his hands from his pockets. Jake's skin was scratched and scraped, colored black and blue and yellow and green with bruises. This time, he was the one who kicked at the sand. "I've told you I'm not leaving. What more can I do to prove myself? After all that's happened to me since I set foot in Fort Worth, a sane man would have caught the first train the hell outta here and gone back to someplace normal. But not me. Here I am, bruised and battered and getting my ass chewed by the woman I love because I'm not proving myself. Why don't you tell me what you want, Katrina? Give me your bloody test so I can pass it and we can get on with our life together."

She shook her head back and forth, back and forth. "No. No. Don't you see, Jake? It isn't something that I can just assign you like multiplication tables! This isn't a game. Life isn't a game. Marriage and family aren't prizes that you seek. You have to want the whole package. You have to do it for us. It can't be about you. And it has to be forever."

"What are you talking about?" he demanded, his tone scathing. "Of course I want the whole package."

Kat continued, "Do you? What happens when you get wanderlust in your shoes and you want to go looking for the lost mesquite tree of Wilbarger county? You can't. Not when you have children. Not when you have *five* children who have been entrusted to your care."

"It wasn't wanderlust, goddammit. I was in a tough spot. I went looking for—"

"Your brother. I know." Kat stepped out of the sandbox and paced back and forth beside it. "And you know what, Jake? I'd probably feel the same way if one of my sisters went missing. I'd probably want to go after them…*unless* I had children to care for. Children dependent on me. A responsible adult's needs come after those of children. You were wrong to go, Jake. So wrong."

"I know." He closed his eyes. Grimaced. "I'm sorry. I wish I could go back and do it over again."

"Well, you can't," she snapped. "We don't get do-overs in life. God knows it would be a wonderful world if we could. I'd give anything in the world to do over a horrible minute on Main Street."

She stood strong in the face of her pain, but he reeled as if from a blow. Silence hung between them for a long moment, until, with desperation in his tone, he asked, "So what do I do to fix it, Kat? Tell me. Please. What do I do to make it up to the children? Make it up to you?"

A tidal wave of despair rolled through her. "That's the problem. Don't you see? You can't. I don't trust you. You left once. You might leave again. I'm not risking the children's hearts again."

"You mean you're not risking *your* heart."

Abruptly the fight drained out of her. She pushed a hand through her hair as her heart pounded and tears pooled in her eyes.

"Honey, please. Tell me. What can I do? There has to be something I can do."

It hurt her to hear him beg. It was…wrong. "Jake, you've given me a fortune I'll never spend, five beautiful children and lovemaking that thrills. You've fulfilled my every fantasy."

"So what's the problem, goddammit?"

Her smile was bittersweet. "Fantasy is merely that. I need reality. It's a fever in my blood."

"Reality? I've tried to show you that you're my reality. What are you talking about?"

"Reality is what my father has with Jenny. What Luke has with Mari. I'm looking for the long run, Jake Kimball, not a fantasy that ends when the sun comes up and the everyday begins. I want a partner. Someone I can depend on. Someone I'll never doubt. Never distrust." She looked at him then, looked hard, as she added, "I need a partner who I know will always be there when I need him. A partner who will be strong, vigilant and true."

He drew in a deep breath. Determination gleamed in his eyes as he said, "All right. Fair enough. I'll give you that, Katrina Kimball. Give me a chance and I'll be that person, that partner."

It would be so easy to give in. The woman she used to be would have given in long ago. Kat shuddered, resisted. "I want to believe you. I do. You don't know how much. But I'm afraid…."

"Don't be afraid, honey. It's gonna be all right. You'll see. I have a niggling feeling that soon, now, everything will be all right."

A niggling feeling. Kat couldn't help but smile at that. "You've been hanging around my father too much, Jake. You're starting to sound like him."

Jake narrowed his eyes and stared at her for a long moment. "That's what you want, isn't it? A man like your father?"

Before Kat could frame an answer to that perplexing question, the kitchen screen door opened and Miranda stood on the back stoop. "Aunt Kat? Your sister is on the telephone. Do you want me to take a message?"

Grateful for the interruption, needing time to think, Kat replied, "No, that's all right. I'm coming." Glancing at Jake, she said, "I, uh…"

"Go on, Kat. I'll wait. I'll wait for as long as it takes."

As she fled toward the house, her emotions a jumble, she knew he wasn't talking about the length of her telephone conversation.

JAKE SHOVED HIS HANDS in his pockets and strolled around the backyard. He certainly hadn't figured on an outburst like this when he sat down to help Miranda with her arithmetic. More fool he for not taking notice of Kat's agitation.

And yet he wasn't sorry for the argument. A couple needed to air their issues from time to time, to cuss and discuss and figure out a way to fix them. Otherwise, those problems would fester and grow into something bigger and even more destructive.

"Well, she certainly aired her issues, that's for sure," he muttered.

Jake took aim at a rock lying in the green grass and gave it a swift kick. As the stone went flying, he wondered if he'd been on target with his last question. Was that the problem? She wanted a man like her father, but she found herself attracted to scoundrels?

As damned tired as Jake was of having Rory Callahan thrown in his face, he had to admit that he did have some scoundrel in him. What Kat hadn't seen or wouldn't acknowledge—or hell, maybe he hadn't shown her—was that he was a lot like her father, too.

"That's what makes me the perfect man for her." He found another stone and sent it skyward with another kick. "I'm Trace McBride with enough Rory Callahan in me to make me interesting."

Not that McBride was the paragon she believed him to be. Oh, no. Maybe that's what he should do, clue her in to her father's nonsense. Show her that Trace McBride had some troublemaker in him, too, by God.

Except, knowing his luck, that'd backfire on him. Instead of getting himself moved into his wife's bed, he'd get his father-in-law kicked out of his. Trace would need somewhere to live, and he'd move into the extra bed in the room Jake was renting.

Jake shuddered at the thought.

Hell, he didn't know where to go from here, other than make sure Kat didn't throw him out of her house. She said she wanted a partner, someone who'd be there when she needed him, a partner she'd never doubt, never distrust. How the hell was he supposed to become that partner if she held him at arm's length?

Jake's wanderings had taken him to the tree swing. Idly, he twisted the rope, then released it to set the swing spinning. Sort of like his emotions, he thought wryly.

The kitchen screen door squeaked open, then banged behind Kat when she stepped outside. Jake's heart gave a little lurch as he watched her approach. The woman was work, no doubt about it, but the prize was truly beyond compare.

Whatever it takes, Katrina. However long it takes.

Even if the waiting damned near killed him.

"Everything all right?" he asked when she drew near.

"Yes. Mari was just checking a couple details about the christening. I told her about the pies, and she said I shouldn't worry. Aunt Claire is bringing lots more than we'll probably need."

Jake gestured for her to take a seat in the swing, and after she did, he gave her a gentle push and pointed out, "Your aunt Claire likes me, you know."

"That's because you make such a to-do over her raspberry tarts."

"Maribeth likes me, too."

"You go on about her chocolates like you do the tarts."

"What can I say? I have a sweet tooth. Your mother also likes me, Kat, and I've never said a word about her tapioca pudding."

"Her tapioca pudding is awful."

"I refuse to comment on that. The point I'm trying to make, here, is that the women in your family are pretty astute, and they have a positive regard for me. That's something I'd like you to think about."

He gave her another push and Kat swung a little higher. Glancing over her shoulder, she smiled at him. "I haven't played in a swing in a very long time."

"Your father told me you'd done a lot of growing up."

"I think that's true. Although, I'm not sure that's entirely a good thing. Maybe I wouldn't be so, well, whatever I am if I took a little more time to play."

Jake liked the sound of that. As much as he wanted to pursue the idea of playing with Kat, he decided he shouldn't let this opportunity to make another good point pass him by. "I reckon I've done some growing up myself. I'd like you to give that idea some thought, Kat. Try to see that in me."

She dropped a foot to the ground, stopping the swing. Jake moved around in front of her. She looked at him with eyes that were round and solemn. "I will. I promise I will. But right this moment I want to play."

He wanted to kiss her then, and the intention must have shown in his expression because she backed up, then picked up her feet, teasing him with a gleeful look as she swung herself beyond his easy reach. She leaned, pumping her legs, propelling herself higher. When she turned her face toward the sunshine, her hair slipped from its pins and fell free, flowing behind her like a golden waterfall. A laugh escaped her, and the joy in it brought an answering smile to Jake's mouth.

The smile died abruptly when, with a whoosh and a roar, flames burst through the roof of Kat's house.

CHAPTER SEVENTEEN

UGLY BLACK SMOKE billowed into the afternoon sky.

Fear unlike any Jake had known before gripped his throat. His feet started moving toward the house even as the reality of what he was seeing made sense in his mind. This couldn't be happening. Not the children. This was beyond bad luck.

This was pure hell.

"The children!" Kat cried.

She ran with him toward the burning house. "Kat, stay here."

"No. You need my help. You can't get them alone."

She was right. The children were in two different parts of the house. He hated leading her into danger, but he had no choice.

He took another look at the house. The fire threatened the girls playing in the attic more than Robbie, asleep in his crib. She'd be safest going after the baby.

His long legs outreached hers, and he called over his shoulder as he approached the house. "The baby. You get the baby and I'll get the girls."

"Yes. Yes." Terror loomed in her expression and her steps faltered. "I can't. I can't lose another child."

He stopped, grabbed her. Gave her a shake. "Kat! The baby? You're with me here?"

"Yes. Yes," she sobbed.

"I need your help!"

She closed her eyes, just for a second, and when she looked at him again, calm determination filled her eyes. He knew then that she'd be all right. "Get the girls. Get our daughters."

The acrid scent of smoke filled his lungs as he burst into the house. He grabbed a kitchen towel on his way through and held it up to his face. *Ah, Penny. I promise I won't let anything happen to your babies.* As Jake pounded up the stairs, he heard Kat cough behind him. It took all his discipline not to turn around to tend to her. *Trust. Hell. I'm trusting you, Kat Kimball. You take care of yourself.*

On the second floor at the end of the hallway, he heard the baby crying. Good. That's good. "Girls?" he shouted. "Girls? Where are you?"

Above him, where the fire raged its worst, the smoke turned day to night, and the heat peeled paint off the walls, he heard the sweetest sound in the world. "Uncle Jake. Help us!"

Up the attic stairs. His eyes burning. Breathing almost impossible. His stomach felt nauseous. Too much smoke. Dammit, he had to keep a clear head.

Mentally he sketched the layout of the attic. A hallway down the middle. Two extra bedrooms on the north side. A couple of storage rooms and the playroom on the south.

At the top of the stairs, he turned south. Flames crackled. The heat intensified. "Girls? Where are you?"

"Here, Uncle Jake!" Miranda cried. He heard many beautiful voices screaming and calling his name. He followed the sound. "We're in the storeroom, Uncle Jake. We can't get out. Something's blocked the door. Hurry. Please. It's getting hard to breathe."

"Something" was a large roof support beam that had fallen and lay propped at an angle against the door. Jake put his back against it, planted his feet and shoved. The beam didn't budge. He repeated his action, putting every ounce of strength he had into the effort.

The beam slowly slid, then crashed to the attic floor.

He had the door open in a flash. The girls were huddled against an open window. "Come on, now. Go go go go!"

They darted toward him, and even as they came, he realized something was wrong. There wasn't enough of them. "Caroline. Where's Caroline?"

"She wasn't trapped," Miranda panted. "She'd just left the room. We told her to go get you to help us."

She must have been downstairs and he hadn't seen her as he rushed through the house. *Please, God, let her be outside, safe and sound, with Kat and the little guy.*

He herded the girls downstairs, swooping Belle into his arms as she bent over, coughing. As they burst through the door, Jake heard the clang of bells heralding the arrival of Fort Worth's Fire Department. Less than five minutes had passed since they'd spied the first flame. It felt like an hour.

Frantically, he looked for Kat, finding her even as Theresa called out, "Aunt Kat!" Jake's heart stood still.

Kat and Robbie, but no Caroline.

He called out. "Caroline? Have you seen her?"

Her voice shook. "No, Jake."

He turned on his heel and rushed back inside.

"Jake!" he heard his wife scream, her voice filled with fear.

The amount of smoke in the downstairs portion of the house had doubled since his first entrance. Visibility worsened with every second. *I won't be able to see her. I'll never find her.*

I have to find her.

He went upstairs, thinking she might have gone to the bedroom she shared with Belle. "Caroline Barrett," he shouted through the smoke. "Now I know you're scared. I know you've been scared for a long, long time. But you have to be brave right now. As brave as you've ever been. I know you can do it, sweetheart. I know you can. Caroline, talk to me, honey. Tell me where you are."

He listened hard even as he searched. Not under the bed. Not in her wardrobe. Not in this room. "Dammit all."

Where else would she have gone?

He stepped out into the hallway. "Caroline, enough of this. You hear me? You tell me where you are, child. Right now." He paused, listening a moment. "Caroline? Caroline!"

Fire burned through the ceiling above him, and debris crashed to the floor. "Caroline Barrett," Jake shouted. "I am your father now, and I demand you talk to me and tell me where you are. Right now, young lady. This is your father speaking."

Heart pounding, fear licking at his soul, Luke held his breath. One beat, two.

"Papa? Papa, I'm in Mama's room. Help me, Papa!"

Jake shuddered and dashed for the room at the end of the hall.

KAT STOOD ON THE LAWN holding Robbie in her arms, Miranda, Theresa and Belle clinging to her skirts and crying as they watched flames eat through the roof of their home and clouds of gray smoke surge into the sky. Despite the chaos surrounding her, she remained amazingly calm.

Jake would find Caroline in time. Kat had complete confidence in the man. For all his talk of fear of fatherhood, Jake's instincts were right on the mark where the children were concerned. He gave them his time, his attention, his discipline when they need it. He still mixed up the girls' names, but now he did it to tease them rather than because he needed color coding to tell them apart. He acted like a father, she thought. A good father.

He would save their child.

"I'm so scared," Theresa sobbed.

"Hush." Kat hugged the girl against her. "It'll be all right. You'll see. Your uncle Jake will save your sister. You can trust him."

Her own words echoed in her mind. Kat's heart, already pounding, beat even faster.

She *trusted* Jake. It was true. She trusted him to save Caroline from the fire. She trusted him to protect *all* these children under *any* circumstance. She trusted him to love them and cherish them and give them guidance and support. She trusted him to be these children's *father.*

"Where is he?" Theresa asked. "Why don't they come out!"

"They will. Trust in your uncle Jake."

Jake Kimball was a trustworthy man. Kat and the children could trust him with anything, with everything. With their lives. Their hearts. He would treat them all like treasures.

"We didn't do it, Aunt Kat," Miranda said. "I promise. We weren't playing with matches or candles or anything. Do you believe me? Please, say you believe me. It wasn't our fault."

"I believe you, sweetheart. Sometimes these things just happen."

"Sometimes it's just bad luck," Belle said. "Right, Aunt Kat?"

Bad luck.

Kat absorbed the words like a blow. Oh, no. Is that what this was? What started the fire? Was *she* the reason her husband was risking his life in a burning building searching for their precious child?

Oh, dear Lord. What's been wrong with me?

All these incidents and accidents Jake had suffered…*she* was the reason for them. She was the Bad Luck Bride. Poor Jake had made the mistake of marrying her, falling in love with her. And look where that had gotten him.

Risking his life again and again because she'd refused to recognize his love. Had she subconsciously required a life-or-death test like Mari said? Was she that shallow?

Shame washed through her. Jake did love her. She knew it for certain. She believed it down to her bones. And his love for her *was* strong—it had pulled him back from Tibet. It *was* vigilant—he showed it in little ways every day. Fixing a loose step of her kitchen step stool. Fussing at her to take a break and put her feet up from time to time throughout the day.

And his love was true. She hadn't missed the batted lashes and flirtatious glances sent his way by some Fort Worth floozies. Jake, who noticed everything, acted as if he didn't even see them. He wanted no one but her. His love was true.

Hers was the love in question. Love she'd refused to acknowledge, even to herself.

Her breath came in fast, shallow pants. Did she really have to have a house burn down to get this through her thick skull? Jake wasn't the problem here. *She* was the problem. Trust *was* the issue, only not in the way she'd thought. It wasn't her lack of trust in Jake that kept the bad luck hanging around, kept husband and wife apart. Perhaps even set their house on fire.

The fault lay in Kat's failure to trust herself.

Jake Kimball was nothing like Rory Callahan. Period. Her instincts had known it all along. Her heart had recognized him all along for the fine man he was. A scoundrel, true, but Jake Kimball was her kind of scoundrel.

And right that minute her scoundrel came running from their burning home, their smiling, sooty daughter cradled safely in his arms.

Kat's heart filled with joy. "See, girls? I told you Uncle Jake would save the day. He'll never let us down."

Some ten yards away from her, Jake stopped and set Caroline on the ground. "Go ahead, honey," he said to the child. "Tell her."

Kat's heart climbed into her throat as Caroline looked up and said, "Right before Mama went to Heaven, she told me Uncle Jake would be my new daddy and that he would take real good care of me and that he'd someday get me a new mommy, too. So, I've been wondering. Can I call you Mommy?"

The girls squealed and cheered to hear the sound of their sister's voice. Kat set Robbie on his feet, then smiled at Caroline and opened her arms. "I can't think of anything I'd like more, Caroline. I'd be so proud to be your mommy."

Her arms were full of the little girl, but her gaze never left Jake. The children were babbling, the house was burning down next to them, and all she could think about was him.

"You saved my babies."

"Our babies."

He was her hero, her love. Her partner. Tears rolled down her face. "Are you all right?"

"Honey, I have never been better."

She drew in a shaky breath. "Jake, about earlier. The things I said. I'm sorry. I was wrong—wrong about so many things."

"Hush, now." He hugged her to him with his free arm. "All that can keep. Let's just enjoy this moment, it's a good family moment. Even though we have no house, all our clothes are gone, and your piecrust is turned to toast, it's about as good a moment as I can remember. We need to wallow in it a bit, I think. All right?"

"All right." But as the girls surrounded them, four beautiful babbling voices, Kat decided she'd try to make it up to him. He deserved a grand gesture, something to prove to him, to her family, to everyone in town, that her love for him was strong, vigilant and true.

And as her parents and sister arrived, their faces wreathed with worry, Kat figured out just what that gesture should be.

The time had arrived for a traditional McBride family wedding.

CHAPTER EIGHTEEN

"IT WAS A BEAUTIFUL CEREMONY," Kat told her sister as they entered the church vestibule following the christening.

"It was, wasn't it?" Mari pressed a kiss to her infant son's forehead, then nodded toward the baby in Kat's arms. "Although I thought Jenna might bring down the ceiling when the reverend sprinkled her with water."

"I never heard a baby cry so loud," Caroline said in awe.

Theresa nodded. "Mrs. Peters said it was shrill enough that even old Buck Laney must have heard it, and he only hears in one ear."

"He has to be listening through one of those ear horns, too," Belle added.

"Our Jenna lets everyone know when she's not happy," Mari said. Turning to Kat, she said, "Your turn, sister. Are you ready?"

"I'm a little nervous," Kat admitted. "There are even more people here than I expected."

"You knew there would be a crush."

"Well, yes," Kat said with a sigh.

Traditionally, McBride family christenings were festive affairs attended by relatives and invited guests. Adding a last-minute wedding to the event—a last minute *McBride* wedding—meant the addition of uninvited guests to the church, too.

Ever since Trace married Jenny way back in '79, McBride family weddings had become known as one of the better entertainments offered to the citizens of Fort Worth. Once word got around town that the McBrides were making this a "two-fer" celebration, the pews at First Methodist had filled to overflowing.

Miranda eyed the wedding gown hanging on a rack, and her eyes gleamed with excitement. "Hurry up, Mommy. I can't wait to see you in the Good Luck Wedding Gown. I think it's the prettiest dress I've ever seen!"

"Of course it is," Claire McBride said as she swept into the room along with her sister-in-law, Jenny. "That's because your grandmommy made it and Jenny is the best seamstress in the world."

"Oh, Claire," Jenny said with a laugh as she scooped her infant granddaughter out of Kat's arms. "Let's get moving, ladies. We have a church full of guests waiting with bated breath."

Within a few minutes, everyone was ready. Claire gave Kat a kiss, took the other twin from Mari and left to take her seat. Jenny handed each of the Barrett girls their bouquets—yellow roses with blue ribbon for Belle, green for Theresa, yellow for Miranda and pink for Caroline. "Y'all wait with your grandfather for a minute, please, and tell him I'll be right out."

With the room empty but for Jenny, Mari and Kat, Jenny said, "I wish Emma were here."

Kat nodded, her smile wistful. "Her absence is the only thing that's keeping today from being perfect. I'm rather perturbed about that."

"We're all rather annoyed at Emma, but let's put that aside for the time being. We've a wedding to attend." Jenny held Kat's face in both her hands. "Be happy, Katrina. I love you with all my heart, and wish for you nothing but good luck in love."

"Thanks, Mama. I love you, too."

After Jenny left Kat and Mari alone in the vestibule, Kat said, "I hope you don't regret sharing the twins' special day with this spectacle."

"Never." Mari fussed with her sister's hair. "This was the best idea ever. A true Menace event."

"Minus a Menace."

Mari sniffed. "Emma had better start sending more letters or, I swear, Papa's going to go after her."

"I wonder where she is and what she's doing, don't you? I wonder if she's found her true love with Alasdair MacRae. She's the last, you realize. First you and Luke, now me and Jake."

"I've considered that," Mari said. "I didn't know if you'd…Kat, has your task been revealed to you?"

"You mean now that it's completed?" Kat gave a little laugh. "It would have been helpful if Roslin of Strathardle had filled us in on that little detail, but yes. I have completed my task." She drew a deep, calming breath, then said, "I've forgiven myself."

Mari nodded, and satisfaction filled her expression. "Yes. Of course. That makes perfect sense." The two sisters shared a look of total understanding, then Mari kissed Kat quickly on the cheek. "Now I guess it's time. Do you know what you're going to say, honey?"

"I know exactly what I'm going to say."

A knock sounded on the door. "Katie-cat?" Trace said. "You ready? They're gettin' restless out here."

"Yes, Papa." As Kat opened the door, she said to her sister, "That's part of the surprise."

JAKE STOOD at the church altar disgusted with himself for shaking in his shiny dress boots as the organ began to play. He hadn't been nearly this nervous the first time he married Kat.

From the corner of his eyes, he saw the McBride boys slip back into the church pews, suspicious-looking bulges in their jackets. Everyone in church knew to expect some sort of addition to the ceremony from the animal kingdom.

Then Jake spied little Caroline walking toward him wearing the color-coded pinafore he'd ordered all those months ago. She was followed by her sisters, dressed similarly, and he forgot his nervousness as his heart gave a little hitch. *Ah, Penny, I hope you know how much I love them.*

Maribeth Garrett followed his nieces up the aisle, and she touched her sapphire pendant, then gave him a saucy wink that made him nervous all over again. He didn't have time to dwell on that, however, because Kat had moved to stand at the end of the aisle on her father's arm.

She was a vision in white, and her beauty took his breath away. Love for her swelled up inside Jake, filling him with a peaceful calm. Then she smiled at him and he knew that he must be the luckiest man on earth.

In the two days since the fire, they'd hardly had any time alone. The one private conversation they did have had been short and sweet. She'd told him she had things to say to him, promises to make him, and she asked if she could do it in front of witnesses as they renewed their wedding vows. Jake would have agreed to anything at that point. The look in her eyes had been downright loving.

As she joined him at the altar, that light in her eyes hadn't changed. Trace McBride glared at Jake out of habit as he handed his daughter over to her husband. They turned to face the minister, who said, "Dearly beloved. Mr. and Mrs. Jake Kimball stand before you now to renew their wedding vows in front of friends and family. Now, because I have experience officiating over McBride weddings, I think it's best if we go right to the meat of the matter, so to speak. Mr. Kimball, you wished to recite your vows first?"

"Yes." After Kat handed her bouquet to her sister, Jake took both her hands in his. "Kat, as I make these vows to you again—with a few additions—know that they are spoken in total sincerity, and with a love that is strong, vigilant and true. I, Jacob Alexander, take you, Katrina Julianne, to be my wedded wife. I promise to love you, comfort you, honor you and keep you, for better or worse, for richer or poorer, in sickness and in health, in good luck and in bad."

Laughter gleamed in her eyes and she smiled as, at her side, Mari Garrett let out an unladylike snort. Jake took a deep breath and continued, "Forsaking all others, I vow to be faithful to you as long as we both shall live."

Then a voice rang out from the back of the congregation. "But will you stay with her, Jake Kimball, when adventure calls? I'm Daniel Kimball and I want you to come with me to Tibet."

Jake shut his eyes and muttered, "Son of a bitch."

"Hold on a second." Trace McBride shot to his feet. "Didn't somebody cancel the brother? Who was supposed to do that?"

"Me." Luke Garrett spoke up. "I'm sorry. I forgot. The twins are keeping me up all night and…well…I'm just not thinking straight these days." Turning around, he called toward the back of the church. "Never mind, Jasper. We don't need you anymore."

Kat glared first at Jake, then at her brother-in-law and finally at her father. "Cancel the brother?"

"You can't cancel me." The bartender from the End of the Line Saloon stepped from a pew and took a challenging stance in the center of the aisle. "Not now. I put on a suit and everything. You owe me fifty dollars."

Jake heard Mari say to Kat, "I thought the wedding excitement would come from the piglets the boys have stuffed in their shirts."

The buzz in the congregation grew louder. Kat pulled on Jake's sleeve. "Jake? Who is that man?"

"Look, I had no part of this. I told him it was a stupid idea."

She stepped toward the front pew. "Papa?"

He smiled winsomely. "It's a long story, Katie-cat.

We'll go into it later. For now, why don't you carry on with the wedding?"

Kat got that look on her face that said they'd be going into it *now* when the squealing started. At first Jake thought it was one of the twins, but then he realized the McBride boys must have let loose their pigs. His suspicion was confirmed when he heard Tommy say, "Holy crap."

The piglets were just a beginning. Some unseen helpers let loose pigeons, prairie dogs and a pair of armadillos.

"Yes!" Wilhemina Peters called out. "Typical McBrides. Typical Bad Luck Wedding."

The observation pushed Jake right over the edge.

He rounded on the woman, strong and determined. "This is *not* a bad-luck wedding, by God. My love for my wife is strong, vigilant and true and nobody—not a newspaper gossip or a scoundrel of a father or a barnyard full of farm animals—is going to interfere and turn it into one."

He grabbed his wife's arm and all but dragged her toward the altar. "Now, where was I? I promise never to take a swing at your father even when he deserves it, which is bound to be often. I'll be kind to your sisters even when they're giving me hell, and I'll love your mother, but that's an easy one because she's a damned fine woman. I'll be a friend to your brothers, although I will swing back at them if they let one fly first. All right, what else? Is there anything else you want, Kat? Ask now or forever hold your peace."

"I...uh...I..."

"Maybe I should tell you I don't want to rebuild the

Braxton house. I bought some land, and I'd like to build our own place. Something that suits us. I like Fort Worth and I want to make our home here. Texans are good people. Now, we'll probably have to go back to England when Robbie gets older because he has that title and everything, but that's something we'll deal with together as a family. And speaking of families…the children. I love 'em. I'm happy to be their father. If you want more babies, I'll be happy with that. If you're fine with our family the way it is, that's all right with me, too. So, that ought to about cover it, don't you think?" He paused for just a second. "Kat? Anything else you want covered?"

"I, uh, no. I guess that's…enough."

"Good. All right, then. That's my wedding vow, so help me God." He folded his arms, glared at her. "Now it's your turn."

"Um…"

"I Katrina Julianne Kimball…" he cued, making a circling motion with his hand.

"Katrina Julianne *McBride* Kimball," she corrected.

"Take me…" Again, the hand circles.

She folded her arms. Tapped her foot. Turned her lips down. But none of that hid the look in her emerald eyes—that soft, warm, loving look—and it seeped into Jake's soul and warmed it, relaxed it. He rubbed his thumb in gentle circles along the inside of her wrist and said in a low, raspy tone, "Ah, come on, honey. Take me. Please?"

"Out to the woodshed, maybe. That's what you deserve. Really, now, Jake. Hiring a man to be your brother? You knew about this?"

"It was your father's idea."

"Hey, now," Trace interrupted. "Watch what you say, boyo. I'm still not sold against shooting you, you know."

"Trace, sit down," Jenny said, pulling him back to his seat.

Jake slipped his arms around Kat's waist and drew her toward him. "Take me, Katrina. Here. Anywhere. Everywhere. Give me the words I've wanted, needed, to hear for so long. Even before I realized it myself."

After a long moment's pause, she nipped at his finger, then said, "I Katrina Julianne McBride Kimball, take you, Jacob Alexander Kimball, to be my husband. I promise to comfort you, honor you, and keep you, for better or worse, for richer or poorer, in sickness and in health, in good luck and in bad, although I don't anticipate any of the latter. Forsaking all others, I vow to be faithful to you as long as we both shall live."

Seconds dragged by as Jake waited, frowning. "And…?"

She sighed. "I promise to protect you from my father."

Following a snort of disdain, again Jake waited, only vaguely aware of the scurrying and scattering of the congregation in the wake of darting animals. "And…?"

"I won't fuss if you need to take business trips of a reasonable length, and I'll always be happy to entertain ideas of, um, more private journeys."

That was almost enough to distract him from what he was waiting to hear. "That's good. I like that a lot. But, Katrina, isn't there something more?"

She sighed, rolled her eyes, then sighed again. "Oh, all right."

Her smile warm and welcoming, Kat clasped her emerald pendant in her right hand. "It was wrong of me to withhold my love, withhold my trust, from you, and I apologize to you in front of God, our family and our friends and neighbors for it. You see, I didn't need you to pass a test of the strength of your love for me. I didn't need a hired brother or a house fire to prove to me that your love is vigilant and true. I was afraid, Jake, and I let my fear and self-doubt blind me to the simple truth. You love me. And I love you."

"Finally," he murmured.

Kat chuckled. "My love for you, like yours for me, is strong, vigilant and true. That is my wedding vow to you."

Then, even as Jake bent to kiss her, she took her necklace off and slipped it over his head. "I think this was meant for you all along, pirate. You found the necklace, Jake."

"I found my family."

Jake took his wife's mouth in a long, loving kiss. As the minister pronounced them man and wife again and asked the McBride boys to please get the armadillo out of the gladiolas, Trace McBride grumbled, "The only thing that makes this bearable is the fact that the scoundrel will eventually get his. The man has four daughters of his own."

EPILOGUE

MUSIC, LAUGHTER and the tantalizing aroma of barbecue floated on the gentle afternoon breeze as the messenger arrived at Willow Hill, where the combination christening and wedding reception was in full swing. Winded from his run, he took a minute to catch his breath and peruse the crowd, searching for the recipient of the telegram he carried in his pocket. There, by the dessert table. The messenger drew a deep breath, then let out a heavy sigh. It was a shame to ruin a celebration this way.

Standing with her husband, wondering how he could possibly eat a third piece of chocolate cake, Kat glanced around at the crowd of guests and took note of the newcomer. Something about the young man's expression caught her attention, and a little ribbon of fear fluttered through her when he began to walk toward Mari's husband, Luke. Instinctively, she reached for Jake's hand.

Jake turned toward her with a smile that slowly faded when he spied the look on her face. "Honey? What is it?"

"I don't know. Nothing good, I'm afraid."

The young man approached. "Sheriff Garrett? I have a telegram for you, sir."

Jake took half a step forward and sideways, shielding Kat as Luke tore open the envelope and withdrew a folded sheet of paper. Kat watched her brother-in-law closely as he scanned the contents. Her stomach dropped to her knees when his face went hard.

Suddenly, Mari moved to stand beside Kat. The two sisters clasped hands as their father demanded, "What is it, Luke? What does the telegram say?"

Luke muttered a curse, then rubbed the back of his neck. "It's from Scotland. A detective in Edinburgh. He says...."

Jenny McBride looped her arm around her husband's. "What is it, Luke?"

"Emma is wanted for murder."

"Murder!" Kat and Mari gasped.

"Not Dair," Jake demanded. "Dair's not dead."

Luke shook his head as Trace ripped the telegram from his grasp. He read it quickly, then his face flushed red with anger. "An old man? They're saying she's murdered an old man? That's a damned lie!"

"I know people in Edinburgh," Jake said, stepping forward. "I'll leave on the first train tomorrow."

"*We* will leave," Luke corrected.

Mari nodded. "All of us. We'll all go."

"No, Mari." Luke folded his arms and leveled a stern gaze upon his wife. "I'll go. You stay with the children."

"No!" Kat's voice rang out, demanding attention. She lifted her hand and clutched her emerald necklace. "No. We must all go—children, too. Mari and I need to be there. Don't you see? We've found our love, completed our tasks, and Emma took off with a man."

"A rat bastard," Trace declared.

Ignoring her father, Kat continued. "She wouldn't

have done that if she didn't have feelings for him. I'll bet anything that those feelings have grown into love. That means we're close. We're so very close to breaking the Curse of Clan McBride."

Mari closed her hand around her sapphire pendant. "You're right. Of course. We *do* need to be there. For Emma. For the whole McBride family." She gazed around at her family members, her expression imploring. "The curse began in Scotland. Maybe it's supposed to end there!"

For a long moment no one spoke. Fiddle music swirled along with laughter in the air as the guests remained unaware of the drama unfolding in their midst. Kat, Mari and their mother shared determined looks. Jake and Luke glanced from their wives to one another and shrugged. Everyone waited for Emma's father to speak.

Finally, Trace McBride threw the telegram into the dirt like a gauntlet. "All right, then. Everyone, go pack your bags. The McBrides are going to Scotland to find Emma.

"And that sorry, no-good outlaw she ran away with…well…he'd damn well better keep her safe in the meantime."

* * * * *

Don't miss Geralyn Dawson's
other BAD LUCK *books from HQN!*
The romance that started it all…
THE BAD LUCK WEDDING DRESS
Mari's story…
HER BODYGUARD
And coming soon…Emma's story,
HER OUTLAW

WIN A DREAM WEDDING DRESS!

HQN Books will award one grand-prize winner the gorgeous wedding dress featured on the cover of *Her Scoundrel* complete with 3 signed copies of Geralyn Dawson's HQN titles (approx. retail value of $420 U.S.).

HQN™
We *are* romance™

To view official rules and to enter, simply visit www.HQNBooks.com or to receive official rules and an entry form, send a self-addressed, stamped envelope to Win a Wedding Dress Sweepstakes 20503, 225 Duncan Mill Road, Don Mills, ON, M3B 3K9.

No purchase necessary.

Entries must be received by January 31, 2006. Open to residents of the U.S. and Canada (excluding Quebec) who are 18 years and over. Void where prohibited.

Odds of winning depend upon number of eligible entries received. In order to win a prize, potential Canadian winners must correctly answer a time-limited arithmetical skill-testing question.

www.HQNBooks.com　　　PHGDPROMO

GERALYN
DAWSON

HQN™

We *are* romance™